eating *crow*

a novel

JAY RAYNER

SIMON & SCHUSTER PAPERBACKS
New York   London   Toronto   Sydney

SIMON & SCHUSTER PAPERBACKS
Rockefeller Center
1230 Avenue of the Americas
New York, NY 10020

He also wants to apologize for the size of this print. It's tiny, isn't it?

First Simon & Schuster paperback edition 2005

SIMON & SCHUSTER PAPERBACKS and colophon are registered trademarks of Simon & Schuster, Inc.

For information about special discounts for bulk purchases, please contact Simon & Schuster Special Sales: 1-800-456-6798 or business@simonandschuster.com.

DESIGNED BY LAUREN SIMONETTI

Manufactured in the United States of America

1   3   5   7   9   10   8   6   4   2

The Library of Congress has cataloged the hardcover edition as follows:
Rayner, Jay.
Eating crow : a novel / Jay Rayner.
p. cm.
1. Food writers—Fiction. 2. Restaurants—Fiction. 3. Remorse—Fiction. I. Title.

PR6068.A9493E37 2004
823'.92—dc22   2004045281
ISBN-13: 978-0-7432-5059-7
ISBN-10:   0-7432-5059-1
ISBN-13: 978-0-7432-5061-0 (Pbk)
ISBN-10:   0-7432-5061-3 (Pbk)

For Matthew, Lindsay and Lois Fort,
and for Jim Albers Jr.

eating *crow*

Preface

I am sorry you bought this book. If it was given to you as a gift, then technically I am not required—or even entitled—to apologize to you. My apology should go to the original purchaser and they, in turn, should say sorry. To be honest, though, I can't be bothered with any of those rigid laws and rules anymore. I can see they are needed for diplomatic exchanges, and as a onetime exponent of the art of the international apology—the leading exponent, I suppose—I was constantly grateful that the Professor had gone to the bother of formulating all the laws in the first place. But they have their time and their place and this isn't one of them.

The point is, I'm sorry this book was bought. Somewhere along the line somebody has been conned by the smart-ass cover art which the art director obviously thought would set it apart from all the other guff on the bookshop shelves (and which, admittedly, did the trick, or it wouldn't be in your hands now). Beautiful trees have been destroyed needlessly to make the paper. Then there's the grievous waste of oil-based ink. And we mustn't forget the obscenely large cash advance paid on this insidious doorstop which will, inevitably, result in the publisher having to spend its remaining money on banal, dead-certain bestsellers to the exclusion of anything new, interesting, or challenging. Finally, of course, there's the waste of your time, should you be one of those people who insist upon finishing a book once they've started it, and I know there are a lot of you out there.

I admit—and under the Professor's first law, I am required to admit—that I am not sorry about absolutely everything in this book. There's some pretty good writing between pages 129 and 133. I like the descriptions of my father, which are honest, and I always will have a warm place in my heart for the tasting menu of chocolate dishes in chapter 29. It really was as good as I make it sound.

As for the rest of it, I think you probably get the idea by now. I'm sorry. I'm just so bloody sorry.

One

It starts with a phone call. I recognize the voice immediately, although not the tone. Usually this woman wants only to make me happy. Today she wants me to hate myself.

"Hestridge is dead."

"What?"

"John Hestridge is dead and you killed him."

"Hang on a second, Michelle—"

"You might as well have put a gun to his head and pulled the trigger."

"How did he die?"

"Of course you want the details."

"As I'm supposed to be responsible, naturally I want details. How did he die?"

A pause.

"Michelle, tell me how he died."

There's a gulp at the other end of the line, as though she is trying to swallow enough air for the task at hand; as if the usual draft could never be sufficient.

"He drank a bottle of whiskey and climbed into the large bread oven as it was heating up. Then he pulled the door shut."

"It sounds like an accident to me, a drunken stunt that went wrong. I can't see how I—"

"He left a note explaining himself and a copy of your review, taped to the outside of the oven."

I thought I could detect a note of triumph in her voice. "I—"

"You killed him, Basset, as surely as if you'd pulled the trigger."

There is a click and then the hiss of white noise. She has gone.

There is something you should know. As a child, lousy with invention, I imagined I was responsible for my father's death. This was a few years before he actually died, and none of the compact dramas I devised ever matched the cruelty of the real thing, which closed him down slowly, an organ at a time. In my daydreams I was the oblivious child in the middle of the road as the truck thundered down upon me. Dad would be the one to push me to safety, only then to take the full force of the impact. I was the little boy who, reaching for a handhold, pulled the stockpot that always stood boiling upon the stove in our house off and over him in a fury of steam and fat as he stooped to tie my shoelace. I was the one he saved from the offshore currents; he was the one who was dragged away by them. And when, rushing home from school, I would find him alive, praying at the stove as he fed the stockpot, or at his desk, his huge, cardiganed back hiding its contents from view, there would be waves of relief, but something else too: a frisson of disappointment. I really did not want my father dead, but I did want to be interesting, and at eight or nine years old I assumed that grief, cruelly earned, would make me that.

You don't need to be a shrink to understand that my father was the focus of my bereavement fantasies because I loved him. Even as a child I could see that. André Basset arrived in Britain in the late 1940s from a small town in the French-speaking part of Switzerland where, as he put it, nobody ever swore or farted. His relationship with his native country was sullen and uneasy. He never once returned there, but he made his living as an architect designing the Alpine chalets that Britain's suburban nouveaux riches loved so much in the sixties and seventies: big, overhanging roofs sloping down to the ground like starched wimples, wood and faux rock front elevation, huge plate glass windows probably shielding an overengineered rubber plant. If you see one anywhere around London it was designed either by my dad or by a Swiss German from Zurich called Peltz whom Dad would only ever refer to, with a derisory snort, as "the little guy." (They don't have much time for each other, the Swiss French and the Swiss Germans; the only thing that unites them is contempt for the Swiss Italians.) It was as if, together in their competition, these two Swiss-émigré architects were rebuilding the country they had left behind, house by house.

My father never lost his French accent, although he did lose quite a lot of French vocabulary which he failed to replace completely with its English equivalent. Language was always a crapshoot in our house: he would "reserve" the car into parking spaces, we were constantly having to deal with things which were an unavoidable "fucked of life," and my brother and I had to make sure that we used lots of "lovely soup" when we washed our hands. He was oblivious to these linguistic pratfalls, and when we small, giggling boys tried to adopt some of them as our family's secret language, he was most insistent that we should not: "What do you mean wash your hands with soup? The word is *soup*. Speak English like I do."

But he did fear that his foreignness could be an embarrassment to us. He tried to make it easier on my younger brother and me by insisting that his surname be passed on with a hardened, rather than silent, final *t,* so that when announcing it now, I always say "Basset, as in hound." He then sullied our Anglo-Saxon credentials by insisting that I be named Marcel and my brother, Lucas, so that we sound like some desperate circus act: Marcel and Lucas, the Flying Basset Brothers. As a kid I hated my name, but it works now, at least in shortened form. Marc Basset is a good name, the kind people remember. It functions particularly well as a newspaper byline.

There was one language, however, in which André Basset was fluent, and that was food. Seventies Britain was fixed in a deathly monochrome of bad taste. It was a country so dismally impoverished that it considered Vesta's range of instant Chinese meals exotic and regarded a tube of Spangles as a worthy substitute for dessert. In our house, though, everything was Technicolor. Even today my oldest friends tell me that our house always smelled of food, although what it really smelled of was the stockpot over which my dad fretted. He was forever topping it up and adding and sniffing and skimming and sipping and skimming again. When he had run out of ideas at his drawing board he would stand in front of the stove and stir. Most evenings he would take a few ladlefuls of whichever stock it happened to be—beef or chicken or, if possible, veal—and strain it into a pan. He would reduce it until he was content. And then at that moment, with the spoon poised at his lip, he would say solemnly, "We may begin."

There were sauces with chunks of earthy morel to accompany steak, and with specks of black truffle for chicken. There were velvet sauces mounted with butter or spiked with cognac or sharpened with orange juice. He also cooked, from Provence, a dense bouillabaisse that was an assault course of fin and bone but which rewarded the effort with dramatic flavors. From Italy came great mounds of homemade silken pasta, and from the confused landscape of Mittel Europe, irresistible strudels and tortes. He did these things to make us happy but also to gratify himself, for he loved to eat and it showed. Just as he built his houses, so he built himself, and me too. We were always bound to be big, my father and I, and while I would like to claim there was a genetic predisposition to these things, I know the stockpot had nothing to do with our DNA. We ate because it was part of who the Bassets were. I can legitimately blame my father's genes for the painful reproach of my feet, with their shattered arches and curled, callused toes, those desperate failures of biology which have kept grinning podiatrists in fees since I was just a child, for he shared my symptoms. But I have always accepted that my size belonged under a different heading, the one marked "learned behavior." When, in adolescence, sex raised its head and I began to suspect that my spectacular failures with girls might have something to do with the female softness of my thighs and the spread of my belly, it was an image of that rumbling stockpot that came to mind, and with it, my father leaning deep into the steam. I held it in contempt, but at the same time, I found the thought of it reassuring.

It was when my father stopped eating that we knew he was ill. The trips from his desk to the stove became fewer and fewer. The spoon was lifted to his lip less and less. I remember him in the autumn and winter of 1982, more asleep than awake and, when conscious, consulting with doctors. There was hushed talk, and later, after all the operations, the smell of stock in the house was replaced by the smell of disinfectant. He became a small man, and because he could not bear to waste the few trips he had the energy to make on visits to clothes shops, he slipped away inside his old ones until my mother began inexpertly to alter them. My father took on the appearance then of an old man stitched away inside a sack. He died in February 1983, shortly before my thirteenth birthday. He was forty-one years old.

Because of my earlier fantasies, I could not escape the feeling that by wishing him dead, I had made it happen. One night I told my mother this, my dear English mother who had been swept up by this belching mountain of a man and then deserted by him. She held me at arm's length, a hand gripping each shoulder as if to stop herself from falling down, and said, "Marc Basset, you are never to blame. You can never be to blame. It is not your fault." Then we both cried, and Luke came downstairs from his bed and joined in too and it was almost like being a family again.

The point of relating all this is that being accused of causing another man's death plays badly with me. Me and death have a history, and mention of it makes me edgy. When I feel edgy I do what my father used to do when he couldn't concentrate. I eat.

After Michelle's phone call I went to my desk in the corner of the living room. I pulled open the Vice Drawer and dragged my fingertips slowly over its high-energy contents. It was well stocked, as it always is. There were a couple of thick bars of Valrhona Manjari, with over sixty percent cocoa solids the king of dark chocolates: intense, fruity, no acidic end, just lots of building flavor. I cracked off a couple of squares and then, for good measure, took another. There were also, from Calabria, some figs encased in dark chocolate and a few soft, dark chocolate truffles infused with tobacco, which I was testing for a friend who is a chocolatier. They have an almost chili heat that comes in slowly and grows, followed by a long finish, a bit like a big tannic red wine. I wasn't yet entirely convinced by them. The flavorings seemed to fight the chocolate. But this was a serious moment so I took three, and the same number of the figs just to be sure. I dropped a square of the Manjari into my mouth, allowed it to melt slightly on my tongue, and then bit into it. Now I could think.

I hadn't known John Hestridge but I did hate him. He was a man for his times and I could say nothing worse about anybody. There was, in the great cities of the Western world at the beginning of the twenty-first century, an appetite for eating that had nothing to do with hunger. It was people like John Hestridge who fed upon those appetites. They created rooms that were uncomfortable and served nonsensical food in them at nonsensical prices. And yet still people came to sit in these rooms and eat this food and they liked themselves for doing so. It led them to believe that at this particular moment, they were in the right place. This drove me insane. But what really broke me up about Hestridge was that he couldn't cook. By his choice of profession he ensured that animals died in vain. He destroyed fish. His sauces were too thick or too thin or just tasteless. His starters were too heavy, his desserts flimsy and insubstantial.

With my free hand I nudged my mouse so that the computer awoke from its slumber. I took another piece of chocolate and pulled up the review I had written of the new restaurant, Hestridge at 500. It had been published by my newspaper two days before.

By Marc Basset

Desperately poor cooking is not yet an offense punishable by execution, not even in some of the more enthusiastic states of the Southern US. But if it were, you could be certain that John Hestridge would be hanging out right now on death row, counting the days. It is only to be hoped that should such justice ever catch up with him, he would have the good sense not to order any of his own dishes as his last meal. No one deserves to leave the planet with that in their stomachs, not even John Hestridge.

And so on.

Not kind, is it? Funny, in a diverting Sunday morning sort of way, but definitely not nice. Still, I wasn't being paid to be nice. I really did hate the food and I had a responsibility to say so. That was what my readers expected of me, wanted from me, even, and I was happy to deliver. I hadn't before dwelt too much on what effect my words might have on the people they were about.

I needed a diversion so I flicked on the television to catch the top stories on the midmorning news. First story: The collapse of the Slavery Reparations Conference in Alabama. Soundbite from Lewis Jeffries III, African-American delegation leader, with a deftly sorrowful speech ("It is for the children of tomorrow that we seek justice, not just for the children of yesteryear"), then a sad nod of his graying head. I found myself admiring the hokey cadence of "yesteryear." Second story: Separatist rebels in region on Russian-Georgian border issue ransom demand for release of American, Canadian, and British aid workers they are holding. Third story: Random, tragic death of entire family in Lincolnshire house fire.

It occurred to me immediately that the third slot was going begging. Journalistic instinct told me that once we'd had twenty-four hours of news cycles, sifting through the ashes, interrogating witnesses and safety experts, something else would be needed to replace the Lincolnshire fire story and a dead chef might well be just the thing. I wasn't exactly sure how they'd spin it, but if Michelle Grey was half the PR woman I thought she was, she'd be trying to get her client airtime right now, whether he was dead or not. It also occurred to me, in the shameless way these things do, that such a story could be exceptionally useful to my career.

The phone rang but I didn't pick it up. I muted the television and turned to watch the answering machine. The beeper whined and then a familiar voice broke through:

"It's me. Where are you? What are you doing, you lazy jerk?" My girlfriend, Lynne, calling me as a displacement activity from whatever it was she should be doing. I reached for the phone, but before I could get to it, she said, "Heard anything from Hestridge's people yet, you vindictive bastard?" There was a peal of rude, throaty laughter. "Call me." And then a click and a mechanical whir as she hung up.

I withdrew my hand from the empty space above the phone and shoved two of the dense chocolate-covered figs into my mouth in one go.

Two

When I was fourteen I was envied by teenage girls. This was because I had larger breasts than most of them. Naturally I found this infuriating, for while I welcomed the attention, I wished to be lusted over rather than envied. Instead, perhaps because of the familiarity of my shape, they looked to me to be their friend, or even their "special friend." Essentially that meant lots of long telephone conversations late at night, but no tonsil hockey and no fumbling. This was intensely frustrating because I wished to fumble with every single one of my special friends without exception, and hoped wistfully that they might fumble back. This would not have been news to them. A horny fat boy was hardly a discovery.

A fat girl who was up for it, on the other hand, was a different matter. That was a truly interesting proposition. As far as my mates and I understood, there was only one in our part of North London. Her name was Wendy Coleman and it was generally assumed that each of us, even the ones with breasts, would have a chance. We merely had to wait, and we would comfort ourselves with that thought, sometimes rigorously. My turn came one warm summer's evening, at one of those parties that seemed to take place every Saturday night at one or another of our houses: cheap cider or Thunderbird, bowls of damp potato chips, and the Clash or the Cure on the tape machine because we wanted to pretend we were tough.

Looking back, I can see that what made Wendy a viable proposition was her pretty face. She had dark, broadly set eyes, full lips, and a curiously small upturned nose. This, combined with the vital intelligence that she was prepared to do more than kiss, was all the mitigating evidence a bunch of cruel adolescent boys needed to off-set her size, which would normally have made her no-go territory. I wonder now if she was even that big. Perhaps, in adulthood, we would merely call her Rubenesque, but when we were fourteen we did not hunt around for adjectives culled from the Flemish School.

I don't recall exactly how it happened. We talked, I imagine. There was always a bit of that. I filled up her plastic cup, probably with Thunderbird, and then she took me by the hand and led me into the shadows in the depths of the garden. I did not look back because I knew every single one of my mates would be watching from the patio, grinning. I simply strolled on, trying to look nonchalant, play-ing out the scene I had rehearsed in my head so many times. She stopped by a large tree beneath which lay a rug (it was the custom for party hosts to place rugs at the back of their garden specifically for this purpose) and she pulled me down upon it. I remember that she drew me down so that I was forced to sit with my back to the tree, and she lay across my lap. For a while we kissed, slopping each other's cheeks with saliva. I tried to get my hand inside her blouse, but she batted me away, and then, as if compensating, moved hers to my belt. Soon my jeans were undone and her fingers were flicking about in the folds of my loose shirt. Finally I felt her hand make contact with my skin and tighten.

Her hand stopped moving, as if she was unsure of her next move. We were still kissing at this point, but clearly her mind was on other things because her tongue was stock still in my mouth and mine was rolling around it like a bolus of dirty clothes on a spin cycle. She had a hold on me now and as she squeezed tighter I let out a yelp, the noise smothered by the contact of our mouths. The cylinder of soft flesh she had clasped was not what she was after, but instead a generous fold of my stomach, and now her nails were digging into me from both sides as she tried to gain purchase. Finally she let go and I let my tensed shoulders sag. It was not the only thing that relaxed. Up to the point when she drove her nails home I had been eager for my moment. But the confusion had been so excruciating that my erection had simply retreated.

She found what was left of it and gave me a few desultory tugs. Then she whispered hotly in my ear, "Let's put the dead man back in his coffin, eh?"

We stumbled back out of the garden and went our separate ways, she somewhere into the house, me into a crowd of my friends still standing outside, awaiting my return. They slapped me on the back and welcomed me into the Wendy club. I made noises full of casual pride and prayed silently that she would not reveal my limp response. (I assumed she would not, using the impeccably flawed logic of a fourteen-year-old boy that it could only reflect badly upon her.) Later, when the Cure's clanking guitars gave way to Lionel Richie's "Hello," slow dances started out on the dimly lit patio. I sat mournfully and watched, as I always seemed to do through the slow dances at the end of parties. Young people swayed and tried inexpertly to slip their tongues into each other's mouths, without the other one noticing until it was too late. Gently the herd of entwined couples rotated about the patio until one of my closest friends, Stefan, was standing in front of me, his mouth already stuck suckerlike across the face of the girl in his arms. He was my slim, attractive friend, solid and toned even at fourteen, the friend no fat boy should ever have, and standing up, with this girl in his arms, he seemed even more solid. My eyes drifted casually down to where he was trying to clutch her ass, and then, sharply, I looked away because I knew what he would be presenting and I didn't want to see that. This was the difference between me and functioning males: hardness. Stefan was hard and solid. I was soft.

I should have got over this, but I haven't. The day after I was informed of John Hestridge's death I went into the office. My editor perched on the corner of my desk, one overtoned buttock clenched about its edge, and yet again I found myself cringing just as I had over twenty years before and so many times in between. Robert Hunter's muscular frame, the comfort he clearly felt in his own skin, his whole physicality, intimidated me. He appeared to understand something fundamental about maleness that had always eluded me. An American friend once told me that my editor looked like the kind of man who should be out on the Wyoming plains, roping cattle. I often wished he were.

Hunter was not looking directly at me. He rarely looks directly at anyone, in case they ask him for something he might be able to give. Instead he was staring out over the gray ranks of newsroom desks. He too had been thinking about where the Hestridge story might be heading.

"This is exactly where we should be," he said, with a gentle nod of the head. "Not just reporting the news, but making the news. Ahead of the curve. Forcing the agenda. Putting our worldview out there."

"You want me to drive more chefs to suicide?"

"Exactly . . . I mean, no, of course not. Can't blame yourself. Never do that. Not your fault he was, you know, teetering. Clearly you opened up a fault line in his, you know . . ."

"Psyche?"

"Psyche. Exactly." A silence fell between us.

He said, as if quoting an editorial he might be writing, "We do not invite events, but we do have a responsibility to understand and interpret them when they occur."

"Perhaps," I said weakly. I flexed my feet within my shoes and felt a sharp, niggling dig of pain where a corn was building on my left little toe. I always look to my feet to deliver me a little agony when I'm nervous, a physical manifestation of my anxiety. It's a learned reflex.

"No perhaps about it. Definitely," he said. A newspaper editor's only currency is certainty, and Robert Hunter's wallet was full. He stood up and raised one open hand in salute to a young woman approaching us swiftly down the floor in a clack of high heels and a rustle of fine brushed-cotton pantsuit.

"There are my boys," she said as she arrived. She reached up to kiss Hunter on the cheek and let her hand rest on the nape of his neck a little longer than necessary. He did not shrug it away.

"Marc, you know Sophie, don't you?" he said, but he did not look at me and neither did she. "From the press office." They were still staring at each other. I smiled idiotically but did not say anything. I had never spoken to her before, but I knew who she was and that was enough.

"Of course he does," Sophie said, her eyes fixed on the boss. "And may I say what a fan of yours I am. So funny. So witty." She turned to me at last. "And this Hestridge business—good for you, I say. Bloody good for you." She punched me lightly on the arm. I thanked her because I couldn't think what else to do.

"Sophie's had a few requests for media with you so I'll just leave you to get on with it, yes?"

"Of course, Bobby," she said. He winked at Sophie, ignored me, and wandered away up the office, sniffing the air like a dog looking for sheep to worry.

We were to visit various radio stations and one television studio, Sophie said as we rode in the taxi from the office. I would be asked pointed questions about the death of John Hestridge and I was to be myself. "A certain amount of regret, I think," she said as she flicked through a pile of papers on her lap, "but don't overdo it and certainly don't accept responsibility. Restaurant business is very complicated. You are merely a reporter, offering the consumer help in making a choice. You know the deal."

And I did. I might have despised Sophie for her professional exuberance and her professional enthusiasm and her professionally glossy hair, but that didn't mean I had to disagree with her. There was a clear marketing opportunity here and the product was me. I had a responsibility to do the product justice.

In one radio studio a middle-aged man with coffee stains on his sweater and yellow teeth said, "Do you feel like you've claimed a scalp?"

And I said confidently, "Not at all. I feel dreadfully sad, for John, for his family, for his friends. But the restaurant business can be very difficult. More restaurant businesses end in failure than success, you know, and in that context, tragedies like this are inevitable."

"You did suggest John Hestridge deserved to be executed."

"It was whimsy."

In another radio studio a woman wearing too much makeup who clearly saw her future in television stared intently at a place between my eyes and said:

"Did you weep for John Hestridge?"

I sighed deeply and said, "I'm not embarrassed to say yes, I did weep a little."

"Out of guilt?"

A light breathy laugh, of the kind I had heard politicians produce. "Not at all." Back to serious voice. "For the loss of a life, cruelly ended by the vicious realities of the restaurant trade."

"Are you one of those vicious realities?"

"I'm just a reporter, there to represent the consumer. I have a duty to report as I find." I reckoned I was doing pretty well and Sophie agreed with me.

In the studios of a late-night news program which was recording an interview for broadcast later that day, powder was applied to my shiny forehead. I shuffled in my seat in an attempt to pull down my jacket so that it wasn't rucking up about my shoulders and squinted at the lights to distinguish my shadowed surroundings. Just before the recording began, the presenter, a whippet-thin man in a suit designed to disguise the fact, leaned toward me, squeezed my knee, and hissed, "Love your column. So nasty. So vicious," before swinging back immediately to camera for his introduction.

"It's being called the New Vitriol, a form of newspaper criticism so aggressive and violent it may even have the power to kill. Two days ago the renowned chef John Hestridge committed suicide. He blamed his despair on the restaurant critic Marc Basset, who the day before had called in his column for Hestridge to be arrested, tried, and executed for crimes against food. And Marc Basset joins me now."

My face was fixed in a completely inappropriate grin. "It was whimsy," I muttered, just loudly enough for the microphone to pick it up.

"Is that what you said to his widow and child?"

"I, er, haven't heard from them yet, but obviously—"

"Let's hear from them now."

I followed the presenter's line of sight to a television monitor sitting on a trolley just behind one of the cameras. Hestridge's wife, Fiona, appeared on the screen, looking pale and red-eyed. A small girl of perhaps five or six was on her lap. The girl was wearing a shaggy white woolen cardigan decorated with little woolly sheep and she had a mess of long dark hair that no one had helped her brush for a couple of days. She looked like a tangled ball of wool.

"Cooking was his passion," Fiona Hestridge said in answer to an unheard questioner off camera. "That's all John wanted to do. It was all he ever wanted to do, and now . . ." Her voice cracked, her eyes closed, and she pressed one loose fist against the bridge of her nose as though she might somehow be able to stanch the coming flood of tears with the ball of her hand.

The wild little girl looked up from her perch on her lap. "Don't cry, Mummy."

And cut.

"So, Marc Basset, how does it feel?"

Three

S ophie smiled warmly and tipped her head to one side.
"It went fine, darling."

"You think so?"

"Absolutely. How's the pork and clams?" I looked at my plate.
We were in a new Portuguese place behind the TV studios.

"It's good," I said, distracted.

"Really?" She looked disappointed.

"No. I mean it's great. Punchy sauce. Great tender pieces of
meat. The seafood's fresh."

She curled up her nose and looked at my plate in disgust. "Oh
dear."

"How can that interview be fine?"

She looked back at me and waved one manicured hand over her
shoulder as if shooing away a fly. "Because nobody remembers the
beginning of television interviews. They only remember the end."

"The bit where I said the stuff about responsibility to the consumer?"

She pointed at me as though I were a promising student who had
stumbled on the answer to a particularly difficult question. "Exactly
that." She leaned forward as if to sniff my plate. "Are you sure you
like it?"

I nodded. "Really. Yes. It's a good rustic dish, well executed.
Authentic, my kind of food . . ."

She tutted and her glossed lips slipped into a delicate pout. "I was hoping you'd hate it."

"Why?"

"In your column, when you like something, you get a bit . . . I don't know . . . serious," she said as she toyed with the herbaceous border of arugula salad in front of her.

"I take food seriously."

"But you're so funny when you hate." She looked up at me and I could swear she was suddenly salivating in a way that she had not done over her lunch. "You have a particular way of communicating disdain which is very special, very *now.*" She spat the last word out, as if pleased to be rid of it. "What was it you said a few weeks ago about that Italian-Chinese fusion place?" She was squinting into the middle distance as if trying to focus on the memory. She looked back at me triumphantly. "That the food would taste better coming back up than it did going down." She grinned.

"Something like that."

"And the new fish restaurant in Margate where all the waiters wear full waders and big yellow oilskins like they're deep-sea fishermen—do they really dress like that?"

"They really do."

"What was it you said that time?"

"Er, it was as if the entire staff were dressed for an exceptionally safe sex party," I said, quoting myself with a shy grin.

"That's it. Fabulous."

"Actually, some of the fish was okay. It was just the tacky theme I hated, which was the point I was trying to make in the—"

She waved me away. "And of course, the brilliant one you did of that Soviet-themed café in Manchester."

"Uncle Joe's Kitchen?"

"That's the one. Didn't you say that you finally understood why the Soviet Union had collapsed?"

"Sort of. I said a bit more than that, actually. It was more of a general critique of Eastern European cuisine which—"

"Oh I know, darling, I know. You say an awful lot. You're terribly brilliant and clever. It's just that certain things you say stick in the memory more than others."

"You really do remember what I write?"

"Of course. How could I not?" She leaned forward conspiratori- ally and whispered, "You do hate better than any other newspaper columnist in Britain."

I nodded slowly because I knew what she was saying was true. I had always preferred writing a bad review to a good one. A good review was a drudge, a desperate struggle for diverting hyperbole. A readable column needs a strong narrative, and nice experiences in great restaurants don't make for good stories. There is no definable beginning, middle, and end, just a constant wash of pleasure. A bad restaurant, on the other hand, is stuffed full of character and intrigue and plot. Terrible places, and the suffering they cause their cus- tomers, make for good stories, and so I had begun to seek them out. I had become the high priest of hate.

That evening I managed a little restraint. I ate only two squares of the Manjari and just one of the tobacco truffles while watching the interview air. Lynne sat next to me on the sofa, unnaturally still, holding my free hand, not daring to look at me in case she grimaced.

When it was over she reached very deliberately for the remote control, switched off the TV set, and after a moment's silence said, "Well, that was okay."

"It was a disaster."

She nodded wisely. "It was an okay disaster."

"I came off as a cynical bastard."

She grinned, kissed me on the cheek, and said, "He's a good interviewer, isn't he?"

"That's not funny."

"It is, quite."

"I've got a reputation to think about."

"Lighten up, Marc. You're a restaurant critic. Not the bloody archbishop of Canterbury."

"He made me look like a self-serving prick."

"Maybe, but you were still the prick that I love. Anyway, I thought you looked rather dashing."

Silence.

"Look, there was no way you could have come out of that looking good. You were set up. Everybody will be able to see that."

"You think so?"

"Definitely. Trust me. It will all be fine."

It will all be fine: one of the most comforting sentences in the English language. No drama. No tension or bathos. Just a gentle, rhythmic reassurance. If I were asked to identify what it was about Lynne McPartland that bound me to her, it would be the way she could say those five words in her low, calm voice and make them certain and true. I needed a woman who could make me believe her, and Lynne was the one. She had been from our very first night together.

By which I mean our *real* very first night, not the actual one, of which I have no memory at all. We were at university together and moved in the same hormonally charged crowd. We must have met at some point early in our first year and become friends in the careless way one does at that age, which is to say without identifying any good reason not to be. I recall her then as imposing, though not as tall or broad. She simply seemed to fill more than her own share of space, by standing still. She was the kind of person who would always get served first at the bar, however crowded it was.

After we graduated I went to London, she went abroad for a few years, and we lost contact. She ended up working for the British Council in Prague, and when she decided to come home, returned to a position in the literature department at their headquarters near Trafalgar Square. Her job was to arrange tours of gloomy Scottish writers to places like Belarus and the Czech Republic which had done nothing to deserve the punishment. She had just started work-

ing there when we met, by chance, in a coffee shop on the Charing
Cross Road. The thick black hair was longer, but other than that she
was exactly as I remembered her, down to the lush lipstick and the
habit of only wearing black or gray and the mocking smile. She
seemed so relieved to come across someone she knew, and so enthusiastic, that I invited her for dinner the next day even though, I realized, we didn't really know each other, not as adults.

That was our real very first night together. She sat at the pine
table in the kitchen of my Maida Vale flat, the flat we would eventually share, sipped delicately from a glass of ballsy red wine (I think
I was going through my Rioja phase), and asked me questions I
didn't want to answer.

"So you haven't made like everybody else and settled down?"

"What do you mean?" I was at the stove, heating a little olive oil
and butter in a roasting pan ready for a lovely fillet of Welsh lamb
that I had marinated in garlic, juniper, olive oil, and a dribble of
lemon juice.

"There's no Mrs. Basset?"

The first wisps of smoke began to rise off the oil and I dropped the
meat into it. It fizzed and whistled and contracted a little in shock.

"There is. Her name's Geraldine, she lives in Northwood, and
she's my mother."

"Very funny."

"Thank you."

"You know what I mean."

I shook my head. "No Mrs. Bassets. No potential Mrs. Bassets.
Never likely to be."

"Why not?"

I swigged from my own glass of wine. "Firstly," I said, waving
my meat fork at her, "point of principle: I can't imagine any sensible
women willingly taking that name and if they wanted to do so I
wouldn't be interested in them. And secondly, a practical point
which makes every other consideration academic: I have displayed a
marked inability to get myself laid."

"Unlucky in love?"

"I don't even get to lust."

She wrinkled her nose. "What's all that about?"

I turned the heat down on the meat and began to spoon the hot oil and butter over the raw upward-facing side. "I don't know," I said, lying. "I'm just not, you know, fanciable."

"Oh for god's sake . . ."

I shrugged and turned to her. "Come on. Look at me. All of me. Women do not want . . ." I held my arms apart, the meat fork reaching upward to the light fixture, and looked down at myself: the enormous chest with the nipples in different time zones, the rounded belly, the heavy thighs and thick calves; the body that made shopping for clothes a nightmare, that made airplane seats a torture, that as a kid had forced me to sit alone so many times at the end of parties through "Sexual Healing" or Spandau Ballet's "True" or something equally irritating by Phil Collins. At the overall hugeness of me.

". . . this."

"What total bollocks."

I turned back to the stove to flip the lamb for a minute or two. The room smelled of garlic and hot, smoky butter. Perfect. "I can only tell you as it is."

"You're not even that big."

"I have a forty-inch waist."

I saw her eyebrows rise involuntarily. She rolled her glass between the palms of her hands as if warming it and said, "You don't look it." She slugged the wine and swallowed, quickly.

"Thank you."

"Just stating a fact." And then: "There must have been women."

"Oh, sure."

"So what happens?"

"You really are intent on interrogating me, aren't you?"

Lynne raised her hands in surrender. "I can shut up . . ."

I clattered the pan into the oven. It would need about fifteen minutes if it was to stay the right side of pink within. "No, it's all right."

I picked up my glass of wine and leaned back against the sink. "We spend one night together, maybe two. And then something happens and—"

"You can't believe a girl fancies you so you do something to screw it up."

"Christ. What are you like after *two* glasses?"

"I'm just guessing. Is that it?"

"Never been good at self-analysis."

She drained her glass. "The way you describe it, you make it sound like a miracle you ever lost your cherry."

"Almost was."

"Oh yeah? How old were you?"

"You're so smart. You guess." Despite myself, I was starting to enjoy this. Normally there would be nothing I would like to discuss less than my heroic failures. But Lynne made it feel almost like sport, and in sport, heroic failures have virtue. It was liberating.

She wrinkled her nose again. "Obviously has to be quite late. Eighteen?"

I jutted my chin upward to say "higher."

"Nineteen?"

"Guess again."

"Older than that? Bless—"

"I was twenty."

"You were at college?"

"Yup. All that time when I should have been shagging around and I didn't sort it out until my third year."

"Anybody I know?"

"Jesus."

"Oh, come on. You know you want to tell me." She grabbed the bottle and refilled her glass. I rolled a mouthful of my own wine over my tongue and swallowed.

"Jennie Sampson."

"Jennie Sampson? Jennie Sampson?" Beat. "Jennie Sampson! I remember her. She was gorgeous. Quiet but gorgeous. Always carried her books against her chest as if she were trying to hide behind them."

"That's the one."

"Shy, though."

"You mean you never talked to her."

"Perhaps. So what happened?"

"What do you mean?"

"What happened? How long did it last? Was it love? Did you propose? Or did you screw that one up too?"

Oh yes, I thought to myself. I screwed that one up. Boy, did I screw that one up. "It just . . . fizzled out," I said quietly.

She tipped her head to one side, looked me up and down, and said, "The only problem is you. You're a very attractive man, my dear. Dark, big, substantial . . ."

I snorted with derision and stared into the depths of my glass.

"No, really. Who wants thin men with their little hips and their pigeon chests? Not me. Give me heft any day, something to get your arms around."

"You're being very kind."

"Jesus Christ." She pulled mockingly at her thick black tresses, as if trying to rip them out. "How am I going to get through to you?" Suddenly she stood up, slammed her glass down on the table, and said, "There's only one thing for it. I'm just going to have to have sex with you. Come on." She strode out of the kitchen and I, obediently, followed, helpfully calling in a small voice, "Second room on the left." In the doorway to my room I hesitated. She turned to me, raised one hand to my cheek, and said, "It will all be fine."

Afterward, when we were done, we lay on the bed and she said, "I thought about jumping you at college but I'm glad I didn't. You'd only have done something childish to piss me off. Now that your secret's out you can't do that because I'll always see through you."

I sat bolt upright and shouted, "Bugger it!"

"I'm not that bad a proposition, am I?"

"No. No. It's the lamb. I've ruined the lamb." The sound of self-congratulatory laughter filled the room: our relationship had been born just as our first dinner together had died.

That was almost six years ago. We were still together, she was still saying "It will all be fine," and I was still happily believing her. Or at least, I had been until that dark February evening in front of the television, with the last of the tobacco truffles finally breaking apart on my tongue and the screen now sitting blank in the corner. A man was dead, a little girl was without her father, and whatever my mother, my editor, or my girlfriend said about not blaming myself, I couldn't escape feeling responsible. It was my review that John Hestridge had taped to the oven door before he climbed inside. Not pages of the *Larousse Gastronomique*. Not the definition of the word "chef" from the *Oxford English Dictionary*. My review. That surely had to stand for something.

Four

She found me in the early hours, hunched in the night darkness, my face steel gray in the glow of the computer screen.

"What are you doing, love?" she said in a thin voice, still drunk with sleep. I didn't look at her. I kept my eyes on the pixeled words on the screen.

"Reading."

"Reading what?"

"Me. My last piece. The Hestridge piece."

"Marc, sweetheart, there's a time for narcissism, and three o'clock . . . no, Christ . . . half past three in the morning is not it."

"Funny."

Lynne moved to the sofa alongside me and sat down in the corner, folding her feet in beneath herself. She picked up an overstuffed pillow to hug to her belly. There we sat, in the darkness, dressing-gowned and chilled.

"You couldn't sleep?"

I shook my head and reached forward to tap the screen, as if it were the guilty party. "I thought this was so bloody funny when I wrote it," I said. "I thought it was clever and smart and—"

"It *was* clever and smart," she said. "It still is. You're brilliant." I heard her yawn but I didn't turn to look. "You know that."

"No. I know. I mean . . ." I swiveled around on my office chair to look at her, hiding back in the shadows for warmth. "I've always been confident about my writing. About my ability to turn a phrase,

to keep people's attention. Whatever. I might have my other insecu-
rities—"

"Yeah. It's the thing that stops you being insufferable, my love. If
you were a smart-ass *and* you thought you were gorgeous, I
wouldn't be here."

"Let me finish. It's a package. I need to believe in the column,
that it's doing a good job, that it's right, to balance the other stuff.
But this Hestridge thing—"

"You can't blame yourself. I've told you."

"I wasn't an innocent bystander."

"You didn't open the oven door and usher him in."

"Lynne!"

"You know what I mean."

"I wrote a column that was the . . ." I hesitated, searching for the
right word. ". . . catalyst."

"Can't we talk about this in the morning? It's so bloody late, it's early."

I turned back to the screen and said, more sharply than I
intended, "Go back to bed."

"Marc . . ."

"Just go to bed and I'll work it out by myself. Go back to bed."

She came and stood behind me, a hand resting on each of my
shoulders. I could smell the familiar, comforting musk of bed and
dressing gown and sleep-sweated skin beneath. She stroked my
neck with one hot hand and I realized how cold I was. "What do you
want to do about it, Marc?" she said gently.

"I want to go and see her. I want to go and see Fiona Hestridge."

"And say what?" I looked up and over my shoulder at Lynne, my
lips pursed as if they were restraining the words.

"I want to apologize," I said. She nodded very slowly and lightly.
"I'm not pretending it will make everything right," I said. "I know it
won't. But it might make her feel a little better."

"And you too?"

I looked back at the screen and shrugged, as if the thought hadn't
occurred to me before. "Perhaps."

She turned me about on the chair so that my face brushed against the soft, underwashed toweling of her dressing gown and the rise and fall of her breast beneath. She held my face in her hands. "Marc Basset apologizing?" she said quietly as she looked down at me. "It must be serious."

I nodded. "It is." We looked at each other in silence through the backlit darkness. "I'll turn off the computer now," I said eventually.

"You do that," she said, and she stooped to kiss the top of my head.

Hestridge at 500 sat on a cluttered, scrubbed stretch of London's Fulham Road, guarded on one side by antique shops selling things that probably weren't, and on the other by interior design shops selling things nobody needed. It was a street of fakery and superfluity and at its nexus was a restaurant that, according to my review, was a celebration of both. I stood a little distance away on the other side of the road so nobody within could see me before I wanted them to, and stared at the frontage through the clatter of the London traffic. The look of the place still infuriated me: the frigid glass and brushed aluminum facade, sounding an overture for the brushed aluminum and concrete interior that I had compared unfavorably in my review to a public parking lot:

. . . only less useful. This is a part of town that could really do with a public parking lot. Here they have built one, and yet—by mistake? by design? who knows with these people?—they have filled it with ugly tables and chairs for the serving of ugly food. Every time I drive past it in future I will have to restrain myself from steering my knackered Volvo straight through the frontage, out of some desperate desire to put it to its proper use.

That was all irrelevant now; my review was superfluous too. I took a deep breath, held it for a moment, and then stepped out to cross the road. It was a little after eleven in the morning, and as I pushed open the door, chairs were being stacked on tables by a busboy who was vacuuming the polished wood floor. I asked for Mrs. Hestridge and he nodded back toward the hard, gloomy depths of the room. I found her sitting at the farthest table, just in front of the back bar (six girders stacked one on top of another and topped with polished granite). She was surrounded by ring binders full of papers and was staring at a ledger, the mass of unruly curly hair that she had bequeathed to her daughter falling down over her eyes. There was a glass of sparkling mineral water on the table, and a cup of coffee, a plate of cookies, a bowl of olives, and a dish of dark chocolate petits fours, all untouched, as though someone had been trying to feed and water her, unsuccessfully. I emerged quietly into the pool of light around her table, dropped from the pinprick track lights up above, the only ones that were illuminated here in the restaurant's lower reaches.

"Mrs. Hestridge . . ."

She started at the sound of my voice and looked up, squinting, as if my face were half-remembered. "Yes," she said tentatively.

"Marc . . . Basset. I've come to . . ." But my words died as she dropped back in her chair and looked me up and down.

"I know who you are."

"Yes. I imagine you would."

We stared at each other in silence for a few seconds until I gestured at a chair by the table and said, "May I sit down?"

"I'm not sure," she said coldly. She looked at the mass of papers surrounding her. "Are you any good at accounts?"

I shook my head. "I'm terrible with numbers."

"Only good with words?"

"I'm not even sure about that anymore."

"No?" Suddenly distracted, she looked back past me, at somebody else who had entered the room. "Charlie, it's all right. You can come out of the shadows. My daughter Charlotte, Mr. Basset. Charlie, this is—"

The little girl emerged on the edge of the pool of light.

"I know who you are," she said in a small voice. "I saw you on the video with Mummy. Mummy says you're the dickhead who made Daddy kill himself."

"Charlotte!"

I closed my eyes and put one hand up to silence her mother. "No, really. It's all right."

"It isn't bloody all right, Mr. Basset. I don't want my six-year-old daughter using language like that."

"But you were the one who said he was a dickhead, Mummy."

"Please, Charlie!"

"Anyway, what does dickhead mean?"

"Charlie, go back upstairs and I'll come and see you in a minute when Mr. Basset—"

"No. Hang on," I said. "Just a moment." I turned to Charlie and got down on my haunches so I was at her level, so that my knees creaked and my ample thighs stretched the thin material of my trousers. "It's okay." I looked at her straight on. Maybe this was the way to do it. Say the words to the daughter. If I could say it to the little girl, get it out there, it would be more real, more meant, more true. I would have played my part and I could go. I chewed my bottom lip for a moment. Charlie stared back at me from beneath her bangs.

I spoke slowly and deliberately. "I am so sorry that the things I said about your daddy's restaurant made him go away—"

"He didn't go away," she said sharply. "He killed himself. In the oven. Back there. In the kitchen." She pointed to a swing door in the corner.

I closed my eyes, sniffed, and tried to recover myself.

"Charlie!"

I raised my hand again to silence her mother. "No, really, it's okay," I said. I paused again and took a deep breath. "Charlotte, I'm really sorry your daddy killed himself after he read the things I wrote." I felt something cold and wet slip down the side of my nose and drop off toward the smooth floor below. Charlotte frowned at me and then looked up and over my shoulder.

"Mummy, this man's crying."

"That's all I need," Fiona Hestridge said, "another weeping male. I've had a kitchen full of them this week."

I said, "I'm sorry," and lifted one open hand to my face to wipe the tears away from my hot cheeks.

"Mr. Basset. Marc . . . come up here. Sit down. Please. Have a drink of water."

I pulled myself up and went to the table. I smiled thinly and sat down. Charlotte sat down next to me and reached across the table for a chocolate. I watched her greedy hand and the stare from her mother that said, "Just the one and no more."

"I really am sorry," I said as the lozenge of bittersweet chocolate disappeared into the little girl's velvet pouch of a mouth. I turned to her mother. "I didn't mean to hurt John or you or . . ." Another tear ran infuriatingly to the end of my nose and dropped off onto the crisp linen tablecloth below.

"Enough, please. Stop," she said. She passed over the glass of water and a tissue. I drank deep, until I could feel the cool liquid flowing through me and calming my breathing.

When I was done, she sat back again and said, "You don't need to blame yourself."

"But really . . ."

She silenced me with a simple shake of the head. "John was severely depressed. Had been for about a year, maybe two. It wasn't the first time he'd tried to do himself in. To be honest, I was surprised it took him so long."

I said "I'm sorry" because it seemed the only thing worth saying.

Fiona let out a sharp, ironic laugh. "Do you want to know the truth? I'll tell you the truth. John was a lousy chef. A really terrible chef. And the real tragedy of it was, he knew it. He knew exactly how bad he was. That was what destroyed him. Not you. Sorry to disappoint you, but that's the way it is."

"There was still no need for me to be cruel."

"Much of what you said was right."

I looked around the gloomy dining room and then nodded toward the ledgers. "Will you sell?"

"Christ no, can't do that."

"Why not?"

"We're doing too well. The place has been packed each service since John died, because of the press coverage. We're doing two sittings in the evenings. I think they were coming in to find out how awful it was, but Ralph, John's sous-chef, has taken charge of the stoves and he can actually cook, so the food's great. I'm afraid that does mean that there are lots of people who now think you're a vindictive monster who hounded someone unnecessarily to his death."

I said, "I think I can live with it."

A chef in pristine whites stuck his head around the swing door to the kitchen. "The first batch is cool enough now, Fiona," he said.

"Thanks, Ralph." She turned to me. "Come through. There's something you should try." We trooped through to the kitchen, where a team of four young men with cropped hair and serious brows were deep into preparations for the lunch service, chopping and arranging, dicing and mincing. On a set of wire trays placed upon a burnished metal work surface stood half a dozen loaves of bread, some round and golden with a light shiny glazed crust, others oval and matte and a darker blue-gray color. Fiona Hestridge picked up one of the lighter loaves, sniffed it, and then turned it over to tap the bottom. It sounded hollow and she nodded approvingly. She sawed the loaf into wedges on a cutting board and then smeared them with a thick layer of pale, creamy butter before handing them around. I took a bite. The bread was warm and had an almost sweet nuttiness, cut through by a just discernible sourness from the yeast.

"Is this a new recipe you're trying out?" I said, my mouth full. I took another bite.

"No, no," she said softly. "This is the first bread cooked in the oven since John was found in it." She nodded toward the huge industrial bread oven in the corner. "I wanted to do something special for when people come back here after the funeral this afternoon so I told the boys not to clean the oven out and just to bake. I think it's rather nice. It will be like having John with us, won't it?" She and Charlie took chunks out of their pieces of bread, happy now to be consuming the essence of the man who had left them so suddenly.

The thick, sodden mush of bread was still sitting in my mouth. I blinked and swallowed and felt it drag itself down to my hollowing stomach. I had eaten enough.

I said, "I should go now. You've obviously got a lot to do before this afternoon."

"You're welcome to come to the funeral. Michelle Grey will be there."

I shook my head. "I don't want to intrude." And I certainly didn't want to be there when the sandwiches came round.

I said good-bye to Charlie, who merely sniffed and took another bite from her bread. Fiona led me out, past the table with the dish of dark chocolate petits fours. Even they didn't appeal after the John Hestridge Memorial Loaf. Outside on the pavement, one shoulder leaning back against the front door, she said, "I really don't think you have to blame yourself. But even so, thank you for coming." She took a sudden deep breath through her nose, her lips pursed, fighting back a wave of the dread emotion she had so far managed to smother.

"And thank you for apologizing," she said, her voice now thin and unstable. "It matters." I nodded. Her eyes were wet and glazed but had yet to overflow. "I'm going inside now," she all but whispered, pointing to the depths of the restaurant. She mouthed the words "thank you" again, turned away from me, and went back inside.

I stood on the pavement for a good two minutes, not daring to move, examining the feelings of lightness and joy that were now seeping into me. I felt my shoulders untense and my breathing become easy. It was clear that something—something very special—was happening.

In the last few weeks before my father died, by then bedridden, he took my brother's battered tape recorder and gave an account of his times which he said was for us to listen to "later," without saying when "later" might be. According to André Basset, his life had been full of "deafening moments": the deafening moment when, as a child, he had discovered the reassuring alchemy of the stove; the deafening moment, in adolescence, when he had become intoxicated by the tight geometry of architecture; the deafening moment in his late teens when he had realized he would have to leave Switzerland to have any hope of happiness. These, he said, "were the moments that deafened me as a person and deafened my life."

Now here I was, experiencing what the Basset brothers always referred to, in memory of their father, as a truly deafening moment. I, Marc Basset, who had never before apologized for anything, or at least not for anything important, who had never before seen the point of repentance, had finally said the word "sorry." And I felt wonderful.

Five

Most people assume happiness to be a basic right, like access to clean drinking water or forty channels of cable TV in hotel rooms. Maybe it's because my dad died when I was young—an excellent excuse for most things—or simply that I'm a gloomy bastard, but I've never felt that way. For me, happiness has always been something I've had to work at. It's not that I loll about constantly with a face like a winter's sky, always on the lookout for somewhere handy to hitch a rope; it's just that the easy, untroubled sunniness enjoyed by others seems to escape me. I don't do sunny.

Which was what made the whole Fiona Hestridge experience so damn intoxicating. I left her restaurant swelling with pleasure. I believed I had been a good person, not just to Fiona but to myself. I had brought succor to the needy and soothed the hurt, and in so doing, I had atoned for my sins. I thought of all these things as I walked east along the Fulham Road, past the locations of no less than three restaurants which had closed shortly after savagings by me. ("The Wooden Table may not be the very worst restaurant in the world," began one, "but I sense that the title is now well within its grasp.") Euphoria is funny like that; it is a pleasure that blinds. I loved myself.

And then I saw him standing, stooped and round-shouldered, examining the contents of an antique shop's window, and in an instant, self-love turned to self-loathing. It was as if somebody had turned up the force of gravity, so that my heart, my liver, my entire viscera were dragged downward toward the pavement by a ballast of guilt. He was very much smaller than I remembered him (for which I immediately blamed myself) and the big, soft, jowly head was now thin and slack-skinned, but he was still recognizable as Harry Brennan, the man whose job I stole.

At the time, a little over four years ago, I was a copy editor on the newspaper's review section. Brennan had been the restaurant critic for almost twenty years and had taken on the kind of legendary status that is accorded those whose achievement is survival. It was rumored that on a trip to the Pacific in the 1960s, he had taken part in a cannibalistic burial ritual for the experience of tasting human flesh. In addition to dog, cat, and snake, which he had tried on a press trip to China, he was also said to have eaten, on separate occasions, both braised otter and roasted badger. It was said that he once dispatched an entire bottle of a 1900 Château d'Yquem, worth six thousand pounds, without offering a single drop to any of his companions at the table; that he had been thrown out of Simpson's on the Strand for eating over three pounds of the prime rib of beef from the cart and only then announcing that he should not have to pay for it because it was overcooked. Even now, long after he had left the field, they told "Harry stories."

He was a scoundrel and a reactionary and his prose was irredeemably pompous ("I journeyed this week to Lombardy, perchance to taste the black jewel of this land, which is the truffle . . ."), but for all that, I respected him because he knew his stuff. He, in turn, liked me. I had become his copy editor first by chance, then by habit, finally by edict. He knew that I cooked and he trusted me to catch his errors, which were, to be fair, few.

Late one morning he appeared at my shoulder in the office and stood wheezing and coughing over me. His eyes were wet and rheumy, and every half minute or so, he lifted one plump, pink fist to his mouth to smother another hacking, fluid cough. He told me, in a phrase that was pure Harry, that he was "held fast within the grip of an infection which puts me at some disadvantage." He was due that day to have lunch at the Noble Scallop, an aging fish restaurant in London's St. James's that he had visited frequently but not reviewed for many years. The management, who were close personal friends, had just employed a new chef. He had no doubt the food would be perfect, he said, but he was not fully equipped to judge. The cold he was suffering from had stolen his sense of taste. He asked if he might borrow mine.

"We shall order the same dishes. I can then make judgments upon texture and presentation, and you, dear boy, can tell me whether the flavor is up to snuff." Of course I agreed. I was flattered by the proposition. And anyway, it was a free lunch.

So we went to the Noble Scallop, where we were seated at a prime corner table. Glassware stood polished and erect. Napkins were unfurled. Brown bread was offered and taken. Naturally the maître d' made a fuss of us; any pretense of the restaurant critic's anonymity was pointless here. We began with a serviceable plate of razor clams in garlic and chili which Harry described as "a studied act of innovation" for a restaurant which had been serving some of its dishes for thirty years. I said all the right things: I described the smokiness of the foaming butter and the sweet aromatics of the garlic and the deep brown nuttiness of the chili, the burn from which was not overwhelming. We polished our plates with the bread, drained our glasses of a slightly overchilled Pouilly-Fumé (Harry drank mostly French wines), and awaited the main course, a dish of roasted cod with cockles.

Harry left the table for what he called "a moment's discreet micturition," and while he was away, our food arrived. I knew, even before the plate landed in front of me, that something was up. The people at the table on the other side of the restaurant should have known. If they had, they did not show it. Maybe they were just being polite, because the cod stank. The smell of a fishmonger's slab at day's end cut through by the acute tang of unemptied trash can hung over the table. I liked my fish dead, but not this dead. I leaned down, sniffed the plate, and gagged. Then I looked about the room. It was business as usual. The maître d' saw me looking around. He smiled and took a step forward as if to come to my assistance, but I waved him away with a cheerful wink and a single raised hand, flat palm forward. How could I announce that the fish was off? Harry was friends with the owners. The maître d' had greeted him as if he were family. Harry would be mortified. Or at least, I didn't want to take the chance that he might be. It wasn't as if we knew each other that well and I certainly didn't want to screw up on this, my first meal out with him.

I knew I had no option. I checked that no one was watching and then swiftly switched the plates so he had mine and vice versa. I sniffed Harry's. It seemed fine. It did not smell poisonous. It was not threatening. He returned, coughing and spluttering and wiping his nose with a crumpled handkerchief, and immediately launched into a story about the time he had caught a chef rinsing his hands in the toilet bowl at a restaurant because the sinks were not working.

". . . and he was there, in his stained whites, bent double over the porcelain, I tell you, his hands plunged into the water right up to the elbow . . ."

At the end of each phrase he took a deep breath, but his cold was so thick and intense that he could breathe only through his mouth. He detected nothing. While he talked he held in one hand a fork, which he waved about to punctuate his story. I glanced down at the toxic plate in front of him.

". . . so I said to the chef, 'Dear boy, is it common practice in this establishment for the kitchen brigade to rinse its hands in the latrines?' "

Occasionally he too looked down at his fish and his fork headed toward it as if he were about to plunge in. Unconsciously, as the fork descended, I would hold my breath. But then, like a falcon teasing its prey, the cutlery would swoop upward again and I would exhale with desperate relief.

". . . and he said, 'If you think this is bad you should see the fahrking kitchens.' " He paused. "The food was rather good, actually."

Again Harry looked down at his plate. The fork went in for the kill. Here he goes, I thought, dicing with death. This is the moment when it all goes horribly, gastrically wrong. But what had started as a small rumbling laugh at his own cleverness soon turned into a roaring, hacking cough, and once more he broke off to smother his furious mouth. I let out my breath, closed my eyes, and waited. Finally Harry's coughing subsided. I opened my eyes.

"You all right, chap?" he said. "You look a little pale."

"I'm fine."

Harry looked down at his plate again. "Lunch, then," he said with a special certainty and enthusiasm, and he smiled at me.

"Yes," I said. "Lunch." I watched as his fork went down and the first rancid flakes of pale fish came up and disappeared into his mouth. He closed his lips around the end of the fork and smiled. "An interesting texture," he said, and I nodded. Doubtless it was.

I'm not sure what I was expecting, but at first nothing happened. We simply ate our lunch. Harry held forth on great chefs he had known and I chipped in with knowing oohs and aahs at the right moment, though I couldn't stop myself from examining his face for signs that something might be awry. We ordered dessert, a pear tarte Tatin each (though, naturally, I wanted the chocolate fondant cake), and we ate it with gusto. I began to relax. Maybe the fish was not that badly off after all. Maybe it was just a little high. Or maybe not.

Shortly after we ordered coffee Harry began shifting about in his seat. Then he began belching, one hand pressed flat against the roundness of his tummy as if to ease the passage of the air. Droplets of sweat formed along his top lip, and the color drained away from his face. Finally, just as the coffee was being poured, he pushed his chair back from the table, stood up unsteadily, and muttered, "You will have to excuse me for a moment. It's all been rather too good."

I watched, appalled and fascinated. I knew what was about to happen. It had been inevitable from the moment the main courses arrived. The only question now was whether he would make it out of the dining room before the fish made it out of him. He leaned forward a little to steady himself against the table. He opened his mouth as if to burp one more time, his hand rested again upon his stomach. There was a small hiss, like air escaping from a punctured bicycle tire, and then he threw up in a raging, creamy torrent that splashed against the table's edge and downward to the floor.

The staff were immediately upon us, cleaning and wiping and lifting poor Harry away to a banquette in the bar, upon which he fell back, his greasy, gray eyelids fluttering with the exertion. I wanted to help, but alongside their professionalism I was only getting in the way. So instead I stood against the wall, feeling childlike with guilt. I had done this to Harry Brennan. Me. Just because I couldn't face a little embarrassment. After he had been sick twice more into an ice bucket placed at his side for the purpose, he gestured for me to approach him. He gripped my hand and stared up at me from the upholstered softness of his makeshift bed.

"Harry, I'm really sorry but . . ."

He silenced me with a sad shake of his head. "There's no time, dear boy," he said in a thin voice, as if the light were fading. "I can't go on. You must do my work for me, now. You must take my place." And then, in a whisper, his head lifted just a little off the bench: "They are expecting my copy by six this evening."

I was horrified. "But Harry, I've never . . ."

He let go of my hand, closed his eyes, and let his head drop back. "You know what to do, Marc. You know what to do." He turned his face toward where I stood, and with a certain elegance, vomited once more, neatly, into the ice bucket.

For two hours I paced about my flat, eyeing the clock. How the hell could I stand in for Harry Brennan? The great Harry Brennan? How could I be him? I sat at the computer and started the review five, six, seven times, but each attempt was clumsy or dull or simply irritatingly stupid. Half an hour before deadline I poured myself a large measure of vodka from a bottle that had been lying in the freezer for a few weeks, just to steady my nerves. It steadied me so well that I poured myself another and then a third. I ate three squares of Man-jari, a couple of white chocolate truffles, and a handful of thickly coated macadamia nuts. Five minutes after that I wrote an introduc-tion that seemed suddenly to make an awful lot of sense:

> You can learn much about the quality of a restaurant's cooking by the speed with which the food disappears into a diner's mouth. You can learn rather more if it happens to come flying out again.

This was what was needed, I told myself. Something sharp. Some-thing deliberate and unflinching. Think of poor Harry lying there, pale gray against the sea green velveteen. Didn't he deserve the truth? Isn't that what he would want? And so I continued to write, a full one thousand coruscating words partly about old restaurants which should know when to give up the game, but mostly about the experience of watching your dining companion throw up. ("It is, I think, bad manners to identify the dishes as they make the return trip.") I filed my copy an hour late and poured myself another large vodka to celebrate.

The next morning, as I was soothing my hangover, Robert Hunter called me from his office. He had read my review. He liked it. He liked it a lot. In fact he liked it so much he had decided to sack Harry Brennan and give me the job.

That's how it happened: I became a restaurant critic because of one poisonous serving of old cod that should have been mine, but wasn't.

Six

Making an apology, I now know, is like initiating a first kiss. It demands bravery. It demands a willingness to be rebuffed combined with a sturdy belief that the moment is right. The apologizer has to be convinced that he can co-opt the apologee into a moment he has artificially created in the hope that it might become more real and therefore less artificial the longer the exchange continues. Professor Thomas Schenke devotes almost thirty pages of his groundbreaking text on international apology to the subject.* He calls it "the maintenance of shared illusion."

On the day I spotted Harry Brennan, of course, Professor Schenke and his six laws and his shared illusions were still some way in my future. I had no support staff to help me make my apologies. I had no team of psychologists employed to analyze the mindset of my apologees. I was flying solo, making it up as I went along. All I knew was that apologizing to Fiona Hestridge had made me feel wonderful and that the sight of Harry made me feel awful again. That he did not move when I said his name, as if it were unfamiliar to him, led me to believe I was about to make some dreadful mistake. He continued staring into the antique shop window. But the Hestridge exchange really had revealed to me reserves of bravery. I called out again.

*Grievance Settlement Within a Global Context, Professor Thomas Schenke, Columbia Law School Press.

"Harry?"

He turned and squinted at me, an old man awoken suddenly from thought.

"It's me. Marc." I smiled broadly, but against his blankness, the smile began to fade. "Basset . . . ," I said, hoping it would help.

Suddenly he came alive. He reached out, clapped me on the shoulder, and barked, "Dear god, the boy wonder himself. The young turk. The sharpest pen in London. What a joy, what a great and kindly surprise, what a . . ." He showered me with enthusiasm as we gripped hands and shook and laughed at the pleasures thrown our way by chance.

I felt like a total shit, which was good. It gave me impetus. Here was the man whose livelihood I had stolen, whose stomach I had turned inside out, whose very life I had ruined, and he was greeting me like a lost son. The familiar knot of guilt retightened in my stomach. I knew for certain I couldn't leave things as they were. This had to be dealt with, and now. If I could apologize to Fiona Hestridge, damn it, I could surely clear the air with old man Brennan.

I waved across the road at a nearby Hungarian coffee shop. "You have time for . . . ?"

"You know, I think I do." He glanced at his watch. "Yes indeed, why not. For old times' sake. Let us away."

We took a table in the window and ordered coffee.

"Cake!" the middle-aged, Mittel-European waitress barked. This was an order, not an invitation.

"Will you, Harry?"

"No, but you must. I insist." He nodded toward the cabinet on the other side of the room. "Have one of those," he said, pointing now at an obscene multilayered mille-feuille of sugared pastry and cream and strawberries and fragile slivers of chocolate. "A young man like you could surely do it justice."

I shrugged at the waitress as if admitting defeat after a long battle. "One of those then, please."

She sniffed. "I bring you cake."

For a moment we sat in silence. I toyed with the silver cutlery on the table and straightened my place mat. Finally I looked up.

"Harry, there's something I have to tell you."

I told him everything, exactly as it happened: That I had never planned to steal his job, that it had been an accident. No, not an accident exactly. A misfortune. A bad piece of planning. That I had swapped the plates out of gaucheness and embarrassment; that I had meant no harm even though I had known I might cause him some.

As I spoke I felt my throat tighten and my mouth become dry. I knew my voice was becoming thinner and more unsteady, and regularly, I looked down at the table, unable now to meet Harry's gaze. For a second I stopped, terrified that I was about to start weeping again.

I took a deep breath and flexed my scarred and battered toes so that a low-voltage current of pain nudged me on. Finally I said, "Harry, I am so terribly, terribly sorry."

He stared at me slack jawed. The edge of his mouth began to edge upward until suddenly the laughter exploded out of him, furious, eye-drenching laughter that seemed wild and hot and necessary. Even when the waitress came with our coffee and my patisserie, he did not stop, and soon I joined in the laughter. She stared at us, appalled, as if our hysterics were as offensive to her sense of decorum as a pair of rutting dogs in her kitchen.

"Cake!" she said as if it were an admonition.

"Thank you," I said as best I could.

When she had left us and we were calmer, I said, "You don't hate me?"

He took a deep breath. "Not at all, dear boy. You want to know what? You saved my life."

"I did?" I cracked the top layer of the mille-feuille with the edge of my fork and scooped a little into my mouth.

"A few days after Bob Hunter sacked me, I went to see the doctor. Touch of the aches in the old ticker," he said. He patted the left side of his chest. "He told me I was a gnat's whisker away from an early grave. Massively high blood pressure, furred arteries. Had to have a couple of them bypassed, actually. Ask me nicely I'll show you the scar."

I swallowed some more cake. "Later, perhaps."

"And my cholesterol level—well, I tell you if it were an Olympic sport . . ."

"You'd have won gold?"

"Exactly. The doc told me to cut out the booze, the fats, the red meat, the salt. Everything. If I'd still been in the job I would have had no chance at all. Dead. Gone. In memoriam Harold Brennan. You did me a favor. I feel bloody marvelous these days on the new regime. Have done for the past couple of years, actually. Peak of fitness. Enjoying life. Can't recommend a healthy retirement more highly."

"Well, I'm pleased," I said as I started to attack the second half of my plate.

"Do you know what my downfall was? I'll tell you." He tapped my plate with the tip of his coffee spoon. "It was the desserts. They were my downfall. *That* would have been a death sentence to me."

I lay down my fork, very deliberately, next to the remaining shards of crisp pastry and the thick whorls of cream. I saw in my mind the sudden perforation of an artery and felt queasy for a few seconds.

"Aren't you going to finish it?"

"Don't think so," I said. "It's good, but . . ."

"Rich?"

"Yes, exactly. That."

"Probably for the best, dear boy."

"Yes." I pushed the plate away. "So, you're really not cross with me?" I wanted to get back to the safer ground of our history.

"No, not at all. Interesting tale. Glad you told it to me. Touched, in fact. But I bear you no ill will."

I felt the same warm lightness that had suffused me after my conversation with Fiona Hestridge. I felt relaxed and at peace. I had a distinct sense of having closed up an aged wound.

Harry Brennan leaned back in his chair. "Good to get things off your chest, I imagine."

"You know, it really is," I said enthusiastically. "I don't want to make you feel like you were just one on a list, but I've made a couple of apologies recently. Well, just the one other, actually. The thing is, it's a good feeling. A very good feeling. It's the right thing to do and it even has its own rewards."

Harry raised one tangled salt-and-pepper eyebrow. "Dear boy, you sound like you have found your religion."

"And the thing is, old man Brennan is right. He's absolutely right. I've found something to believe in."

"Marc darling, that's great. I'm pleased for you. But that still doesn't explain why I come home to find you standing in the middle of the living room wearing only your underpants and smeared with dust and dirt."

I looked down at myself. Lynne had a point. It wasn't the prettiest of sights. "Enthusiasm, I suppose," I said. "I just wanted to get going."

"With what, exactly?"

"Those." I pointed at two shabby cardboard boxes on the sofa, their corners reinforced with packaging tape, which I had only recently dragged from the loft. Above us, in the living room's ceiling, the hatch was open and the smell of old dust and paper hung in the air. "I was wearing a suit and I didn't want to get it dirty. I couldn't see any point in putting on jeans just to crap them up so . . ."

Behind me the television was on and tuned to a news channel. I turned to watch, distracted by the sound of Lewis Jeffries III. The slavery reparation talks in Alabama had broken up again and a crowd of African-American men, the armpits of their once crisp cotton shirts stained with sweat, were gathered about their delegation leader as he prepared to make a statement to the media.

"Our search for a way to heal history's wounds goes on, though they be deep and grievous . . ."

"He's a class act, isn't he?"

"Marc!"

"Hang on a second."

". . . but until our fellow Americans accept the stain of their past there can be no hope of reconciliation . . ."

I walked over and peered at the screen. "I recognize her," I said absently. "Don't know where from, but . . ." A white woman about my age, dressed in too structured a blue suit for too hot a day, stood at the back of the crowd, watching. She was with the crowd but not of it. I touched the screen with one index finger and felt the static that had collected upon it. "You are so bloody familiar, lady . . ."

"Marc!"

". . . who the hell are you?"

"Marc, for god's sake!"

There was a click and the television went off. I stood up and turned around. Lynne was standing, her weight rested on one hip, with a look of just contained anger upon her face. She held the television remote control in an outstretched hand, pointed now at me, as if it were a weapon.

"Please, will you tell me what is in those boxes that is so damn important?"

"Yes. Of course. Right." I walked over and started rummaging through one of them, suddenly aware that I was essentially naked and beginning to feel a chill. "Photographs," I said. "Old stuff. Me with friends at school. Outings. Later stuff of teenage parties." I picked up a handful of the pictures and started shuffling through them, discarding them back into the box in a fall of dust and crumbling paper as I went. "Me on holiday when I was a kid." I stopped at one image: me and Luke, both being held aloft by my mountainous, bare-chested dad, all three of us grinning at the camera, somewhere pine-forested and hot. I must have been about seven, Luke five. "Me with Dad."

"Marc?" Her voice was softer now, almost careful, as if she were trying to coax me out of a dark cave.

I turned to her and smiled reassuringly. "No, honestly, love, it's fine. I'm fine. Hang on." I carried on going through the pictures. "Sometimes you need pictures to remind you of all the things you've done, don't you? All the people you've screwed over. The mistakes you've made."

Lynne was standing next to me now as I flashed through my youth in a set of garish, creased images. All she said was, "I see."

Finally I found the picture I had been looking for. It had been taken at a friend's party: There was the living room, empty of furniture. (It was customary to remove it all, in case it got trashed.) My friends were sprawled about on the floor, cans of beer and bottles of cheap wine at hand. A few couples were deep in their various clinches in the corners. At the center of the shot, the reason for this picture, apparently, was a pile of adolescent boys sitting on top of each other in a heap, four deep, grinning at the camera. Stefan was on top. I wasn't in the heap so I must have taken the photograph, but I'm sure I thought the pile of humanity bloody funny. We must have been about fourteen or fifteen at the time, a point when, if you are drunk enough, piling on top of each other can be hilarious.

My interest in the image lay elsewhere, though, off to one side: a dark-haired, rather pretty, rather large girl, sitting with her back to a fitted cabinet and staring up at the camera with complete disdain.

"There she is," I said, resting the top of my thumb against the blurred image of her face.

Lynne squinted at the image. "Who is she?"

"Someone I knew when I was a kid," I said, distracted once more. I heard Lynne sigh with irritation.

I turned to her. "She's a girl I used to know called Wendy Coleman," I said. "And I owe her an apology."

Seven

My mother comes from one of those old English families which have always believed in giving service to the state, much as popes have always believed in God. Whenever there was a colony that needed ruling or a war that needed fighting, a people that needed subduing or exploiting or indoctrinating, you could be certain a Welton-Smith would be on hand, ready to help out. There were Welton-Smiths at Trafalgar and Balaklava and Ladysmith. They helped Cromwell rampage through Drogheda and Wexford in 1649 and still managed to be cheering at the coronation of Charles II a few years later. They skippered slave ships into Jamaica, ran tobacco plantations in Kentucky, and mined diamonds in South Africa. Buccaneering and valiant they may have been. Political radicals they were not. There are members of my mother's family who are still not convinced that giving women the vote was a terrific idea.

The nearest thing they had to a revolutionary was my mother, Geraldine. Damn it all, but the woman married a bloody foreigner. She never claimed the title, of course. I don't think it would ever occur to my mother to make claims for herself. In any case her brigadier father did it for her. Roger Welton-Smith continued to decry the "unsuitability" of her love match right up until his death, which occurred a good few years after the death of the son-in-law he was complaining about.

My father, on the other hand, liked to think of himself as a maverick merely because he had left Switzerland. His family never understood why he went. Who would willingly leave a country so rich in scenery, grass, cows, and bells to put on them? I remember once his twin brother, Michel, whom I never met, writing him a letter, passages of which Dad read to me:

"The yellow gentians in the meadow above the house are in bloom, though Maman insists they are only weeds." Dad crushed the letter into a ball and threw it in the bin. "In Switzerland, Marc, 'Flowers in Bloom' is classed as headline news."

His was the politics of opposition, to most things. He read broadsheet newspapers by sitting sideways at the breakfast table and holding them aloft, spread full, as though the task of consulting them was something only he was built for. Then he would exhale in fury at whatever story had caught his eye, so that if you were in front of him, all you would see was the wide, crackling sail of newsprint which would buck and bow out toward you each time he let free another belch of furious air.

"So Mr. Brezhnev and Mr. Nixon sign nice treaty to limit war. Now I feel safe."

I recognize that we weren't exactly a family of urban Marxist terrorists. But in practical terms I see now that there was an innocent radicalism about the way our household functioned. Even before my father's death my mother worked four days a week in a local solicitor's office, and because my father worked from home, his was the presiding influence. He did all of the cooking, of course, and he soon inculcated us into its rituals so that the stove became a place of male bonding. We didn't clean it much.

My mother had other fiefdoms but they were defined solely by her talents. She understood, for example, the ways of our monstrous old boiler and its polyphonic arrangement of hiss and clank, all of which completely escaped my father. I took this free-floating division of labor to be entirely natural, which it was, though not compared to what went on in my friends' houses. For most people in the 1970s, gender politics was still something that happened only on the evening television news, more spectator event than contact sport. I like to think my family's arrangement gave the Basset boys a proper understanding of, and respect for, women.

I like to think this, but plainly it didn't. How else can I explain the appalling way in which I, like my friends, treated Wendy Coleman? We saw her in terms only of the things she might allow us to do (or, as in my in case, fail to do) rather than who she was. I'm not suggesting for a moment that there was even the slightest element of coercion involved, because there wasn't. The abuse she suffered at our hands was purely verbal and emotional and, for the most part, out of her hearing. But still, we did deny Wendy respect, and for that alone I felt she deserved an apology. I knew it would be a unilateral act and I had already worked out that I would first have to make her aware of the hurt before apologizing for it, but that did not deny the imperative to do so. She had the right to hear the word and I was hungry to say it. (You will accept from this that even before I had heard of Professor Schenke's book, I had by myself begun to work out the psychosocial complexities of apologizing.)

She was easy to find. Her parents still lived in the same house, and when I telephoned, they told me she was now a podiatrist at a small practice in the same corner of North London. I flexed my feet within the hard casing of my shoes and felt once again the sharp insult where the smallest and most pathetic of my toes, salt-crusted with corns and calluses, made contact with the leather. I made an appointment with her secretary.

Wendy Coleman saw me the next day in her small white-tiled office, which smelled sourly of disinfectant just as our house had done when Dad was ill. There was only one meager slash of color, provided by a huge photograph of a dissected foot that hung on the wall, flaps of beige, graying skin pulled back to reveal the bloodless tramlines of tendon and muscle that had long ago been separated from their owner by a practical incision above the ankle. Wendy did not look up from her notes when I came in. She waved at the large articulated doctor's chair in the middle of the room and said:

"Take a seat, please. Shoes and socks off. Don't touch anything."

I did as I was told. I am always compliant in podiatrists' offices. My feet, the final joke upon which the whole ludicrous charade of my body is based, demand nothing less.

She snapped on a pair of thin white latex gloves and turned to look at me. She was exactly as I remembered her, save for a little harder-boned definition to the softness of her face. She wore a blindingly white coat, so that against the blank tiling, she seemed almost to be a part of the room itself. She had remained a woman at ease with the space she filled.

"Hello, Wendy. It's Marc . . ."

"Yes," she said. "I've already seen your name in the book." This coolly, as if I were merely proving the accepted fact of my stupidity. I felt horribly exposed (which is to say, even more exposed than I usually feel in a podiatrist's chair, with my shoes and my socks off and my trousers rolled up and my feet on full display). It felt good. It felt right. An apology demands humility, and you cannot be anything other than humble before a woman who is willing to repair your feet.

With one hand she examined the toes on my left foot, pulling the smallest digit up and away from the protective custody of its larger brothers. With the other hand, and without looking, she picked up a sliver of steel scalpel.

"Your tendons are tight, and a regressive locking of the joints, particularly in the small toes, is causing you to walk increasingly on the balls of your feet, leading to a buildup of callused skin underneath and a roll inward, thereby depressing the bridge." She sniffed. "You should consider having the toes broken and reset."

"Do you do that sort of thing?" I said. "Break bones?"

"No," she said. "I deal only with soft tissue." I looked for a smirk, an acknowledgment of double entendre, for any recognition of the past, but there was nothing. She was a woman at work. Methodically, head bowed, she now began to cut away at my little toe; slicing, whittling away at the rough sleeve of hardened flesh.

Each stroke of the blade raised the possibility of pain, suggested it, without delivering on the promise, like the suggestion of chili heat at the end of a tobacco chocolate. Fragments of my skin sugar-dusted the floor about her.

I said, "Do you like feet?" A podiatrist once told me that of all the fetishisms—latex, rubber, dwarves, amputees—the one that most appalled him was foot fetishism. That, he said, was truly aber-rant behavior.

"Feet are straightforward," she said. "The other end of the body from the mouth, so there's no emotional rubbish . . ." She paused for a second as she started to dig into the crumpled eye of the corn on my little toe. "And with feet there's always a solution."

"What solution?"

"If worse comes to worst, you cut off the foot."

There was silence in the room, save for the buzz of the overhead track lights and the self-sufficient murmur of a small clinical fridge.

"I didn't just come here because of my feet," I said eventually, as she lifted my left foot up a little and began to work on the callused motherlode beneath.

She said, "Hmm?" But she did not look up. I sensed she was enjoying herself, in a quiet sort of way.

"I came because I wanted to say sorry." For a second she hesi-tated, the blade poised over the ball of the fourth toe, as if she were trying to recall a face or a name or a smell. She went back to work.

"I wanted to apologize for the way we—I mean *I*—treated you when we were kids." Up to this point I had been sitting up a little in the chair, tensing my neck, so I could look down at her as she worked, but now that I had revealed my reason for being there I felt I could re-lax. I lay back and stared at the ceiling. The chair was my confes-sional; Wendy Coleman, my priest. She moved on to the other foot.

"We were just adolescent boys, dosed up on hormones, and well, I think that made us a little crazy. That's not an excuse. More of an explanation, really. There are no excuses, of course not, but we were cruel to you and . . ."

I was on a roll now, comfortably negotiating the emotional land-scape of apology. We had talked ill of her, I said, seen her less as a person than a challenge, and that was wrong. I hoped she didn't mind me explaining all of this, I said, but I wanted to deal with the past. I finished up with, "So anyway, I don't expect you to accept my apology or like me for it, but I did just want to say it." She was dabbing at my feet now with a little astringent disinfectant, which did not so much sting as remind me that all the time there had been living skin buried down there. Now she lay down her cotton balls, job done. She got up and pulled off her gloves as she walked back to her notes.

"You can put your shoes and socks back on now," she said as she wrote. "Do not leave it so long next time before you are seen, and if you think for a moment that I have spent even a minute of the last twenty years considering you and your little friends, then you are tragically mistaken." This without even a pause for breath or a change in intonation, so that it took me a second or two to notice that she was acknowledging a word I had said.

She turned to look at me. "You were a sad bunch of tossers who could never get it up and I only feel sorry for the poor women you have all doubtless convinced to be your partners. That will be forty-five pounds. Pay at the front desk."

And that was it. I paid at the front desk and left. The buzz was sub-tler than those produced by the Hestridge and Brennan apologies. I would even call it mellow, but it was sweet for all that. The Wendy Coleman account had been closed and I liked the feeling very much. Back home, in the corner of the living room above my desk, I assembled the Wall of Shame, a patchwork of photographs of those who deserved to hear from me. Over the next few days I began vis-iting them.

For Marcia Harris I prepared a soup of white beans and vine-ripened tomatoes, thick with chopped chervil. Marcia was a butcher's daughter from Merseyside who at university had undergone a conversion to vegetarianism of such ferocity and vigor that she had broken off all links with her family. She took to wearing only rubber shoes that squeaked wherever she went, so you could hear her coming. Despite her refusal to have anything to do with them, her bemused parents continued to send her checks. She called them "blood money" and set fire to each and every one, with which guttering flame she lit her rank hand-rolled cigarettes. Short of cash, she turned to her friends for the occasional meal, "just to see me through," but would nevertheless patrol our kitchens like a customs officer angling for promotion, sniffing out animal products. This infuriated me.

One night I made her a minestrone soup using a rich veal stock as the base. I waited until she had eaten two bowlsful before telling her. She screamed and ran out the front door. I chanted "baby-cow juice, baby-cow juice" at her as she threw up into some tired rose-bushes. Then I took from the oven the spare ribs I had prepared in anticipation of her departure and ate the lot.

I took her the white bean and tomato soup in a cobalt blue pottery tureen that I had purchased especially for the occasion. She stood at the front door of her mansion block in deepest South London, where she now practiced as an aromatherapist, with her arms crossed, and said, "Why should I trust another bowl of soup from you?"

"Because it would be bizarre for me to repeat the stunt again after nearly fifteen years."

"And this isn't bizarre?"

I shrugged and bowed my head. "You don't have to accept my apology. I just wanted to make it. I'm really sorry. I was not respectful of your views." I placed the tureen on her step. We both stared at it.

I said, "Are you still a vegetarian?"

"Yes, but I eat fish now."

I nodded. "I like fish." She smiled thinly, picked up the soup, went inside, and closed the door. It was, to be honest, only a division two apology. My genuine sorrow at what I had done and relief at having atoned for it were undermined by my deep-felt hatred of vegetarians. I noticed that she was still wearing rubber shoes, although I didn't hear them squeak. Still, I stuck a gold star on Marcia Harris's photograph to indicate that she had been dealt with.

For Miss Barrington I prepared a more complex dish. Ellen Barrington was our home economics teacher at Northills Secondary and I was her star pupil. She was the kind of round middle-aged woman who had always looked middle aged. She smelled just slightly of coconut—the aroma of a hair product, I think—and called every dish an "amiable attempt," apart from mine, which were always "the genuine article." She was unmarried and filled much of her time leading out-of-school activities, the most beloved of which was the Northills Brigade, a team of wannabe chefs who entered interschool competitions. I was, naturally, its captain. In my third year, when I was fourteen, we made it to the English finals, to be held in Birmingham, but the cook-off was scheduled to take place on the same day as a party which I was desperate not to miss because I had been told a girl who was going to be there might, quite remarkably, be willing to kiss me.

I was so certain of my kitchen skills, and so contemptuous of them, that the final seemed a pointless reason for missing the party. The morning of the contest I went into the back garden and, when I was sure I was out of view, smashed my arm against the corner of the garden wall five or six times, until a massive, bleeding bruise marked its length. I went inside and told my mother that I had fallen over. She took me to the hospital where they said it wasn't broken, but put it in a sling anyway. By then the school minibus had left. Without me there to cook the star turn, an almond soufflé (in which most of the sugar was replaced by marzipan whipped into cream), the team didn't even make it into the top three. Miss Barrington was, I heard later, distraught, but she didn't show it to me. The following Monday in school she was genuinely concerned. And I never did get a kiss.

Miss Barrington had retired. I went to her little house in the privet-hedged, mock-Tudored suburbs, where she greeted me with a big hug. She still smelled of coconut. I had brought with me all the ingredients, and there, in her neat and scoured kitchen, with its pristine spice rack and its one-cup French press, I prepared the soufflé I had failed to make so many years before, while explaining myself. She watched me in silence.

When it was finished, the pillow of beige soufflé tumescent above the ramekin's rim, I placed it on the kitchen table and sat down opposite her. She took one mouthful, pursed her lips, and a single tear rolled down her cheek. "One of the very special things about a life in teaching," she said, gulping down air, "is seeing those you have shepherded through the confusions of childhood turn into such nice adults." She reached over and gripped my hand. "You're a good man, Marc Basset. A very good man." I'm not embarrassed to say it. I wept too.

At a meeting in a local pub I apologized to Marcus Hedley, whom Stefan and I had taunted when we were just ten or eleven because he once wet himself while listening to the *1812 Overture* during music lessons because, he said, it was so exciting. When I had explained myself, Marcus and I got raucously drunk and sang along to "No More Heroes" by the Stranglers on the pub jukebox.

I apologized to Karen and Richard Brewster, two former colleagues of Lynne's at the British Council, because I once got so drunk at one of their parties that I quietly threw up into their laundry basket and then didn't confess. I also bought them a new laundry basket to make up for it.

On the spur of the moment, I even apologized to our garbagemen for having put grass cuttings in the wheelie bin, which contravenes local council bylaws prohibiting the leaving of garden waste for collection. It wasn't much of an apology, but it did help me to start the day on a little high. It was an espresso of apology. I cut out a picture of a wheelie bin from the local newspaper (which for some reason always contains photographs of wheelie bins) and I added it to the Wall of Shame. Then I stuck a gold star on it, to indicate that the matter had been dealt with.

Lynne tried to be understanding but I could tell she was confused. In the mornings, before going to work, she would stand in the doorway to the living room, silently watching me as I made adjustments to the Wall, sticking up gold stars or adding a new image.

One morning she said, "Are you nearly done, then?"

I laughed. "Done? I don't think so."

"Oh." And then: "Who's left?"

I was cutting out the photograph of a chef. I had once described him as "the David Koresh of the restaurant world" for the messianic devotion he inspired in his fans despite the generally demented nature of his dishes. (Seared herring fillets in a raspberry vinaigrette, anyone?) "There's loads of people, actually. This guy, for example." I held up the cutting. "He might be a truly awful cook, but that didn't mean I had to humiliate him. The customers would have told him in the end, and if they didn't, what business was it of mine?"

Lynne said, "Now you're beginning to scare me."

"I'm just saying perhaps there are limits to criticism."

"Are you planning to apologize to every chef you've ever given a bad review to?"

"I'm not sure yet. Maybe."

"And then? Will you stop?"

"Listen, Lynne, I haven't apologized to my brother yet."

I heard her mutter "sweet Jesus" under her breath as she retreated from the room. The front door slammed shut behind her.

Eight

One dull Sunday afternoon, when I was eleven, I spent two hours torturing my brother. I cannot now remember why I decided to do it, save that Luke was two years younger than me and that younger brothers, sodden with optimism, deserved to be tortured. Psychologists would say my behavior was born of a festering and deep-seated hostility toward the family member who, by mere fact of birth, had unseated me from my position of primacy within the household. I would have told you that he was an annoying little shit who always managed to make me look like I was in the wrong.

The method of torture was simple and devious but, ultimately, grossly effective. I made a sound at him once every three minutes or so for two hours. It was a kind of high-pitched braying noise, a sharp hee-haw on helium. Mum was out somewhere, but our father was in, working at his desk on another of his suburban chalet designs. We had been told not to disturb him on pain of death, and I knew that Luke could not call upon him to intervene just because I was braying at him like a prepubescent donkey. And so, all that afternoon, I followed him about the house, hee-hawing.

Hee-haw. Hee-haw.

At first, when we were watching TV together—it was an episode of *Hart to Hart* or *The Pink Panther Show*, something like that—he didn't appear to be all that bothered. He merely looked over at me irritably from his corner of the settee and sighed at my obvious stupidity. After a while he became more intrigued. He'd say:

"What d'you do that for?"

And I'd say:

"Do what for?"

I'd turn back to the television.

Next he tried ignoring me. He kept his eyes fixed firmly on the screen and barely flinched at each new squeak. But soon his patience gave out, as I knew it would.

"Hee-haw."

"Shut up, Marc."

"Hee-haw."

"Marc!"

"What?"

"Shut up."

"Hee-haw."

"Shut up, shut up, shut up!"

And onward through that long, gray winter's afternoon, until the daylight failed and the sound was driving him nuts; until he was trying to punch me and I, being bigger and stronger, was refusing to allow him the feeble pleasure. He pursued me around the house making a sharp keening noise, like a strangled goat, lashing out at me, fists and feet flying. Eventually Dad came roaring out of his office. He stood at the bottom of the stairs staring up at us on the landing, his huge, shoeless feet planted flat and splayed on the parquet.

"What is the bloody rocket going on out here?"

"It's Marc. He's . . ." He looked at me, trying to work out exactly what it was I was doing. ". . . teasing me." He knew how feeble it sounded. I did my "I'm just as confused as you, Dad" face.

Our father shook his head. "You," he said, pointing at Luke. "Grow up."

"And you, leave your brother alone." He stomped back to his office and shoved the door shut.

The moment I heard the door close I, naturally, made The Sound. Luke burst into tears and curled up in a tight ball on the upstairs landing carpet. Which was when I stopped. His will was broken. He was mine now. I left him sobbing on the floor.

A few hours later the family Basset gathered in the kitchen for supper. Dad had slow-roasted a shoulder of lamb in red wine flavored with rosemary and garlic and our plates had just been filled when, without looking up at Luke across the table, I made The Sound again; gently, quietly, as if it were no more than a sigh of pleasure.

"Hee-haw."

Luke screamed, picked up a full glass of water, and threw it at me, glass and all. I ducked so that the glass sailed over my head and smashed against the wooden dresser behind me. He was shouting at me now, throwing cutlery at me, trying to clamber across the table to pull my hair out. André Basset was on him in a moment, grabbing hold of him beneath the armpits and pulling him away bodily from the table and out of the room.

He was still shouting "shutupshutupshutupshutup" as Dad dragged him up to his bedroom.

Mum looked at me, genuinely startled. "What in god's name was all that about?"

I shrugged. "I have no idea. You know Luke. He's always been a bit"—I leaned toward her and dropped my voice to a whisper—"special."

She said, "Don't be so bloody silly." Then we cleaned the kitchen.

Even now, more than twenty years later, I could not look at Luke seated at a table laid with the rigorous geometry of a dinner setting without seeing him explode across it at me in a shining fury of glassware and cutlery. This evening as I entered the restaurant he merely slipped back in his seat and jutted his jaw upward in greeting. His perfectly carved and shapely jaw. My little brother is me, only in focus: his waistline is narrower, his features more definite and assured, his hair tamed rather than rising up in some spirited revolt. His feet, of course, are shapely and boast a definable arch.

Luke is the kind of man who can wear a cheap suit well. Despite this he chooses to wear only expensive ones because he is a distressingly wealthy lawyer and can afford to do so.

As I sat down, he said, "A definite four."

"A four?" I nodded approvingly. "Chair or table?"

"Chair."

"A good sign."

Our father, displaying the Swiss precision he tried so hard to deny, told us when we were boys that the quality of a restaurant could be defined by what it did with your napkin when you left the table to pee. If the waiters ignored it so that it remained in a neglected crumple on your chair, it was a substandard place undeserving of his—or our—attention. If they folded it back into the original arrangement—fan, mountain peak, or, Lord preserve us, swan—and positioned it on your place setting, they were trying too hard. True quality was a single vertical fold, the prepared napkin then laid over the back of the chair, for that presumed the meal to be a work in progress and the napkin a tool. We Basset boys had, in adulthood, adapted the napkin test into a formal competition, awarding one to five points for how intrusive waiters were when performing the act, whether they managed to get the job done before you came back or if they changed the napkin altogether on grounds of staining. It was a remarkably consistent indicator. Very few restaurants that scored four or five on the napkin test served poor food.

Tonight we were in a new place called the Hanging Cabinet, near London's Smithfield meat market. The proposition: great cuts of perfectly reared organic meat, classically prepared. The décor was pure meatpacker chic: bare brick walls, sanded floors, elegant bare lightbulbs; the kind of understated minimalism that £130 for two buys you in London at the beginning of the twenty-first century. Here hollowed-out beef bones, sealed at one end, were used as vases for a single blood red tulip. Bread was served in the cranial hollow of an upended sheep's skull that rocked back and forth on its ridged peaks. The Hanging Cabinet was not shy about its intent.

When we had ordered, Luke said, "Lynne called me."

I jutted out my bottom lip fiercely and dropped my aitches. "You 'avin an affair wiv my bird?"

He grinned. "Yes, of course, but in my youthful foolishness I have let the cat out of the bag by telling you she called me."

"An elementary mistake."

"Indeed. I shall learn next time."

"Does she know about your size problem . . ." I nodded toward his groin.

He opened his eyes wide. "Yes, she's afraid she won't be able to fit all of me in."

I recoiled in disgust. "Aw, thank you, Luke. That's a delightful image."

He scratched the back of his neck and looked away over my shoulder. "Actually, she thinks you're going bonkers."

"Yeah? In what way."

"Oh just, you know, generally. She's a bit concerned."

I grabbed a heavy-crusted chunk of bread from the sheep's skull. "Don't worry about it."

"I'm not worrying about it. I've always known you were a mal- adjusted prick. But Lynne, you know . . ."

"What did she say?"

Luke shrugged. "That you're on some major apologizing jag. Saying sorry to everyone. Chefs, teachers, garbagemen. She tells me you even dug out Wendy Coleman. Is that true?"

I chewed my bread and nodded. "It was good to see her."

"Did she slip her hands down your—"

"Stop it, Luke. Let's be a little more adult about this."

He rolled his eyes and I immediately regretted the phrasing. He bowed his head sarcastically and said, "Sorry, big brother of mine." We were silent for a moment, weighing up the overloaded baggage of a brotherly relationship.

And then: "Is she still, you know, a big girl?"

"Didn't notice," I lied. "Irrelevant. Not what I was there for."

He sighed irritably. "And what *were* you there for?"

"To have my feet done."

"Eh?"

"She's a podiatrist."

"Big Wendy's a podiatrist?"

"We each of us follow our calling."

"I think that even beats Stefan's decision to join the army."

"Let's not go there."

He reached for his own bread.

"So, seriously, what are you up to? Should me and Mum be getting you committed?"

I shrugged. "It feels like the right thing to do, that's all. Actually, it's why I invited you here tonight."

He leaned back in his chair. Now he was interested. "Go on."

Our food appeared and we began to eat. "I've thought back over our childhood and, you know, I just want to say sorry. I treated you badly."

Now Luke was flustered. He scraped away chunks of meat from the oxtail bones on his plate. "That's what big brothers are meant to do, isn't it?"

"Why should we just accept convention? That day I made you so antsy you almost leapt over the dinner table, for example. It was—"

Luke laughed. "It was ingenious."

"It was horrible."

"Does it matter?"

"I think it does. I feel terrible about it. I'm sorry, is all."

He nibbled his lip and looked embarrassed. "How's your food?" He pointed at my plate of roasted pork belly with pickled plums.

I laid down my knife and fork and pushed the plate away. "Dismal. The crackling is flabby, the fat hasn't been rendered. It's a soggy waste of good meat."

Luke narrowed his eyes. "Do I sense a Marc Basset special coming on? How about, 'The only meat that ought to be inside the Hanging Cabinet is the chef's'? Something like that. You can have that one for free."

I smiled thinly. "I don't think so," I said, shaking my head. I called for the menu and ordered again, this time choosing the steak and kidney pie.

"What in god's name are you doing?"

"I don't want to leap to conclusions. Maybe it's unfair to judge a place on just one dish."

"Marc . . . ?"

"I'm serious. They've got a whole menu, and from it we've chosen just the pork belly and your oxtail and—how is it, by the way?"

He looked at his plate. "Fine. It's braised oxtail."

"Good. You see? If I'd judged the kitchen on mine alone it wouldn't have been fair."

"Lynne's right. You are ill."

"Bollocks. I'm merely refusing to accept that everything has to be done the way it's always been done." I hesitated. "Anyway, where was I?"

"Er, apologizing to me for that noise-torture thing which I thought was hysterical."

"No you didn't. You tried to kill me."

"Okay. I didn't like you for it, but I don't care about that now. It's called personal history. You can't rewrite that."

"No, you can't. But you can reassess it. Historians do it with world events all the time. Just wars become evil wars. What looked like a smart policy at the time fifty years later becomes an outrage. Why can't people revise their own histories?"

They took away my pork belly and replaced it with the steak and kidney pie, the dark stew held in beneath a golden dome of puff pastry. I cut through the crust, and a burst of steam escaped ceilingward. I tried a couple of pieces of steak.

"Bugger!"

"What is it?"

"Gravy's insipid." I chewed on another piece of beef. "And the meat hasn't been in there for long enough."

Luke raised his hands. "See? This place is crap. Admit defeat."

"Service is good. The bread is fine. And it got a four on the napkin test. That has to stand for something. Pass me the menu." My brother let out a little whimper, an echo from a Sunday afternoon so many years ago. I chose a sirloin steak, rare, with fries and a béarnaise sauce. By the time it arrived, Luke was sitting with an empty plate in front of him. He watched me hawklike as I cut into the caramel-browned meat. It yielded softly to the knife, folding back to reveal its glossy purple innards. It was a fantastic steak. Finally the cow had been given a reason to die.

"See?" I said, carving happily. "I knew this place could do good."

"It's a steak. They grilled you a steak and you want to give them a medal?"

"The simplest things are the hardest to get right."

"No they're not. They're the simplest to get right."

"That's just cynicism, Luke."

"I've had enough. I'm going to call for the bill and a straitjacket."

Nine

Later, back at the flat, I emptied the Vice Drawer of its brittle store of Manjari and poured myself a large vodka. Lynne was out, hosting a reading by a bunch of gloomy Czech writers, and wouldn't be home until much later. The place was mine. I stoked up the computer, finished the chocolate, and swilled the vodka around my mouth to strip away any residue on my tongue. It was time to write.

By Marc Basset

Once, in this column, I claimed that a dish I had eaten had tasted like dog food, only without any of the grace notes. I said of another that it would probably taste better coming up than it did going down. I have used words like "effluent" and "slurry," "contagion" and "toxic scum." I once called for a chef to be tied to a pole in a market square—any pole, any market square—and pelted with platefuls of his own glutinous mash. I suggested another might like to try grilling one of his own kidneys, to see if he would then treat the poor, maligned organ with a little more respect. Most recently I argued that a chef should face the death penalty for the crimes against cooking of which he was guilty.

I said all of these things partly because I really did hate the dishes I had been served, but mostly because I believed that my job as a restaurant critic was to serve you, the readers, not necessarily by providing information but by presenting you with something readable and entertaining. To judge from my mailbag I had good reason to believe that like the Parisians who crowded about the guillotine, you appreciated these sudden outbursts of violence.

I see now that I was serving you badly. Cruelty may entertain us for a moment, but it is a transitory and, ultimately, feeble pleasure; a tiny one compared to the pleasures of a good meal easily taken. I have concluded I should be finding you fewer cruel jokes and more good meals. And so, from here on, you will no longer find anything negative in this column. If I tell you about a restaurant it is because it is good. If I mention a dish it is because it is worth eating. Life is too short to be wasted on the substandard. I shall, instead, seek out for you only the diamonds in the rough. Which brings me, rather neatly, to the Hanging Cabinet in Smithfield . . .

I finished with a few rapturous words about my steak and Luke's oxtail. I printed it out, scribbled *Lynne, if you're sober enough, have a look at this* across the top, and went to bed. It was to be the last restaurant review I would write for a very long time.

"He'll sack you."
   "No he won't."
   "I'd sack you."
   "You're not Hunter."
   "No, I'm your girlfriend and I'd still sack you."
   "It's the hangover talking."
   "It's the girlfriend talking with assistance from the hangover."
   "Why will he sack me?"
   "Because your columns will be boring."
   "What's boring about good restaurants?"
   "Nothing. It's reviews of them that are boring."
   "Not necessarily."
   "Yes, necessarily. It's the way you are. You write better when horrible things happen to you. Happiness makes you gauche, at least in print."

"Maybe that's the way I was. Maybe I have woken up to nice experiences."

"This isn't you, Marc. None of it's you."

"Maybe it's just that you don't like the idea of me moving on—"

"And what? Discovering yourself? Finding the real you? Listen, if you're thinking of going for a spot of rebirthing, give me a warning so I can lay down a few towels."

"All the apologies I've made will be worthless if I merely carry on writing nasty reviews. I'll be creating new victims to whom I'll need to say sorry. What's the point of that?"

"Now we're getting somewhere."

"What d'you mean?"

"You said it. What's the point of apologizing to people? You asked the question."

"No, what I said was—"

"You said, 'What's the point?' I heard you and you're right."

"It's about . . . it's about sorting through the things I've done wrong."

"No it's not. It's about enjoying the purging of guilt. It's all about you wanting to experience extremes again."

"Again?"

"You've always done it. You pretend to be so cool and still, an emotional dead calm, but really you're just swinging between the ends of the scale."

"No I'm not."

"Absolutely you are. Marc Basset is unattractive. Marc Basset can't get laid. Marc Basset hates this restaurant, loves that one, is the best writer. Adores his dead father—"

"Lynne!"

"Okay. Unfair. But only a little. You major in self-pity and self-congratulation. Nothing by halves. So now you're hooked on this apologizing thing because you like the ride. In fact, shall I tell you why you should rewrite this column? Because if you carry on shit-bagging restaurants, that will give you a whole bunch more people to apologize to and you'll just love that."

"There's no point in rewriting it."

"Why not?"

"The paper already has the copy. I sent it last night."

"Oh, terrific. Did you also write 'Please sack me now' at the bottom? You might as well. In fact, why don't you email them? Go on. Press the self-destruct button. 'Dear Robert Hunter, I don't want my job, Yours sincerely, Marc Basset . . .' Marc! Marc, are you listening to me. Marc!"

The television was on in the corner of the room, muted. I had been staring at it studiously as a way of avoiding eye contact with Lynne, but now something really had caught my attention. The news was on, and even though the sound was off I could tell that the item was about the international aid workers being held on the Russian-Georgian border and efforts by their families to get the various governments to do something to secure their release. I had seen the huddle of parents and siblings being interviewed once before: their skin, slack and gray from worry and lack of sleep; the blinking mothers trying not to weep; the tense jaws; the heads tipped attentively toward the interviewer. This time they were standing outside the heavy gray doors of the British Foreign Office on King Charles Street in Whitehall, where presumably they had just met ministers who had tried, and failed, to sound reassuring.

It was not they who interested me. It was the woman advancing up the street behind them toward the entrance who I was looking at, the same woman I thought I had recognized in items from outside the slavery reparations talks in Alabama, days before. This time I really did recognize her. I pointed at the screen.

"Look at the way she's holding those books out in front of her."

Lynne turned toward the screen, irritably. I was pointing now. She said, "Who?"

"Her. Coming toward us. Look. It's her. Don't you remember?

That's exactly what she used to do at university. The books. Up and in front of her, a bit defensively. Hiding herself—"

"No it isn't."

"Yes it is. It's—"

"So what if it's her? What difference does it make? It doesn't make any difference."

"You know it does. You know what I did to her. You know what happened."

"You think I'm the person you should be discussing this with?"

"If there's one person I should say sorry to, it has to be her."

"Shit, Marc, there's only so much of this I can take."

Jennie Sampson. Even just the sound of her name could make me think of myself as repulsive. We were students together in York, where we both studied politics, she intently, me with deliberate casualness. For two years and seven months we barely exchanged a word, even though we were often in small group tutorials together. When we passed each other on campus, we would find ways to look at the ground or the trees or anywhere else but at each other because we had both grown tired of saying only "hello" with a fixed grin. She was intense and earnest, and although she made an effort to indulge the latest fashions, there would always be something—the terribly sensible shoes on her feet, or a beige cardigan worn over a zipper top—which suggested she couldn't really be bothered with it all. She had a fine narrow nose, delicate lips, and she wore no makeup. I always thought of her as more than just a little pleased with herself.

Then one morning, out of nowhere, she came to my aid. It was a tutorial on the Paris Commune and I was arguing that it had come about not through some hunger on the part of Parisians for equality, but instead out of their feelings of superiority over and hatred for the rest of France; that the decision to throw up the barricades was merely an expression of cosmopolitan disdain at its most acute. The Parisians simply hated everybody else. It was a great theory save in one regard: I had done no reading whatsoever and had nothing with which to support it. I had plucked it out of the air because I was bored of listening to the tutor, a tiresome man who insisted on calling everyone comrade. He had been arguing that the project emerged out of a genuine belief in the invincible logic of organized equality, and while I appreciated the sentiment, I was irritated by his smugness. I held my ground for about five minutes, and then, just as I was thinking I would have to admit defeat, Jennie waded in magnificently. She cited this history of Paris and that. She quoted Racine and Hugo. She described, in terrifying detail, the machinery of French local government. But it was the last line that stuck with me:

"As Bocuse wrote in his seminal history of the French peoples, Paris is not a place but a state of mind, which defines itself solely by what it is not. And what it is not is France." There was silence. The tutor's nose twitched. He sniffed. Then he looked at his watch and told us he would see us all next week.

Afterward, outside, with the wind blowing harshly through the stone canyons of the modern campus, I thanked her.

"But that last quote. Where did you get that one from? Who is Bocuse?"

She chewed her bottom lip and looked down shyly at the ground. "Paul Bocuse."

"The chef Paul Bocuse?"

She nodded.

"He wrote a history book?"

She shook her head. "No, I made it up. I needed something to deal with that little arse."

I smiled. The word "arse" seemed so much harder and ruder and *mean,* coming from Jennie Sampson.

"So you chose a great French chef?"

"I was reading one of his books last night and it was the first name that came into my head and, well . . ."

"You read recipe books?"

She blushed. "It's kind of a hobby of mine."

"Are you serious? I can't believe this. I thought I was the only one who . . ."

She came over to my studio the next night, bringing with her a simple and rather nicely executed onion tart. (I supplied a main course of duck that I had confited myself.) We ate dinner and she looked at my collection of cookbooks, and eventually, standing there by the meat section, we kissed. It should have been straightforward after that. There should have been a series of simple maneuvers that would lead us easily from standing to lying, from dressed to naked, from aroused to spent. And there would have been had the man involved not been me.

I hadn't stayed a virgin until my twentieth year by chance. It was a part of me, like my battered feet and my ungainly thighs—and it all dated back to that desperate night with Wendy Coleman when she had tried to get hold of me and failed. The experience had been so dismal that two years later, when something approaching sex next offered itself, I was so terrified I would fail to attain the necessary hardness that I remained inconsolably soft.

This second humiliation led to a third and a fourth and so on until, quite reasonably, I found myself running away from women unless I was horribly and unattractively drunk, in which case there was no chance at all. I wasn't impotent. I had no trouble doing it by myself, and I did, rather too much at times. For a while I even wondered if I were gay. I overcame excruciating embarrassment and purchased a gay mag from a small newsagent's in King's Cross. Swiftly I realized that didn't do it for me. The pictures were startling and informative and full of pink flesh, but they weren't arousing. If the thought of sex with other men did not get me going when I was by myself, it was not going to work when I was with someone. Homosexuality wasn't the solution. My virginity had begun to hang about me like a bad smell. By the time Jennie Sampson rolled up, I was more than a little desperate.

And yet, halfway through that evening together, I suddenly became convinced that she could be the one. Everything about it seemed right: the setup, the apparent mutual interest, this clinch now on my makeshift bed of two single mattresses slapped down on the floor. Which, of course, was when I began to panic. Surely it couldn't all go wrong again? Or perhaps it could. How could failure be turned into success when the most important part of the equation—me—had not changed in any way? I heard myself begin to make a speech:

"I just want you to know I'm not going to have sex with you tonight."

"No?"

"No. I just don't, not on a first night. Never have, never will. There's this belief that, you know, men have to perform. That we immediately have to be able to generate these impressive erections to order, whereas women, well, they can just lie there and hope they get into it, and if they don't, so what."

"Really?"

"Yeah, there is. I think it's quite oppressive, actually, although nobody's ever going to be bothered to start a campaign or anything, are they? I mean, 'Save Men from the Oppression of the Erection' isn't really a rallying cry, is it?"

"No, I suspect not."

"Then there's the faking thing. Well, you might be able to fake an orgasm, but men, you know, we can't fake our erections, can we? You'd always find us out, and so, the thing is, well, I just wanted you to know that this is the way it will be tonight and . . ."

She was smiling at me. Then she reached out to brush a few stray strands of hair away from my eyes and said, "That's fine, Marc. We'll just lie here and do this. This is nice. This is lovely." And she kissed me again.

Naturally, half an hour later, I was no longer a virgin.

Ten

The first words I said to Jennie the next morning when we awoke were the last words that had been floating about my head as I drifted off to sleep the night before. They were, "Thank you." I was festering with gratitude.

She leaned back from me in the bed, yawned, and said, "My pleasure," as if she had only bought me a drink.

We agreed to meet later that morning in the Basement Bar, a dimly lit coffee shop in the student union that smelled of stale food and fresh coffee, where the hungover and furtive went to escape daylight. The walls were lined with high-backed booths that were ideal for hiding in. Tucked away in there, nobody could see anybody else, which was why most people went to the Basement Bar. It was why Jennie and I suggested it as a meeting place. We liked the idea of being cloistered away together with our curious knowledge of each other. I arrived early, bought a coffee, and was heading toward one of the farthest booths when someone called out my name.

"All right, Marky Marc."

It would have been easy to acknowledge the call and move on. I could have raised one hand in salute and continued toward that farthest booth. In the Basement Bar nobody's need for space was ever questioned. The problem was I had time on my hands and time is the enemy of good decision-making. The names of the two lads who had called me over don't matter now. They were just hyperhormonal men, the big beasts of the student savanna, nostrils open for the scent of an available pheromone. I knew instinctively that if I sat down with them, talk would soon turn to the pressing matter of sex. For these men sexual conquest was a sport to which they offered their own commentary. Too many times I had found myself an uneasy and counterfeit coconspirator. I had sat in too many of these booths listening to this sex talk and, still surprised by my own lack of experience, had chipped in with a special arrangement of knowing guffaws and wisecracks which kept me in the conversation without ever drawing me too close to its center.

This morning was different. As of the previous night I was what my doctor would have called a sexually active male.

"Young man, are you sexually active?"

"Well yes, Doctor. Yes I am. I am sexually very active. I was sexually active last night, as it happens, thank you for asking."

I deserved a place in that booth. I could join the herd out on the savanna. So I slipped in along the warm leatherette bench, scrounged a fag, and sipped my coffee. Off went the conversation, this chatter of capability and willingness, and at some point, buoyed up by success, I joined in. Looking back, I can now see the flow of that conversation spreading out like a mighty river with its tributaries and bifurcations. I can still identify the narrative beats along the way which would have allowed me to send the talk off down another channel; streams which would have left me innocent and unsullied. But the truth is—and I accept this now—I just didn't want to. I wanted these boys to know that I was one of them. I wanted them to hear me boast about sex. Most of all I wanted them to hear me boast about sex with Jennie Sampson. I needed them to know about it because somehow it would make the whole event seem so much more real. Naturally, in the desperate pursuit of this realness, I was more than willing to lie.

When one of them said, "Is Jennie Sampson a shouter?," I answered in the affirmative, even though all I remembered from the night before was the warmth of her breath on my neck and the hum of the fridge in my dour kitchenette.

But I was flying now, writing my own story lines, crafting my own narrative arc. "She howled," I said. "I thought someone might call the police, she was so bloody noisy. Seriously, I was so worried I . . ."

It took me a few seconds to notice that their gaze had lifted from the Warner Brothers animation of my face to a place just up and behind me. Their lascivious smiles had subsided to be replaced by something closer to a smirk. I said, "What? What is it—"

"Hello, Jennie," one of them said cheerily.

"Yeah, hello," the other one said, just as eagerly. "We were just talking about you."

I swung around. She was standing at the end of the table, a pile of books gripped tightly to her chest. She was blinking and even in the gloom I could see tears beginning to form. God knows how long she'd been in the Basement listening. She could have been in the next booth, her head rested back against the divider that separated us. However long she had been there it was long enough. Behind me the boys started sniggering.

I tried a welcoming grin and said, "Actually, we were just talking about . . ." But it was pointless. She sniffed and blinked so that her eyelids fluttered beautifully, and she mouthed the words "You bastard" at me. Then Jennie Sampson turned and fled. We left university without saying another word to each other.

Once you finally recognize someone it's hard to imagine how there was ever a time when you failed to identify them. Watching Jennie stride toward me now, down the wide, empty space of the corridor that led to the Foreign Office entrance hall, she was so very much herself that I felt only foolish. How could I not have recognized her? The carefully designed swish of her loose black trousers and the matching jacket may not have belonged to the Jennie Sampson I once knew. There may now have been a pair of sculptured heels beating out a confident rhythm on the checkerboard stone-tiled floor where once there would have been the silence of flat soles. But none of that interfered with the essentials. She was still recognizably Jennie Sampson, the woman I had humiliated.

I had turned up unannounced shortly before one on the off chance that she might need to break for lunch. If she hadn't been available, my great plan—and it really was no more developed than this—was to leave my number in the hope that she might call. I didn't need to. The receptionist had announced tersely, "Ms. Sampson will be down presently," and now here she was, hard-faced and businesslike. She reached out to shake my hand, as though I had arrived for a pre-arranged meeting, and said, "I read your column occasionally. You know your stuff but you are sometimes unnecessarily cruel."

"Yes. You're right. I'm attempting to deal with that. It's why I—"

"Walk with me," she said, looking toward the bright rectangle of daylight beyond the open doorway. "I have a package to deliver." She lifted a manila envelope held in the crook of her neatly tailored arm, before turning to stride out into the sudden clamor of the busy London street. I rushed to catch up, feeling clumsy and uncomfortable beside her self-containment.

"As I was saying, it's why I came."

"Yes?" This impatiently.

"I wanted to talk to you about us—well, me. About what I did to you a long time back."

"Go on."

"Good. Yes. Right. The thing is, I've been thinking back to, you know, our time at York together and the way I—well, I lied about you. It was a horrible, dreadful thing to do, nasty and cruel and thoughtless, and I came here today to see you because I wanted to say sorry. I don't expect you to accept it just like that, but—"

"Hmm."

"—I still feel it's the right thing to do."

We were walking briskly now, she clearing a path through oncoming pedestrians, her gaze fixed dead ahead, me all but skipping to keep up. I felt like I was trying to sell her something she didn't need—which was, I suppose, the case.

"Because there's no point apologizing if you already know some-one's going to accept it, is there? I mean, it's got to be for its own sake, hasn't it?"

"Yes?"

"And it doesn't matter how much time has passed, does it?"

"No?"

"The thing is, you know . . ." I was hunting around, trying to work out exactly what the thing was, when the phrase came to me. "The thing is, there's no statute of limitations on a hurt."

I had walked on a few yards before I realized she had stopped. I turned back to her. Suddenly she was alert.

"What did you say?"

"Erm, that there's no, you know, statute of limitations on . . ."

"Yes?"

". . . a hurt."

"Did you read that somewhere?"

"No, I just—"

"It didn't come from a law book or—"

"I just made it up, I'm afraid."

"And to be absolutely clear, you're saying sorry to me?"

"Well, I'm trying to, yes. That's the plan."

"Apologizing?"

I shrugged. "I suppose so. I don't expect you want to hear it, but—"

"No no no. I do want to hear it. Really." She seemed excited now, as if she had just caught sight of an item in a shop window she had been trying to find for months. She glanced at her chunky watch and said, "Do you have half an hour to spare? My place is not too far from here, just over in that building, actually."

"You live in a government ministry?"

"In one of the tied apartments. A perk of the job. I'm moving out soon. What I'd like to do is . . ." She stopped as if trying to calm her-self. "I know this might sound a bit weird, but I'd like to get you down on camera. A small digital thing I've got for recording meet-

ings and stuff. Would you mind? Would you? It would be very help-
ful to me."

"What about your package?"

She looked down at the manila envelope as if she had forgotten it
was there.

"It can wait," she said.

I had no reason to refuse. If she wanted my apology recorded
then that was her right.

She took me to a single-room apartment high up inside one of
the Treasury buildings, a grand echoing space of dark parquet floors
and long windows that flooded the vault with light. There was a
neatly made double bed and, by it, a clothes rail hung with black
pantsuits and white blouses. In one corner was a starkly modernist
kitchen and, above the work surface, a shelf heavy with thick-spined
cookbooks. She asked me to sit down on a pale cream sofa in the
seating area while she went to retrieve something from a cupboard
in the wall by the bed, which I hadn't even known was there until she
thumped the panel and it sprang open.

"Here we are," she said. She came back carrying a tripod and a
camera so small it seemed unlikely it would be able to fit all of me
into its narrow frame. She fumbled around trying to get the two
pieces of equipment connected to each other and a minidisk into its
drive and the whole kit pointed in the right direction. Finally she
seemed satisfied that everything was in place. She pulled up a chair
so she could sit next to the tripod and reached up to press the con-
trols.

"Can you see a little red light on the front, just below the lens?"

I looked away from her to the camera. "Er, yeah. Yes. I can see
it."

"Great. It's recording." She looked back from the control panel to
me. "So, in your own time."

I pointed at the camera. "Do you want me to do it to the lens or to
you or . . ."

She leaned forward, resting her elbows on her knees and her

head on her hands as if bracing herself. She said, "Doesn't matter. Whatever feels comfortable. Talk to the camera or to me. Really. Whatever works for you."

"Okay," I said. And then: "From the beginning?"

"Absolutely. From the beginning." She smiled encouragingly at me.

"Right. Here goes." I closed my eyes for a second, then opened them and looked past the camera at Jennie. She had presented me with the perfect opportunity, a way to move the apology on from being simply a momentary rush of self-serving emotion toward something much more profound, a performance piece that would have a life above and beyond the set piece. I was apologizing for posterity. The arguments with Lynne, the tense exchanges with my brother, the intensity of the previous days faded away. I was focused on the event.

"I treated you badly and for that I am terribly, terribly sorry. Some people might say it's such old history that it doesn't matter now. That we were practically kids. I don't see it that way. I wasn't a child. I was an adult who behaved as a child. And the irony is that it was you who helped me into the adulthood I then failed to grasp."

Jennie tipped her head to one side and smiled at me.

"We don't need to pretend, do we? I am, I hope, mature enough to be able to say it without embarrassment. You took my virginity, which was a gracious and lovely thing to do, and I should have been only grateful to you. But instead I violated the trust you placed in me.

"I am also, I hope, enough of an adult to understand why I did it. I wanted to belong. That was all. There was this club from which I had been excluded for so long, a ludicrous club, the boys' club. But I still needed to feel a part of it and you gave me the perfect opportunity."

I hesitated for a second and she nodded at me, urging me to go on. I had been wondering whether to give her my newly developed and impressively acute analysis of why men are the way they are when it comes to sex. Now it seemed she wanted anything I was prepared to give. "You see, the thing about men is that, deep down, they know their involvement with the reproductive act to be tiny, insubstantial, the work of seconds." I snapped my fingers. "And yet women . . . women are the makers. They create. We just have sex. But you produce lives, and somewhere deep down within us, that leaves us feeling desperately inadequate, which, frankly, is exactly what we are. Our value in sex can be measured in centiliters, and not very many at that. So what do we do to make up for our redundancy? We boast. We make up stories, mythologize ourselves in an attempt to fill the chasm in our identities. The only way we can face being ourselves is if we've already rewritten the plot.

"But you need a plot to start with and before you came along I'd never had one. I'd sat for years listening to boys talking themselves up and all the time wanting to know what was true and what was false. I wanted the vital intelligence. You gave it to me. You made me a man and I went and behaved like one."

I swallowed hard. Looking at Jennie's face now, I suddenly had a memory of her standing in the gloom of that basement coffee bar, those books clutched hard to her chest for protection. I blinked and felt a tear begin to roll down the side of my nose. The moment was so intensely real. So true.

I went on. "None of that is an excuse, though. It's just"—I sniffed as another tear rolled down to join the first—"my feeble attempt to explain to you what happened that morning. I will never excuse myself. You were right to be upset. You had every right to be furious." I took one more gulp of air. "I'm sorry, Jennie. I'm so terribly, terribly sorry. For everything."

There was silence. Eventually she said, quietly, "Have you finished?"

I nodded and mouthed a "Yes."

She clapped her hands together and the spell was broken. "Marvelous. Bloody well done. Excellent. Really very excellent." She jumped up and stopped the camera. "Would you like a tissue? Glass of water? Anything?"

"Well, a glass of—"

"Be a dear and fetch it yourself while I sort this out. Shelf above the sink over there." She pulled out the minidisk and scrawled something upon its label in felt tip.

"Oh, and Marc," she called across the room, "could I have a phone number for you? Mobile? Pager? Anything?"

I gave her my mobile number and she wrote that on the label too. She led me to the apartment door and said, "Listen, I've got a couple of calls to make and so forth, but you can find your way out, can't you? Yes, of course you can." She clasped my hands in hers. "Look, Marc, thank you for coming. It was great. Really. I do appreciate it. And you know, I'll call you, very very soon. Okay? Yes? Great."

And suddenly I was standing outside on the street again, trying to work out exactly what had happened.

Eleven

Three days later I was invited to see Hunter in his office. He was leaning against the edge of his desk, legs outstretched, heels dug into the carpet to brace himself, as if this were the only way for a man of natural authority to hold a meeting. He waved me to a chair in front of him and, in a single continuous movement, slapped the two sheets of paper that he was holding with the back of his free hand.

"Just reread your column."

"Yes?"

"Marvelous stuff. It will set the agenda. Force a debate."

"Thank you."

"Get them talking about us."

"Which is what we want."

"Precisely."

"Good. I'm pleased because it means a lot to me. Emphasizing the positive is an important move, I think."

"Hmm." Hunter shuffled the sheets of paper.

"We ought to encourage our other critics to go the same way. Why tell people something's rubbish when there's so much good stuff out there?"

"Yes. Of course. Up to a point." He looked over my shoulder and out through the glass office walls behind me, surveying the newsroom for signs of inactivity.

"How do you mean, up to a point? Don't you think we ought to stop being rude for rude's sake? I thought you liked the column. You just said . . ."

He fixed me with a worryingly sudden smile. "I love the column. I adore the column. It will make a huge splash and you will be terribly famous. The thing is, we think there might be a way of getting two hits from it."

"How so?"

"A touch of recidivism perhaps?"

"I'm sorry?"

"Here's the great Marc Basset telling us about all the things he loves, and then, a few weeks hence, when you're ready—no rush— you visit a restaurant that's gut-rottingly awful. A gastric pit."

"Then I can't write about it."

"No no. That's the thing. You do. Suddenly, a flash of the old anger illuminates the page. You wanted to be positive, but the truth is, there's too much awfulness to be ignored. It's your duty to expose it . . . and so on."

"Hang on. You're making my head spin. You want to run this new column with the intention—the *intention*—that within a few weeks I should go back on my word and slag things off again?"

"That's the way to force the agenda."

"That's the way to alienate the readers."

"Marc, old chap, you're a terrific writer. Bloody funny. All my girlfriends love you. But you need light and shade, rough and smooth. Too much of the same and you become bland."

"I've just written a column announcing the death of negativity—"

"So we get a Second Coming. Hurrah!" He waved the papers above his head in mock celebration. "The readers want their critics to be critical. That's what they expect."

"I'm sorry. I can't do it. I can't lie to the readers."

"No one's asking you to lie."

"I can't mislead them. Once we publish this column I will be duty bound to stick to the spirit of it. If you insist that I do otherwise, I'll just . . . I'll just . . . I'll just have to quit."

"It's a pity because you've done such a good job." He stood up and walked around to sit behind his desk. He threw the sheets carelessly to one side like so many used tissues and studied his computer screen.

"I want to carry on doing a good job."

"And you will, dear boy, you will. But perhaps for somebody else."

Back at my desk I phoned Lynne on my mobile.

"I think I've just resigned."

"What do you mean?"

"Well, technically I think I can argue that Hunter sacked me. It was constructive dismissal."

"It was that bloody column."

"Don't shout at me."

"What did Hunter say, exactly?"

"He wants to run the column, but he wants me to go back on my word and start writing knocking copy again within a few weeks." Off to one side there was a cheer from a group of my colleagues crowded around a computer terminal. I shoved a finger in my free ear to muffle the sound.

"And you refused?"

"Sorry. Say that again. It's a bit noisy here." I looked over at the huddle. A woman turned round. It was Sophie from the press office. The moment she saw me she tried to smother the broad grin on her face by biting her glossy bottom lip. I mouthed "What?" at her, but she shook her head and turned back to the group to whisper. They all turned to look at me. One or two appeared embarrassed to see me there, but others clearly thought it was the funniest thing that had happened all morning. I stood up and walked toward them, the mobile still pressed to my ear.

"I said, did you refuse to do what Hunter asked you to do? Marc? Are you listening to me?"

"Well, I . . ." One by one, as I approached, the crowd moved away from the computer, as if they had thought of something far better to do, until I had a clear view of the screen. A pixeled video was playing in a window: a man was talking directly to the camera, his face pink and blotchy. As I moved closer I could see streaks of tears running down his cheeks. The audio was too low for me to be able to make out the words, but I didn't need to recognize the voice for I already recognized the face. The video was of me, apologizing to Jennie.

I said, "I'll call you back," and ended the call before Lynne could protest.

Sophie was the only one left standing by the desk. She looked sheepishly from the image on the screen and then back to me. "If you ask me, darling, it's a lovely apology."

I stared openmouthed at the image of myself peering into the camera. "How did it get onto—"

"Everybody's got it," she said quickly, as if this made it better. "Somebody down in marketing had it emailed to them and they emailed it up here and now . . ." I looked around the office, and as I turned, I sensed people ducking their heads down behind their terminals so as not to catch my eye. Somebody walked past and barked, "Great performance, Marc. Deserves an Oscar."

I opened my mouth to reply, but he was already trudging away up the office. I pointed at the screen. "Everybody in the office has seen this?"

"Everybody in every office, by the sound of things. You're turning into rather a cult figure, actually. Not that you weren't one already." Into my mind came the image of ten, a hundred, a thousand computer screens, all playing this self-pitying, tear-splattered video, this minor miracle of garish emotion and digital multimedia. How had it become an email? And now that it had been emailed, how many people in Britain had seen it? How many in America? How many in the world? I felt suddenly as if I were stalking myself from every humming computer terminal on this floor and the one below and the one above.

I leaned toward the computer and heard myself say, "I'm sorry, Jennie. I'm so terribly, terribly sorry. For everything." The Marc Basset on the screen blinked a couple of times and then the image faded to black.

I phoned Lynne back.

"You haven't seen anything of me on the Net, have you?"

"What?"

"Nobody's emailed you anything?"

"Marc, talk to me. Did you refuse to do what Hunter told you to do?" She hadn't seen it. Yet.

"I had to. It's the principle of the thing. There's no point me attacking people if—"

"Marc, do not use the *A* word."

"—if I'm then only going to apologize to them."

"Then stop bloody apologizing. Go back to Hunter's office. Tell him he's right. Tell him you want to file a different column. Get your job back. Get on with your life so we can get on with ours."

"Is that all that matters to you? That I keep the money rolling in so we can keep having fun?"

"No. What matters to me is that you stop mucking about and get on with being the Marc Basset I know."

"Or is it just that you don't like the Marc Basset I'm becoming? Is that what it is? You want me to stay the way I was because you can deal with that."

"Listen to yourself, Marc. Look at what's happening to you. You've lost your job. You're behaving as if you've lost your mind. And you know what, the way you're going, you're going to lose me too."

"Hang on. There's a call waiting."

"What?"

"I won't be a second."

"Bloody hell, Marc, you can't just expect me to . . ."

I put her on hold and clicked onto the other call. In less than a minute I was back.

I said, "Sorry about that."

"Who was it?"

"Jennie Sampson."

"What does she want?"

"She says she needs to see me urgently."

"And you're going?"

"Actually, there's something important I have to talk to Jennie about too."

"More important than your job?"

"Look, sweetheart, we'll talk later tonight. Yes?"

"Don't make promises you can't keep, Marc Basset. Who knows how long Jennie Sampson will want you for?"

She led me along great echoing corridors and deep into the building. As I trailed behind her I said, "Why did you do it, Jennie? Why did you do it?"

She shook her head and, without looking at me, said, "I didn't. Honestly. You have to trust me on that."

At a heavy wooden door she stopped, her hand on the handle. She leaned toward me conspiratorially so that the plastic pass which dangled about her neck swung out to meet me. Its brush felt curiously soft and intimate. She said, "Everybody here is terribly interested in you," then she opened the door.

There were half a dozen people in the functional room. One was sitting at a stubby conference table with two others looking over his shoulder at a file which lay open in front of him, their own passes hanging loose over the first man's shoulders. Another was messing about with a VCR that sat on a bulky cart with a large television mounted above it. In the far corner an older man, perhaps in his sixties, was standing by an open window exhaling smoke from a cigarette held close to the knuckle, so that he smothered his mouth with his long-fingered hand each time he took a drag. His winter gray hair was cropped neatly and the expensive weave of his expensive gray wool suit caught the light. Another, more disheveled man, who wore a whole garland of plastic cards about his neck, stood close by with his back to the window watching the room, although it was obvious the two had been talking while looking in opposite directions. As Jennie showed me in he pushed himself away from the wall in midsentence.

From behind me I heard Jennie say simply, "Stephen Forster, meet Marc Basset."

"Mr. Basset, a pleasure, really, a pleasure. Come in, come in. Let me introduce you to . . ." He was looking back past me. "Or later, Jennie, do you think?"

"Recording first, perhaps?" she said.

"And then?"

"And then. Exactly."

"Splendid. Yes. Come this way, Marc. Guest of honor up here, I was thinking." He patted me on the shoulder as he led me to a seat by the window while he took the top of the table. From here I could see that a small digital camera had been connected to the video, the lens turned away from us. The others in the room took their places. Only the man at the window did not move. He gave me a considered half smile and then turned back to exhale over the rooftops, as if my arrival had interrupted a great thought. A fierce rush of blue-gray smoke slipped from his lips through the window. He put out his cigarette on the outside windowsill, flicked the stub across the rooftops, and then in an elegant movement that immediately made me feel clumsy, took his seat at the other end of the room. In the middle of the table, covered by a crisp white cloth, lay what looked like a tray.

Forster said, "Let's get started. First we'll have a look at Jennie's tape again just to remind ourselves why we're all here today." Everybody muttered in the affirmative. "Joe, could you do the honors?" A younger man in jeans and loose tartan shirt at the far end of the table reached over to just below the television and pressed a button.

I recognized the camera a split second before I heard Jennie's voice on the tape saying, "Can you see a little red light on the front, just below the lens?" And then there was my face, worryingly massive and greasy on the television screen, squinting into the lens. I gasped and Jennie grabbed my hand. "Don't worry," she whispered. "It's all going to be okay."

I could not see how any of this would ever be okay. Sure, I had done a bad thing all those years ago. I had betrayed Jennie's trust. And perhaps she had recognized, in the intensity of my apology, some of the profound pleasure I had gained from my recorded confessional. But was it really fair to humiliate me like this? Did that justify setting up this "meeting" so she could grind me deep into the dust? I wasn't sure which was worse: the video being emailed anonymously across the world or me being forced to sit here in this room where the ordeal was so intimate and enclosed.

Up on the screen, my face three feet wide, I was saying, "We don't need to pretend, do we? I am, I hope, mature enough to be able to say it without embarrassment." Everybody leaned toward the set, desperate not to miss a word. I remembered what was coming next. I closed my eyes and heard my recorded self say, "You took my virginity, which was a gracious and lovely thing to do . . ." Voices in the room muttered: "Oh, well done." "Terrific, excellent." "Spot-on." I opened my eyes again and looked at them. If this really was a setup, it was a peculiar one. I looked over at Forster, who threw me an avuncular wink before turning his attention back to the screen.

I was now deep into my speech. "You see, the thing about men is that, deep down, they know their involvement with the reproductive act to be tiny . . . women are the makers . . . that leaves us feeling desperately inadequate . . . Our value in sex can be measured in centiliters . . ." That last line got a small laugh, although whether of ridicule or recognition I couldn't be sure. They all seemed genuinely gripped. And onward went my televised self, my eyes now becoming glassy. "I wanted the vital intelligence. You gave it to me. You made me a man and I went and behaved like one." I watched myself blink hard. The picture moved into a tight close-up on my face. I couldn't recall Jennie touching the camera at this point, but clearly she had, or perhaps she had been holding a remote control. However she had done it, my eyes—my moist, imploring, cow eyes—now filled the screen as a single fat self-pitying teardrop escaped to roll down my nose.

I felt sick. My humiliation was complete. Jennie had got her revenge.

Maybe Lynne was right. Maybe I was being a fool. I was throwing my life away in pursuit of . . . what? Catharsis? Righteousness? An overdeveloped interest in the past? It had already gone too far, now that anybody with an Internet connection could witness me at work. In that instant I concluded that the time had come to give it all up. Strip down the Wall of Shame. Phone Hunter and make nice. Rebuild my relationship with Lynne. Reclaim my life.

But there was that muttering again: "Oh, great. Fab." "Spot-on . . . just what we're looking for." When I reached the climax of my speech—"I'm sorry, Jennie. I'm so terribly, terribly sorry. For everything"—everyone in the room slumped back in their seats and started applauding. I'm sure one of them shouted, "Bravo!" Joe reached over and paused the picture on my tear-streaked face, teeth just bared, cheeks coloring a blotchy pink.

Forster called the meeting to order. "Right, everybody. Now we have all seen what we are dealing with, let's fill in poor Marc." He turned to me. "How much do you know about what you're doing here?"

"I don't . . . I'm not sure I—"

Jennie jumped in. "I thought it would be better if I let you explain."

"Fine," Forster said. "Introductions first. My name is Stephen Forster and I am Deputy Undersecretary in FO26, which essentially means I have responsibility for relations with the United Nations and so forth."

He indicated the middle-aged man across the table from me who wore a brown tweed jacket and a mismatched tie with too fat a knot. "Francis Wilson here is head of Historical and Verification."

"Very excited to meet you, Mr. Basset," he said. "You really do have spectacular antecedents. Your file is remarkable." He patted the fat manila folder in front of him.

"Er, thank you," I stammered. "I think."

"Next to him is our very own Will Masters from Legal." Masters, my age and dressed with a determination to prove it—suit by Boss; shirt, probably by same, buttoned to the throat; rimless glasses—raised one open-palmed hand in salute. "Hi!"

"Joe there is from Psych."

"Psychiatry?"

"No no no," Forster said soothingly. "Psychology." As if that made things clearer.

"Obviously you know our own Jennie Sampson."

"I don't know what she does."

Forster nodded. "Jennie?"

"Er . . . liaison, I suppose," she said with a grin.

"Yes," Forster said, "*special* liaison," with knowing emphasis on the "special." "Next to Jennie we have Satesh," he said, indicating a young, neatly dressed Asian man in steel-rimmed glasses. "Satesh works with me at FO26." Satesh leaned across Jennie to shake hands.

"And finally, down at the other end of the table, we have Maxwell Olson, on temporary assignment to us from our friends at the US State Department."

"Just call me Max," the American said, with a smile dripping with shared purpose. "I'm here to tell you, son, my government is very interested in what you have to offer." I muttered another thank-you because I couldn't think what else to say.

It was time to take control. I took a deep breath. "Fine. Lovely to meet you all, I'm sure. I'm delighted everyone's so very excited by me. Now, can someone please tell me what I am doing here?"

Forster leaned back in his seat and nodded slowly. "Of course. Of course. Tell me, Marc, what does Professor Thomas Schenke's name mean to you?"

Twelve

I shook my head. "Never heard of him."

"And why should you?" Forster said. "Not much of a prose stylist, our Mr. Schenke. Unlike you." Everybody else around the table laughed knowingly, including Jennie, which irritated me. I said nothing.

"For all his failings as a writer," Forster said, filling the silence, "Schenke has nevertheless become the founding father of a new and exciting strand of international relations theory known, in diplomatic circles, as 'Penitential Engagement.' "

"Sounds fascinating."

"Oh it is," he said, ignoring my stab at deathly irony. "Penitential Engagement is the future."

"The very near future," Max Olson said dryly from the other end of the table.

"Indeed," Forster said. "I'll give you a copy of Schenke's book when we're finished here, but for now let me précis." He leaned toward me as if taking me into his confidence. "According to Professor Schenke, the conduct of calm international relations is being stymied by the enormous weight of emotional baggage that world history has given us. There are too many countries, too many peoples—call them what you will—with unresolved grievances. If we could resolve the issues of the past, then the conduct of world affairs in the present would be that much smoother."

Again Max Olson chipped in. "All it requires is for one half of the world to be willing to apologize to the other."

"Apologize for what, exactly?" I said.

Forster sat back. "Take your pick: slavery, colonialism, the Opium Wars, Cromwell's campaign in Ireland, the Rwandan genocide, support of apartheid—"

"Is that all?" I said tartly.

"No, no," he said. "There are endless cruelties for which an apology is applicable and, dare I say it, appropriate. Indeed a lot of the background work has been done. It's fair to say that we've worked out the how, where, what, and when of international apology."

Olson jumped in again. "But we're still looking for the who."

Forster nodded. "Exactly. What's important is finding the right person to make the apology. Or apologies. The identity of the apologist is crucial."

I sat back, incredulous. "You mean you're actually going to start doing this?"

"Oh, absolutely," Forster said. "All the important global players are right there behind it, partly because of the economic benefits, which you can read about for yourself later. The main point is that an Office of Apology is being established at the United Nations in New York, with a research and registration secretariat. Many countries have nominated their apologists. The one thing it is missing"— he slowed down now and spoke very deliberately—"is a Chief Apologist."

The whole table stared intently at me.

"And you think I'm the one . . . ?"

Forster nodded slowly. "We have been searching for the right individual for many months."

"Who's 'we'?"

"Britain and the US," Max Olson said. "It was agreed at a special session of the steering group in Geneva four months ago that as Britain and the US carry the burden of apologizable events, the Office of Apology would accept whomsoever we nominate."

"Although others have been involved in the decision to nominate you," Forster said. He nodded toward the screen. "A digitized copy of Jennie's video was sent electronically to every single member-state delegation at the United Nations in New York."

I leaned toward him. "It was emailed?" He nodded slowly. I looked at Jennie. She whispered, "Sorry." I turned back to Forster. "Which is how my face came to be on every damn computer screen in my office?"

Forster pressed his hands together as if he were praying. "Regrettably it appears one or more of the UN delegations forwarded the video to friends or associates outside diplomatic circles, and for that I apologize, though I believe they only did so because they were so impressed by the passion you displayed. Either way it was never our intention to embarrass you."

Jennie leaned over toward Forster, like a pupil eager to impress. "It has had a positive effect, though, hasn't it, Stephen?"

"Oh yes, indeed. Your apology has rather taken on a life of its own."

Jennie again: "It's become the most emailed video in the history of the Internet, actually." It was quickly becoming regarded as an icon of the weblog movement, she said. In an age when the monolithic corporate websites were being overtaken in popularity by the diaries and electronic jottings of millions of individuals determined at last to grab control of editorial content for themselves, my video had come to represent an ideal: the use of the Internet for the expression of intense and personal emotion. My video was the victory of the individual. And it had happened in a matter of days. She squeezed my arm fondly. "There are millions of copies out there now."

I shook my head in disbelief. "And that's good because . . . ?"

Forster smiled indulgently at me. "You have to understand, Marc, that bureaucracies are, by their very nature, terribly conservative. They don't tend to recognize talent until it has been recognized elsewhere." He waved at the table. "Those of us here were certain from the moment we viewed the tape that you were the man for the job, but it took the sudden and informal success of your apology to Jennie for others to see your virtues too. In the past twelve hours we've had dozens of messages of support from other UN member states encouraging us to go forward with your nomination. Even the French appear to be impressed by what you can do." I couldn't help but feel a shiver of pride flow through me.

I said, "You're serious, aren't you?"

"Completely. There's a conference at Dayton, Ohio, in a couple of weeks' time, and we want to be able to announce your name then."

I looked over at the television screen, still filled with the damp cheeks and bloodshot eyes of my remorseful face. "Why me?" I said.

Forster nodded very slowly. "Francis, will you . . . ?"

The man across the table with the badly knotted tie opened the file in front of him. "The key phrase is 'Plausible apologibility,' " he said, enunciating each syllable as if it belonged to a foreign place name. "Under the Schenke Doctrine no apology can be made unless the apologizer is entitled to make it. Which means that if somebody is to apologize for an event of great or even midrange antiquity, there must, on their family tree, be a person who was directly involved with that hurt." He looked down at the papers in front of him. "Your tree on your mother's side is remarkable. You have plausible apologibility over, well, pretty much everything: Welton-Smiths were deeply involved in the slave trade, obviously big in various colonial administrations, and were enthusiastic prosecutors of military campaigns throughout the eighteenth, nineteenth, and twentieth centuries. Frankly, there have been few atrocities in which a Welton-Smith was not involved."

"I've never been so proud," I said.

The historian's eyes lit up. "So you should be, so you should be. It's a truly stunning historical record."

"And that's all on my mother's side?"

"Indeed."

"What about on my dad's side?"

"Oh, well," the historian said, closing the file, "he was Swiss so he gives you plausible apologibility for almost everything else." A ripple of knowing laughter went around the table, which Forster silenced.

"Joe . . . ?"

"Thank you, Stephen. What matters, Marc, is not just your historical antecedents, which as Francis says are remarkable. It is who you are, too. There's no point us nominating a Chief Apologist who has nothing to say for himself or no way to say it. But you . . . well . . ." He gestured toward my tear-drenched face on the television beside him. "It's all up there to see, isn't it? You clearly have massive reserves of empathic understanding, plus a profound ability to live fully within and through the moment." He looked at the sheets in front of him and ran his finger down a list. "Fiona Hestridge described you to us, and I quote, as 'the authentic voice of remorse.' Ellen Barrington used the phrase 'convincingly anguished.' Even Marcia Harris called you—"

"You've been spying on me?"

"Just doing a little research," Forster said, cutting in.

He reached across to the white cloth in the middle of the table and pulled it away to reveal a silver dish full of dark chocolate, cocoa-dusted truffles, and glossy chocolate-coated nuts. He pushed the dish in front of me. "You're among friends," he said. I hesitated for a second, both infuriated by the knowingness of the gesture and attracted by the high-quality product in the bowl. I took a Brazil nut and focused on how my teeth slid through the dense outer layers to reach the crunch at the center. I ran my tongue around my teeth.

"I've told you I've never heard of this Schenke guy. Shouldn't I meet him before we go any further?"

Forster sniffed and studied the ceiling. "Oh, I don't think that's necessary."

"But I know nothing about international diplomacy."

"That's the point," Forster said, looking back at me. "It's what makes you ideal for the job. A Chief Apologist plucked from among the usual suspects would have no credibility at all. A former restaurant critic with an interesting backstory—"

"What do you mean, 'former restaurant critic'?"

"We heard you had resigned. Isn't that so, Jennie?"

"That was what I was told by Sophie in the press office at the paper. You did resign, didn't you?"

Max Olson got up and walked to the window. He lit a new cigarette and rested his elbow on the high windowsill like a cocktail party guest propping himself up at a marble mantelpiece. "Mr. Basset," he said, killing a flaming match with a quick, deliberate flick of his wrist, "you are worrying too much about what has been. My government . . . our governments are in a position to make you an offer which it would be foolish for you to refuse."

Forster said, "You will have your own team of advisers—historians, psychologists, political, legal, everything you need—many of its members drawn from around this table. And Jennie here will go along with you as your chief of staff to take care of admin." I turned to her and she raised her eyebrows as if to say, "How about it?" I shoved a crumbling truffle into my mouth and felt its soothing liquid fall across my tongue as the soft center of salt caramel broke out from the chocolate's heart.

"They are superb," I said, pointing to the bowl. "L'Artisan du Chocolat?" I said, naming my favorite chocolatier on Lower Sloane Street.

Forster said, "Jennie, are they . . . ?"

She nodded. "Gerard sends his regards."

"He knows his chocolate, does Gerard."

"Of course," she said. "And so do you."

I took another, and then a third. The room was watching me. "Okay, then. And if I say yes, what will I get?"

Forster said, "Will?"

The lawyer picked up a sheet of paper. "Diplomatic status, from

Her Majesty's Government, as necessary. The apartment on the twenty-sixth floor of the Millennium Hotel at number one United Nations Plaza, rent free, naturally, plus another official residence, to be decided, in Geneva. A tax-free salary of two hundred and fifty thousand dollars per annum as an advance against point zero zero one percent of the Schenke scale differential plus—"

"Hang on a moment. Point zero zero what of what?"

Will Masters put down the sheet and took off his glasses. "It's a little technical, Mr. Basset, and I suggest you read up on the Schenke scale in the book. I also have to advise you to get independent legal advice on this contract and I will happily suggest some names of good people who can help you through. But be assured that the minimum you will receive is a quarter of a million dollars a year, payable in monthly installments, which could be topped up in a significant manner depending upon your performance."

"What do you call significant?"

He replaced his glasses and returned to his sheet. "Best to read the book," he said, distractedly. "All expenses will be taken care of, naturally, and you will have a minimum severance payment of two years' salary—half a million dollars—this contract to run, in the first instance, for two years blah blah blah." He put down the sheet. "There's a lot of other stuff here about domiciles, jurisdictions, and your nationality—which may, at times, have to be flexible—but those are the main points."

I shoved two Brazil nuts into my mouth in quick succession. $250,000 a year as an advance against point zero zero one percent of something. "A lot to think about, isn't it?" Forster said. I nodded because my mouth was too full.

He slid a book across the table to me. "Go home. Read this. And call us," he said. "But do it quickly. There's only fourteen days before Dayton kicks off and we need you in place by then."

Thirteen

Dick "Crawfish" Anheiser, who earned his name as a young man working the shrimp boats out of Freeport, Texas, first told his mama he would eventually be a millionaire when he was twelve years old.

"An' I'll be doin' it the decent way," he told Dolores Anheiser, "sellin' decent stuff to decent folk."

In 1948, on a trip to San Bernardino, California, where he hoped to establish himself in the burgeoning car wash business, he stopped at a roadside restaurant for a hamburger. It was run by two brothers called Maurice and Richard McDonald and appeared to be turning a brisk trade. His experience of the McDonald brothers' new Speedee Service System, a production line for hamburgers, convinced him that his business ambitions were misplaced. He telephoned his younger brother Jimmy back in Texas, told him that he was going into the restaurant business, and offered him a job. Reckoning that McDonald's was already well positioned to dominate the West Coast, the Anheiser brothers made for Raleigh, North Carolina, where in 1949 they opened their first branch of Dick's Dogs, a roadside restaurant specializing in extralong hot dogs dressed with chili sauce or mustard, fried onions or Dick's famous hot cheese sauce.

The business was a great success, and by the late 1980s, a mixture of franchising and company-funded expansion had created an empire of 2,237 restaurants in forty-eight states of the Union. Crawfish Anheiser was a very wealthy man and he had become so decently, just as he had promised his mama. Then, one February morning in 1989, his clean record was put in jeopardy. A manicurist called Rosalie Romaro sustained second-degree burns in a branch of Dick's Dogs in Gallup, New Mexico, when an egg-yolk yellow fountain of cheese sauce, overheated by a machine fault, squirted out of a Big Dog Number One onto her bare thigh. She spent three days in the hospital and felt unable to wear split-thigh skirts ever again because of the unsightly scarring. As is the custom, Romaro sued Dick's Dogs.

The tort came at a difficult time for Crawfish Anheiser. He was in the advanced stages of a deal with the Cheezey Pizza Corporation of Oregon which would enable him to slip quietly into retirement, his fortune intact. CPC, which controlled around a third of the Dick's Dogs stock, suggested that their lawyers handle the Romaro situation given their experience in the area. (They had recently settled a case in which a nine-year-old boy had sustained burns to his knees when the bottom fell out of a Cheezey Pizza box while he was watching television.) At first Crawfish agreed. "Ask me 'bout hot dogs and I'll tell you all there is to know," he told his brother Jimmy. "But I leave the big words to the professionals."

A month later the lawyers reported back. They had secured what they believed to be an advantageous deal. Romaro had agreed to accept an out-of-court settlement of $10 million, in return for which Dick's Dogs would in no way admit liability or be called upon to express regret.

Crawfish was appalled. Ten million dollars seemed an awful lot of money for one squirt of Dick's famous cheese sauce. "Have you tried sayin' sorry?" he asked his lawyers. "Isn't that the least this lady deserves?" The men in suits almost fell off their chairs. If Crawfish Anheiser apologized, then the company would be left open to countless other claims, they said. The cost could be astronomical. Crawfish demurred. "I promised my late mama I'd be decent," he said, "an' I shall." CPC were furious and pulled out of the takeover deal for fear of future liabilities. They sold all their Dick's Dogs stock, thus forcing the price down, which made a huge dent in the old man's paper fortune. Still, he kept his word.

In September of 1990, nineteen months after the injury, Crawfish Anheiser met Rosalie Romaro at her mobile home in the desert just outside Gallup. He apologized profusely for all the pain and discomfort she had been caused. According to a report which subsequently appeared in the *Gallup Independent,* the old man even wept upon seeing the scar and said, "Oh my, the terrible things my dog done to your pretty skin."

Romaro was so moved by his gesture that she agreed to settle the case in return for just $500,000, a statement of apology, and a personal signed photograph of Crawfish, which she kept by her bed.

Although there were subsequently a number of other claims against the company, the damages paid out by Dick's Dogs over a ten-year period never amounted to more than $3 million. Each time, Crawfish made the apology himself. He was forced to remain as chairman of the company for a few years more, but that meant he was able to ride out the recession of the early 1990s. When he did eventually find a buyer—the Tastee Taco Corporation of Nevada—they paid almost double the amount CPC had been prepared to pay just six years before.

"It just shows," Crawfish Anheiser said at his retirement party, "that sayin' sorry really does bring its own rewards."

The Romaro case would probably have remained an obscure footnote in New Mexican legal history were it not for a student at Columbia University Law School called Karen Stewart, whose uncle was an attorney in San Jose. One Thanksgiving he mentioned the Crawfish Apology to his niece, just after she had poured gravy on his arm by mistake. Stewart was so intrigued that she made it and other similar apologies the subject of her graduate thesis. An exhaustive search produced just enough examples of corporate apologies and their outcomes to enable her to conclude that the minimum cost-benefit of the apologetic approach to civil actions (as against paying out while denying any liability and not saying sorry) was twenty-three percent to the defendant. Sadly for Stewart, the legal profession was unimpressed by her hard work and she ended up as a divorce lawyer in Cleveland.

The lack of interest was not surprising. There are only two types of lawyer in the field of civil claims: those representing plaintiffs, who are paid a significant proportion of the final sum secured, and those representing defendants, who dream, at some point, of representing plaintiffs, which is where the big money is. Neither group was interested in research that would reduce the size of the ultimate payout. The academic journals, knowing their readership well, thus declined to publish the paper.

Only one person showed any interest: Stewart's supervising professor, Thomas Schenke, an expert in international law. His had not been a sparkling career. If Schenke were to be remembered at all, it was as the author of a deathly tome on the problems of multilingual tribunals and the complexities of interpreting legal jargon from one language to another in real time. Behind his back his colleagues joked that the book was a more interesting read in Dutch than English, as long as you understood no Dutch.

But Schenke had one ace up his sleeve. For a decade, since the end of the Cold War, he had been working on what he originally called his theory of event overload. While Francis Fukuyama was wowing the media with his notion that the fall of the Berlin Wall meant a victory for liberal democracy and the end of history—that future events would now be dominated by little more than spats over who would get to stage the next Olympics and whether any French pop music was worth listening to—Schenke had concluded exactly the opposite: that Soviet rule had been a massive scab, which, now wrenched off, would lead to a raging gush of bad blood. He came to believe, correctly, that an enormous number of newly exposed and ancient unrighted wrongs would clog up the processes of international politics, with injured parties constantly bringing their antique wounds to the negotiating table. Furthermore, an ever more globalized world would lead to an acceleration in the number and depth of new grievances. Schenke pointed out that while the eleventh century had produced only two events of any note—the Norman Conquest of England in 1066 and the taking of Jerusalem by the Crusaders in 1099—the last decade of the twentieth century had alone produced dozens on a similar scale from the Balkans to West Africa, from East Timor to the Arabian Gulf. Each of these in turn had its roots in a set of unsettled grievances. Unless something was done to lighten the planet's historical ballast, the future would be a more chaotic and dangerous place in which to live.

Schenke had identified the disease, but until Stewart's paper landed on his desk, he could offer no cure. The model of corporate apology provided the solution. Surely the principles could apply just as easily to nation-states, which were increasingly being called upon to make financial amends for the sins of their forefathers. Wars demanded reparations. The excesses of colonialism required compensation. Could not an apology, earnestly and sincerely given, reduce the size of these monumental payouts? He first raised the thought in an article for *Foreign Affairs,* the journal of the Council on Foreign Relations, in which he shamelessly appropriated Stewart's research as his own, an act of plagiarism for which he later had to apologize. Schenke's apology was apparently so impressive that Stewart settled her claim against her former professor for no more than a fifty-dollar Borders voucher and a new copy of a Webster's English dictionary. Curiously, the offense, which in most circumstances would have been enough to end an academic career, served to inflate Schenke's reputation. A rare and impressive link was made between the man and the theory he propounded; he had, by his own flawed actions, proved that it had potential.

The Schenke Doctrine was already the talk of international diplomatic circles when his book, *Grievance Settlement Within a Global Context,* was published a year later. Diplomats and politicians liked the sound of Penitential Engagement. They wanted the chance to show that they cared. Schenke's argument that the apology could only be taken as genuine if it was completely separated from the size of any compensation payments eventually made also appealed. It made mollification the primary responsibility, from which all others flowed. Now their job was to make sure everybody felt okay about themselves. When one critic argued that the Schenke Doctrine was "merely an attempt to bring the values of Oprah and Ricki Lake to the negotiating table," the professor was defiant. "Perhaps we could all learn a little more from daytime TV," he said.

In the closing chapters of his book he proposed the foundation of an Office of Apology under the auspices of the United Nations. In Appendix 1, he published the six guiding laws under which all international apologies should be offered:

Appendix 1:
Professor Thomas Schenke's Six Laws of Grievance
Settlement Within a Global Framework

1. Never apologize for anything for which you are not sorry.
2. Never apologize for anything for which you are not responsible.
3. Only apologize to those who have suffered the hurt (see point *i* below), or their legitimate heirs.
4. Never link the wording of an apology to the shape, scale, or form of any settlement that may follow (see point *iv* below).
5. Never blame others.
6. There is no statute of limitations on a hurt.

Schedule of sublaws, definitions,
and implicatory conditions

i) *Hurt*—the term, recognized in international law, for any physical, mental, or moral injury to a person or peoples.
ii) *Self-definition*—a hurt is defined as such by those who allege they have suffered the injury (be it physical or mental).

iii) Self-direction—any people or peoples who have
   declared themselves a victim of a hurt have the moral
   right to appoint their representative or representatives,
   without interference from any outside body.

iv) No apologee may define or assume, from the shape,
   form, or scale of the apology they have received, the
   shape, form, or scale of any settlement that may follow.

Appendix 2 described the Schenke scale that Will Masters had
told me about. It laid out a complex mathematical formula which
had been used to calculate the size of reparation and compensation
payments that would be made where no apology had been offered
for a hurt. Most of these amounts ran to billions of dollars. Alongside them, as a comparison, was the expected figure if an apology
had been offered, still using Stewart's original twenty-three percent
figure as a baseline. The gap between the two numbers was
described as the Schenke scale differential, of which I would be due
point zero zero one percent. I understood that Appendix 2 was no
more than an academic exercise; that it was an attempt by the professor to attach some hard numbers to his lofty theories. I already
recognized that some apologies might be refused and that others
might have no effect whatsoever on the size of the eventual payouts.
Still, even with my tenuous grasp on mathematics I could see what
all this meant. Most of the Schenke scale differentials amounted to
billions of dollars, of which I was being offered a thousandth. This
was serious money. For being an emotional mess. For being in touch
with the real me. For doing the very thing that had been giving me
so much pleasure.

I put the book down and looked over at the two fatly packed suitcases, standing sentry by the living room door, which had been there
waiting for me when I got home. I looked at the sudden gaps on the
living room shelves, the signs of disengagement from a previous
life. It was just as Stephen Forster had said. I had an awful lot to
think about.

Fourteen

The old Manjari wasn't going to do it tonight. I needed substantial comfort food, a dish that would fully engage me. Naturally, being British, this meant cooking something Italian.

I heated a little olive oil in a heavy-bottomed iron skillet and, when the first wisps of smoke escaped the surface, sprinkled the pan with flakes of dried chili that fizzed and bubbled in the liquid. I imagined my father standing behind me, watching me as I cooked, as he had done so many times. I could feel the sound of his voice in my chest, a deep and sonorous echo from the past.

"Step back, little one, or the fumes from the chili will choke you."

I turned away from the skillet for a moment. "I know, Dad. I've done this before."

"Everything takes practice, Marcel."

"So you always told me."

"And I'm telling you again."

"Pancetta now?"

"Yes, now."

I dropped the fingertip-sized chunks of smoky bacon, with their lush, marshmallow white ribbons of fat, into the pan and spread them around with a wooden spoon. They turned in on themselves as the heat sucked the moisture from the fat and began to brown. On a chopping board I crushed a clove of garlic with the flat of my knife and then I chopped it up.

"Not too soon with the garlic."

"I know, Dad. I'm just getting it ready."

"It will scotch if you put it in too soon."

"I said I'm only getting it ready. And the word's 'scorch.' "

"Such a big boy now. He knows so much. What wine are you using?"

"An Australian sauvignon blanc."

"Australian? Things so bad you couldn't afford French?"

"You get more for your money with Australian."

"So spend more money and get French."

"Dad, things have changed a lot since you were about. Australia makes great wines."

"If you say so. If you say so. Now with the garlic, Marcel. Now!"

"Don't bark. I'm onto it."

I gave the fragments of garlic only thirty seconds in the bubbling oil before adding a third of the bottle of wine, scraping away at the caramelized lumps of bacon and chili on the base of the pan as the liquor went in. I put down the bottle and tipped the spitting, boiling pan of liquid up a few degrees to gain more purchase on a few particularly sticky lumps of pork. Suddenly a sheet of flame, tinged blue at the edges, leapt from the skillet.

"It's on fire, Dad, it's on fire!"

"Calmness, little one. The flame is your friend. It is just the alcohol burning away. Let it do its job . . . there, it has gone."

"Thanks, Dad. It's good to have you here." I threw some coils of butter yellow tagliatelle into a pan of bubbling water.

"What is the fish you bought?"

"Clams. Lovely big ones."

"Good. You spent money."

"With seafood anything else is a false economy. Unlike with the wine."

"Marcel, I believe you on the wine."

I tipped the shellfish into the skillet, where they tumbled and rolled against each other like so many rounded pebbles in the surf.

Immediately they began to open. I shoved a saucepan lid over the top, so that they would steam.

"Now we wait."

"Yes, Marcel. But there's time to chop the parsley and the . . . what are you doing?"

"Grating a little Parmigiano."

"Parmesan? With shellfish?"

"They work brilliantly together. The Parmesan is a natural source of monosodium glutamate which emphasizes the meatiness of the seafood."

"What is this monosodium gluty—"

"Glutamate, Dad. It's a flavor enhancer. A manufactured form is used in Chinese cooking, and with seafood it—"

"Stop, stop. My head is spinning with all this . . . this . . . chemistry. When did cooking become such a science? Have I been gone so long?"

"Yes, you have. You've been gone far too long."

It was time. I drained the pasta, retaining just a little of the starchy cooking liquid for the serving dish to keep the ribbons of tagliatelle moving. Then I poured the entire contents of the skillet—crisp shards of pancetta, clams, and the dense, rust-colored cooking liquor—over it all. Next, the green flakes of parsley and the shavings of cheese. Carefully I began to turn the ingredients together so that the pasta became coated with the sauce and the shells became caked with the cheese and over everything were the little flakes of chili that I had started out with.

"It looks beautiful, little one."

"Thanks, Dad."

"You haven't forgotten what I taught you, then."

"How could I forget?"

I lifted a shell and sucked the soft little mollusk from its hiding place. It tasted of the sea and of the cheese and the wine and at the end came the sudden lift of chili heat.

"It's good?"

"Very good." I spooled a few ribbons of pasta onto my fork. "I wish you were able to try this. You'd have liked it very much." For a minute or two I simply ate, enjoying the all-consuming physicality of the process: the lift and suck of the clams, the spool of the tagliatelle, the slurp of the rich, rounded liquor. I wiped my hands on a paper towel and drank a little of the grassy wine.

"What am I going to do, Dad? Am I going to New York?"

"You're asking a dead man?"

"Who else do I have to ask?"

"You can't talk to your . . . what is her name?"

"Lynne."

"Lynne. Lynne I think I would have liked. A sensible girl. You can't ask your Lynne?"

"She's the one I want to ask. She's my best friend. I always talk this stuff over with Lynne. But . . ."

"If you do go it will be the end?"

"Yeah. She's hardly a disinterested party. Anyway I think it may already be the end. Things haven't been good lately."

"No?"

"She thinks I've lost it."

"Have you?"

"I don't know. I was offered a quarter of a million dollars a year today just to carry on doing what I've been doing. And millions of people appear to be obsessed by a video of me that's flying around the Net. So it can't be all that bad."

"It sounds good to me."

"Thanks, Dad."

"Sometimes, Marcel, you just have to move on. It happens to us all. It happened to me when I left my family. Now maybe it is happening to you."

"Do you think so?" I heard the delicate rattle of keys in the front door. "Do you think so, Dad?" But he was gone, and there standing in the living room doorway was Lynne. She looked down sheepishly at her suitcases by the door, as if she had not expected me to come home before she had removed them, and then back up at me apologetically. Her eyes were bloodshot, and her hair fell in tangled folds that were even more unkempt than usual, as though she had been burying her hands in them.

She said, "I didn't know when you'd be back."

"Are you hungry? There's enough here. I could put some in a bowl and—"

"No. It's okay. I've already . . ." She waved in the direction of the front door, as if there were a table just out of view beyond it. She walked over to a desk and picked up a couple of books, studiously checking the covers before holding them to herself in a way that immediately reminded me of Jennie; not the confident, self-possessed version I had met today, but the more delicate creature from years ago, cowed by the world.

We both opened our mouths to speak at the same time and then shut up.

"You first," she said.

"No, you."

She nibbled her bottom lip. "I'm moving out. I think it's for the best, just until—"

"Where are you going?"

"I'm, er, staying with Luke. Your brother said I could crash at his place until I find somewhere—"

"You don't have to."

"No, Marc. I do. We're not . . . we're just *not,* are we?"

"No, I mean you don't have to because I'm not going to be here. I've been offered a job."

"Oh?"

"The United Nations."

She tipped her head to one side and fixed me with a look I had seen many times before, the one that, with a sweet, mocking intensity, said: Just what kind of fool are you? For a moment it cut through the embarrassment and the fury which were weighing her down. I told her about the job, about the terms, about the things I was being asked to do. When I was done she stared at me silently for a moment.

"So you're going to teach the world to eat humble pie?" she said eventually.

"Well, I'll be based in New York so I suppose I'll be teaching the world to eat *crow*."

"Do you know any good recipes for crow?"

I laughed. It was a nice feeling. "Apparently I do. I'm told it's why they want me for the job. I make the best crow pie east of Long Island."

"First catch your crow—"

"Exactly. First catch your crow."

She looked around herself, as though the room were suddenly unfamiliar. Until that point I think she had understood why she was bailing out on me. I had disappeared off down my own tight emotional rat hole, and it was a gap into which she was unable to follow. But now this job offer suggested something else. Apparently I hadn't turned into some maladjusted clown. There was meaning here, a pattern that was to take me on an adventure.

"I was emailed that video of you apologizing to Jennie Sampson this afternoon."

"Oh."

She raised her eyebrows as if to say, Yes indeed: Oh!

She said, "I thought it was rather touching, actually."

"Really?"

"In a buttock-clenchingly embarrassing way."

"It does have a high buttock-clench quotient, doesn't it? Still, that's what they want to pay me for."

She attempted a smile and said, "I'm pleased for you, Marc, really—"

"The thing is, I won't need the flat because I won't be living here, and you don't really want to stay at Luke's. He was never the tidiest of boys. Have you looked under his fridge? There are life-forms growing under there. Whole families of microbacteria. There's more culture under Luke's fridge than there is on his bookshelves. Seriously, he's—"

She allowed herself a full grin. "Stop it, Marc. When are you going?"

I shrugged. "Soon, I think. They want me in New York as soon as possible, so . . ."

Lynne played with the keys that she still held in her free hand. "Look, maybe I'll just hang on to these and come back when you've gone."

"You don't have to go at all."

"I think I do, honey. It's better this way. Give you some space. Give both of us some space." And then: "I'm pleased for you. It's a good thing, this, I'm sure."

"*We're* a good thing."

Suddenly she looked unbearably sad. I wanted to reach across and embrace her, but the distance between us was too great. "Will you come and see me in the States? Maybe I could cook you one of my special crow pies."

"I'd like that," she said, but from the droop of her shoulders and the way she turned her gaze from me to the books she was holding, it was obvious Lynne did not like the idea at all.

Too often we only identify the crucial points in our lives in retrospect. At the time we are too absorbed in the fetid detail of the moment to spot where it is leading us. But not this time. I was experiencing one of my dad's deafening moments. If my life could be understood as a meal of many courses (and let's be honest, much of it actually was), then I had finished the starters and I was limbering up for the main event. So far, of course, I had made a stinking mess of it. I had spilled the wine. I had dropped my cutlery on the floor and sprayed the fine white linen with sauce. I had even spat out some of my food because I didn't like the taste of it.

But it doesn't matter because, look, here come the waiters. They are scraping away the debris with their little horn and steel blades, pulled with studied grace from the hidden pockets of their white aprons. They are laying new tablecloths, arranging new cutlery, placing before me great domed wine glasses, newly polished to a sparkle. There are more dishes to come, more flavors to try, and this time I will not spill or spit or drop or splash. I will not push the plate away from me, the food only half eaten. I am ready for everything they are preparing to serve me. Be in no doubt; it will all be fine.

Fifteen

Sitting at a back table in a small fondue place that I found two blocks north of Union Square in New York City, I could pretend that everything was fine. It was called the Matterhorn Café and inside the air smelled unself-consciously of dairy fats and hot wine. The boss was a Swiss Italian called Bruno who every evening occupied the last booth before the kitchen door, his huge belly wedged in against the tabletop, from where he directed his staff of young Czech waitresses, each as pale as he was dark.

The interior gave out mixed signals. The walls were paneled in old varnished pine planks, and each of the booths had its own carved, overhanging faux roof, as if it were an Alpine chalet. But the table-cloths were of red and white laminated gingham and stacked about the walls were bulbous bottles of red wine, their bases encased in baskets. It turned out that Bruno, fearing New York wasn't ready for a Swiss fondue joint, had tried to run a Swiss Italian trattoria here instead (lots of grilled meats with heavy cream and mushroom sauces and attitude) only to discover that Manhattan definitely wasn't ready for one of those. So he had gone back to Plan A and begun serving fondues. Now they came: the middle-aged couples from the outer boroughs who remembered fondly their young-married years in the early 70s when fondues were somehow chic, and the gay boys from the Village who thought there was something kitsch about the place, and the confused former restaurant critic with a new job at the United Nations who was wondering if he had made the biggest mistake of his life.

This retreat to the Matterhorn Café had nothing to do with my dad, though I can see why some people might assume so. André Basset may have been Swiss but he was endlessly dismissive of the fondue.

"One thousand years of civilization and this is the best they can do? A gallon of boiling wine and ten pounds of cheese? This they call cooking?"

He hated any trend and fondues were exactly that when I was a kid, so he would have nothing to do with them. It was my mother who was determined not to be left out. The fondue was the only thing I ever remember her cooking before my father died and then just the once. I have scant memory of the dish itself, save the smell when it was cooking and that I burned the roof of my mouth on the hot, molten cheese. I have better memories of my mother dipping chunks of French bread into a little glass of kirsch that she, and only she, had at her side, before dipping it into the pot. She did this with every piece of bread and with a marked precision and daintiness, as if it could not be a proper fondue unless the rituals were observed. I remember my father glowering and my mother giggling uncontrollably, and us little boys joining in too because Mum, who was always steady and cool, was so very funny when she laughed. (We didn't join in, though, with her shouts of "mountain boy" at Dad, which made him blush.) The next morning Dad made our breakfast and Mum stayed in bed because, he said, "she has become ill." He hummed to himself as he warmed the milk for our porridge, the stove his domain once more.

In a strange city the Matterhorn Café reminded me of who I was. The main event, a *fondue des Mosses* from Vaud made with Gruyère and Appenzell, was good. There was no aftertaste of raw alcohol or uncooked cornstarch, and alongside it they served plates of *viande des Grisons,* those exquisitely fragile slices of Swiss air-cured beef that could put a Harry's Bar Carpaccio to shame. There was also a neighborhood feel to the place. I noticed the same guys in there night after night. The balding fellow in the checked sports jacket up at the bar. Green salad. Plate of cheese, basket of bread, and the sports pages of *USA Today*. Then, a few booths behind me, an older guy with a graying buzz cut and a black suit, a steak and a magazine—fishing or cycling, always some kind of red-meat outdoor sports—whom I would pass on the way to the toilets at the front by the door. At the Matterhorn Café I could be one of them, another single man who needed dinner and who chose to take it here, where he belonged. Christ knows, I didn't belong anywhere else in the city. I worked that one out early on.

The gatekeeper for the United Nations, the single person with the power to grant access to the headquarters of the most overarching internationalist organization the planet has ever seen, was a soft-cheeked middle-aged woman with pencil lines for eyebrows, a saggy gullet, and a name badge that read *Nora*. She peered over the counter of the tight, circular reception desk at the suitcases scattered about us.

"You the team from UNOAR?"

"Yes," Jennie said tersely. She rocked back on one heel. She had done exactly the same when she discovered there was no limo to meet us at the airport: one foot back, rocking on the heel, as if by keeping all the movement below the knee, no one would notice her irritation. Then she muttered to me, "No one who flies first-class should ever have to take a cab. Remember that, Marc. No one. First-class. Ever." She sent Will Masters and Satesh Panjabi to join the taxi line.

Now it was happening again.

"You got bags?" the receptionist said.

"Yes."

"They been through security?"

"Naturally. Can you call the UNOAR secretariat's office and tell them Marc Basset is here?"

"There's no one in the UNOAR office." This as if lecturing an idiot. Nora pushed herself back on her office chair from the curve of desk and barked at a colleague a few inches away over her shoulder. "Doreen? Who'd'we call for UNOAR? Larry?"

The other woman didn't look up. She kept on punching away at a computer keyboard. Just kept on pushing those buttons. "Yeah, Larry. Extension twenty-seven sixty-four seven."

"I'll call Larry Zwegller."

"Fine. Please do."

And then he was there, a small man in a cheap blue suit with a big bunch of keys hanging off his belt and a film of sweat clinging to his top lip.

"You the UNOAR guys? Larry Zwegller, Facilities." Vigorous handshakes all round, as if the human contact might save him. "Jesus, but am I pleased to see you. Sorry the greeting isn't more, you know, fitting, but what with the situation an' all . . . You got bags? They been through security? Good. Hey, Tony? Tony here will deal with the bags. Check 'em, won't you, Tony? We leave 'em here and we'll take elevator seven. I'll show you around and then, you know, then you can get to work."

We stood in the lift, the five of us trying not to notice the smell of dry cleaning fluid and sweat coming off Zwegller's suit.

"So the thing is, Miss . . ."

"Sampson. Ms."

"Sure, Ms. Sampson. The thing is, arrangements have been a bit . . . anyway, just expect a bit of noise up there."

"On the fifteenth floor?"

"Fourteenth, fifteenth, sixteenth—take your pick," he said wearily, looking upward as if through the lift ceiling he could see something the rest of us could not.

The lift doors opened on that very special kind of chaos only a failed attempt at organization can create, like the disruption of a beautiful place setting after the meal has been eaten. There were huddles of men, backs against the corridor wall, hunched down on the old gray linoleum-tiled floor shouting into mobile phones, surrounded by arcs of strewn paper. Through office doors we could see people jabbing each other in the chest across desks and others shouting into telephones or at each other, or both. Weaving in and out of them were tidy young women, with fixed smiles and shiny heels, carrying stationery supplies from one place to another as if a sense of purpose might save them from being swallowed up by this clutter of noise and motion.

"Ladies and Gentlemen," Larry said, deadpan, "welcome to the United Nations Office of Apology and Reconciliation."

We stepped into the thick broth of shout and accusation. Jennie flinched and pressed one hand to an ear to help herself think.

"What in god's name is going on?"

Zwegller leaned into her. "We had to come up with a plan for the desks," he said, all but shouting to make himself heard. "So some guy—"

Before he could finish, a short dark man with a Velcro strip of mustache battered him on the shoulder. "Mr. Zwegller, it is intolerable. We must be moved. My people, we cannot take this offense. We must—"

"Whoa, whoa, whoa there. Which delegation?" Zwegller leaned his ear toward him.

"I am from Armenia. The Turks are on the next desk. Do you know about the Armenian genocide by the Turkish? Do you know of this stain on the world's history? We cannot tolerate to be so close to these . . . people." He spat out the last word. "And the Kurds, they are there interrupting our arguments with the Turkish and saying their claim is newer and so should take precedence. It is intolerable, heinous—"

"Okay," Larry said. "Okay. Listen. I am only Facilities. I do desks. I do telephones. Not stains on history." He hesitated, apparently looking for a solution. "I may be able to do screens, though. Maybe I get you a screen to separate you from the Turkish delegation as a stopgap? How's that?"

The man looked mollified. "You are a good man, Mr. Zwegller."

"Here to serve, my friend. Here to serve."

He turned back to us with a big see-what-I-mean shrug. "So
some shmuck, he set the desks up geographically. End result, we got
Israelis sharing a desk pod with the Palestinians, the Australians
with the Aborigines, the East Timorese with the Indonesians. It's a
friggin' disaster, I tell you. 'Scuse my French. So anyway—"

"Why doesn't the secretariat sort this out?" Jennie said, leaning
back in to him.

Larry Zwegller blinked for a moment, then nibbled his lip.
"Okay, lady. What we have here is what I think is called a communi-
cation breakdown. Let me get you to your offices and I'll, you
know . . . then we can talk. And step carefully. As you can see, my
friends, there are people who've just shifted out of their desks altogether and are camping out in the corridors. UNHCR is thinking of
popping up here to have a look-see," he said and grinned encouragingly, but none of us grinned back.

On this side of the fifteenth floor, which faced into Manhattan,
were the delegations from the European and Near Eastern special
interest groups who had been invited to research and register their
apologizable hurts. The Middle and Far East, Africa, and Australasia
delegations were on the floor above, Zwegller shouted at us, where
they would eventually be joined by Financial Control. Historical and
Verification was meant to be on the floor below, along with Legal
Affairs, Psychology, and ancillary services like Transport and
Accommodation. We pushed through a set of new double doors on
the East River side of the building and the noise immediately subsided.

"And this," Zwegller said, with a dying fall, "is the secretariat."
There was a long, thickly carpeted, newly painted, and deserted corridor off of which stood a set of deserted offices filled with empty
desks and bare bookshelves, each offering a lovely, unbroken view
of the East River. We padded slowly through the silence.

Jennie said, "Where is everyone?"

"Just through here, Ms. Sampson, if you please, ma'am."
Another set of double doors and into an anteroom where two young

women, with nothing to do, jumped up from behind empty desks and straightened their skirts. "Alice, Francine, good to see ya, let's take these good people onward." They led us through a last set of doors, to a massive corner expanse that looked out in one direction on uptown Manhattan, and in the other, over the river. There was modern window seating padded in caramel-colored leather, a sofa area, and a couple of separate goldfish-bowl offices. There was tasteful modern art. There were healthy rubber plants. There was the gentle hum of air-conditioning.

I went and looked out at the view of the city, this vast, shuddering creature that looked calm and at rest compared to the craziness out beyond the doors behind me.

Jennie said, "So . . . ?"

"We have this situation."

The secretariat were the bureaucrats who would be responsible for the day-to-day running of UNOAR: overseeing the compilation and verification of hurts, the staging and financing of apologies, the work of various other apologists scattered about the globe (of whom I was, notionally, the head). Normally, secretariat-grade UN employees move to each new task without a murmur, but here they had made an exception.

"These guys, apparently, they don't do feelings," said Zwegller, whom I was coming to like. "They do administering. They say to their line managers, in this department maybe, 'I'll be required to have emotional responses.' This, they say, is a dangerous business. At the least, they say, they run the risk of passive empathizing."

"Passive empathizing?"

"These folk, they're worried they'll start having feelings just by being near you."

"So?" Jenny said, rocking back on her heel again.

"You know how it is. It's about the money. They wanna raise— like we don't all want one of those. So anyway, none of them will come in here till management sorts them out. In the meantime, it's just you, me, and Alice and Francine here."

We all stared at each other in silence. Francine stepped forward.

"Mr. Basset, can I say how much I loved the video of your apology? I'm just so looking forward to seeing you emote in person."

On my first full day in New York, instead of going to the office, I started walking the streets, and late that afternoon I found the Matterhorn Café. I went there every evening after that and ordered the same thing—fondue, salad, a carafe of white Jura—until on the fourth night the waitress didn't even give me the menu but simply said "The same?" and I nodded. I snatched a couple of mobile phone conversations with Jennie—she had handed us each a new mobile at the airport—but she was always brisk and businesslike. She told me she was "getting to the bottom of things" and that I should "get settled in." Will Masters called me once, to check a couple of details on my contract, and Satesh phoned to see whether I wanted to take in some new Finnish movie with him, at an art house on the Upper East Side. I told him no thanks, I was getting enough gloom and angst at work. He laughed and said everything would be sorted out soon enough.

On that fourth night at the Matterhorn, just after my fondue had been placed on the burner in front of me, Jennie appeared at my side. She was wearing jeans and no makeup and her hair was pulled back and tied with a simple black velvet band. It was like seeing your teacher outside school.

"I didn't think fondue would be your kind of thing."

"A fine dish," I said, skewering the first piece of bread. "You want to?" She sat down and they brought us another fork. She leaned into the steam. "It smells pretty good."

"Over the past few days I have come to consider the fondue the height of gastronomic endeavor."

"How so?"

"You look at this bowl. What's in it? At base nothing more than grapes and milk. If you broke it down to its constituent parts you would have just a bunch of grapes and a big jug of milk on the table.

But happily some genius has gone to all the trouble of turning those grapes into wine and that milk into cheese. Imagine life without cheese. Can you? Can you imagine life without cheese?"

"I can imagine life without Edam."

"Oh sure. And we could probably lose that weird smoked German stuff in the plastic skin."

"Anything that's been processed, actually."

"Of course. But apart from those—could you imagine a world without cheese?"

"No. No, I couldn't."

"Exactly. And then what happens? Someone comes up with a glorious plan to combine these two ingredients which are themselves the pinnacle of culinary invention, to create yet another dish. The fondue is indulgence squared."

I dunked a piece of bread deep into the fondue and felt it take on the weight of the molten cheese. Quickly, before the bread fragmented and dropped away to be lost in the depths, I put it in my mouth and whipped it off the fork. Jennie watched me eat.

"You can be a real nerd sometimes," she said. "You know that?"

"Thank you. For a long while I have only aspired to nerd-dom. Now I appear to have achieved it."

We ate in silence for a minute.

"They've settled the dispute," she said.

"That's good news."

"The first admin officers started moving in this afternoon. A new desk plan for the delegations has already been drawn up."

"Excellent." I dragged another piece of cheese-clogged bread out of the bowl.

"I thought you'd like to know."

"I do." I was about to plunge another piece of bread into the pot, when a thought occurred to me. I lifted my fork and pointed it at Jennie, accusingly. "How the hell did you know where I was?"

She smiled. "We had you tailed," she said. "For your own safety."

"You what?"

"Alex and Franky here," she said, nodding over my shoulder. "Your security detail." I turned around. The man at the bar in the loud checked jacket and the crew-cut guy in the booth with the magazines grinned at me and each raised a hand in salute. I managed a feeble wave back.

"You had me followed?"

"You're an emotional bloke, Marc. That's why you got the job. I knew this would be a stressful few days, but I didn't have time to baby-sit you, so—"

"I didn't need baby-sitting."

"Of course not. That's why Alex and Franky have been employed to keep an eye on you, just to check everything is fine." She leaned in toward me. "You're an important man now, Marc. We have to take great care of you."

I slumped back in my seat. "Is this what the new job means?"

"You'll get used to it. And Franky and Alex are great guys. You'll like them. Trust me."

"So what happens now?" Languidly I skewered another piece of bread. Fondue may well have been the pinnacle of gastronomic achievement but it was also getting boring.

"There's a big file on your desk. Tomorrow morning you go in to your lovely big corner office and you start reading."

"Yeah? What's the file about?"

"Oh, you know. Your family's total complicity in the creation and maintenance of the US slave trade."

"Aaah, that," I said, and pulled the bread off the fork.

Sixteen

Chocolate has played an important part in my life. It has comforted and reassured me. It has focused and fattened me. It has indulged me. And one afternoon, many years ago, chocolate almost helped me kill my brother.

It was another dull Sunday, a few months after the annoying hee-haw incident, and our parents had been foolish enough to leave us alone together for a few hours. They thought we were now friends. They thought that, at base, we approved of each other. But how could we? Remember: Luke was nine; I was eleven. We were of different species. Still, for the first half hour we managed a certain peaceful coexistence, like two ancient enemies who can't even be bothered to rattle the sabers anymore. He sprawled on the sofa in front of the television while I turned my attention to the high mantelpiece on the other side of the living room and the Lady Bountiful that stood upon it.

The Lady Bountiful was a box. It still is. The joints are half-lap, as befits a casket made around 1796. It is a foot square and it is fashioned of thickly waxed, blackened oak. In the middle of the tightly fitting hinged lid is an oval silver plaque. It bears the legend *William Welton-Smith* in a pinched italic. Beneath that are the words *The Lady Bountiful*. This, my mother told me, was the name of a great merchant ship of which her ancestor William had been owner. The vessel was wrecked in 1794 off the coast of South Carolina, a little north of Sullivan's Island. According to the story, William Welton-

Smith had considered the *Lady Bountiful* to be the foundation of his great fortune and felt its loss keenly. To commemorate its part in his making he salvaged just enough of the oak deck to make this box. It had been passed down through the family to my mother's uncle, her father's elder brother, who in turn bequeathed it to his niece.

I recall her using it, at first, as a jewelry box, although it was no place for valuables. There was a lock on the front but the key had long ago been lost. Inside she padded it with small, self-stitched linen bags of kapok and overlaid these with a lining of purple satin, tacked into the base. Much of her modest collection of jewelry—some fine-link silver bracelets, a delicate gold chain with a teardrop of amber as a pendant—lay free upon the satin bed. Other pieces—rings, brooches, a pearl necklace—were encased within separate boxes that then went into the Lady Bountiful. I came to associate the smell of that open casket, the mustiness of a dusty cupboard over-laid by the floweriness of the heavy wax, with nighttime glamor, for it was opened only when my parents were preparing to go out for the evening. I now know that some of the aroma was the slick of per-fume that she would apply before choosing her jewelry and which would cling to the necklaces when she had taken them off, but to me it was all of a piece.

One Christmas my father gave my mother a new jewelry box of burgundy leather which held special compartments for bracelets and ridged cushions for rings. There was even a lock on the front, the key to which she placed on her key ring. The Lady Bountiful now became free for another purpose. The padding and the satin were removed and it was lined instead with that year's leftover tissue-thin Christmas wrapping paper.

Then it was filled with chocolate. And so it began. Occasionally something of quality would find its way in there: a few rectangles of buttery Italian praline wrapped in greaseproof-lined gold paper, or a cellophane bag of misshapen truffles heavily dusted with a bitter cocoa powder the color of rust, both gifts from clients of Dad's who saw in his Alpine chalet designs the exotica of what was still then called "the Continental" (as in "Continental breakfast" or "Continental quilt"). But for the most part the box contained what I would later come to call, dismissively, Civilian Chocolate. There were bars of Cadbury's Dairy Milk with the minimum cocoa solids needed to keep them in one piece at room temperature. There were the glucose overload of Mars bars, small bags of Maltesers, the loose contents of a tin of Quality Street, their garish wrappers a more potent reminder of Christmas than the lining paper could ever be.

The thing I remember most about the Lady Bountiful was its fullness, for Dad appeared to refill the box more quickly than Mum ever allowed it to be emptied. (It was a long time before I clocked that he was attacking the contents every night after we went to bed and refilling from a private store he kept in his desk.) It would come down off the mantelpiece irregularly, usually on Sunday evenings as some sort of consolation for the impending threat of school the next day, but even then its pleasures would be rationed. Mum would say, "Only three, Marcel," and as my hand slipped inside she would reach out to squeeze my growing love handles, unfairly accentuated by the action of me needing to bow down to peer inside because she held it so close to her. "Just like your papa," she would say, with a shake of the head, so that the chocolate also became a guilty consolation for some small token of motherly humiliation.

To be left alone that Sunday afternoon was to be offered unchallenged access. While Luke sprawled, I dragged over a chair from the kitchen table and brought the Lady Bountiful down onto the ancient rug. I killed a Mars bar first, then a packet of Maltesers. Next I broke off a few chunks of Dairy Milk, and then a few more. Every now and then I looked up at Luke who was desperately trying to ignore me. He could sense danger here. Yes, I was the one breaking the rules, but somehow he suspected that, no matter what he did, it would rebound upon him. (Well, of course—he was my younger brother. He had "fall guy" written all over him.) I finished the bar of Dairy Milk, unwrapped some of the Quality Street, particularly the square ones with the liquid-soft caramel centers, stuffed them in my mouth, and threw him a bag of Maltesers. I needed allies and he was the only other person in the room—Luke had to eat. He lobbed them back at me unopened and returned to staring at the television. I chucked them back to him; he back to me. I weighed the bag in my hand. I chucked it up in the air a couple of times to feel its unexpected weight. Then I threw it back again, but hard, with a serious flick of the wrist, so that it crashed into the side of his head with a stinging crack. I imagined the little balls of chocolate-coated honeycomb shattering within the bag, a contained explosion of crisp recrystallized sugar. He yelped, pressed one shocked hand to the side of his head, and burst into tears. I grinned at him.

Now he was upon me, a simple leap of unexpected grace. This was nothing like the kitchen table lunge. That had been a dam-burst of uncontrolled psychotic rage. This was lithe and focused, and I, weighed down by a stomachful of dissolving chocolate, was immediately thrown back onto the floor where my head cracked against the place where the rug ended and the floorboards began. From that point onward the afternoon could only end badly. We were both hurt and fighting for survival. I lay dazed for a second, and then, using what little energy had not been sapped by the effort of digestion, righted myself and lunged at him. Luke did the only thing he could in the face of my size advantage, rolling onto his back and kicking out with one shoeless foot, but for once I was too quick for him. I dodged the foot and the moment his leg reached full stretch, leapt up and straddled him.

Luke's legs were irrelevant now. He could kick all he liked but he could not reach even the hollow of my back, and with my knees pinning his arms to the floor, he could not hit me either. All he could do was scream but I knew a way to deal with that too. The unopened bag of Maltesers lay just a few inches away. I picked it up and ripped it open with my teeth while my other hand took hold of his jaw and wrenched his mouth open.

"Eat them, you little dickweed!" I shouted. "Eat them!" And with one deft action, emptied the entire contents of the bag into his mouth, the shiny chocolate balls spilling deep and sudden into the froth-flecked cavity. He tried to say something, but all except the most guttural of noises was swiftly smothered, so that he could only stare at me bug-eyed and arch his head upward at me imploringly. I grinned at him again. Job done.

It was a good minute before I realized he was choking. He had managed to push some of the Maltesers out of his mouth with his honeycomb-crusted tongue so that now I could hear the hard rasp from the very depths of his throat as he fought for air. But it was the way the veins on his neck stood proud and erect that finally told me something was wrong. His neck looked muscular and developed. Nine-year-old boys do not have muscular and developed necks. Would that not be a stupid way to go? Killed by a Malteser?

I rolled off him.

"Luke, are you . . . ?"

He bucked onto his side, his tongue lolling out of his mouth, tears running down his cheeks, his whole head jerking upward with the effort of trying to clear his windpipe of the mash of confectionery. The color was draining from his cheeks.

"Luke, speak . . ." I knew now that the situation was serious but my vital intelligence went no further. All I had was a clatter of images harvested from the limited range of information offered by early 1980s British television (the television which was still talking to itself, oblivious to the real drama unfolding on the carpet in front of it).

So I did what I had seen done. I turned Luke over onto his front, reached underneath him to clasp my hands about his chest, and then squeezed him to me with as big a wrench as I could manage. He writhed in my arms, limbs uncontrolled and loose. Once. Twice. Three times. And then, with a huge barking cough, the coagulated ball of half-dissolved chocolate and fractured honeycomb and a few whole Maltesers shot out of his mouth and landed with a deadened splat on the carpet. Luke let out a deep, weary sigh and fell forward, gasping, onto the floor.

I brought him water to drink. I loosened his clothes, and when he still appeared drowsy I helped him upstairs, undressed him, and put him to bed. Downstairs I cleaned the carpet and hid the evidence—those empty chocolate wrappers—in the trash can outside and returned the Lady Bountiful to its place on the mantelpiece. Occasionally I looked in on Luke but he was soon asleep, and when my parents returned, as day faded into evening, I told them my younger brother had suddenly fallen ill. My mother took over then, flitting up and down the stairs, taking temperatures and drinks, and all that evening I sat curled in the corner of the sofa, eyes fixed on the television screen, waiting for the call from upstairs which would announce the game was up, but it never came. Later that night while my mother was again upstairs, Dad looked inside the Lady Bountiful. He saw that it had been pillaged and challenged me on it and I quickly confessed to that minor crime, grateful for the opportunity to confess to anything at all. He nodded gently and said, "Better for special occasions," and never mentioned it again.

Luke never said a word about what happened that afternoon either. I was grateful to him for his silence and that was the key. In that moment when I rolled off him and pulled him to me and dislodged the wedge of confectionery that was killing him, I think we recognized something about each other: that we were all we had. On more than one occasion after that I took the rap for his crimes, and I always looked out for him at school. It was why that particular insult didn't need an apology. All the sorries had been said, however silently, and Luke knew it. The next Sunday and any Sunday after that when the Lady Bountiful came down off the mantelpiece, I abandoned my seniority and let him go first. After his experience that afternoon I wouldn't have blamed him if he had turned away from the contents of the box altogether, but he was still a nine-year-old boy and it was still chocolate.

The Lady Bountiful had taken on another layer of significance. All families have stupid secrets, secret because they are so stupid, and the rituals around the Lady Bountiful were one of ours. We were the Bassets and we ate chocolate because Dad was Swiss. And it was kept in a box that was made from a ship that had been owned by one of Mum's ancestors. And chocolate in that box had almost helped me kill my brother but had ended up bringing us closer together. When I set up the Vice Drawer in my desk at the flat I was trying both to sate an appetite and re-create a fragment of my childhood. It was my tribute to the Lady Bountiful. After Dad died, the box stood untouched for months, as if to open and eat from it were to somehow forget that he had gone, until one spring morning Mum, in a quiet rage, snatched it from the mantelpiece and threw the moldering contents in the bin and ripped out the lining so that it crumpled in a shower of discolored paper from that Christmas so many years before. She took to storing postcards and letters in there from friends, from family, and eventually, once we had left home, from Luke and me. I found it hugely comforting that it still played a role in the story of my family.

I would feel the same way about it now, I'm sure, were it not for the file that Jennie had placed on my desk in my lovely corner office while I was slacking off in the Matterhorn Café, the file that contained a new story about the *Lady Bountiful*. The one about its part in the bloody slaughter of 265 men, women, and children.

Seventeen

If I have committed a crime it is not one of ignorance or stupidity. It is one of accident of birth. Not that this makes me feel any better about the detail of the story. Some of what I had known was true. I did have an ancestor called William Welton-Smith and he was a merchant, of sorts, but although he did own a great three-masted ship called the *Lady Bountiful,* that was not its original name: it had been launched at Nantes on the French Atlantic coast in 1783 as *Le Zéphyr,* a pretty name for a ship with an ugly purpose, for it was, of course, a slaver.

Welton-Smith purchased the 157-ton *négrier,* as the French called their slave ships, in 1791, eager for the extra "cargo capacity" that the larger French vessels afforded over their English counterparts. He quickly changed its name to the *Lady Bountiful,* a choice which, according to Francis Wilson from Historical and Verification, who had compiled the file that Jennie gave me, was as good a measure of the man as "any we could hope for." The Lady Bountiful was a character in George Farquar's popular eighteenth-century play *The Beaux' Stratagem*, a grotesque woman determined to make as much public play of her charitable acts as possible. It was the perfect choice for a man like Welton-Smith, who had once described charity as "the foulest vice of the indolent rich." His *Lady Bountiful* was not intended to be bountiful in any way, at least not to those carried in its hold.

In the late spring of 1794 she collected a cargo of 368 African slaves from the port of Cacheu on the coast of Guinea-Bissau, 34 of whom were dead of disease and malnutrition by the time she arrived off the Eastern seaboard of the United States in September of that year. The remaining 334 were carried onward toward the port of Charleston, South Carolina, where Welton-Smith was awaiting their arrival. The ship never made it. On the seventeenth of the month they ran into what was called, at the time, a "fearsome tempest," what we would call a hurricane. Remarkably the *Lady Bountiful* survived intact, having been swept onto a sandbank early in the storm. The crew's control of the vessel's cargo was less robust. At the height of the storm a group of African men broke free from their chains and, having released their fellows, took control, chasing those crewmen who did not die in the revolt away into the lifeboats. The Africans' mistake was to delay escaping onto dry land in the hope of being able to refloat the ship.

Welton-Smith, who against all advice had spent the darkest hours of the tempest in a rackety boathouse just outside the town, the better to watch the estuary for any sight of his ship and its precious cargo, only found out what had happened two days later, when half a dozen of the crew made it ashore. Welton-Smith was so outraged by the news that he immediately toured Charleston's taverns and inns offering a month's pay to any man who would come with him to take back his vessel, which proposition met with instant approval; there was no shortage of violent, restless men willing to take his shilling from among the wretched and scabrous hordes that were the feature of any American port in the late eighteenth century.

It took twelve hours for the flotilla of fishermen's yawls and skiffs to make it along the estuary and out to the sandbank off Sullivan's Island where the *Lady Bountiful* lay beached, its masts broken, its hull leaning into the sodden ground as if putting its shoulder to the shore. Favoring the blade over the unpredictability of the musket, it took the horde just two more hours to finish the job, although their enthusiasm undermined the intended outcome, preserving neither vessel nor cargo. Stories were later written of that day. According to the many lurid quotes which Francis Wilson had excavated, the *Lady Bountiful* was, by day's end, awash with "blood that did course upon the decks" and the remains of "the children slaughtered still in their mothers' grip."

It seems the narrative became infected with a certain hyperbole, as so many of these eighteenth-century seafaring tales did, in the journey from eyewitness to professional storytellers. We know from Welton-Smith's own business accounts, for example, that later in the month he sold 69 slaves, all of them presumably survivors of the rebellion on the *Lady Bountiful*. Still, that means at least 265 men, women, and children died on the deck of the ship and that they died by the blade.

According to the record, Welton-Smith boarded her just once more after that to "ascertain whether it might be salvageable, and reassuring himself that it was not, to remove a number of personal effects." It did not say what those personal effects were but I had a pretty good idea what one of them was. Did he wash the blood from the pieces of oak that he cut from the deck that day? I suspect not. William Welton-Smith was not the kind of man to fear an ugly stain. I imagine he relished it, this dark slick of human blood soaked deep into the wood's tight grain; I can just see him enjoying the detail of the story as he explained to the carpenter how it came by its unique markings. Now if anybody ever questioned his resolve he need only show them the oak box that had been made from those pieces of wood and tell them of the day he fought to take back what was his.

He had good reason to keep a memento of the *Lady Bountiful* because it proved more valuable to him as a wreck than it did in one piece, so fully was it insured. He did not buy another ship but instead used his money to invest wisely in the ventures of others, and became so wealthy that he was able to found a bank which he later handed over to two of his sons. In the 1820s, in a successful attempt to mitigate their Englishness, the boys shortened their surname to Welton and moved their interests to Louisiana. There they invested heavily in the newly emergent cotton crop, establishing the Welton-Oaks plantation at St. Francisville on the eastern bank of the

Mississippi, its great house approached along an avenue planted with fine saplings which, as they reached maturity, gave the plantation its name. For the next century the Welton family occupied a pivotal position in the public life of Louisiana not merely as slave owners and businessmen—although they were certainly that—but on the bench and in the statehouse and, when necessary, in the Confederate forces. They were the politicians who opposed slavery's abolition and the justices who enforced the law, and the officers who fought the Civil War in its defense. And even after slavery was abolished they were there as arch segregationists. Were there Weltons in the Klan? It is hard to imagine any self-respecting Klan meeting east of the Louisiana Mississippi that would not have had one of the Welton boys in attendance, warming his hands at the friendly glow of a burning cross.

In 1821 William Welton-Smith returned home to London from Charleston a wealthy man. He died a few years later, and his legacy—money, title to property, and that damn box—began its journey down the root and branch of the Welton-Smith family tree until it landed on our mantelpiece, the aroma of fresh blood replaced by the sweet confectionary smell of sugar and cream and cocoa beans.

I place the file on my desk, lean back in my chair, close my eyes, and at some point, I suppose, begin to doze. Into my mind, unbidden, comes the image of myself when young. Before me is the box, held on my mother's lap. She lifts the lid and I reach inside. The contents are no longer Civilian-grade stuff. This is quality product: fine ganaches and properly dipped centers and hefty bars of Manjari. My hand does not hesitate inside the box. I take out one rectangular soft center, the surface almost ebony in darkness and with a distinct shine. I place it in my mouth and feel the exquisite tempered shell crack against the force of my tongue. And then into my mouth rushes a liquid center that is hot and metallic; it is a burst of something very human and unwanted. I wake up suddenly and involuntarily swallow. The taste is gone.

* * *

Although Professor Schenke devotes thirty pages of his book to the "maintenance of shared illusion in the penitential process," he still fails to offer anything of use on the practical aspects of saying sorry. At one point, clearly straining to manufacture something, he announces that "Making an apology is like plucking a chicken: it requires love, determination, and attention to detail," which is both clumsy and false. Committing bestial acts upon a chicken may require determination and attention to detail and, if you're really emotionally involved, a certain amount of love, but plucking one demands none of those things. All it requires is stamina and a non-allergenic response to feathers.

Even so, in the first hours after reading the file, I was sorely tempted to send one of my security detail out to the Ely Live Poultry Market over on Delancey Street to get me a feathers-on bird in the hope that a bit of plucking would give me inspiration. (I admit I also liked the image of Franky, with his Special Services buzz cut, struggling through the subway, a dead chicken under his arm and that take-no-prisoners look upon his face.) I abandoned the idea when I realized I was merely looking for a displacement activity. Still, I held fast to the notion that I needed a vehicle for the apology. For Marcia Harris I had made the soup. For Miss Barrington it had been the soufflé. Harry Brennan had received his in the coffee shop over cake, even if he hadn't eaten any. And the founding apology to Fiona Hestridge had taken place within the logical surroundings of her late husband's restaurant. The unifying principle here was that I knew these people or, at least, understood who they were and the context within which I was saying sorry to them. I knew nothing about Lewis Jeffries III beyond his role as a figurehead for the great African-American hurt. The one thing I knew for sure was that I felt really bad: about the massacre on the *Lady Bountiful,* about my family's complicity in the crimes of slavery, about the box and the chocolates and my ignorant hunger for them. I didn't want to say sorry. I *needed* to say sorry.

"Well, that's a good thing," Jennie said, when she stopped by my office the same morning I read the file. And then: "Have you been crying?"

"Oh, I just get a bit, you know—it's heavy stuff."

"Should I go get Francine? Wasn't she eager to see you emoting or something?"

"Jennie!"

"Sorry. How about one of these to cheer you up instead?" She pulled a dinky oval box from a bag at her feet. "They're Garrison Chocolates from the Chocolate Loft down on West Twenty-third. Have you been there yet? Very good. The Madagascar Vanilla is particularly special."

I ran my tongue about my teeth as if searching for the residue of the taste just gone.

"I won't, thanks."

"Wow. You really have got it bad."

"Perhaps it's time I went to see Professor Schenke?" I said suddenly. "Just to talk through what's expected of me?"

She chose a chocolate and popped it into her mouth. "Don't worry about Schenke," she said, studying the confectionery as if deciding whether to take another. "He'd only distract you."

"From what? I haven't got a clue how to do this apology. Maybe he could help me. Maybe he could . . ."

She tipped the chocolates toward me so that the contents shone in the light. "Are you sure you won't?"

I shook my head. I thought of explaining to her all the things that weren't in the file, about the box and the Basset family traditions, but I couldn't.

"What have I got myself into, Jennie?"

"Marc, trust me. You're the right man for the job. Sleep on it for twenty-four hours, and if you don't feel you're getting anywhere, we'll pull the team together to help you out."

The next day they pulled the team together. Francis Wilson came up from Historical and Verification on the fourteenth floor, in the same ill-fitting jacket and ill-tied tie he had been wearing the day I met him at the Foreign Office in London, to deliver stuttering lectures on slave trading in the Carolinas in the eighteenth century. Will Masters and Satesh Panjabi together gave me an account of the negotiations so far, which amounted to a series of conferences in various grand historical buildings across the Southern US, all of which had ended in a communiqué declaring a commitment to keep having more roundtables.

"And which grand historical building is going to host my meeting?"

Satesh glanced down at the sheet in front of him. "The Welton-Oaks Plantation House in St. Francisville, Louisiana."

I scoffed. "Welton-Oaks? Oh right. Very cute. Very nice. Who came up with that one—the United Nations Office of Clumsy Symbolism and Photo Ops?"

"Marc," Jennie said soothingly, "it's Lewis Jeffries' home. He's lived there for over a decade. You're just going round to his place to say sorry."

"Which also just happens to be my family's ancestral home?"

"I told you, Marc. You weren't chosen for this job by accident. The whole Welton-Oaks connection is key to the apology."

"Very good. Excellent. Welton-Oaks it is, then. Perfect." I was holding a small pad of paper and I tried to look severe and statesmanlike as I scribbled a few notes. "Who else will be there with him?"

Satesh shrugged. "No one. It's just you and him."

"Really? No other members of the Slavery Reparations Committee? No media?"

"You want your moment in the sun?"

"No, no. I just assumed Jeffries and the committee would want as much publicity as possible."

"The news media will be at the bottom of the drive waiting for the announcement," Jennie said. "If we allow them in there's a risk they'll contaminate the apologibility zone."

I nodded sagely. Until that moment I hadn't known there was such a thing as an apologibility zone, let alone that it could be contaminated.

"As for Jeffries being by himself, they've invoked their right under Schenke's third sub-law to nominate their own representative."

"And that's Jeffries?"

"He's chair of the committee so it makes sense. They've specifically said they didn't want it turning into a circus with big delegations on both sides. They want the apology one-on-one, you and Jeffries, no one else, and that's what we're doing."

I scribbled more notes on my pad. "I really think I ought to go see Schenke, you know. To get his thoughts on how to approach this. And to pay my respects."

There was a sharp intake of breath from the group, which made me look up.

"Bad idea," said Satesh, too quickly.

"Really no need," said Jennie.

"A waste of your time," Satesh added.

I looked from one to the other and back again. They smiled reassuringly at me and then, uneasily, at each other. I placed my notepad down on the table in front of me. "I need a little time to think on my own," I said, and I slipped my pen into my inside jacket pocket. The meeting was over.

Eighteen

I heard the Professor's house before I saw it. He lived outside the town of Olivebridge on the edge of the Catskills, a couple of hours' drive north of Manhattan, and as I approached the address my secretary had obtained for me from his publishers, the narrow wooded lane echoed with the sound of breaking glass and over-revving car engine. I was so distracted by the noise that as I turned into the drive, I almost went bumper to bumper with another car coming out. A middle-aged woman, graying red hair pulled back into a ragged ponytail, her lips pursed, wound down her window to talk to me. I leaned out of my own open window toward her.

"You going in there?" she said. She looked tired and seemed eager to get away.

"I was planning to, if it's the home of Professor Thomas Schenke."

She looked back over her shoulder as if to remind herself of where she'd come from. "Oh sure, you've found the place." She turned to me and said quickly, "Listen, honey, do yourself a favor. Turn the car around. Go home. Be kind to yourself."

I looked up the sloping gravel drive at the wooden house with its shady veranda and view out over the treetops. An old plum-colored Cadillac was parked up next to a tightly packed store of logs. It looked peaceful.

"I think I'll pop in for a moment," I said. "I've driven a long way to get here."

"If you take my advice, you'll drive even further to get away from this place." She blinked and let her fingertips tap lightly on the steering wheel.

"I'll back up so you can get out," I said, and she nodded gratefully.

"Don't say I didn't warn you," she said, and she turned out of the drive so fast her wheels screeched on the tarmac. I parked up next to the other car, stepped around the remains of two smashed beer bottles on the front path, and climbed the steps to the front door. I pulled on a chain mounted by the door that rang a small bell above my head. There was silence.

I called out his name. Still nothing, save for a creak from behind the solid wooden door. I squatted down so I was level with the letter slot and said his name again, quietly. "Professor Schenke . . . ?"

"Has the bitch gone?" The voice was harsh, as if its owner had been shouting. He seemed to be sitting on the other side of the letter slot.

I looked back at the empty drive. "The lady who was here?"

"Lady? She's a witch."

"She's gone."

"Good."

"Professor, my name is—"

"What are you doing here? Another fucking apology groupie? Here for absolution?"

"Absolution? No. I'm—"

"You want to hear me say sorry, don't you? That's what they all want."

"I'm Marc Basset, Professor. We spoke briefly yesterday."

"Basset? Basset?" He paused. "The shyster UN-patsy Basset? That Basset?"

"You told me to come." I was still hunched down by his letter slot and my knees were beginning to ache from the strain.

He said, "I did?" and sounded genuinely surprised.

"Perhaps if you opened the door I could introduce myself?"

There was the sound of locks being turned and safety chains being slipped from their holding place. I pulled myself up. A man flung open the door, but turned and walked away into the house so quickly that I didn't get a good look at him.

"I told you to stay away," he shouted back at me as he slipped into the shadows. "I tell them all to stay away."

"I'm really sorry if I misunderstood you, Professor Schenke. I asked if I could come to see you and I thought you said you'd be here, which I took to mean I could drop by." It is true he had slammed the phone down after that, but I had assumed his closing words to be an invitation from a busy academic lost in his own thoughts.

"I've changed my mind," he barked from somewhere deep inside the house.

I followed his voice to a study at the back. Its shelved walls were packed with books and most of the floor space was covered by tottering piles of yellowing journals. Light filled the cramped room from a wall of windows that presented a view of the tree-carpeted Catskills, and the sun caught motes of dust and old paper that hung in the air. Schenke was sitting at a desk behind a copy of that day's *New York Times,* the broadsheet held full spread in a way that reminded me immediately of my father.

"Professor . . . ?"

He dropped the paper. "What do you want?" He was a wiry man in his fifties, and everything about him—his clothes, the bags beneath his eyes, his wild wavy hair—hung down, as if the force of gravity affected him more than others. His steel-framed spectacles were pushed up atop his long forehead, and when he jutted his head toward me the lenses scattered the sunlight about the room, which made me squint.

"I was wondering whether we could discuss the practicalities of the international apology?" I said. It sounded pompous, but it really was the point of the trip.

"You want to know about practicalities? I'll tell you about fucking practicalities. There's no hot water 'cause the boiler's blown, my car's up shit creek, and now that witch of a cleaning lady"—he waved toward the front door—"has walked—"

"I heard breaking glass."

He stood up, leaned across the desk at me, and shouted, "She made me throw the bottles at her!" He sat down and started reading the paper again, laid flat across the desk. "It was provocation," he muttered to himself. "That's what it was. Undue provocation. That's what I'll tell 'em. Call me a slob, will she?"

"Maybe I chose a bad day. Perhaps I'll go now and we can sort out another time when—"

"Hah! What's a good day? Define a good day for me, O Mighty Chief Apologist. The man who knows everything. Where did they find you anyway?"

"Well, I—"

"Some snotty jerk profiting off my hard work."

"I don't think that's fair. I'm only trying to do a job that—"

"Another lazy little shit like all the rest of them, leeching off me. Sucking me dry."

"Professor Schenke, I don't see how I can be accused of doing anything to you."

"You're like the rest of them." He leaned back in his chair and picked up the paper to hide behind. I watched him in silence. He did not move. All I could see were his two wrinkled thumbs pressing so hard against each outer edge of the paper that it began to tear. I decided to try another tack.

"You know, Professor, you're not at all what I was expecting."

He snapped the paper down. "What were you hoping for? Snow-fucking-White?"

"Jennie, he's vile."

"We did try to keep you away from him."

"He's paranoid. He's raving."

It was the next morning and she was sitting on one of the sofas in my office, her hands clenched nervously in her lap. I paced up and down in front of the window, my gaze fixed on the view of the river.

"I really don't think you should worry about Professor Schenke."

"He seemed so angry about everything."

"Yes, anger is one of his problems. I believe he came up with the first draft of his apology laws as part of the homework for an anger management course he was sent to."

"Sent to?"

"By the courts. He was the subject of a restraining order. It was a while ago, though." She crossed one leg over the other.

I stopped and stared at her. "You're telling me that the founding father of Penitential Engagement is mentally unstable?"

"It doesn't undermine the quality of his scholarship."

"No?"

"Absolutely not. His blueprint is still valid. It merely means the Professor isn't the right man to be involved in the process. Which is why you've got the job."

I turned back to look at the East River, sparkling beneath an early summer blue sky. I watched the tugs drag themselves through the water and the smoke billow from factory chimneys in Queens on the other side and thought about this furious man in his mountain aerie, raging at the world through the mocking sunlight. Angry at every-thing and nothing at all. Furious with me. And then retiring to his desk in his book-infested study to write works of great moment.

That was when it struck me. Going to see Professor Schenke hadn't been a mistake. On the contrary. It had been exactly the right thing to do. By discovering what a monster he was, I had given myself the freedom to pursue my apologies however I saw fit. I wasn't beholden to Schenke. He wasn't my master and I wasn't his slave. The mystery had gone. It was as if he had ceased to exist.

I turned to Jennie and said, "Let's get the team together again."

She threw me a wink. "That's my boy."

Later that day Joe Phillips came up from Psychology, still looking like a Gap billboard, all loose denim and unironed plaid, clutching hours of videotape of Lewis Jeffries III in action: giving lectures, taking meetings, milking cows . . .

"Milking cows?"

"Yeah, sure," Joe said. "He owns a few purebred Friesians down at Welton-Oaks. Makes his own cheese and butter, apparently."

"He wrote a book about it," Satesh said, flipping through a pile of paper. "Here it is. *The Deepest Furrow: An African-American on the Land*. It was, er—hang on . . ." He read the summary quickly. "It describes it as a, quote, polemical memoir reappropriating for African-Americans their traditional role as custodians of the land rather than merely slave labor working upon it, etc., etc., unquote. Published four years ago."

Joe nodded as if he knew all this already. "Jeffries is a complex chap, Marc, who has managed, quite remarkably, to keep a foot in both urban and rural black American culture while maintaining an impressive profile in academic circles. He still teaches law at Xavier in New Orleans, regularly publishes, both books and in journals, sits on god knows how many committees . . ." He was leaning on the top of the huge flat-screen television in the sofa area of my office, the picture fixed on a close-up of one of Jeffries' hands clutched about an engorged bovine teat. He stood up and pointed the remote at the machine. "Anyway, if we just move this along . . ." He wound the tape forward. "Here's some very precious footage shot just before the substantive talks at the Georgia statehouse last year." We all leaned in toward the screen.

"Okay, what I want you to look at here is the straight back, the arms not crossed but open and laid on the table, palms up, head bowed slightly here . . . and again . . . in deference to the other side of the table without indicating self-abasement. Either this chap is as honest and open as they come or he's read a lot of books on how to appear so. Look now . . . he reaches across to take something from that small bowl in front of him, nuts or something . . ."

I watched carefully.

"And instead of tipping the bowl toward him, which is a closed-off, exclusive gesture . . . there we are . . ."

Beneath the lights in the room the white porcelain of the bowl gave off a sudden glare on the screen which, just for a split second, obscured the whole image. This business with the bowl and the nuts intrigued me. It looked so very precise.

". . . he tips it to one side slightly. He can still see what's in there, but he's not excluding anybody, he's—"

I stood up. "Joe, hold the picture there."

"Marc, I don't think we need to—"

"Freeze the picture."

I studied the screen. For all the nodding I had done and the insightful questions I had asked and the oohs and the aahs, nothing anybody had said to me had moved me an inch closer toward a viable vehicle for the apology. Perhaps there was something in this nut-bowl thing.

I said, "I know what he's doing."

Joe looked at the television. "He's choosing nuts. He's tipping the bowl and choosing nuts."

I shook my head. "It's far more specific than that. He's not just choosing nuts. He's choosing *specific* nuts. He's picking out all the macadamias and who can blame him? I'm a sucker for them too. Macadamias are fabulous things. Could you, you know, start the tape again . . . There—see? Pick, pick, pick. Out go the macadamias." Triumphantly I said, "The man likes his food. That's what pushes his boat out . . ."

I sat back down in my seat and turned to Jennie, but I could see from the look on her face that she had already got it. "Fried chicken, potato salad, gumbo . . . ," she said.

". . . macadamia nut pie . . ."

She tipped her head to one side. "Is there such a thing?"

"Who cares, Jennie? If you can make pecan pie you can make macadamia pie. We'll find him a recipe. Or we'll invent one."

"A menu of African-American soul food. The real thing."

"Exactly."

"We'll need cookbooks."

"Lots of them."

"And a big house with a huge prep kitchen. Marc, it will be a triumph."

"I will apologize to him for the appalling crimes of slavery over a lunch like he's never had."

"I said you were the right man for the job," Jennie said. "I just knew you were right." She reached over and squeezed my hand. Around me the rest of the team was nodding enthusiastically, even Will Masters. They broke into a round of applause and I felt a warm glow of anticipation break over me: I was only days away from the huge emotional release of a real apology.

Nineteen

There were many things I loved about Lynne McPartland; her cooking was not one of them. She was lousy, unburdened by either technique or good taste. In the early months of our relationship this was a terrible problem because she refused to accept it was so.

"I've survived into adulthood on my own food well enough, thank you," she said one evening, when I offered a little constructive advice. "I think I can get along just fine without you now."

I did wonder. The casual manner in which she cut up raw and bleeding pieces of meat on our wooden cheese board threatened us repeatedly with poisoning, and even the dishes that came out the way she intended promised a certain measure of gastric distress. She refused to believe, for example, that the order in which ingredients were introduced to each other was of any importance. If Lynne attempted a coq au vin you could never be sure whether the onions would be sweated down before the wine hit the pan or after, uncooked. She insisted upon frying garlic to a bitter brown crisp before allowing anything else near it. And then there was her love of cupboard condiments. One evening she watched me beat a little red currant jelly and Dijon mustard into a lamb *jus*. This flicked a switch; the secret to flavor, she concluded, lay in the sticky jars that crowded our cupboards. This was the vital intelligence I had kept from her. The next evening I found her spooning neat strawberry jam into a fish pie "to add a touch of sweetness." The liquor from a jar of pickled onions became a particular favorite "to add an oniony acidic edge" and no

Lynne McPartland dish was ever complete unless half a bottle of Heinz Tomato Ketchup had been upended into it.

I took to patrolling the kitchen whenever she was cooking, like a prison guard watching for escapees. I couldn't help myself. I knew terrible things were happening to innocent ingredients and it was my duty to protect them. Unfortunately, I didn't have the guts to face the situation head-on. Instead of just telling her to cease and desist I would hover by her shoulder and say things like "Are you sure you want to put that smoked salmon in the pan before you've scrambled the eggs?" or "Salted anchovies in the mushroom risotto?" She would become ever more hunched over the stove, as if convinced she could hide its tragedy from me.

Inevitably my frustration boiled over, and in the worst possible of places: a review. It was a London hotel restaurant specializing in the fusion of Turkish and Austrian cooking, the resulting horrors served up on overengineered lumps of white porcelain by Villeroy & Boch or Royal Doulton. Koftka schnitzel. Caramelized aubergine puree strudel. And so on. As I put it:

> The last time Austria and Turkey were introduced to each other was on the field of war, and the result here is no less murderous or bloody. Why had I come? After all, if I genuinely wanted to eat food this bad I could have stayed home and got my girlfriend to cook dinner. What's more, she wouldn't have charged me fifteen percent for the dismal service. The service would have been equally as dismal. She just wouldn't have charged me for it.

I told her it was a joke. I told her lots of things, but she was still furious, and rightly so. Yet it did the trick. A division of labor developed in our household which gave us a certain balance; we filled in each other's gaps and made a kind of whole. I did all the cooking and the washing up. She attended to the rest of the domestic duties, at which, in any case, I was terrible. This suited me perfectly for I was, by nature, a solitary cook who both wanted and needed to keep control of everything that happened in the kitchen. I suspect that even if Lynne had been a good cook I would have done everything in my power to keep her out of there. She could have the bathroom and the living room. She could have the hallway and the bedroom. The kitchen was mine. I was not a team player.

This was what made my first three days down in Louisiana so curious and special. There in our house by the heavy waters of the Mississippi, Jennie and I cooked together, hemmed in by volumes of recipes from Camille Glenn and Craig Claiborne, Bill Neal and Jeanne Voltz and the Culinary Institute of America. We fried chicken that had been dusted only with flour, after Glenn, and then fried some more that had first been soaked, *pace* Claiborne, in milk and Tabasco, and decided we preferred it unsoaked. We tried our hand at Frogmore stew, thick with lumps of smoked sausage and shrimp from the Gulf of Mexico and hacked-up ears of corn. I made a wild rice gumbo, spiky with cayenne and andouille, and Jennie cooked crawfish in a huge pot that took up half the stove and steamed the windows, and the two of us swapped spoons to taste and check and advise. We took turns beating our grain to make hominy grits until our forearms ached, and boiled them up with salt and butter. We practiced gently kneading buttermilk biscuit dough so that the gluten didn't become overdeveloped and the biscuits too tough. We cooked up a pasty milk gravy that looked no more appealing for being made according to the instructions. We even tried to invent a macadamia nut pie, using a pecan pie recipe, but it wasn't a success.

"This tastes like something died," Franky said after trying it, and as Franky was a Southern boy and wore a pistol in the holster strapped to his chest, it didn't seem right to argue.

"Franky knows his pie," said Alex approvingly, as they sat side by side at the breakfast bar in the kitchen, jackets off in the early summer heat, a little sweat staining their shirts, tasting our efforts.

"So we make Key lime pie instead," Jennie said. "And just chocolate-coat the macadamias?"

Franky and Alex agreed. "That's all you need with a fine
macadamia," Franky said, heavy with the wisdom of the world
bequeathed by a childhood in Alabama. "A good overcoat of chocolate."

It felt good to be in that kitchen, cooking hard alongside Jennie.
We understood each other. So when late on the second day she
asked me how my meeting with Max Olson had gone at the Dayton
Air Force Base—my "Max Moment," as she called it—I felt relaxed
enough to tell the truth.

"I think he meant it to be special," I said. "But in truth it was just
bizarre."

Following Schenke's second law—that no one can apologize for a
hurt unless it is their responsibility—it had been deemed necessary
to invite individual nations to appoint their own representatives to
deal with areas of "local penitential interest" which would fall outside of my purview. For example, because I had opposed South
Africa's apartheid regime during my student days, and had even
played a part in The Struggle (by refusing to shop in my nearest supermarket, which insisted upon stocking cans of South African
pineapple rings), I clearly wasn't the best person to say sorry. Instead
the job would be falling to a Dutch apologist. Likewise the French
apologist would be dealing with various issues in North Africa and
Indochina (although I would get to keep the Vietnam War because of
the American connections in my family and a certain unwillingness
by the French, the former colonial power, to admit they had anything
to do with it at all). An Italian countess had been chosen to deal with
Ethiopia and Albania, and a trio of Germans had been appointed to
do nothing but say sorry to Israel for the grievous hurt of the Holocaust, on a monthly basis, for the next two years.

A former KGB man called Vladimir Rashenko had been
appointed by Russia to say sorry for all the things it had done to its
neighbors during the Soviet era, "which is particularly fitting," Jennie said as she led me toward him across the ballroom of the airbase

conference center where the UNOAR inaugural meeting was being held, "because dear old Vlad was directly involved in most of them." Around us the opening cocktail party was in full swing, and the room was packed with UN diplomats and apparatchiks, many of whom Jennie seemed to know.

"You're kidding me?" I said, trying to keep up.

"No, really. He was a wonder with the cattle prod and the thumbscrew, apparently. Wrote the KGB handbook on modern interrogation techniques."

Rashenko was a huge man of muscle gone to fat, his heavy Slavic head pedestaled upon a neck as thick as my thigh. Seeing me, he rose from his seat, his cavernous, double-breasted, midnight blue satin suit pulling against itself like a sail catching the wind, until he was looking down at me from somewhere near the ceiling. And then, without warning, he burst into tears. Hefty sobs made his shoulders heave and roll as he wrapped his arms about me and pulled me deep into the padded, sweaty cell of his man-cleavage. He muttered something damply into my ear about being really sorry for the Cold War and all the general unpleasantness it had caused and said he watched the video of my apology to Jennie every evening because it was "inspire-ration-al." He let go of me and returned to his seat, his face suddenly impassive once more.

"And that's it?" I said to Jennie when we had escaped back to the other side of the room.

She smiled. "That's his schtick. Rashenko cries a lot when he apologizes. Look . . ." He was on his feet again, another startled man swept up in his arms, tears dribbling down his cheeks. "I'm told it goes down very well with other Slavs."

"I'm glad it goes down well with somebody."

"They all have a routine of some sort, actually. Watch the Italian girl . . ." On the other side of the room an elegant woman in a red Chanel suit was standing at a table deep in conversation with a balding mustachioed man. She was taking off her expensive jewelry, piece by piece.

"Once the Greek apologist has gone she'll put it all back on again to be ready for the next one. Apparently she has some teasing speech about stripping herself bare before you. The French guy quotes Molière endlessly, you know."

I scanned the room.

"It all seems a bit . . ."

". . . unsubtle?"

"I was going to say 'calculating,' but 'unsubtle' just about does it."

"Exactly, Marc. That's why you're here. True empathic engagement is an art." She jabbed me in the left side of my chest. "You feel it *here*." She started looking about the room as if searching for someone. "Plus you'll cook up a mean gumbo, I'm sure. Ah, there's Max. Let's go see him. I know there's something he wants to show you."

Jennie left us together while she went off to work the room. Max immediately walked me toward the door. "Come on, son. I want to get us out of here before Rashenko gets his hands on me."

"You've met him, then?"

Max gave a weary nod. "Met him? I'm on temporary assignment at the Russian Federation so it's unavoidable. I've had a lot of damp shoulders, I can tell you."

"You're no longer with the Foreign Office? I didn't know."

"Busy, busy, busy," he said simply. "Always busy."

A small golf buggy was waiting for us in the evening gloom. Max took the wheel and drove us out to one of the aircraft hangars, a cigarette tucked neatly between his lips so that the smoke streamed over his shoulder as we drove. At the hangar an engineer in greasy blue overalls unlocked the sliding doors and we slipped through the gap into the darkness, illuminated only by a blade of light from security lights outside. Max took a new cigarette from a pack in his pocket and cupped his hand around the guttering flame as he lit it, a discrete pool of orange warmth illuminating half his dry, angular face in the blackness. Somewhere off beside me I heard the solid clunk of a switch being thrown, then another, and a third. Away at the far end of the hangar, banks of arc lights expanded into life.

A floor-to-ceiling theatrical backdrop hung across the entire width of the hangar, shimmering silkily in the light. Before it was a podium set up with a lectern and microphones from where, tomorrow, my appointment would be officially announced. Printed on the vast expanse of curtain was a black-and-white photograph. A man is outdoors, kneeling on the ground at the top of a short flight of broad steps, his body stiff and upright. His hands are clasped in front of him, very pale against the blackness of his raincoat. His head, with its elegant swept-back receding hair and long forehead, is bowed so that his gaze appears to be fixed on a spot on the ground perhaps two feet in front of him. He appears oblivious to the large crowd that surrounds him at a respectful distance. Many in the crowd are holding cameras and, like the photographer who took this picture, recording the scene. This was clearly an important moment, although I didn't recognize it.

Max Olson was looking up reverentially, as if stopped by a memory. He took a drag on his cigarette and exhaled, the long plume of smoke guttering in the beams of light around him.

"Warsaw," he said gravely. "December 1970." He didn't look back at me. He waved the hand holding the cigarette at the image. "Do you recognize him?"

I said I was sorry but I didn't.

He laughed. "No need to apologize to me, young man. Not for that. It's Willy Brandt . . ." He sounded the *W* in Willy as a soft Germanic *V*.

"Chancellor of West Germany?"

"Very good. Chancellor of West Germany. Arguably the greatest postwar German chancellor. Do you know where he is?"

"Well, you said Warsaw . . ."

"He's at the memorial to the half-million Jews of the city's ghetto murdered by the Nazis."

"And he's . . ." I hesitated, wary of failing the test. ". . . Apologizing?"

"A seminal moment for West Germany," Max said, approvingly.

And then, with a weary shake of his head: "Jesus, but it was cold that day."

"You were there?"

"Oh, sure. I'm back behind the fat army guy in the peaked cap. You see him? Well, I'm just to the right and back a little with the—"

"I'm sorry. I can't quite—"

"I was there, is all. And afterward Willy says to me, he comes to me and he claps me on the shoulder and he says, 'Max, maybe I should get some thicker pants . . .'"

"You knew Willy Brandt?"

"I was attached to the embassy in Bonn for a while in the sixties and seventies." This, as if it were obvious. He fell silent again and took another long drag on his cigarette.

"This is our man, Marc, poster boy for the Penitential Engagement crew. There's not been a gesture like it since."

"Not even Clinton in Kigali in 1998?"

He turned and fixed me with an amused, fatherly grin. "You've been doing some reading."

A little, I said. My office had prepared a few briefing papers for me and I had tried to read as much of them as I could. There had been one on Bill Clinton's trip to Rwanda, while still president, to apologize for the world's failure to intervene in the Rwandan genocide.

Max sniffed the air irritably. "Shall I tell you something about Clinton at Kigali, Marc? Shall I?" He wasn't looking for an answer, but I nodded all the same. "You know he was only there for two hours?" I nodded again. "And that he never left the airfield?"

"There were security concerns and—"

"The engines on Air Force One were never turned off," he said, enunciating every syllable so I didn't miss the point. "All the time Billy Boy is on the tarmac wearing his bleeding heart on his sleeve and saying his wise words about the one million dead who aren't there to hear him, there are four Rolls-Royce engines back there, all powered up and ready to go." He took a final drag on his cigarette, then dropped it and ground it under the toe of his shoe. "If you go round in the car to say sorry to a neighbor, it's always good to turn off the engine. Just for a minute at least. Don't you think?"

I nodded wisely again.

"No, Marc," he said, pointing up at the image in front of us, "this is your man." He walked over to me, placed a hand on my shoulder, and together we studied the gargantuan picture. "I just wanted Willy Brandt and the heir to his legacy to spend a little time together." Tomorrow, he said, would be a circus. For now it was just me and him. So we stood there in silence, looking up, and I tried to think grave thoughts about Lewis Jeffries and slavery and I wondered whether I ought to do the apology on my knees, just like Willy, but abandoned the idea. Kneeling was one thing. Kneeling and talking at the same time was quite another.

Disbelieving, I said, "I am the new Willy Brandt?"

"*Time* magazine made him their Man of the Year for that," Max said.

"Really!"

"I thought you'd be interested." I blushed at the bubble of enthusiasm in my voice. "No need to be embarrassed, Marc. A little ego is a good thing. You think Willy didn't check his hair right before kneeling down? That he didn't straighten his collar? He knew the world would be watching. And they'll be watching you too, kid. Don't be frightened. Trust me. You're going to be a big, big star."

Jennie was leaning over a work surface, making final corrections to my recipe sheets.

"Would you have preferred to stay at the conference, then?" she said without looking up.

"Christ, no. I was grateful to be able to escape early to come here and cook. That's the thing. The day after my Max Moment, when I'm standing up there next to the UN secretary-general and he's making his big 'dawn of the empathic era' speech to introduce me, do you know what I was thinking? I'll tell you. I was thinking how bloody cold Willy Brandt's knees must have been. That was the only thought in my head."

Jennie looked up at me. "That's fine, Marc. That's just fine. It proves you're human, not some weirdo policy wonk."

"Like you?"

"Exactly. You're not a weirdo policy wonk like me." Looking back now at the neatly annotated pile of paper in front of her, she said, "We're ready," and I knew she was right. There was no more time for agonizing or recipe checking. There was no more time for tasting. After all, it wasn't as if we'd been cooking these past three days to sate our own hunger.

At a few minutes past nine the next morning I found myself halfway down a great alley of ancient trees, their heavy engorged roots reaching out across the ground toward me, their branches above me leaning in toward each other as if conferring over my suitability. As a mark of my humility I held in my arms two heavy brown paper sacks of Wal-Mart groceries and I was wearing chef's whites, the loose-fitting jacket buttoned high at the neck, which encouraged me to stand with my chin just up, as if I had been called to attention. Behind me, strung out along the verges of the road that ran past the end of this driveway, were three dozen television trucks, many of them connected by a thick umbilicus of cable to their up-load satellite dishes ranged along the top of the levee that bordered the road. And ahead of me was the imposing white clapboard and porticoed Welton-Oaks Plantation House, where Lewis Jeffries III was waiting.

It was time.

Twenty

The front door was unlocked, as I had been told it would be. Inside, the wooden-floored, wood-paneled hallway smelled heavily of furniture polish and freshly cut flowers. A grandfather clock ticked to itself at the bottom of the stairs. I went through the open doorway to my left, as Jennie had instructed, into a formal reception room dominated by an expanse of shiny oval dining table and a white fireplace. Above the fireplace was a portrait of a Mr. George Welton in breeches and red jacket, a hunting dog at his side, a pile of dead game birds at his feet. There was a look of quiet satisfaction on his face: the job is done; the birds are dead; the meal can be prepared.

"Would you like me to introduce you to the family?"

I almost dropped my groceries, startled that anybody had managed to enter the room without my hearing. I turned around. Jeffries was standing by the table in a loose-fitting dark suit and dark blue shirt open at the neck. The fingertips of one proprietorial hand rested lightly on the tabletop as if he were about to check it for dust.

"He raped at least six of his house slaves."

"I'm sorry?"

"Your ancestor." He pointed up at the portrait. "George Welton. He raped six of his house slaves, fathered seven children by them, and was probably responsible for a murder or two." This, as if he were discussing the provenance of the table. "Lewis Jeffries. Good to meet you."

Clumsily, I placed the sacks on the floor and we shook hands. I said, "Yes, well, we've moved on a bit from then as a family. Less of the rape and murder."

Jeffries nodded slowly. "Probably for the best."

"None of the rape and murder, actually."

"Indeed."

And then, faced down by his quiet and his poise, I began talking, letting free a flood of inconsequential words: how good to meet you; to have this opportunity; to make amends; to bring an end to this epoch; this scar on my history; on our history; on all of us, really, because slavery, ooh, a terrible thing, yes, a terrible thing really, and . . .

Just as quickly as they had begun my words dribbled away to nothing. Silence. Out in the hallway the grandfather clock marked time.

"Was that the apology?"

"Er, no."

I took a deep breath. Now I began to explain myself, slowly: that the apology for the great injustices and hurt of slavery would be made over a lunch of traditional dishes from the American South which, in a formal act of penance, I would be cooking for him. Hence the chef's whites. I went through the menu enthusiastically: the fried chicken and cornbread and gravy. The gumbo and the Frogmore stew and crawfish. The Key lime and pecan pies and the chocolate-covered macadamias.

Lewis Jeffries blinked. "Young man," he said slowly and deliberately, "do you think my people won their freedom from slavery so we could eat that low-rent garbage?"

"Well, I—"

"No. We did not win our freedom from slavery so we could eat that low-rent garbage. I hate fried chicken. I hate milk gravy. And if the Federal Government of the United States of America is planning to cook me a meal, I expect something rather more sophisticated than Frogmore stew." He looked me up and down. "You want to make me believe you mean it when you say sorry? Then you better cook me filet mignon and seared foie gras. That is the way to this black man's heart."

"Yes."

"I also have some thoughts on the wines."

"Of course."

"You can keep the chocolate-covered macadamias, though."

"Jennie?"

"How's it going?"

"It's going bad."

"Bad how?"

"He doesn't want the Frogmore stew."

"So don't make it. Dump the Frogmore stew. There are other things on the menu which will—"

"No, no. He doesn't want any of it. He calls it low-rent garbage."

"Aah." A pause. A hiss of static on the cell phone. "What does he want?"

"It's complicated."

"How complicated?"

"Very complicated. Larousse complicated."

"Oh!"

"Exactly. If I were in London or New York I could probably get most of this stuff together in an hour or two, but out here . . ."

"Do you think he might be able to help us with suppliers?"

"I can ask him. He should have a few ideas. But there's also the wines to think about."

"The wines?"

"Yeah, the professor's got thoughts on wines. And believe me, they aren't going to be stocking these at Wal-Mart."

"I'm going to need help with this, aren't I?"

"Yes, rather. Perhaps we can get someone to lend us the National Guard. That should just about do it."

"Very funny."

"Only trying to break the tension."

Another silence. And then: "Actually, they might not be such a terrible idea."

"Jennie?"

"Call me back in ten minutes with a list of ingredients and any thoughts on suppliers that you can get out of Jeffries. I've got some calls to make."

"Jennie?"

"Marc. You've got the list?"

"Yes."

"And you think you can pull it off. Can you actually cook this?"

"Yes, but it will now have to be dinner, not lunch."

"Sure, dinner. But you must still hit the six o'clock deadline so we can get the declaration on the networks. This is UNOAR's big moment and we mustn't screw up. They'll be going to us live at 6:30 PM."

"I understand, Jennie. An early dinner." Another few seconds of static. "I so wish you could be in here with me, helping me cook."

"I know, Marc. I do too. But I just don't have the plausible apologibility." Jennie Sampson: ever the sweet, weirdo policy wonk.

We let the disappointment hang heavy between us until she said, "The list, Marc."

When I was done and we had checked the details, she said: "Okay, here's what's going to happen."

I listened, and when it was my turn to speak I said, "You're kidding me, right?"

She wasn't kidding me. In the ten minutes between our conversations the White House had been advised of our problems. They had asked the Department of Defense to offer us all necessary assistance, and they in turn had scrambled four Apache attack helicopters out of the US Army's Joint Readiness Training Center at Fort Polk, 125 miles northwest of us.

"Three of them have external tanks for extra range," Jennie said, as if helicopter gunship specifications were a regular part of her daily duties, "so they can make round trips to Florida and Texas at a push. The fourth will only be able to do the run to New Orleans."

Throughout that morning and early afternoon the Apaches beat up the warm Louisiana skies. One flew directly over us at low altitude, rattling the window frames and giving the TV crews outside something to shoot for the rolling news networks, who took the pictures live. It was heading for Seagrove Beach in northwest Florida, the location of Sandor's, "the best restaurant in the Southeast," according to Jeffries. There it hovered for ten minutes, whipping the sand into great stinging clouds and drawing its own crowd, who stood looking upward, hands shielding their eyes from the dust and the sun, as it winched up a quart each of the finest beef, fish, and veal stock. Then it turned back on itself and flew twenty-five miles west to the seafood market at Destin, just south of Niceville, for half a dozen plump live scallops on the shell.

Another chopper flew due west from Fort Polk to Houston, where it hovered over Central Market to collect a fresh piece of Québecois foie gras that had arrived only the day before, a single imported Perigord black truffle, a bunch of baby asparagus, and a packet of vanilla pods; roasted California almonds and sweet, hand-made marzipan; free-range eggs, cheesy French *beurre d'Isigny* from Normandy, and pots of unpasteurized light cream. The third headed even further west into Texas, pushing the bird's envelope as far as it would go, to collect the finest aged beef fillet available in the state for tournedos Rossini.

"Tournedos Rossini? Don't you think that's a bit—"

"Old-fashioned?"

"I was wondering."

"Young man, when you have created a dish as robust and venerable as tournedos Rossini you may dismiss it as old hat. Until then—"

"No problem, Professor Jeffries. I'll get the beef."

The fourth helicopter made for New Orleans, where it hung lazily in the air above the French Quarter Wine Merchant on Chartres Street while the staff dug out the bottles: the Montrachet Domaine de la Romanée Conti 1989 to go with the starter, the 1921 Château d'Yquem to go with the dessert, and the big-fisted 1947 Château Pétrus for the main course in between. It was a mark of Jeffries' confidence that he had made the choice of these wines sound random and spontaneous, as if they were just a few of his favorite things chosen from a much longer list rather than a trinity of the greatest wines of the twentieth century, their combined value enough to purchase a small house down by the ocean.

The Apache was already heading back toward Welton-Oaks when Jennie told me the bad news. I found Jeffries in his book-lined office on the first floor, watching the coverage of the military maneuvers on the news channels.

"Nice to see an effort being made," he said, without taking his eyes off the screen.

"Absolutely. Of course. One problem. We couldn't get a bottle of the forty-seven Pétrus so we've substituted a forty-six."

He looked up at me pityingly. "Even my pool boy knows the forty-six Pétrus is rough as a dirt track. It's old, is all. Like a senior citizen who's forgotten his own name." He tapped a finger against one graying temple. "Not all there." He turned to the screen and began flicking between the coverage from CNN to Fox to MSNBC and back again. "It has to be the forty-seven." I made to leave. "Or the forty-five. I am a reasonable man."

So the helicopter turned tail midjourney and went back to New Orleans to swap the '46 Pétrus for a '45. Still, by 1:30 PM the Apaches were circling the great house and coming in one by one to hover low over the neatly manicured back lawn where, ever so gently, they winched down their goods. Now I could cook.

I seared three of the scallops for a couple of minutes each side in a hot skillet, and served them with an honor guard of crawfish tails on a vanilla-infused sauce. It was made with the light fish stock mounted with a little cream and foamed to within an inch of its life using a handheld, battery-operated cappuccino beater. I made the tournedos Rossini by the book, literally, using the recipe in a copy of *Larousse Gastronomique* that had been flown in to me: the lobes of foie gras and the slices of black truffle sautéed first in butter alongside the bread to make croutons. I seared the medallions of beef so they were still blue in the middle, and arranged it all in a tower, toast at the bottom, then beef, then foie gras and truffles, before deglazing the pan with Madeira to make the sauce. The lovely green asparagus formed a cordon about the edge. Finally, having received no direction on the dessert, I made my almond soufflé, certain nothing could go wrong, and nothing did.

I did not eat but instead stood service beneath the portrait of George Welton, a little way behind Jeffries, in the long, late-afternoon shadows. When he had finished the soufflé he took a sip from his five-hundred-dollar glass of d'Yquem and called for a second glass and the chocolate macadamias. He filled the second glass with the Sauternes, pushed it gently across the table to the place opposite him, and indicated that I should sit. Jeffries took a handful of the nuts, popped a few into his mouth from a closed, protective fist, sat back, and nodded for me to begin.

I started with the story of the box and my hunger for the chocolates it contained, dropping back to link this to the story of the Welton-Smiths, and then went further back still to the very birth of the Atlantic slave trade. Carefully, expressing regret with every dark narrative beat, I brought it forward again through my comfortable childhood built, I now understood, on the ancient proceeds of slavery inherited by my mother, to this moment in this room. The story came naturally and organically, each step leading to the next. I was lucid and convincing, the prince of contrition; the king of penitence. I did not weep, for the naked, bleeding emotion was present in every word.

My last line was a model of simplicity and elegance: "I, my family, and the peoples of Britain and the United States of America now apologize to the African-American community for the crime of slavery." No ornament. Just words turned to the purpose for which they were designed.

A gentle smile settled on Jeffries' lips. He took a few more macadamias from the bowl, popped them in his mouth, and chewed. Finally he said the one thing for which I hadn't prepared myself.

Twenty-one

I'm sorry?"

"No need to apologize again, Mr. Basset."

"No, I mean, I don't understand. What did I do wrong?"

"You did nothing wrong. Indeed there are elements of your speech which I find myself admiring. I'm just not a big fan of this whole apology thing in general." This, with an airy wave of one hand, as if my words had settled in a light haze above his head.

I glanced at my watch: 5:40 PM. Looking out the open window, I could see in the distance the satellite dishes and aerials of the television trucks preparing for our moment. This was not good. Not good at all.

I said, "What is it you don't like?"

"Mr. Basset, if you apologize for making me a slave, what does that make me?"

"Well, I—"

"It makes me a slave, Mr. Basset. I remain the victim of the offense for which you apologized. In short, the act of apology only serves to emphasize victimhood."

"Well, I'm not sure—"

"It emphasizes the fact of our history and therefore makes us prisoners of it."

"I don't think of you as a slave."

"Thank you, Mr. Basset."

"What I mean is, it's a real apology. I'm genuinely sorry."

"Of course you are, Mr. Basset. You are genuinely sorry that my great-grandfather was born a slave."

"Exactly. I'm very sorry about your great-grandfather."

"I understand that. But nothing you say can change the fact. Randall Jeffries will still have been born a slave."

5:43 PM.

"What is it that you do want then, Professor Jeffries, if not an apology?" I could feel the panic rising, the stickiness of tongue and the shallowness of breath. I didn't want to screw up my first assignment. Not now. Not after all that Montrachet and Pétrus, d'Yquem and Apache.

Jeffries looked up at a corner of the ceiling, as if trying to draw up a mental list. "What is it I want?" he muttered to himself, mockingly. "Just what is it I want?" He looked back at me. "I know! Same as the white folks. A condo in Florida and a Lexus with the executive walnut trim."

"But you already have this place. What do you want with a house in Florida?"

"This house? Oh, Mr. Basset, you think I own this? On a professor's salary?" He roared with heavy laughter. "No no no. It's owned by a trust. The committee thought it would be cute if I lived here to make a point." He took another sip of the wine. "In any case, you are being too literal. What I'm saying is, all we want is your money. Only with economic muscle, the economic muscle we are due, will you stop thinking of us as slaves, for our history will no longer be relevant. As I say, a condo in Florida each and a Lexus with walnut trim should just about do it. And maybe a GPS and onboard DVD player."

I stood up and walked over to the window. Heavy tropical rain clouds had rolled in to darken the sky to a gloomy smudge above the oaks. A bloated wind blew through the branches, and down in the lane at the bottom of the drive, sharp white television lights were fizzing into life.

5:49 PM.

My cell phone vibrated. It was Jennie's number on the screen; presumably she was calling to see how we were doing. I imagined that anxious tinge that comes into her voice when things aren't going precisely as she planned them. I turned off the phone without answering it.

"Did you need to take that?"

"No, it can wait. Professor Jeffries, if you don't approve of apologies, what are we doing here?"

"A fair question. Two points." He raised a single, bony finger. "One. There are many in the African-American community who do want an apology, and for entirely laudable reasons. They want recognition of their hurt, and nothing I say will convince them that this is other than a reasonable and useful demand."

"And the second point?"

"Process."

"Process?"

"Yes, process." He ate a few more of the macadamias. "These are very good, by the way."

"Thank you."

"As was the whole meal."

"My pleasure."

"You must give me the recipe for the sauce that went with the scallops."

"I will, Professor Jeffries, I will. Forgive me. Time is a little short. What do you mean by 'process'?"

He stared sadly into the nut bowl. It was almost empty. "We are involved in a process here. The federal government has bought into the idea that any compensation package must first be preceded by an apology. Once an apology has been made and accepted, they will simply have to move forward to the question of money. They will have no choice. That is the process which in the interests of compensation, I too am willing to participate in."

"I'm sorry, Professor Jeffries. Under the Schenke laws—"

"—'no apologee may define or assume, from the shape, form, or scale of the apology they have received, the shape, form, or scale of any settlement that may follow.' Sub-law four. I know my Schenke, Mr. Basset."

"Of course you do. I was just saying—"

"And sub-law four is the most phony of the lot because everybody knows that the whole point of Schenke is that it should result in reduced compensation payments, which means everybody has already made assumptions about the scale of the cash settlements that will result. But I will tell you this, Mr. Basset, I will tell you this. The African-American community will not be settling for a twenty-three percent reduced payment simply for hearing the word 'sorry' from your lips, however finely said. We'll be going the whole nine yards. Only suckers will settle for less."

"I see."

Another interruption from the long-case grandfather clock outside, as if tapping its foot in irritation.

"Don't worry, Mr. Basset. There are a lot of suckers in the world. There are still those who will settle for less and you will still get your cut."

A grubby silence fell between us.

"What time is it?" he said.

I looked at my watch. "Five to six."

Jeffries nodded slowly. "We better get to work, then, if we're going to make the six-thirty bulletins."

"Get to work?"

"We need to write ourselves a new apology." He stretched in his chair and yawned. "Yours was good, but it will never fly with my committee."

"Oh." I looked mournfully at the wooden floor. "Just so I know— for future reference, what was wrong with it?"

Jeffries smiled indulgently. "A little too . . . cute?" He stood up and made for the door, humming to himself. "I think in your country they'd call it 'chocolate box.'"

I felt cross: I'd put a lot of effort into this afternoon. I'd cooked

like a demon and pulled off something remarkable. My speech had
been thought through. It was the product of care and planning. And
now, as with everything I'd done that day, Jeffries was undermining
it. I'd come into this for the buzz of apology. I wanted to feel the
warm glow of emotional wounds salved. Now all I felt was humiliated. I wasn't going to stand for it.

"Professor Jeffries. I know I'm new at this job, but I also know
you can't go writing the text of apologies made to you."

"Can't I?"

"It's against the rules."

"And that matters because . . . ?"

"How do you know I won't spill the beans?"

He looked me up and down. "Anybody can see you're having the
time of your life, Mr. Basset. You're not about to put that in peril
now, are you?"

". . . And these wounds, though they shall never be bound up, are
now recognized. The pain and hurt that has passed from generation
to generation, from father to son, from mother to daughter, is our
pain too, for we the perpetrators accept our guilt. The tongue that we
now share, that was forced upon the peoples of Africa by our ill
deeds, is overburdened by the language of domination but ill
equipped when it comes to the making of amends. Only one word
presents itself, a tiny word compared to the magnitude of the task
set before it, but we offer it now in all humility, for it is all we have.

"That word is 'sorry.' We are sorry for the grievous crimes of
slavery, sorry for the centuries of deprivation, sorry for the river of
blood that we have caused to flow. On behalf of myself, my family,
and the peoples of Britain and the United States of America, I ask
now that you accept both this apology, late though it be, and the sincerity with which it is given."

Jeffries stared silently at the piece of paper in his hand before
carefully folding it away. Above us the early evening rain thundered
its applause onto the huge golfing umbrella under which we were

sheltering. The photographers' shutters clicked and whirred while the television cameras fixed us with their steely gaze, their magnesium lights causing our shadows to dance against the underside of the canopy. I stood still, impassive, at Jeffries' side. He spoke again.

"Those were Mr. Basset's words to me this afternoon. They are fine words, considered words, and on behalf of the millions dispossessed by history, I now humbly accept them. The work to settle slavery's debt has begun." He tucked the sheet of paper into an inside jacket pocket and turned away to give individual interviews while reporters started their match-play commentaries to camera.

Standing next to me, speaking in a half whisper, Jennie said, "That was a beautiful speech, Marc, really beautiful—"

"But they weren't my words," I whispered back. "They were—"

She silenced me with one delicate finger pressed lightly against my half-open lips. "I know, sweetheart. They were the words of history speaking through you."

I said nothing.

I couldn't see what else I was supposed to do. Call the cameras back and confess? Interfere with the "process"? Jeffries was happy enough. The television people were getting great pictures. And if Jennie wanted to believe I had written that speech, so full of rich African-American rhetorical cadences, what right did I have to disappoint her?

Anyway, as the man said, I was having the time of my life.

Twenty-two

A few hours later Max sent me a text message.
It read: WILLY WLD B PROUD.

Max hadn't put his name to it, but his signature was there in the message. I was sitting in a roadside diner a few miles from Welton-Oaks, with Jennie and Satesh, Will Masters and the security boys. We were slugging cold beer and eating fried chicken and talking in the busy, self-important way of people who have been working too hard for too long but who have finally closed the deal.

I slumped back into the warm leatherette of our booth, cell phone in hand, reading the glowing screen, on pause from the banter.

"Marc?"

"Text from Max."

"Oh yes? What does he say? Share it with the class."

"Nothing. Congrats, is all."

"Come on. Full citation please."

"Jennie . . ."

"Don't be shy."

"Oh god. He says . . . , 'A fine day's work. Yours. Max O.' "

It was less embarrassing than the real thing. The crowd looked nonplussed but remembered to smile encouragingly, before returning to the retelling of their part in the day's heroic narrative of helicopters and vintage wines and satellite feeds.

I have no idea whether Willy Brandt would have been proud; I didn't need praise from dead men. Still, if Max was impressed and this was his way of saying so, that was good enough for me. As the evening wore on, and the beer softened my mood, I became increasingly comfortable with my role in the day's events. Did it matter that the words were not mine? Hadn't they become so? It was like when I was a kid and I used to claim Luke's crimes as my own. I remember once he smashed a neighbor's greenhouse window with a stick intended for the horse chestnuts lodged high up in a tree (he never could throw), and in taking the rap, I also inherited the legend of the crime. Mum used to tell the story over and over, with nannyish indulgence, as if it were proof of my tendency to mischief, until even Luke forgot he was the guilty party. A piece of family history was mine. Couldn't the same apply here?

There was more than enough encouragement to think that way. Three days later we flew in a private jet to Zambia for the annual congress of the African Union, where I was to follow my first apology for slavery with a second to the entirety of Africa. There is nothing better calculated to give a man faith in himself than flying in his own Gulfstream V executive jet. Before Jennie, before any of this, I had only one wealth ambition: to be rich enough to need never to turn right ever again as I boarded a transatlantic flight. That shows the narrowness of my aspirations. I thought only in terms of business-class leg room for my ludicrous thighs and in-flight meals on bone china. Now I knew better. The true definition of success is being on first-name terms with the pilot of your Gulfstream V. Mine was called Chris.

If I needed any further encouragement, there was also the presence on board of a reporter from *Time* who was to profile me. She was a tall, big-limbed Midwestern woman of Scandinavian stock called Ellen Petersen, who favored long earrings that emphasized the length of her neck. She wore beige canvas trousers with ancient scuffs at the knee and Timberland boots and a black canvas jacket with an awful lot of pockets. She had dressed for an overland trip by Jeep to somewhere remote; we were headed for the Holiday Inn Hotel and Conference Centre, Lusaka.

Jennie said, "She looks like the kind of woman who would positively enjoy clear-air turbulence," and I couldn't argue.

Her interview technique, though, was soothing. They were the sort of questions you would never ask yourself but which, in the answering, help you take a position.

"So, tell me: what qualities does an apologist need?"

"Oh, I don't know, Ellen. An understanding of the self? A willingness to free your emotions? It's hard to say."

"You must be capable of feeling genuine remorse?"

"Absolutely. And you also mustn't get carried away by the surroundings in which you're feeling it. All of this: the private jets, the white leather seats—you have to keep it real."

"Is that tough?"

"It's just a case of remembering who you are. Where you're from. Have you tried the Roquefort, by the way? It's on a plate up by the galley. Very good. It's just about the only thing that can withstand the deadening effects of altitude on the taste buds."

"Of course—you were a food critic."

"A restaurant critic, actually."

"That background? It informs what you are doing now?"

"An interesting question, Ellen. I do think it gifted me an understanding of how people can come to feel pain."

"Pain you inflicted?"

"Ultimately, yes. I'm not proud of it, but perhaps some good came in the end from . . ."

And so on, question after question. During the flight. Over drinks at the opening reception. As we checked out our apology room, with its heavy armchairs in brown velour and its overactive rubber plants and its French windows overlooking a courtyard of wilting palms. Until she became just another part of the team floating about this curiously sealed corner of Africa: air-conditioning; poolside drinks service; the sickly sweet back smell of decaying vegetation.

Late on the afternoon of the first full day she drew me aside.

"Listen, I'm getting great words but we need to discuss pictures. Is there any chance of something . . . ?"

"Yes?"

". . . penitential?"

"How do you mean?"

"Perhaps I could have a photographer in for the apology itself?"

"Absolutely not. It would contaminate the apologibility zone."

"Well then, could we sort something else out? The better the images, the more space I'll get up in the front of the book."

"What were you thinking?"

"I don't know. Head in hands? Tears, maybe. Something like that."

"Come on, Ellen, I can't do that. I've been talking to you about keeping it real and now you want me to fake it?"

"All I'm saying is, the better the art, the more the space, the bigger the audience for what you want to say."

"Sorry, Ellen."

"Well, think about it."

The idea of stunting anything in this hotel was ludicrous given how much of the genuine article was going on about us: the AU Congress was to be the site not just of my apology, but of many other nation-specific acts of penitence. It was as if the Dayton conference had been lifted up from one continent and dropped onto another—the cast list was the same. A tiny, balding Frenchman in a beige safari suit could be seen rushing about the corridors, frayed volume of Molière in hand, from the Tunisians to the Algerians, from Mali to Cameroon to Chad, apologizing for the excesses of his country's particular brand of colonialism. The Portuguese were slated to deal with both Angola and Mozambique on the morning of day two, while the Dutch were spending almost a whole afternoon cloistered with a delegation of South African bishops. We could hear them singing.

In the bar I ran into Rashenko, who according to rumor had been bursting into tears on the shoulder of any African delegation leader he happened across, just to be on the safe side. In penitential terms Soviet involvement in Africa during the Cold War was a gray area.

"Mr. Basset, I am so sorry . . ." He reached down to embrace me, his eyes flooding. I backed off.

"Vladimir, we've already done this."

"We have?" He hung over me like a giant ape about to scoop up its young from the forest floor.

"Back at Dayton."

He thought about it, then grabbed me anyway and sniveled into my neck. "I'm sorry, I forgot. Such a bad man. I am such a bad man."

The combined efforts of all these apologists, along with those of the Italians and the Belgians, so overwhelmed the media center that press conferences for the announcement of each new apology had to be limited to thirty minutes, in an attempt to get through them all before the congress concluded. At one point on the final day so many different apologists and delegations were meeting around the hotel that the apologies were being made quicker than the media center could announce them. They were stacking up like jets over an international airport.

My contribution, to the president of Zambia (which this year was chairing the AU), was scheduled to be the last of the entire event. It should have left me with time to sit by the pool and work on the text of my apology, but on the evening of the first day we ran into trouble.

An advance group of us had just grabbed a table in the hotel restaurant. Jennie, Will, and I were checking out the menu (Caesar salads, Maryland crab cakes, rib eye steaks and home fries—exactly what you would expect from an international hotel in Africa) when Satesh bounded up, panting slightly.

"Just seen Max."

I said, "Olson? He's here?"

"Working with the Sierra Leone delegation. The thing is—"

"It's hard to keep up with him."

"I know. He gets about. The point is—"

"Did you ask him to join us? You should ask him to join us."

"Marc! There's a situation developing, a serious one."

According to Max, Cyril Masuba, the president of Sierra Leone, was coming under heavy pressure from both opposition politicians and the military back home to extract from me a slavery apology specific to his country. This shouldn't have been an issue. Under Schenke's third sub-law, which propounded the doctrine of self-direction, I was obliged to abide by the AU's decision that the apology should be made to the head of state of whichever country happened to be holding the chair at the time, in this case Zambia. But there were practicalities here. Masuba was the first successful civilian president Sierra Leone had enjoyed in years. He was a liberal and a democrat and he had balanced the competing powers against him with immense skill and tact.

"If he doesn't get his apology," Satesh said, "it could destabilize him, and result in a coup."

"And that in turn could destabilize the entire region," Will said. "Thousands will die."

"Exactly. We've been here before."

Silence. Jennie looked around the table. "Okay. What are the options? Will, what happens if Masuba gets his apology?"

He shook his head. "Disastrous. First up, we'll come under immense pressure to supply every one of the fifty-two other AU states with their own site-specific apologies. Put aside the logistical nightmare of trying to research and deliver those apologies—which is impossible within the time frame—we'll also be trampling all over the sovereignty of the AU and contravening sub-law three of Schenke."

"Not an option, then."

"Positively illegal, I'd say."

"Satesh?"

He took off his frail, steel-rimmed glasses and rubbed his eyes. "Let's find an excuse to delay the apology. Say Marc's been taken ill or just announce that the text of the apology needs more work. Something. Give Masuba breathing space to argue his case back home and return when the ground is ready."

"By which time," Will said, "another country will demand their own apology." He shook his head. "In any case, no one will believe us, when there have already been so many other successful apologies here. We'll undermine UNOAR. We're meant to be above this sort of dirty politics. We get caught up in this and . . ." He didn't need to finish the sentence.

Another pause. Around us diners clinked cutlery against porcelain. Slowly Satesh looked up, as if he had just surprised himself. "What about the Frankfurt Maneuver?"

Will allowed himself a half smile. "The Frankfurt Maneuver? That's a thought."

Jennie sniffed irritably. "What is the—"

Satesh interrupted. "In the early nineties, there was a series of meetings between the European Union and some of the former Eastern Bloc countries in Frankfurt to discuss moves toward inclusion. Hungary, Poland, Czechoslovakia as then was. The Russians protested that they should be in on the talks, which was unacceptable to the Hungarians and the Poles. To everyone, actually. A couple of the backroom boys at the Foreign Office surmised this was simply the Russian culture of pride."

"They accepted the likely outcome but they didn't want to lose face," Will said.

"What did you do?"

"We set up a cocktail party to precede the opening dinner," Satesh said. "The Russians were invited for drinks and then hustled out the door before the serious business began. That way they could go home and tell everyone they had met the EU and the former Warsaw Pact powers and engaged in amicable discussions, blah blah blah."

Jennie said, "I like the sound of this. But we can't throw a drinks party just for Masuba."

I leaned into the table. "No, but we can throw a drink *over* him."

They turned to look at me irritably, as if the child who had been allowed to stay up for dinner with the grown-ups had just interrupted. "Hear me out. We get Max to arrange for Masuba to take up position in one of the bars when it's quiet. Middle of the afternoon, say. I come in, strike up a conversation, order a drink, and accidentally on purpose spill it all over him. Then I love-bomb him with apologies for the mess, sorry for this grievous stain, all of that."

Satesh slapped the table with one open-palmed hand. "We get one of the boys from the Sierra Leone press corps into the room to witness it."

"And then," Will said, "we brief him when he comes to us for a quote that we cannot possibly comment on a private meeting between the Chief Apologist and the president."

"But," Jennie said, "we don't deny anything."

"Exactly," Satesh said. "It's the apology that never happened. Enough to dig Masuba out of his hole, but slight enough to protect the integrity of the main event."

"Okay, Satesh," Jennie said. "Set it up with Max. For tomorrow PM if possible." Satesh wasn't listening. He was staring across the table. We all followed his line of sight to where Ellen Petersen was seated, head down, furiously taking notes. We had become so used to her presence that we had forgotten she was there. Alerted by the silence, she looked up to find us watching her.

"What? What is it?"

"Ellen," Jennie said quietly, "you can't report any of this."

She looked down at her notes and then back up at us. "I didn't hear anybody say it was off the record or—"

"Ellen," I said self-importantly, "we're trying to save lives here. You report any of this, and it will be wasted effort. People will die."

She closed her notebook very deliberately. She put the lid back on her pen and placed it across the notebook as if laying down her weapon. She looked at me.

"Okay. Quid pro quo?"

"What are you thinking?"

"That photograph?"

"I won't stunt anything."

"My magazine would not allow anything to be contrived. It must be authentic. We need to capture an authentically penitential moment."

I let this pass. "And that notebook stays shut?"

"You have my word."

"Meet me tomorrow morning in the foyer."

"Foyer?"

"Lobby."

"Done."

The next morning Ellen Petersen got her photograph, something spontaneous and sharp, as I happened to rub my face with both open hands. Later that day Cyril Masuba got his apology, as I emptied a glass of Perrier over his navy blue, brass-buttoned blazer. After I had loudly showered him with words of regret and sorrow at the mess I had made I placed a hand on each of his shoulders, pulled him to me, and whispered in his ear, "Now you may go home and tell whoever you need to tell that you had a private meeting with the Chief Apologist where he expressed regret over a number of issues. We will not contradict you."

"Thank you, Mr. Basset," he said, with a shy nod of his head. "You have the gratitude of my people."

"Think nothing of it, Mr. President."

At 3:00 PM on the third and final day of the congress, I settled into the warm embrace of a brown velour armchair opposite the aging president of Zambia and delivered the slavery apology. Essentially it was the Jeffries text but recombined with an element of my family's story, which made the sentiment my own. The old man sat across from me, a solid meaty hand placed on each armrest, chin down on his chest, lips pursed, listening. When I was done, he sighed heavily and closed his eyes for a minute, until I thought he had fallen asleep. He opened them again and in thickly accented English said only, "History will remember us both."

Which was fine by me. If history needed people to remember, why shouldn't it recall me? I was back in the game, back in charge of my own emotions. The buzz was there and it was rich and it was profound and it was fulfilling. Together we had done a good thing, the president and I.

As we boarded the Gulfstream for the flight back to the States, Ellen Petersen said, "You're a sharp political operator."

I said, "Don't make too much of that. I prefer to think of myself as an ordinary man who happens to be in extraordinary circumstances."

"I like that. An ordinary guy in extraordinary circumstances. Very good."

"How do you think the magazine will play it?"

"It depends."

"On what?"

"Oh, the usual things. The outcome of the German elections. Whether the current round of the world trade talks reaches a conclusion. Acts of God."

I liked the sound of this. Marc Basset was now jostling for position with Acts of God.

Marc Basset; Acts of God.

Acts of God; Marc Basset.

I could see how this would be a tough call for any editor.

Twenty-three

At the German general election the incumbents were returned. The latest round of the world trade talks in Zurich ended in a stalemate. And there were no earthquakes, floods, or other divine interventions that resulted in major loss of life. As a result Ellen's profile made the cover of that week's *Time:* a huge close-up of me, my face hidden behind my fleshy, feminine hands.

The headline read: WHO'S SORRY NOW?

Beneath it was the subhead: *The man who can't get enough humble pie.*

The article began: "Marc Basset is an ordinary guy in extraordinary circumstances."

Other interview requests followed.

". . . and we've had one from a Mr. Robert Hunter in London," Francine said, reading from a long list in her message book. "Told me to say hi, wonders whether you'd like to write a diary of a week in the life of the Chief Apologist. He says it can be as positive as you like."

"Nice."

"He sounded lovely."

"Jennie, is it okay with you if I just tell him to fu—"

"Don't burn any bridges, Marc."

"You deal with it, then. Tell him I'm . . ."

". . . really sorry, but up to your eyes?"

"Exactly."

Jennie scribbled in her own notebook. She said, "There's one invitation I think you should accept. Helen Treasure's people called. They want you for Sunday night."

This was an unrefusable offer. Treasure's program, *Powertalk,* was a clear hour of live one-on-one chat with People Who Count. Millions watched it, coast to coast, though less for the razor-edge insight than the Kleenex moment. Somehow Treasure always got her interviewees to weep on camera: vice presidents, senators, retired generals—all of them had sobbed in her armchair. If you only ever watched *Powertalk* you would presume the United States to be ruled by a tight coterie of emotionally incontinent men. Through it all, Treasure would remain clear-eyed, her glossy lips pursed in close-up sympathy, head tilted to one side. The words "Just take a moment" had become her catchphrase. Well, I was done with the weeping thing. I had wept for the world. I would not need a moment.

We flew south in the jet to Washington, DC, took a couple of suites at the Willard, and ordered lousy pasta from room service.

"You want me to come with you?" Jennie said, spooling up another forkful of overcooked, underseasoned linguine.

"I think I can handle Treasure by myself," I said.

I was collected from the hotel at sundown by a television company limo, which drove around two sides of the White House, as if giving me the tour. We picked up Pennsylvania Avenue going west, and then turned south again to an industrial-looking block tucked away in the shadow of the Watergate complex. In the middle of the building, reached through corridors overlit by buzzing fluorescent tubes and past darkened scenery stores, stood Treasure's set. It looked much like the hotel suite I had just left: overstuffed sofas and armchairs; heavy, rucked floral drapes; priapic-standard lamps. And in the middle of it all, Helen Treasure, a hostess waiting for a party to begin, knees together, shapely calves shining in glossy tights, one high-heeled foot tucked demurely behind the other.

Just before broadcast, I eyed the box of tissues hidden out of sight behind a cushion and said, "I don't think you'll be needing those tonight."

She looked down at the box.

"Those, honey? They're just for retouching my lipstick during the breaks."

She gave me a fearsome smile of icing sugar–white teeth that made the corners of her eyes crease away into cracks of expensive skin-care products, and said,

"Trust me, dear. It will all be fine."

Now why did she have to go and say a thing like that? It was reverse psychology. In the past, when I heard those words, they were being used to soothe an anxiety which Lynne had identified before I had articulated it. This time all it did was make me question whether I ought to be more anxious than I was. I found myself eyeing the tissue box like it was a bottle of hard liquor that I might later need to slug from.

At first the interview was straightforward. She asked me what Jeffries was like. She asked me all the Petersen questions about being in touch with my emotions. She asked me how it felt to know that a video of one of my apologies had been emailed across the world. I said it felt odd at first but that, given time, you can get used to anything. "I just hope people got something out of it."

She fixed me with another ice white smile that I took to be more punctuation to the conversation than encouragement. "In your country they refer to eating humble pie, I think. Here we also eat crow. Does the difference in language cause you any problems?"

"Indigestion is the same the world over, Helen. It doesn't matter what meal caused the problem, does it? We're all people. We've all got feelings and that's the level I work on."

"Tell me how you got started in this game."

So I told her: about Hestridge's suicide and the effect it had on me. About Ellen Barrington and, without naming her, Wendy Coleman. ("We don't need to go into details, Helen, for the lady's sake.

But let's just say I treated her badly and I needed to face up to that.")
I didn't talk about Harry Brennan because who needs to hear about
an old man losing his lunch? But I did make it clear I'd done a big
number on myself before embarking on the job.

"My, that's remarkable Mr. Basset. You really did apologize for
everything you had ever done wrong."

Suddenly, into my mind came a memory and I shivered under the
hot studio lights: an ancient garden shed, a single shadow of two
people intertwined cast against the battered, clapboard wall, and one
pretty boy's face caught in an expression which said only, "What
have you done to me?"

"No, Helen, not everything. There is something left." And I
began to talk.

Her name was Gaby Henderson and I loved her, although that barely
does justice to the car crash of overwrought emotions. We met at
university when we were both eighteen, at a party. The only curiosity was that we had not met before, because we took a number of the
same courses in our first year and we already knew people in com-
mon. They had mentioned her, discussed her vivacity and her
appealing eccentricities as if she were an exotic island they only got
to visit occasionally, but none of the things they said did her justice.
She had short dark hair cut in a gamin bob, dark eyes, and a laugh
that made you feel like you were the only person in the room. I want
to compare her to Audrey Hepburn in *Roman Holiday,* because men
always want to compare the women they have loved to Audrey Hepburn in *Roman Holiday,* but that doesn't do her justice, for she had
none of the worrying vulnerability or faux innocence.

Later I learned that she had made all the long, silky, ankle-length
skirts that she insisted upon wearing, which suggested an instinctive
understanding of her own long, lissom body. She read books by
Anaïs Nin, which sounded like a filthy thing to do even before I got
to read a single page, and collected records by people I had never
heard of, like Chet Baker and Bobby Darin. She knew how to cut

cloth on the bias. She knew how to make a martini. She knew a lot of things.

I invited her out to dinner, to an American place in town used by the richer students. I was convinced the sophistication of the gesture would win her over, but then appetite kicked in and I ordered the one thing on the menu I could not resist. There was, I can see now, no chance of her falling for me when my fat cheeks were smeared with spare rib sauce and my fingers spent most of the evening in and around my mouth as I tried to rip the meat from the bones. Gaby didn't recoil in disgust. She laughed at my jokes and I laughed at hers and at the end of the night she put her hands around my neck and said, "That was really lovely. You're really lovely. Let's do it again." She kissed me on the cheek. I floated home.

We did go out again. To the cinema. To the pub. For weekend afternoon walks in the park. She held my hand. She still laughed at my pathetic jokes. She still only kissed me on the cheek. It took me about three weeks to clock that this one was getting away from me; that I was heading again for Most Favored Friend status. Two months into our "friendship" I got drunk on Thunderbird wine at a party and told her I loved her.

"Oh, Marc. I love you too. You're lovely. I'm just not *in* love with you."

Bugger.

The next morning, terrified I'd blown my chances for good, I phoned her. I said: I get a bit emotional when I'm drunk. You know how it is. I'm really sorry. Ignore me. What a fool I've been. What a terrible fool. She said: No, darling. It's fine. It was really lovely that you felt so comfortable with me to be able to say that.

"Lovely" was a big word with Gaby Henderson.

She came over to the student house I shared and I cooked her dinner, which clearly impressed, because she knew her way around a kitchen but had met few boys who did. Soon we began cooking together. We even held dinner parties for our university friends, great overinvolved tableaux of neomaturity, complete with guttering candles and ice buckets for bottles of German Hock. Our friends watched us, working together at the stove or bringing dishes to the table. After we had served the main course I would sit at the head of the table and Gaby would stand by my side, a hand resting lightly on my shoulder as we took their compliments. And our friends would say:

"Look at you two. Like a married couple."

I would glow because the bond between us had been recognized. But of course, we were not a couple or anything like it. One night I went round to her house to collect her for a party. I was directed upstairs to her bedroom by her housemates, where I found her getting ready. We were talking about the night to come when, as she opened the wardrobe door and without looking at me—without even glancing, to acknowledge my presence—she pulled off her T-shirt. She was braless.

"Hope you don't mind," she said, as she riffled through her clothes looking for a new top. "But it is only you."

I had dreamed of seeing her naked, often more than was strictly healthy. And now I was being granted a viewing because I was only me. Oh, how I wished I was someone else. That night I got very drunk again.

It was not, I think, an accident, that Gaby hadn't met Stefan. No fat boy should ever introduce the girl he loves to his thin, good-looking friend, so unconsciously or otherwise, I kept them apart. I had been to visit Stefan in Bristol, where he was a student, but whenever he suggested coming to stay with me for the weekend I came up with a reason for why he should not. I was a realist, though. I knew he would have to visit me in York one day, and that when he did, my two closest friends would meet. The moment they did so, the outcome wasn't in doubt. These were two very attractive people sizing each other up. I could tell from the look Gaby gave him that when Stefan got round to seeing her naked it wouldn't be because *he* was only *him*. We were sitting in a pub not far from my house. I feigned tiredness, withdrew from the field, went home and sobbed. I did not want to witness the first kiss.

It could, I suppose, have been worse. Gaby and I at least remained very close, even when Stefan came to visit, which was nearly every weekend. Sometimes we formed a little triumvirate, Stefan, Gaby, and I, our friendship reasonably equal and balanced all the way up to the bedroom door, which they closed behind them with deliberate finality as they set about inventing sex. She did still confide in me, which was something, and she had the sensitivity not to talk too much about their coupling when we were together, which was more than could be said for him. I had comforted myself that the affair would be short-lived because Stefan's always were. He would see how far he could get, squeezing the juice from the lemon until it ran dry, and then move on. But this one was different. They stayed together for the rest of that first year at university and into the second.

"I always thought falling in love would be really scary," Stefan said to me late one night as we were sitting, just the two of us, in my bedroom, getting stoned on a little grass. "But it isn't, you know. It's the easiest thing in the world. I really think I've found the one for me."

I said, "I'm really pleased for you," but I wasn't. I fantasized about him falling under a bus or a train. The tragedy would force Gaby to turn to me for support and comfort, and swept along on a wave of emotion, she would finally realize that I was the one.

"It's a terrible thing that Stefan died the way he did," I heard her saying in these dramas of mine. "But at least we finally discovered our true feelings for each other."

"Yes," I would reply, "something good came from the tragedy. I know Stefan would be happy for us."

Although the relationship hadn't yet failed as I had expected it to, I held fast to the notion that it would eventually buckle under the strain of their separation at different universities. Naturally I assumed this would happen because Stefan would give in to his urges and run off with someone else, whereas Gaby would remain faithful. It didn't work out like that.

It was the spring term of our second year. Gaby and I were at a Saturday night party, the usual crowd. For some reason Stefan couldn't be there that weekend. It was late, we were drunk, and she was sitting on my lap, head rested into my neck, the gentle curve of her back eased into the softness of my belly. We were people-watching, swapping opinions on friends we had known for years and whom we now felt we could see in a new light, courtesy of the distance and feverish newfound adulthood provided by college life. Into our field of vision strode Gareth Jones: broad shouldered; meaty thighed; testosterone enhanced. Gareth played football. Gareth played rugby. He was studying engineering. Gareth was the kind of boy who, when we were 15, would have been first onto those heaps of adolescent males that we thought it hysterical to build at parties. Gareth had always been quick to laugh at my jokes, which meant he was fine in my book, although as far as I could recall he had never given me anything to laugh back at.

I said, "Now there's a big piece of male hormone."

"Gareth?"

"Yeah. I've always thought of him as a friend, but you know what? I don't really know why. We've never had anything in com-mon."

"I've always rather fancied Gareth."

"What?"

"Not in a hearts-and-flowers way. Only in a *phwoar* way. You know, a what's-in-his-trousers sort of way."

She turned to look at me sleepily. "It's okay to say these things to you, isn't it? I mean, it's okay to fancy other people when you're with someone else, isn't it? Doesn't mean I don't love . . ."

I stroked the back of her head. "Don't worry. I'm not going to go mouthing off to Stefan."

She kissed me on the cheek. "You are such a good friend. Don't know what I'd do without you. It's so lovely to be able to say what I'm thinking." She turned back to look at Gareth. "He really does have a lovely ass."

Of course I wasn't going to tell Stefan. My plans were much more sophisticated than that.

Twenty-four

In my defense I must emphasize that there was nothing calculated about my plan. It was entirely opportunistic. That said, the general notion had been in my head for a few weeks. The way I saw it, I would be doing everyone a favor if I helped Stefan and Gaby to break up. I considered it my duty to do so. Stefan was clearly dangerously in love with a girl whose thoughts were elsewhere. It was incumbent upon me as a friend to bring about the inevitable conclusion at the earliest opportunity, because the longer this sham of a relationship went on, the more the end would hurt. By the same token, I had to save Gaby from unintentionally hurting Stefan more than necessary—an act which I knew would distress her greatly— while also freeing her up for the relationship she was meant to be in. Which is to say, the one with me. Gareth would, of course, only be a catalyst. Anything which occurred between them would be temporary, for while the inside of his trousers might be mildly interesting, the inside of his head wasn't. All of this was obvious to me.

Another party, then. A few grams of potent grass in my pocket and Stefan nowhere to be seen. Arriving later from Bristol, Gaby says. Gareth smoking hand-rolled cigarettes by a tree out back of the house, one knee up, foot back against the trunk, watching the world go by. I suggest to Gaby that we slope off to an old shed at the back of the garden to smoke a joint but announce sadly that I have no cigarette papers. This is a lie, for they are in a jacket pocket, snug against my chest. The lie is necessary. I approach Gareth, who swiftly agrees to join us. A few papers in return for sharing a joint? Who could refuse? It's a good deal. I hurry the two of them away into the nighttime shadows, giggling excitedly to each other. Just as we disappear around the shrubbery I look back and see Stefan step out of the house and into the back garden, his weekend backpack still slung over his shoulder. He is looking for us, but we're out of sight before his eyes focus in the gloom. He'll see us soon enough.

Inside the shed one corner is illuminated by a pale wash of light from the house, breaking through the trees outside. I use it to see what I'm doing while I roll the joint. The light casts a huge fuzzy shadow of me against the wall, hunched and round-shouldered. Gaby is perched on a pile of bags containing bark and peat, her long, slender legs braced against an old shelving unit containing pots of paint. She looks comfortable and self-contained there, the delicate folds of her skirt hanging down to the floor. Gareth is leaning back against the gray clapboard side of the old shed, holding the same position as he did against the tree. There really is very little to Gareth. It doesn't matter whether you move him from one place to another, from one situation to another. He still looks the same.

They watch me silently, exchanging expectant glances. When the construction work is done I light up, the knot of twisted paper at the end bulging dangerously with flame that makes the other two laugh naughtily, before it falls back to a flickering, smoldering kernel of hot red. Quickly the smell of peat and bark and rubber hosing is smothered by the sweetness of the grass. I take a couple of puffs and pass it around. Gareth takes a deep drag, the peaks and hollows of his hard-jawed face illuminated by the burning joint for a moment. He goes into a comedy spasm of coughing when he can't hold down all the smoke. We giggle. Gaby reaches out to stroke Gareth's shoulder.

She whispers, "Are you all right?"

He looks up. "I'm very all right," he whispers hoarsely. They hold the look and giggle again.

I smother the surge of jealousy. I can deal with this. I have been jealous for months now. These days it is a general state of mind with me. It directs what I am doing. But this jealousy is different. It is a means to an end and the end is suddenly very close.

I say, "I'm just popping outside for a sec." They don't even look at me. This makes sense. Why would two attractive, stoned people who fancy each other bother to look at me?

Outside I sat down on the damp grass and waited, hugging myself to keep warm. How long would they need? How long did these things take? I had no idea, but I knew I had done my bit. In front of me I could hear the thump of music and the echo of laughter from the house. Behind me I could hear the occasional creak and whisper. I was the pool of dead calm between them.

I pushed myself up from the lawn and wandered back to the house. Stefan was still standing in the back garden, nursing a drink, staring into the darkness. He saw me and cut straight to the point.

"Have you seen—"

"I've come to take you to her."

"Where have you—"

"In the shed, having a quick . . ." I mimed pulling on a joint held between thumb and fingertip at my puckered lips.

"Aaaah!"

"Yes, aaah! Come on before they hog the lot."

We trudged into the depths of the garden. Only when we came within a few feet of the shed could I hear the creaking of the old wooden frame. It was rhythmic and continuous, like the sound a new pair of leather-soled shoes makes on a polished stone floor. Stefan noticed nothing, of course. He wasn't primed to listen out for sounds. All he knew was that his girlfriend was in there waiting for him and that he was anxious to see her. He stepped ahead of me so that it was his hand which reached to open the door first.

I heard Gaby gasp as the door opened, and then the world stopped. She stared at us over Gareth's shoulder, eyes wide, her open mouth a big black "ooh" of surprise in her lovely white face. She was still sitting on the peat sacks, but her bare knees were up and separated to make room for his hips. With one hand she held on to his neck. The other she rested back on for support. Curiously, from the neck to the waist, her clothes were perfectly in place. Below that it was a sudden tangle of his shirttails and her rucked skirt and his jeans slumped to the ground about his knees as if deflated. Stefan stared at the mess of limbs and clothing, his mouth open. He closed his eyes for a second and opened them again, but the scene remained the same. Gareth stared straight ahead over Gaby's shoulder, motionless, as if hoping that by keeping still nobody would notice him there.

Gaby said, "Stefan, I'm . . ." He pressed his lips together, shook his head to silence her, turned and walked away back to the house.

"Go after him, Marc," she whispered, her voice now thin and frail. I nodded and gently closed the door, as if it were to their bedroom.

I didn't catch him. Stefan walked out of the garden, out of the house, and out of my life. He returned to Bristol that evening on the last train. Two months after that he dropped his courses and joined the army. As proof of my impressive insight into the male condition I would like to be able to tell you that he was overcompensating for the blow to his machismo, but as we never spoke again I would only be speculating. I wrote to him a few times, at an address in Scotland provided by his parents, but he never replied and after a couple of years I gave up. A few years later I heard from his mother that he had left the army and now worked "in security" somewhere in West Africa. Gaby moved out of the house she had been living in, but only so she could move in with Gareth Jones and he quickly made it clear there was no space there for me. In those circumstances our relationship could do nothing other than wither on the vine. I had wanted to separate Stefan from Gaby. In the process I separated myself from them as well.

I grabbed a handful of tissues from the box and tried to stanch the deluge. I knew my face would look a mess before the unforgiving lens of a television camera but there was nothing I could do about it.

In any case there was no room for vanity now, for this was the last personal apology I had to make and this studio was the only place I was ever going to get the chance to make it. I could feel a camera bearing down on me. I turned and stared directly into the lens.

"Stefan, I don't know where you are or what you're doing or even if you're still alive." A break of a few seconds, to wipe my nose. "But if somehow you're watching this, I just want you to know . . . I want you to know I'm sorry. I'm so bloody sorry for what I did to you. I'm . . ."

One of Treasure's exquisitely manicured hands reached across and squeezed my knee. In a trembling voice she said, "Just take a moment . . ." I looked up. Tears were coursing through the layers of foundation on her face, like a flash flood turning dusty hillsides to mud. She grabbed some tissues from the box for herself and tried to mop her eyes but succeeded only in smudging her makeup, so that great black, misshapen shadows appeared beneath them.

I took a deep breath and held up one hand, palm forward. "I'm okay, Helen. Really. I'm"—my breathing came in great, sobbing gusts—"I'm . . . fine."

A final statement to the camera. "I don't expect you to accept my apology, Stefan, but it's all I have left to give you." My lips began trembling. I could feel the camera tightening on my face. In a whisper I said, "I'm so sorry."

And cut to Treasure. "From the boiling cauldron of emotion that is the *Powertalk* studio"—sob—"good night . . ." She raised a tight fistful of tissues to her nose and, for the first time in her career, turned her face away from the camera.

As the limo drew up, Jennie was waiting for me on the steps of the Willard Hotel, holding my overcoat. She opened the door and, without saying a word, helped me out, throwing the coat loosely over my shoulders as if I were a prize-fighter who had just come out of the ring. I was drained and empty and it was a relief to be with someone to whom I did not need to say anything or explain myself. The silence was comforting. She led me through the lobby and into the lift. She led me along the corridor and through our suite and into my bedroom. It seemed entirely natural that she should stay here and sit me down on the edge of the bed and undress me, her fingers carefully unbuttoning buttons, and emptying sleeves and untying shoes; that she should fold back the covers and help me to slide between them. It was natural that she should remove her own clothes, and that having dimmed the lights and closed the door, she should climb into the bed next to me. It was exactly the way things were meant to be.

"I'm sorry."
　　"Marc, it's fine. It's . . ."
　　"You're laughing."
　　"I'm not."
　　"You are. You're laughing at me."
　　"Well, it is quite funny."
　　"It isn't funny. It's not happened to me for a very long time."
　　"No, I mean, it's just—"
　　"What?"
　　"I get into bed with the Chief Apologist and he immediately . . ."
　　"What? Spit it out."
　　"Apologizes to me."
　　"I'm just a bit embarrassed, is all."
　　"You don't have to be embarrassed. It was a stressful night. You were strung out. It was our first time together . . . well, almost our first time together, and—"
　　"Anyway, I'm sorry."
　　"It's quite sexy, actually."
　　"What is?"
　　"You. Apologizing."
　　"Is sexy?"
　　"A Chief Apologist apologizing is kind of sexy."
　　"You actually find the word 'sorry' sexy?"
　　"Ooh, go on. Say it again."

"Sorry."

"Whisper it in my ear."

"Sorry."

"Hmm. And again. Breathe it on my neck."

"Sorry."

"Fancy another whirl?"

"I refuse to apologize to you if it doesn't work out again."

"I wouldn't expect you to."

"Promise?"

"Shut up and come over here."

Twenty-five

My father died in my sleep, and from the moment I awoke I knew by the silence that he was gone. There is never silence in the house of the dying, even in the darkest hours of the night. There are always people talking in muffled voices behind closed doors or spoons being clinked restlessly against mugs in the kitchen. The morning Dad died there was none of this, and long before I came downstairs and found my mother alone at the kitchen table, I knew what had happened. Even now, waking to silence, I can be flattened by the anxiety of loss. I am that child again, reminded anew that Dad has died and fearful that there is unfinished business between us, the nature of which I cannot quite recall. Then I hear the inane murmur of a radio in someone else's kitchen, or the background soundtrack of birdsong, and the day begins. I distrust silence.

In my thickly carpeted bedroom at the Willard Hotel in Washington, DC, I thought of my father only for a second or two, with a dull confusion about where I was, before the muffled sounds of chanting voices expanded through the fifteen-hundred-dollars-a-night quiet. Jennie lay asleep next to me. I slipped quietly out of bed and pulled on a bathrobe that did not fit me (they never do in hotels; the sleeves are always too short). In the suite's sitting room I tried to see what was going on at street level, but the windows did not open and we were too high up for me to get any view.

"What's the noise?" Jennie was standing in the doorway yawning, wrapped in a sheet, her long hair in a tangled spray over her shoulders.

"No idea. Demonstration of some kind. Can't see."

She yawned again. "I'll send Franky or someone from security to check it out." She stumbled back into the bedroom.

I stayed at the window, my cheek pressed lightly against the hard, cool glass, listening to the crowd, recalling the complex events of the night before with a gentle satisfaction. The phone rang but I didn't move. Jennie picked it up.

She shouted from the bedroom. "Will says turn on the TV."

"Sorry?"

"The television. Turn it on."

"Which channel?"

To the phone: "Which channel?" A silence. Another shout: "He says a news channel. Any of them." My finger was already on the button.

It took me a few seconds to focus on the face: the pink, over-flowing eyes, the tear-smeared cheeks, the lips on the edge of a child's uncomprehending pout.

"Jesus."

From the bedroom Jennie said, "Marc, are you getting this?"

"It's me."

"Which channel are you looking at?"

I searched the screen for the ident logo. "Fox."

"Try CNN. Channel fourteen."

"They've got me on both."

"Hang on. You're on MSNBC too and"—I heard the soundtrack change on the television in the bedroom—"CBS."

There was a knock at the door. It was Satesh. "Have you seen . . . ?"

"We're looking at it now. They're all playing it."

"Where's Jennie?"

"In my bedroom. I mean . . . the bedroom." Satesh looked at me quizzically. I said, "It was late last night and . . ."

"Oh."

This was a new one on me. What is the correct procedure when one work colleague has just acknowledged that you spent the night in bed with another work colleague? All I could manage was, "Thank you." He bowed his head graciously, the diplomatic Sherpa, here to serve.

Another knock at the door. Will, followed by Franky. In his slow Southern drawl my bodyguard said, "I think you should go see what's happenin' outside."

"We're a little busy right now."

He was insistent. "Hit channel one, dude," he said.

I did as I was told. A crowd at least a hundred strong was pictured standing outside the main entrance to the hotel. Some of them were holding homemade posters. One read, WE'RE SORRY TOO.

A reporter was working his way along the crowd, microphone in hand. He stopped at two young women, all honey-chestnut hair and bleached teeth.

"Why have you come down here today?"

"We just wanted to show our support for the Chief Apologist," the first girl said, nodding her head with sincerity.

"Yeah?" said her friend, her voice rising in a questioning intonation. "We just think he's, you know, so brave?"

"Is there a message you have for Mr. Basset, if he's watching?"

The girls looked at each other, grinned, and then leaned into the microphone: "We're sorry too!"

I blinked at the screen, and flicked channels. "We need more televisions up here."

"There's a media facility in the basement," Will said. "Lots of TVs down there."

"What are we waiting for, then?"

He looked me up and down. "You and Jennie to put on some clothes?"

The room was a fully equipped television control room for outside broadcasts from the Willard Ballroom, where important men in dinner jackets regularly came to give implausibly dull speeches for broadcast on C-Span. There was a long mixing desk, and on the back wall, thirty-two plasma TV screens hung in rows four deep and eight across. We switched them all onto different channels. Five were showing reruns of *The Simpsons*. Three were carrying various parts of the *Star Trek* franchise, and one, reassuringly enough, was screening *Sesame Street* ("Today's program is brought to you by the letter *W*").

The other twenty-three were covering the reaction to my appearance on *Powertalk*. It had, we discovered, become the highest-rated edition of the program in its history, as friends and family implored each other by telephone to stop whatever they were doing and switch over. In an age of reality television, when authentic emotion was so commonly sought but so rarely found, I was being praised for displaying feelings of such depth and intensity that commentators had been moved to reclassify the broadcast as, by turns, "ultra–reality television," "meta–reality television," and even "reality-max."

On one news channel a former US secretary of state was busily crediting me with ushering in a new era of peace and security.

"With this guy in the Chief Apologist's chair," he said in a growl, "the world can get back in touch with its emotions."

On another they were running footage from New York of the United Nations secretary-general, a tiny Sri Lankan man, standing before a phalanx of news cameras, wiping the tears from his eyes.

"Mr. Basset's empathetic capacity shows the way forward for those of us struggling to mediate in today's complex world," he said. "We've got the right man for the job. Now I'm going to telephone my brother in Colombo to apologize for not making it to his wedding." (I heard later that Schenke had also issued a statement through his publishers that day, but his comments about me were so vitriolic and so freighted with expletives that they had chosen not to release it.)

I immediately recognized the people being interviewed on a third screen, even though it had been more than fifteen years since last I saw them, and time had been cruel. The on-screen caption read *Swindon, England*. And below that: *Gaby and Gareth Jones*. They were perched on the edge of a sofa and on their laps they each held a small blonde scrap of child, their eyes wide, presumably at the tangle of cables, lights, and people hiding behind the camera. Whatever soft summer fruit blush Gaby had once boasted was now gone. There was a fullness to her cheeks and a heavy curve to her shoulders and a general heft. The years hadn't treated Gareth well either, nudging his razor-sharp frame far out of focus. (This proves what I always say: it is far better to start out overweight than to become so. That way you disappoint no one, least of all yourself.)

"We want to thank lovely Marc Basset," Gaby was saying, "because without him we would never have found each other. Isn't that right, Gareth?"

"Yeah."

"And if we hadn't got together there'd be no lovely Vicky and no lovely Tom, would there?" She stroked her children's hair. "Right, Gareth?"

"Yeah."

"And like Marc, we want to send Stefan our love, wherever he is."

"Yeah. Wherever."

I scanned the screens for an interview with Stefan, but all anybody had was a shot of him as a student, all sharp jaw and crisp blue eyes and you-know-you-want-me smile. However, there was a live two-way with Robert Hunter, perched on the edge of an office desk in London. "Marvelous chap. All-round pro. And terrifically emotionally engaged."

"You bastard!" I shouted at the screen. "That's why you sacked me."

I heard Jennie laughing. "Marc," she said. "It doesn't matter anymore, does it?"

She was right, of course. I had entered a new phase in my job where what people who knew me thought of me was far less important than what people who didn't know me thought of me. This is the definition of modern celebrity, and whether I liked it or not, this was now my status.

"At the beginning," she said, lecturing me on the flight back to New York, "you had legitimacy because people like myself and Max thought you'd be good at the job. Now you have legitimacy because the news networks have accepted that you are good at the job and my opinion is therefore irrelevant, which is as it should be. Although, for what it's worth, I think you're brilliant." She kissed me lightly on the cheek, in full view of the rest of the team.

There were huddles of media waiting to greet us wherever we went, asking for my response to the world's response to my response to Helen Treasure's questions.

"It's very humbling, actually," I said, or "I just don't want to let anybody down" or "If I can help other people to make the apologies they need to make, well, I'm pleased." I meant it. I knew how good it felt to say sorry. I knew all about the tension and release. I was more than ready to turn a few more people on to it. In time we began to hear stories about apology clubs springing up across Europe and North America where friends and extended family would meet to conduct formal "apology ceremonies," using versions of the Schenke Laws adapted to these more domestic circumstances. Newly videoed apologies began to circulate about the Net via email, just as mine had done, and people set up weblogs devoted entirely to saying sorry to friends that they had hurt. I was approached by a publisher to produce an apology handbook for a mass audience—outlines of apologies for specific circumstances, ideas for locations and ceremonies, that sort of thing—but had to decline due to pressure of work. The handbook was later, logically enough, published under Schenke's name, although—thankfully—ghostwritten.* Apology clubs soon overtook reading groups as the community activity of choice.

In New York the office filled up with tumescent bunches of flow-

---

This Sorry Business: Apologies for Home and Hearth, by Professor Thomas Schenke, Heartfelt Editions.

ers and boxes of exquisite chocolates from well-wishers who had read about my passion in *Time*. We gave them away to hospitals and charities across the city. I was invited to the openings of Manhattan art galleries and cocktail bars, films and plays, to book launches and charity events. One evening Jennie and I were asked to the launch of a new caviar joint on the Upper East Side. Between us we dispatched half a kilo of golden Almas caviar, the most expensive foodstuff on earth at fourteen thousand dollars a kilo, which we ate off the back of our hands in the correct fashion, under the gaze of television news cameras crowding around the plate glass windows that gave onto the street.

"This one I'm not going to apologize for," I told the reporters outside as we left. "It's my money and I can damn well spend it as I like." I could tell the New York media appreciated this light, unstuffy approach to the heavy responsibilities my office carried.

Most nights we went out in a big gang, Franky and Alex riding up front, the rest of us in the back with a bottle of something chilled on the go to help us wind down from the pressures of the day.

And there were pressures. One morning Franky and Alex came to see me, faces as dark and brooding as a gray winter's day.

"Who died?"

Alex said, "Nobody . . . yet."

They had received a letter postmarked Mississippi making death threats against me which they said they did not have the luxury to ignore.

"What does it say, exactly?"

Alex took a frail sheet of paper from the leather folder in his hand and in a deadpan voice began to read: "You nigger-loving Zionist scum . . ."

"Zionist scum? I'm not even Jewish."

". . . watch your back. We will get you and we won't be saying sorry to no one. We will hang you from the trees like the scum-bag—"

"Let me see this." It was a single piece of lined paper torn from a student notebook and scrawled upon in purple ink. There were a lot of words in capitals and some of them were underlined three times.

"Boys, this is a nut. We used to get these all the time at the newspaper. Rule of thumb: colored ink on lined paper equals crazy person. I mean, what's this stuff at the bottom about looking out for 'kiddies in wheelchairs for they too may be the footmen in the coming Aryan militia'?"

"It says the threat is everywhere."

"Well, I know, but—"

"Sir, we must take seriously each and every threat to the physical integrity of your person."

"You're talking about my safety?"

"Sir, yes sir."

I folded up the paper and gave it back to them. "Franky, Alex, do what you feel you have to do, but please don't go overboard. Promise me."

Franky said, "The response will be proportionate," which meant for the most part that all vehicles in which I traveled, including the jet, were checked over before I got into them, and all post was x-rayed twice before Francine and Alice opened it. This I could live with as long as it didn't get in the way of the job at hand, which now shifted into another gear.

I flew to Drogheda to apologize to the Irish taoiseach for Oliver Cromwell's bloody rampages through Ireland. In a moving ceremony in Ho Chi Minh City, I apologized to a group of saffron-robed monks for America's ill-judged adventures in Vietnam. I headed south to Australia and a fading sunset at Ayer's Rock. There I told the appalling story of my nineteenth-century ancestor Jeremiah Velton-Smith and his vicious treatment of the Aborigines who lived on his sheep station, before offering a complete and unreserved apology to leaders of the community for the deprivations their people had suffered at the hands of white Europeans. On a frantic whistle-stop tour of the Indian subcontinent, I apologized in turn to India, Pakistan, and Bangladesh for the general mess the British had made of independence and partition, and then I went even further east to the city of Nanking, where I apologized on behalf of the British, the Americans, and the French for the ruinous Opium Wars.

They were happy times. I was getting to travel the world, meet interesting people, and apologize to them. I was being treated as if I were possessed of particularly special insight, and as the successful apologies piled up, I came to see why this might appear to be so. Luckily, I also had a girlfriend who kept me grounded and in touch with the real me. Around Jennie I never felt self-conscious about my love handles.

The idea that there could be any other benefits or pleasures to be taken from this job seemed ludicrous, but that just shows how even the most expansive of imaginations can fail. One morning Jennie came in clutching a letter, and this one hadn't been ripped from a student's notebook and it wasn't written in purple ink.

"Sweetheart," she said, handing it over, "you've just graduated."

Twenty-six

As a kid I harbored rock star ambitions. I had no singing voice. I played no instruments and I had no plans to take lessons. Nevertheless I presumed that alone among my peer group, I was the person most suited to the job of rock god. In this I was exactly the same as every other teenager. Later, when I established myself as the star of Mrs. Barrington's Northills Brigade, I concluded that my future lay not onstage but behind it, as chef to a rock star, which I felt represented a precociously realistic assessment of my own talents. Having made that career choice, I set about identifying the artists who warranted a place in my record collection according not to my tastes, but to theirs. I was interested only in musicians and singers who had an interest in food and wine and who might, therefore, be worthy later on of my services.

I scoured the pages of inky must-read music magazines like the *New Musical Express* and *Melody Maker* for snippets about the gastronomic adventures of rock stars. Gossip about lobster and champagne was not good enough. Anybody could waste money on those. It was a hollow victory of hard cash over ignorance. I was looking for the unlikely individuals who understood the importance of visceral pleasures and they were a tougher find, although they did present themselves occasionally. For example, in one *NME* interview I discovered that David Bowie liked to relax by reading Italian cookbooks, and that he made his own pasta from an exclusive brand of durum wheat flour which was flown to him wherever he happened to be in the world, from a small shop in Bologna. This was fortuitous because Bowie had, by general consent, just executed a remarkable return to form with the release of his album *Let's Dance*. It was cool to say you were a Bowie fan; cooler still, I decided, if your fandom was grounded in true Bowie gastronomic esoterica ("Yeah, he makes his own game and porcini tortellini, actually. He's a master of the Trattorina Pasta Machine"). Similarly I discovered that Dave Gilmour of Pink Floyd had an impressive wine collection, and this too was okay, because *The Wall* was still regarded as a must-own album.

Other passions were less easy to sustain. For a long while I was a huge fan of the Rolling Stones, which had a certain camp retro-chic, even in the mideighties. My interest was based on an interview Mick Jagger had given to *Melody Maker* in which he revealed he was building a collection of fine clarets and ports. Later, however, I discovered he was buying these solely as an investment for his kids. There was no way I could sustain our relationship after that. I sold all the albums and tore down the Jagger posters. And it was simply impossible to claim you liked Chris de Burgh, however many cases of premier cru Bordeaux he happened to have ferreted away under that Irish castle of his. *The Lady in Red* was a crime against pop and no volume of Château Margaux could mitigate the offense.

In time, of course, I came to understand that some recordings were great regardless of the diet of those who made them. Somehow I don't think the Clash ate well before recording *London Calling*. It is a hungry record, fueled by a knowing emptiness in the pit of the stomach. Indeed I realized that most rock stars eat badly until they retire and have no need of a chef, the intricate orders for backstage food merely a part of the continuous power games that these people play rather than anything linked to appetite.

And yet I never lost my rock star fantasy. It still played in the mental movie theater that is always open somewhere in the deeper recesses of my mind. Sometimes, though, fantasies get to become reality, if only for a moment. The letter Jennie had handed me suggested just such a moment was upon me.

"U2 want me onstage with them?"

"It's the honor all international statesmen dream of."

I was incredulous. "Bono himself has asked me to join him onstage?"

"That's what it says. I've been talking to his people. They've got Jimmy Carter penciled in to join them in Detroit, and Bob Geldof's going to play half a set in New York. They're suggesting you for Philadelphia."

"Tell them yes."

Franky and Alex were not pleased.

"There are security considerations."

"Franky, a former president of the United States is doing this."

"But we have had specific violent threats against you."

"No. We have had one letter from a knucklehead with only half his share of chromosomes who probably lost his virginity to his own sister."

"Our job is to look after your safety, sir."

Jennie intervened. "Boys, Marc will be accepting the invitation. Make the arrangements." Jennie understood. You did not say no to Bono.

On a close evening in late summer when the air smelled sweetly of dust and gasoline, we drove in a convoy of stretch Lincolns through the superheated, low-rise streets of South Philadelphia to Veterans Stadium. The band was already onstage when we arrived (my one concession to the boys' security worries) and we could feel the growl and rumble of the bass lines echoing toward us through the belly of the building. Over and above the bass came an endless roar, like a ceaseless wind blowing through a ceaseless forest. It was the noise of seventy-five thousand people in one place for one reason. Everything about this stadium was monumental: the great, black, sooty walls of the corridors they led me through, each wide enough to accommodate an articulated truck; the huge shadowed ramps and vents; the endless coils and lines of duct-taped cables and that crushing sound which did not so much increase in volume as we neared its source as stretch out to hold us.

When I reached the edge of the stage, there was a dam-burst of crystal clear sound; of guitar and drum and bass and crowd. U2 were finishing a track, something from *Achtung Baby* which, to my embarrassment, I only half recognized. As the final chords played, Bono did that careful backward walk upstage which rock stars do, booted heels lifted high as dressage horses might, to avoid an unseen trip or fall. He looked toward me in the wings, his eyes shielded by heavy shades, and nodded. It was the boost I needed. He was holding the stage with comfort and familiarity and soon, he was saying, I would do the same. I heard him introduce me with a simple elegant sentence about "the planet's conscience" which made me blush, and that was it. I was on. He handed me a radio mike, and placing one arm up and around my shoulder (he really is terribly short), he led me out to the end of a runway built deep into the crowd.

"Ladies and Gentlemen, the Chief Apologist of the United Nations."

Night was falling over Philadelphia. I remember the deep, clean ultramarine of the sky and the starbursts of the stadium lights and the epileptic flash of cameras rippling across the crashing waves of faces. I admit I froze there for a few seconds, my feet placed square on that salient of stage, looking out at the mass of humanity stretching away from me and up high above me. At last I opened my mouth, and powering into the microphone until I feared the sound might distort, I said the one thing everybody in that stadium wanted to hear me say:

"I'm so sorry."

Back came the roar, echoing toward me:

"WE'RE SORRY TOO!"

It was a truly deafening moment, as my dad might have said.

There was a press conference afterward, held in a grisly basement hospitality room, where the usual bunch of reporters asked me the usual bunch of questions about how I felt. This was only to be expected. I was, after all, a spokesman for emotion now; I was the crown prince of authenticity, the high priest of empathy.

"Mr. Basset, how did it feel?"

"It felt good, Janice."

"Did the response surprise you, Marc?"

"Mike, I'm constantly surprised. I've been surprised every day since I took on this job."

"You mean you didn't expect this kind of response?"

"What can I tell you, Dick? I hadn't been onstage with U2 before. I had no idea what to expect."

"How have your old friends back in London responded to the global interest in you?"

It was the solid, rounded Englishness of the accent amid all those American voices that threw me. I looked to where the question had come from. There was the thick black hair. There was the lush lipstick. There was the familiar uniform of black and gray.

I opened my eyes wide and said, "Lynne? What the hell are you doing here?"

We went off together to the dressing room which had been set aside for me, where I poured her a glass of wine from the huge array of bottles that had been set out. She looked at the crowded table.

"You expecting a lot of people?"

"No. Nobody, actually. They always set out this much stuff, wherever I go. Maybe they think I'm an alcoholic. A bit embarrassing, really."

"But not that embarrassing."

"No, I suppose not. Getting used to it." We stared at the bottles. I said, "So tell me, why are you here?"

"New job," she said cheerily. "After we . . . after you went to New York, I decided it was time for a bit of a career change. Reckoned there was a vacancy in journalism, what with you having left the business, so I got myself onto one of the British Council's journals."

"And they sent you to a U2 gig?"

She smiled sheepishly. "No. I'm covering a British Council event over in Chicago and I heard you were coming on so I wangled a ticket and a press pass."

"I'm glad you did. It's good to see you."

She looked deep into her glass. "Marc, I just wanted to say, you know, I'm sorry—"

"Hey, somebody's apologizing to me."

"Shut up, boy. I wanted to say I'm sorry I doubted you. It looks like you've done some brilliant stuff. The slavery apology, the thing in Ireland, that set piece down in Australia. Pretty cool."

"Thank you."

"I could do with a little less of the weeping."

"Well, you know. Sort of comes with the territory."

"It's just good to see you happy."

"Despite the tears?"

"Yeah. A very clever trick, crying a lot and being happy at the same time."

"Thank you. I am happy. It's all a bit weird but, you know—fun. How about you? A new job. That's great, isn't it?"

She looked doubtful for a second, as if she were mentally review-ing unreliable evidence. She nodded her head just a little too vigor-ously. "Yes. Terrific. I'm having a ball, actually. Lots of fun. Lots of travel, interesting people. I've seen a bit of Luke back in London, by the way. He's coming out here soon, isn't he?"

"Yeah. In a couple of weeks."

"Terrific."

"I hope so. Should be good."

A deathly silence fell between us, broken only by the muffled roar from the stage above us. "Listen, Lynne. The way we broke up was . . ."

She waved me away. "Stuff happens, Marc. You had to do what you had to do and—"

"I know, but . . ."

There was a knock at the door and Franky put his head round. "Transport is waiting, brother. Got to go."

"Okay, Franky. Give us a second. Lynne, it looks like I've got to—"

"No, of course. Just wanted to say hi and now I've said hi and I'll—"

"Come on, walk with me up to the car. Security can slip you back into the stadium from there."

Together we trudged up through the corridors, flanked by Alex and Franky, with me muttering embarrassed inanities about how silly it felt sometimes to have so many people on my staff. We had just turned a corner, bringing my car into view where it was idling by a service bay, and I was about to say something to Lynne about how she should get in touch the next time she was in New York, when Alex shouted, "Threat at three o'clock!" Everything happened with furious speed after that. Franky all but picked me up, rushed me the last ten yards to the car, and chucked me bodily through the door, which slammed shut behind me. To my right I heard girlish shrieks and saw the glint of chromium spinning away from me in the gloom.

As the car sped away I managed to pull myself up on the back-seat and look out the tinted rear window just in time to see three women in wheelchairs rolling away down a ramp and Alex standing over them, his pistol drawn.

Satesh snapped around from the front passenger seat. "What was all that about?"

"Sir, we identified a threat to the Chief Apologist, sir," Franky said from behind the wheel.

"Shit. Really? Are you okay, Marc?"

"I'm fine. Just a bit shaken."

"Suppose that means you didn't get to talk to the members of the US Women's Olympic Paraplegic Team that we had arranged to meet you on your way out? What a shame."

I looked at Franky witheringly.

"Sir, we thought we had identified . . . I mean we had identi-fied . . ." His words drew to a halt.

I looked back out the rear window at the retreating hulk of Veter-ans Stadium, floodlit now against the night sky. There was one image that stuck in my mind. It was not the women in their wheel-chairs, turning around and around and around like riders on a fair-ground waltzer, or even Alex, jaw tensed, both hands gripping the butt of his gun. It was Lynne staring back after the car with that old look on her face. The familiar one that said, Just what kind of fool are you?

Twenty-seven

One morning, waking alone in my New York bed, I discovered my hipbones. At first, feeling beneath the covers, I wasn't sure what to make of these two hard ridges. The large man is all too aware of his body's geography, but not of its geology. We do not dwell on questions of muscle mass and bone structure, because to do so, we must first make excuses for all the flesh that hides them and it is easier not to broach the subject at all, even with ourselves. Still, here they were, just south of my belly-softness, these two nodules of bone pointing diagonally toward my groin. I climbed out of bed and stood naked before a floor-length mirror. Now I understood why I had been so unself-conscious with Jennie. There was nothing to be self-conscious about. The love handles had all but melted away. The weight had fallen off me.

This made sense. I suddenly realized I had not eaten a single memorable meal in months. The Almas caviar blowout didn't count. There are no calories in caviar. That's why thin rich women eat it. We also gave away those chocolates I was sent after the *Powertalk* appearance. And I had spent the weeks traveling around the world missing eating opportunities which once would have been the point of the journey. In Ireland the old Marc Basset would have sought out the very finest soda bread and oysters and langoustines. In Vietnam he would have insisted on being taken to the best place in town for pho, that fabulously intense beef noodle soup which is the cornerstone of Vietnamese cookery. He would have eaten crab claws in

Mumbai and smoky kebabs in Karachi and great platefuls of barbe-
cued shrimp in Australia.

This Marc Basset did none of those things. Obviously I ate
meals, but in the distracted manner of the busy man. I do not even
recall whether any of the food we ate was good or bad. Back in London such a thing would have been unthinkable. The quality of the
food was the thing. In my old life the shape of each week was
defined more by the meals taken than the people I took them with;
my knowledge of the city was dominated by my recall of where the
useful restaurants were located. This new life had no need of useful
restaurants.

One way of looking at all of this is to say that I had lost my
appetite, but as I saw it I had simply found new ones that did not
concern what I put in my mouth. That afternoon I went to Fifth
Avenue and bought suits by Paul Smith, one with a subtle pinstripe
of rust, another in an outrageous houndstooth check. In Kenzo I
bought fitted shirts in charcoal gray and steel blue rather than the
billowing unfitted numbers in which I used to put my trust. I went to
Boss and bought trousers that didn't need to be belted high across
the belly to keep them in place and silky turtlenecks of the sort I
would once never have considered for fear they would make me
look like I had breasts. (Which I did.) In the old days, although I
fantasized about the creation of a better-dressed version of me, I
was realistic enough to know that I would barely fit into the chang-
ing cubicles in these shops, let alone their clothes. It was all different now. I no longer needed to look, desperately, to see what size
they went up to, because I wasn't even top of the range. I had a new
toy to play with and the new toy was my body.

Paying for all of this was not a problem. I had become a wealthy
man, even if at first it had not seemed the likely outcome. The first
settlement arising out of my apologies was the one for American
slavery, and just as Lewis Jeffries had predicted, our careful words
had not influenced the final reckoning at all. The US government
awarded the African-American Slavery Reparations Committee

every last cent they asked for, in billions of dollars of direct personal, business, and educational grants and endowments to African-American banks and community organizations, to be paid out over the next twenty-five years. There was no Schenke differential for me to take a thousandth percent of, a disappointment I accepted manfully. Then came the slavery settlement with the African Union and everything cheered up remarkably. The AU were offered and accepted a full twenty-five percent less than the predicted sum, a differential of billions, one thousandth of which came my way. This constituted the vast majority of my earnings, but there were also smaller amounts from the settlements in Ireland and Vietnam, on the Indian subcontinent, and with Australia's Aborigines, all of which helped.

One day Max telephoned me and asked how it felt to be rich.

"To be honest, it's a little unreal," I said. "I know the money is there but I don't quite know what to do with it, beyond buying a few good suits."

"How do you mean?"

"I don't think I've worked out how to be rich."

"Let me sort you out," he said.

He sent me a man with prospectuses and computer-generated income forecasts who talked about tax-free environments and sustainable investments and who used my first name an awful lot in conversation. He suggested gilt-edged bonds for stability, new technology for growth, and natural mineral exploitation for adventure. All of this sounded like the kind of stuff a rich man should do, so when the documents came my way, I signed them.

Still, I tried not to wallow in ostentation. On Luke's first night in New York, for example, I avoided the wood-and-leather-trim American bistros down in the Gramercy district and introduced him instead to the simple pleasures of the Matterhorn Café. We ordered a *fondue des Mosses* and talked about the past, but I didn't eat much.

"You not hungry?"

"I've eaten it before."

"When's that ever made a difference to you? Remember that Italian place in Swiss Cottage? You ordered the same pasta thing there six nights in a row. What was the dish . . . ?"

"Tagliatelle with pancetta and artichokes."

"That's it. Pancetta and artichokes."

"It was an experiment. I was checking out the consistency of the kitchen."

"No you weren't. You just liked eating it."

"Maybe I've changed."

"Maybe you have. Mum told me to take you out and get some proper food inside you because she thinks you've changed too much. She says you look ill. She phones me up every time you're on TV."

"Terrific. I lose a bit of weight and you two want to call in the doctors."

He spooled some molten cheese onto a piece of bread and popped it into his mouth. Without looking at me he said, "Remember Dad."

"Blimey, Luke. All I've done is lost a bit of what I didn't need."

"I'm just saying, that was how we knew Dad was ill, wasn't it? When he started losing the weight."

"I have not got an inoperable cancer."

"I'm only telling you what Mum was saying."

"Well, you can tell her I'm fine."

"Why don't you tell her yourself?"

"I will."

"You know she doesn't call you because she thinks you're too busy."

"That's crazy."

"But you have been busy."

"Sure. It's one of the reasons I've thinned down a bit."

"A bit?"

"But I've not been too busy to talk to my own mother. I'm never too busy for that."

"I'll tell her."

"No, it's fine. I'll tell her myself."

"Are you sure you won't eat some more?"

"My appetite's gone. It's probably the bowel cancer."

"Shut up, Marc."

Jennie was away for the weekend so together we toured the heavy redbrick bars of the East Village and the Bowery. I wanted Luke to see that I had purchase on the city; that I was comfortable here amid the late-night hum and the expectant rattle of cocktail shakers. "You'll love the next place," I would say as we clambered out of the cab. "They mix the best martinis in town" or "At this one they have forty-eight different flavored vodkas."

And yes, maybe I was a little too insistent about him enjoying himself. But he was so determined not to be impressed by anything I was doing or anywhere we went that I couldn't help myself, particularly after the third killer cocktail. I'm not trying to blame him for what happened. It was all my own doing. But let's just say that he made it easier for me to behave in the way I did.

We were in a bar on Union Square, slugging beer, when I was approached by a couple of young women, one hiding shyly behind the lightly tanned, bare shoulder of the other. Both of them were blonde, and as I recall, both had names which could end in a *y* but ended instead in an *i*, the dot on the top doubtless drawn as a heart when they signed their names. They were called Mandi and Traci or Suzi and Kirsti. Something like that. Luke and I were leaning back against the bar, our conversation having all but trickled away to resentful grunts and nods.

One of the girls said, "I'm sorry to bother you but are you . . . ?"

I was accustomed to this kind of thing by now. I was on television a lot and it was natural that people should recognize me and wish to speak to me. I smiled and said, "Marc Basset, yes."

Beside me I heard Luke sigh with irritation. The girls giggled. "We were wondering," said the bolder of the two, "if you would . . ."

"Yes?"

"Say it to us."

"Say what?"

She looked coyly at me from under her bangs. "You know. It."
Her friend giggled again.

I leaned in toward her, and as I did so she pulled her hair back
behind her ear and presented her long neck to me as if it were an
expanse of smooth upper thigh. "You mean . . . ," I dropped my
voice to a whisper, ". . . I'm sorry." I heard her gasp and she exhaled
damply against my cheek.

She said quietly, as if she had all the time in the world, "Again."

"I'm. So. Sorry." I looked up over her shoulder at her friend
watching us, her eyes wide.

I said, "Would you like a go, too?" She nodded but said nothing,
her lips just slightly parted. Now she pulled back her hair and I
whispered into her ear and I could feel her shiver. The two girls
looked at each other and laughed again.

The first one said, "It's so hot."

"In here?"

"No. You. Whispering like that. It's . . . you know?"

"Oh."

"Do you live far from here?"

I turned to Luke. "You can find your own way home, can't you?"

Let's freeze the image there for a moment and review the situation.
Remember, Jennie and I had only been a couple for a month or two. It
wasn't as if we were married or living together. There were no kids involved. We didn't even own a dog. It was just a gentle friendship that
had grown into something more in the pressure cooker environment
of the job. Anyway, Jennie wasn't there and Mandi and Traci were, and
they were offering something which even had I been sober—which I
fully accept I wasn't—would have proved an attractive proposition.
For years I had whined on about my failures with women and my inability to seize the opportunities when they came my way. But I was a
new Marc Basset now. The old excuses didn't work anymore. I had a

suit by Paul Smith and a shirt by Kenzo and two very attractive blondes from somewhere big and wide and flat (Nebraska? Iowa?) who wanted to go to bed with me. Just where, exactly, was it written that I had to say no? Where? Nowhere, that's where.

I was woken by the sound of the bedroom door opening but I didn't raise my head from underneath the covers. I focused on the unexpected feeling of the smooth, warm bodies on either side of me and on the dull throb behind my eyes, cruel reward for the night just gone. Next I heard her calling my name quietly, as if hesitant about waking me.

"Marc?"

Initially I was overcome by panic. I could see this might not be the best of situations. But almost immediately that feeling was swept away by a wave of something more intimately associated with anger. She was meant to be away for the weekend. She was meant to be doing her own thing, and surely, so was I. Wasn't I allowed a secret life? Wasn't I allowed to do the things that other people got away with?

I heard her flick on the overhead light and then imagined her surveying the tangle of discarded clothes on the floor at the end of the bed; threaded through it, the little straps and lacy panels that had proved so endlessly fascinating to me the night before.

She said, "Marc?"

I pulled myself up from under the covers and so did the girls.

"Hello, Jennie."

"Hi there."

"Hiya."

She stared at me. She stared at Mandi. (Or Traci.) She stared at Traci. (It may have been Mandi.) She looked at me again and said, in a thin, overwhelmed voice, "Aren't you going to say something?"

I yawned and rubbed one sleep-crusted eye with the ball of my hand. "What were you thinking of, darling? An apology?"

"I just . . ."

"Dream on, Jennie. It's my day off."

Behold: a monster is born.

After Jennie had run from the apartment and the girls had scooped up their clothes and dressed and said their perky good-byes, I went to the kitchen to make coffee. I found Luke in there.

He said, "So tell me, when exactly did you become such an arsehole?"

"I'll make it right."

"Will you?"

"It's my thing. It's what I do. I make things good again."

"Looks to me like what you do is fuck things up."

"Stuff happens."

"Oh, right. Two airhead blondes in your bed is just one of those things that happens."

"They were very smart girls, actually."

"Really? What have they got? A masters degree each in fellatio and frottage?"

"I know what this is."

"What what is?"

"This. It's the green-eyed monster."

"You think I'm jealous?"

"It's like I said last night. I've changed. I've moved on, and you don't like it."

"You're right about that. I don't like what you've become."

"What? Successful, rich, famous—"

"At the risk of repeating myself, I was thinking more along the lines of 'arsehole.' "

"You're going to have to get over this, Luke."

"What you did to your girlfriend this morning—"

"What I did to my girlfriend this morning was stupid and insensitive and clumsy. I know that. But the thing is, Luke, I can deal with it. I can make it right. I'm a professional. I can make anything right."

Behold: the monster is now only on nodding terms with reality.

Twenty-eight

Jennie announced the end of our coupling in a memo circulated to senior members of the staff. It said, "The relationship between the Chief Apologist and his chief of staff has concluded. This will in no way interfere with the running of his office." I was in awe. She had dispatched our affair in just twenty-five words, and not one of them was an adjective. It wasn't a "close" relationship or a "personal" relationship or even, heaven forfend, both. The word "sadly" would have sat neatly at the front of the statement, but she had chosen to do without it. She could have written, "Don't worry about me. I'm fine. Really," at the end. But she didn't. She stuck to the essentials. We were. Now we aren't. That is all. Carry on.

This was all the more awful for me because I really did feel guilty. It wasn't just the offense, although that was bad enough. It was the familiarity of the victim. In my role as Chief Apologist I had performed the same apology to a number of different people, but I had never needed to apologize twice to the same person for different things. I felt guilty for being in a position to feel guilty again. Unfortunately a surfeit of guilt is no help in the apology business, particularly when adjectives are so scarce. Doggedly I had a crack at it anyway, at the end of one of our morning meetings.

"Jennie, I just wanted to say, about what happened in my—"

"There is nothing to say, Marc."

"No, but really, Jennie, I think I owe you—"

"I'm not interested."

"But—"

"Nope."

"Really, I—"

She was already on her feet. Glumly, I watched her leave, her files held tight against her chest. It was all terribly discouraging. Nobody had ever refused one of my apologies before. I found myself examining the possible reasons for this failure. Jennie had mistaken my personal feelings of guilt for the kind of professional guilt I exercised as Chief Apologist; that it really had been just another day at the office. I could see how such a mistake could be made. This made me feel better about the rejection, but it didn't deal with the guilt itself which was still there, gnawing away at me. I knew what I had to do, though. I had to find someone else to say sorry to. That would cure it. That would be my magic bullet. Of this I was certain, if nothing else.

The very same day I went into a department store and, instead of holding the door open for the elderly lady coming in behind me, let it swing back. I spun about eagerly to say sorry, but she scowled at me and backed away as if I were a crazy person. I had forgotten I was in New York, where unexpected acts of kindness to little old ladies are regarded as an overture to some con or ruse, which, in my case, I suppose it was.

I tried my hand at petty larceny by stealing a copy of the *New York Times* from a newsstand at Grand Central Station, but I had failed to consider the impact my notoriety might have on the adventure. When I returned fifteen minutes later to admit my guilt, not only did the news vendor refuse to accept my apology, he also refused to accept my money.

"I know who you are," he said. "You're doing great work. Have this one on me. Come by any time. Be my guest."

I had been too modest. I needed to do something which would actively disrupt and inconvenience. While traveling across the city in a cab, I noticed a NO FOOD OR DRINK sign stuck to the greasy plastic barrier that separates driver from passenger. I offered him an extra ten bucks to stop at the next coffee shop and wait for me while I purchased a large cup of coffee, which I promised to hold carefully. I brought it back to the cab, this bucket-cup of full-fat foam and mud-colored liquor, and as we moved off, spilled it all over the backseat. When I attempted to make amends, the driver told me not to worry and asked, instead, for my autograph.

I even tried hanging around a pathway junction in Central Park I knew to be popular with joggers in the hope that I might be able to trip some of them up, but I just got kicked in the shins. I went home feeling sorry only for myself, which wasn't the plan at all. Willy Brandt would not have been proud.

It was another week before I found someone who would let me say sorry to them, and that was at the Palais des Nations in Geneva. They could hardly refuse; it was what we were all there for. We were attending the First Close-Proximity Apology Round, a new forum designed to bring together, in a neutral environment, sets of nations which held various grievances against each other. They would meet in neighboring rooms within the cool, echoing interior of the United Nations headquarters in Switzerland and make their apologies in sequence. This first session had been timed to coincide with Germany's monthly apology to Israel for the crimes of the Second World War. Taking my plausible apologibility from my father, I would be saying sorry on behalf of Switzerland to both Israel and the World Jewish Congress for the Swiss banks' mishandling of monies belonging to Jews murdered in the Holocaust and for the refusal by the authorities to grant asylum to those fleeing persecution by the Third Reich.

The plan was that Israel would then apologize to representatives of the Palestinian people who would be waiting in the next room. The Israelis had agreed to do so as long as the Palestinians in turn apologized back to Israel for the violent acts that had been committed against them by various Palestinian terrorist organizations.

By chance, outside one of the meeting rooms, I met Max, who was there on temporary assignment to the German delegation. The expected cigarette was there between his yellowing fingers, and as he spoke, he exhaled a long gray mist.

"Have you heard?" he said. "The Israelis and the World Jewish Congress have laid on food."

"It's a catered apology?"

"And how! Chopped liver, bagels, some great new green pickles. It's like Katz's Deli in there."

"How do you think it will go?"

"It should go fine as long as we don't have too many people going down with indigestion." He laughed at his own joke, the sound soon dissolving into a ripe, bubbling cough from somewhere deep at the bottom of his lungs. We agreed to meet later for dinner.

For my apology on behalf of the Swiss, I dug deep into my father's prejudices about the country. I talked about the excess of bureaucracy. I talked about the ghoulish fascination with order; the preoccupation with hillsides and cows; the love of meadow flowers. "My father used to tell me that in Switzerland the blooming of the gentians was headline news." That, I said, was the problem. The Swiss looked at the details and never took in the bigger picture. "We look clever and considered. But really we are nothing of the sort. We were so enamored of our own beauty that we failed to see our flaws, and as a result we treated your people badly. We were a disgrace to the civilized world, to ourselves, to everybody." I spoke for a short while about how wretched this killer combination of arrogance and efficiency made me feel, before concluding with, "I'm so very, very sorry."

Everybody seemed very moved by my speech. A few of them wept and they even gave me a big bag of bagels to take away as a token of their respect. For my part, though, it felt more professional than emotional. I recognized it was a job well done but little more than that. I could imagine my father standing in the corner of the room, arms crossed, shaking his big, fat soft-cheeked head at the idiocy of it all.

"So the Swiss are boring boogers? And for saying this, they will pay you?"

"They pay me for the apology. The bit about the Swiss is the way to get to the apology. And it's *'buggers.'*"

"That's what I said."

"Of course."

"Me, I would have told them the truth about the Swiss for free."

"Now you want my job?"

"I'm just saying. For free. Maybe I would even pay. To be rude about the Swiss, I would pay."

I came out feeling only more frustrated.

Thankfully I didn't have much time to dwell upon it because I was immediately called to an emergency meeting. The previous night, Satesh told me, the Israelis had demanded that the Palestinians not only apologize to them but find someone else to whom they could also apologize.

"They are insisting upon a longer chain of apology," he said. "I think they feel there's safety in numbers." Historical and Verification had thrown up a family from Ramallah whom the Palestinian militias had failed to protect back in the 1940s. "Apparently three generations of this family were killed in an ambush by a company of British soldiers."

I said, "That should be just the thing, then."

"It is. A representative of the family was flown in early this morning and the Palestinian apologist is in with them right now. But there's a general feeling that we should have a second apology to the family, something to deal with the massacre itself, just to tie up any loose ends."

"Good idea."

"Guess the name of the commanding officer of the British soldiers involved?"

"Hit me."

"Captain Roderick Welton-Smith."

"Uncle Roddy?"

"You know him?"

"Knew him. My mum's older brother. Dead now."

"A real personal connection, then?"

"I didn't like him much. He always called me fat boy."

"Well, a chance for you to make him a better man than he was."

"Oh sure. My speciality. When do we do this?"

"Twenty minutes."

The apologee was a thin, wiry man in late middle age, with black eyes and a light covering of graying stubble about the chin. He wore a pinstripe suit that had seen better days and, beneath the jacket, a dark woolen tank top over a beige, wide-collared shirt. When we were introduced, he took my hand in both of his and in faltering English said only, "I thank you to be here."

An interpreter stood at his side and I invited them both to sit. Obviously there was no time to prepare anything on the scale of the Swiss apology, but I had no doubt I could wing it. This, after all, was my territory. A little bit about my family and its colonial adventures. Perhaps mention the slavery and the *Lady Bountiful* stuff to prove just how much a part of my family's life all of this was. Use the phrase "the dark stain of history" because that always goes down well, and then move on to the "deepest sorrow" conclusion before the "sorry, sorry, sorry" finale. I was confident that each narrative beat would lead me comfortably on to the next. I had started out in this game by extemporizing. It would be good to give it another go.

I was on the closing straight when it happened. I don't even recall being terribly distracted. As far as I was aware, I was doing the job very well. I was even beginning to enjoy the process, taking satisfaction from the knowledge that my uncle would have hated anybody saying sorry on his behalf for any of his actions. It made me all the more contrite and penitent. Still, as I was talking, the thought crept into my head, like a cat trying to slink unseen into a room, that because of this unexpected apology I was going to be late for my meeting with Max. I glanced down automatically at my watch. Unfortunately, my jacket cuff had slipped down my wrist so I had to reach down to pull it back. Now it was a two-handed operation, a whole-body affair, and as I tipped my head to one side to get a clear view of the watch face I could hear the two men opposite me shifting restlessly in their seats. I looked up. They were both regarding me with total disdain. The old man turned and said something to the interpreter, who translated:

"He asks if we are keeping you from something more important."

Believe me, as the world's leading practitioner of the art of the international apology, I know: it is impossible to come back from something like that.

Twenty-nine

That was when my feet started to hurt again, both little toes bitching against the hardness of my new leather shoes. My feet had not given me grief since the day Wendy Coleman saw to them, but they were at it now, punishing me for the casual cruelty of my footwear choices. It was as if they had been woken by the day's events from a long and restful sleep.

"You hungry?" Max asked as I limped into the taxi, and I realized that I was, for the first time in many months. The combination of aching feet and an aching hunger was comforting. It was a Marc Basset I recognized. Back in London my feet had always hurt. Back in London I had always been hungry. Or, at least, I had always had an appetite, which could amount to the same thing if you were being kind.

We were driven out across this tidy city on the lake, along darkening, well-swept streets, and up into the hills. An old wooden chalet lay hidden at the end of a long drive, its presence betrayed by the warm buttery glow of candlelit windows flickering through the trees. Max told me he had borrowed it from a wealthy friend, as if we should all have friends with beautiful houses to borrow, as if we all did.

We were shown into a warm, wood-lined room with a view out over the lake, where in the darkness a mother-of-pearl moon hung low and heavy. A table had been laid for a dinner of many courses. I sensed that other than ourselves and those here to serve us, the house was empty. As soon as we were seated we were each brought a taster on a glass plate frosted with ice: a disk of white chocolate the diameter of a golf ball but only a few millimeters thick. On top was piled half a teaspoon of Osetra caviar.

"The chef has told me we must eat this in one go," Max said as if challenging me. I looked down at the plate. The dish was clearly intended to make the eater feel by turns curious and uneasy. Fish and chocolate? Together? What empty-fridge desperation had dreamed up this nightmare? Instead I felt excited, like a skier who has been off the piste for far too long staring once more down the slope. I knew how to do curious food. The muscle memory was all there. It was just a matter of pushing off. We slipped the white chocolate disks into our mouths.

The taste was sublime. There was the clean measured saltiness of the eggs and the sweet creaminess of the chocolate, and then a separate flavor that emerged shyly out of the two. It reminded me of the savory backtaste of the salt caramels I had once loved back in London, only more so. White chocolate and caviar made me homesick.

I said, "That was extraordinary."

Max looked up over my shoulder and gestured for the server to step forward. He placed before me a printed sheet. I read it.

"A chocolate menu?"

"My friend also lent me his chef," Max said proudly, "and I've had him hunting around for a few chocolate dishes that we thought might amuse you."

After the white chocolate and caviar came a soothing gamy soup of woodcock, flavored with dark, unsweetened bitter chocolate, chili, and crisp pieces of pancetta. That was followed, as a fish course, by lobster on the half shell, in a pungent lobster *jus* the color of terra-cotta. Once it had been placed upon the table, another server approached holding a fine beige muslin pouch, one hand gripped tightly about the neck of the bag, the other held flat underneath where it bulged with what looked like ground spice of some kind. He leaned over and, with delicate precision, shook the bag across my plate, dusting it with what turned out to be a fine, earthy cocoa powder that only pointed up the sweetness of the shellfish.

For the meat course we were served thick pink slices of venison, carved tableside and laid one across the other over pieces of caramelized fennel and Jerusalem artichoke, the whole drizzled with a fruity chocolate sauce that played terrifically against the ripe field-and-meadow flavor of the meat and the anise kick of the fennel. We finished with a delice of chocolate with a glazed shell that glistened and shone beneath the candlelight. At its heart was the most ear-ringingly intense chocolate mousse I had ever tasted, and to keep the mouth alive, the base had been filled with shards of popping candy that fizzed and crackled on the tongue. I ate this meal like a man who has just discovered the pleasures of food, holding each mouthful for a second longer than necessary so that the flavors might have a chance to develop, eyeing the menu between courses as we talked, trying to guess what result the combination of ingredients listed on the sheet might achieve. I felt settled and unburdened by the ballast of anxiety which I realized had been weighing me down for weeks now.

At the meal's end I asked for mint tea and they brought me fresh leaves in a glass of hot water, trailing wisps of aromatic steam. With it came a plate of chocolates including those salt caramels from London which, Max said, had been flown in that afternoon.

"Chocolate to Switzerland?"

"The chef cares only about the very best products. Not their origin."

I put one in my mouth and felt the liquid center flow out across my tongue. When I was done I said, "I am terribly touched, Max. You did all this for me?"

"My spies told me you were in need of a little care."

"Who's been snitching?"

"Franky. Alex. They were concerned. Said you'd been chasing your tail a little. To quote Franky"—Max dropped his East Coast patrician tones in favor of something swampy from the Deep South—"'Like a rack-*coon* in heat.'" We laughed.

"They're good boys, those two," I said. And then: "It has been a bit crazy recently."

Max leaned back and lit a cigarette, killing the flaming match with the same quick flick of the wrist that I remembered from our first meeting at the Foreign Office. He observed me like I was a new exhibit at the community museum. "You do a difficult job, my boy, and don't ever allow yourself to pretend otherwise. No surprise if it gets on top of you sometimes."

I told him what had happened that afternoon during my apology to the Palestinian.

"What did you tell him?"

"Said I was on medication and needed to check when my next dose was due."

"Did he believe you?"

I grimaced. "Don't think so. He refused to shake my hand at the end."

Max rolled his eyes as if to say, There's no accounting for folk. "One apology out of so many. Don't worry. Everybody else thinks you've done great."

A relaxed silence fell between us. I looked out of the window at the dark, oily, nighttime slick of Lake Geneva, far below. "Do you know this is the first time I've been to Switzerland? I seem to recall I even have a flat here somewhere that comes with the job."

"I think you're right, though you're staying at the hotel with the rest of the crew?" I nodded. He took another drag. "Your dad never brought you here?"

"Oh, he talked about us all going one day, but . . ."

"He died when you were a kid, right?"

"I was thirteen. Almost thirteen."

"A bum deal."

"Exactly." I held my breath before saying what had come into my mind. "I can't get him out of my head at the moment, actually. Keep hearing his voice."

"There's always unfinished business."

"You're not wrong. It's like there's this big conversation we were meant to have, one I keep trying to have."

"Nothing shameful there. I talk to the dead all the time."

"You do?"

"Those who will listen," he said with a thin smile. He tapped his ash.

"Problem is, they don't always answer back the way you want them to, do they?"

"No."

"Maybe I'm asking for too much. I suppose I'm just still angry with him for, you know . . ."

"What are you after? An apology?"

"Nice idea. I don't get too many people apologizing to me in this game."

"Well, if it helps, I know how you feel. I was way too young when my old man died, too."

"Really?"

"Oh, sure."

"Well, then."

"Exactly."

"How old were you?" I leaned in to him, intrigued.

"Me? Jeez. Let me think. It was so long ago. I was . . . yeah. I was forty-seven."

I sank back into my chair. "Very funny."

"I'm serious, Marc. There's no good age. I was forty-seven and I still hadn't finished the great conversation. Angry as hell, I was. Talk to any guy who's lost his pop and they'll tell you the same thing. There's never a good age."

"Are you telling me to lighten up?"

"Lighten up?" He took another deep drag and coughed ripely into his linen napkin, which he pressed primly to his lips. He stubbed out the cigarette. "Not the phrase I had in mind. But I was just thinking to myself, the job you've been doing, it's forced you to take a lot of things very seriously."

Now I was curious. "So what *are* you saying? That I should quit?"

"I'm saying maybe you need a change of scenery, a chance to enjoy a few of the simpler pleasures. I think you need to find a life which is just, how should I put it, a little less important?"

"Well, I'm open to suggestions."

"Why don't we call for a small *digestif*?"

"Tell me you haven't got one of those foul chocolate liqueurs. Not that Mozart stuff. There are limits."

"It's okay. You can trust Max. No chocolate liqueurs."

Professor Thomas Schenke's first penitential work, *Grievance Settlement Within a Global Context,* had become the kind of crossover success of which publishers can usually only dream: a serious, expensively priced academic text, with all the intellectual cachet that brings, which also sold to a general readership. The edition for general readers came complete with an "apology card," for it was discovered that while hundreds of thousands of people had bought the book, very few had read more than a few pages. The card enabled these guilty readers to send the professor a note, care of his publishers, apologizing for not having made more of an effort. A quarter of a million people did so, though it's unlikely he appreciated the gesture.

It was, of course, only a matter of time before Professor Schenke produced a sequel. (There had already been two follow-ups to the mass market text for domestic apologies, although these merely offered more scenarios rather than developing the initial premise.*) The new book, *More Grievance Settlement Within a Global Context*, a proof copy of which Max gave me that evening, took as its starting point the successful establishment of UNOAR and welcomed that which had already been achieved. "The world has made a great

---

A Very Sorry Business: Further Apologies for Home and Hearth and *Sorry Situations: Perfect Apologies for Weddings, Funerals, and Bar Mitzvahs,* both by Prof. Thomas Schenke (with others), Heartfelt Editions.

effort to pluck its apology chicken," the good Professor wrote at one point in the introduction, which proved his writing style hadn't improved with practice. That effort, he said, must continue, but new challenges lay elsewhere. As well as opening up ancient hurts, the end of the Cold War had, he argued, proved a victory for the free market over the corporatist approach. It was unthinkable now that any moderately developed economy would choose a nationalized energy or telecommunications system when it was accepted that the private sector could do a better job more cheaply. In fact, he said, the private sector could do everything more cheaply: education, health care, pensions, you name it. Big government had gone on a diet, taking inches off its waistline, and far less was now expected of it. As the state had retreated, so private corporations had advanced to fill the vacuum, taking on more and more of the state's traditional responsibilities.

Naturally with these new responsibilities would come something else: an increasing likelihood that corporations would cause great hurt. People always screw up, as Schenke didn't think to put it, but should have done. "In the future it will be the multinational corporation which will be called upon to make apologies," he wrote instead. "And once again there will be sound economic reasons for doing so."

On the face of it this read like a simple return to the commercial tort–avoidance which had got the ball rolling in the first place; a little squirt of hot cheese sauce onto a lovely bare knee here, a spilled cup of coffee there. But Schenke, to give him his due, was thinking far more ambitiously than that. "The great apologizable events of the twenty-first century may be a land inadvertently poisoned by a mining company, an ancient hillside wrongly deforested by a logging company, a people displaced by a new hydroelectric project." In conclusion, he wrote, "there are a whole new flock of chickens ripe for the plucking."

Max warmed the bell of his cognac glass between his palms.

"The thing is, my boy, these corporations will need qualified, experienced people to make their apologies for them."

"They won't be setting up their own internal departments to deal with it?"

"Why bother? Unless they're either unlucky or criminal, most of them will only have to make one or two of these big apologies over, say, a twenty-year period. Far better to outsource the work to professionals with serious credibility."

"What are you proposing, Max?"

He sipped his drink. "A private consultancy. You, me, Rashenko."

"Rashenko? That sob-monster?"

"Don't worry about him. Turns out he was just a bit depressed. He's been much better since they put him on the happy pills. And he has terrific contacts east of the Urals, which is bound to be a big market for us."

"What's the incentive? I mean, why would I want to do this? I'm not saying it's a bad idea, just—"

"No rush, but when you get a chance, have a look at the text. Schenke makes a clear point that in the commercial sphere, the market will set the fees. I've been talking to a few informed guys and they say we could charge anywhere from one to three percent of the Schenke differential for our services."

I gasped. "One to three? That's thousands of times what I'm getting now."

"And I'm here to tell you, many of the settlements will still be measured in the billions of dollars."

I stared out the window again. "You're talking about enormous sums of money. I'm already rich. What would I want with more?"

"Forgive me, Marc, but you are no more than comfortably off."

"So what do you call rich?"

He lit another cigarette. "Simplest measure?"

"Yeah, simplest measure."

"Enough so you can't ever spend it all."

"What's the point of that?"

"A fine rule for life, son: only losers die poor." He raised his eyebrows and sucked noisily on his cigarette again, content he had closed down that part of the conversation. "And of course," he said, "in the private sector there will be far less of the pressure you're under now. No organization takes itself more seriously than the United Nations. I think you'd thrive outside of it."

I sipped a little of my own cognac and felt it strip away the cocoa burr on my tongue. "And what do we call this venture of yours?"

"Of ours, Marc. Of ours. It will be a partnership. Rashenko, Olson, and Basset Associates?"

I shook my head. "The acronym is ROB. Not good for a money-making venture."

"The other way round, then?"

"That's BOR, which hardly suggests dynamism."

"We can decide on the name later," he said. "For now, read the book and have a think. This might be exactly the change you need."

I said I would, and thanked him for a remarkable meal.

Back in my restaurant critic days I made a point of ordering dishes according to appetite rather than what I thought might challenge the kitchen. Nonprofessionals only ordered what they wanted to eat, and I believed I had a duty to be as normal a diner as possible. There were a few exceptions. If a dish showed up on a menu which read like a car crash—black pudding spring rolls in chili jam, for example, or grilled scallops with strawberry-scented laksa—I would order it "so you don't have to." But for the most part I let taste be my guide. Occasionally, as we all do, I would get in a rut, ordering, say, grilled sardines three weeks in a row because I had my grilled-sardine head on. I would then argue, week after week, that the grilled sardine is a great test of any chef, when really it only tested my capacity for grilled sardines.

Still, at least I was exercising free will. Talking to Max that evening I realized that for many months now, my free will had been on holiday. Events had come my way and I had engaged with them unquestioningly. I had been living according to the set menu rather than going à la carte, and then dealing with the indigestion. Perhaps it was time to put appetite back in charge. Perhaps it was time to choose what I really wanted. In front of me lay the plate of chocolates. There were some oblong ganaches and a few dipped centers and a couple of those rust-dusted truffles. In the middle was a single shiny tablet of the darkest chocolate I had ever seen. I picked it up and put it in my mouth. It was delicious.

Thirty

I awoke to the sound of my own heart thumping angrily in my ears. My cheeks felt hot and swollen, and when I tried to breathe, a feeble hiss squeezed itself into my lungs. I threw back the quilt, assuming it was the thick hotel bedclothes about my face that were restricting the supply of oxygen, but it made no difference. I was trying to gulp down great drafts of air but all I was getting was feeble sips. This was when it occurred to me that I might be dying.

I reached out into the darkness to find the phone, and just as I managed to get a hand around the receiver, the bed bucked and kicked and chucked me onto the carpet. Now the floor tilted furiously, desperate to roll me into the corner. Then the bedside table threw itself on top of me. All the time I kept a grip on the telephone. The telephone would save me. I was certain of that. The telephone was my friend. I found a button to punch, a mouthpiece to speak into, but I had nothing to say save a savage rasp, for my throat was closed and my breath gone. In the darkness I could hear furniture throwing itself in all directions, trying to find me. There was a feeling of panic, but something else too: a distinct curiosity. In my mind I kept hearing the words "perhaps it was something I ate perhaps it was something I ate perhaps . . ." over and over. And there, half lit in the darkness, was Harry Brennan, shaking his grizzled head at the sad inevitability of it all. "Indeed, dear boy, perhaps it was something you overate." Would this not be the most vainglorious of ends: to be killed by your dinner?

I must have lost consciousness, for the next thing I sensed was light flooding the room and then the repeated calling of my name in a French accent, as if someone were trying to get my attention from far away. Events passed now in single images, like the frames of an incomplete movie storyboard: my body being thrown onto its back; a hard cushion shoved under my neck; a sharp, painful blow to the throat and then, oh thank you, thank you so much, hurt me again if you must but keep it coming, for here is a rush of sweet, soulful air to the lungs, and here another.

I am on a stretcher now, strapped in beneath a red blanket, chandeliers flashing over me. And now in a car. Or a van. I feel another sharp punch, this time to my arm. And a voice saying, "Try to relax, Meester Bassay. Try to relax." How interesting, I think to myself. The French pronunciation of my name. Maybe they have mistaken me for Dad. No no. Silly me. Dad's dead. Aha! Perhaps I am too.

I awoke again, this time in a hospital room, to the unsettling pip, pip, pip of a heart monitor. I know some people find this sound reassuring, an irrefutable proof of life, but I didn't. While the man connected to a heart monitor is clearly now alive, he was also very recently nearly dead and this cannot be a good thing. To my left, asleep in a chair, jacket off, empty holster showing over white shirt, was Franky, head back, snoring. A pale wash of gray morning light illuminated the thin curtains behind him. My body ached, and from somewhere below my chin, I could hear the suck and blow of air. I reached down and found a hard plastic tube protruding from my throat. I was intrigued. Just for a second I placed one fat fingertip over the hole the air was coming from, and I choked. This, too, could not be a good thing.

My retching woke Franky. "Brother. You're back with us."

I opened my mouth to say "Are you sure?" but nothing came. My vocal cords were being denied the necessary rush of air to allow for speech, courtesy of the emergency tracheotomy, and I was a sudden mute.

"Don't strain."

He called the nurses, who arrived with their uniform of crisp white and their certainty and their impeccable command of five languages. They took my blood pressure and removed the tube from my throat so that the air flow redirected itself back to my mouth, and they sealed up the wound. They opened the curtains, as if genuinely interested in the view, gave me tepid water to drink through a straw, and sat me up. Later they told me to sleep. Ready to be dependent, I did as I was told.

That afternoon I was visited by a doctor. He was a lean man of my own age with dark eyes and the relaxed air of one who knows he is not about to lose a patient.

"You are a lucky man, Mr. Basset," he said, this time with a hard final *t*.

"I am?" I croaked, my feeble voice squeezing itself out through my wretched, battered throat. "In what way, exactly? I am in the hospital and I have a hole in my throat. What's lucky about that?"

"You had a lucky escape," he said as if humoring me. "The night manager of your hotel, he is trained as a paramedic by our fine Swiss army. It was he who found you and he who performed the emergency procedure on your . . ." He tapped at his own throat as if the correct English had eluded him. "Without it you would be dead."

Automatically my hand went to the soft cotton mound of the wound's dressing.

"What did he use?"

"A Swiss Army knife, I think," he said brightly, flicking through my notes. "The spike for getting stones from horses' hooves." Even in my addled state this seemed to me so very Swiss: my hotel manager carried a penknife that was clean enough for use in surgical procedures. I could imagine my father reacting to this news with a snort and a glance to the heavens. Only in Geneva!

I was told I had suffered a massive angioedema, a severe inflammation that had caused my neck to swell, blocking the airways; in short, my own body had attempted to strangle me.

"An allergic reaction?"

"Quite so."

"To what?"

"This we will have to discover, sir." And sooner rather than later, he said, for the reaction had been too severe to allow it simply to show itself again at a moment of its own convenience. He suggested I remain in the hospital for a few days while they attempted to identify the cause. This suited me fine. A hospital is the right place to be when one has cheated death, if only to remind others of the seriousness of what has happened. The pip, pip, pip had its uses. I wanted to be here with these sweet efficient nurses.

"Very well," my doctor said. "We will soon begin. In the meantime, is there anything we can do to make you more comfortable?"

I flexed my toes. "Could you send me a podiatrist?"

Later that day I gave a junior doctor a list of everything I had eaten in the previous forty-eight hours, including a course-by-course description of the dinner I had shared with Max the night before. I assumed he would be impressed, jealous even, but he wrote it down as if I had listed the contents of my sock drawer. Ah yes, white chocolate with caviar, of course, and lobster with cocoa powder, you say? And the venison was prepared how? Well naturally, with a chocolate sauce.

I told him I had once worked as a restaurant critic, that there was nothing I didn't eat "except chicken feet."

He looked interested and scribbled a note. "No chicken feet. Why, sir, no chicken feet?"

"Clearly you haven't eaten them; they're disgusting." I grinned; the doctor sniffed and crossed out the note. There was no place in this examination for jokes about chicken feet.

Now earnest-looking women came to me and made various scratches on my forearms with sharp implements. They studied the resulting red welts and muttered something to me about false positives. Every few hours they fed me little plastic capsules which they refused to identify, and asked a nurse to sit by me "in case of reaction."

"What? My throat's going to close up again?"

The nurse indicated a small box the size of a glasses case. "We have the injections. It is the only way to be sure. There is no risk." I dared not question her.

We sat together watching old movies, the nurse and I, and flicked over occasionally to the news reports of my hospitalization, and I could not help but wonder how much Professor Schenke had enjoyed the announcement of the misfortune that had befallen me. All of this was a useful distraction while I awaited my body's attempt on my life. There were other entertainments: a visit from Satesh, who brought another sack of bagels from the World Jewish Congress; a phone call from Max full of guilt and recrimination, but I told him he should not blame himself. It was my body which had attempted the hit, I said, not the food we had been served.

Shortly after lunch on the third day we got a reaction: a red rash the color of unripe raspberries on the back of my hands, hives on my cheeks, and then down my neck and onto my knees, great red swellings and blotches that did no favors to my newly attractive body. The nurse looked and called a doctor to look too, and they studied me with great curiosity as if intrigued by the cruel jokes genetics could play, until I dragged their attention away from my sad, mottled thighs and they pumped me full of antihistamine and adrenaline.

"What is it, then?" I said as the cocktail began to take effect. "What's the killer ingredient?"

"I do not know," the nurse said. "This is a blind test with placebos. Only the doctor knows. He will see you this evening."

I was left alone to ponder the identity of my assassin. While I was waiting Jennie came to see me. She sat next to my bed, dressed in one of her dark pantsuits, one leg crossed tightly over the other as if waiting for a seminar to begin.

"Just wanted to check you were still alive," she said coolly.

"I am. Just about."

"I mean, obviously I would be quite happy if you lost your genitalia to a threshing machine, but I didn't want the inconvenience of your funeral."

"You told me I had nothing to apologize for."

She shook her head. "I told you not to apologize, which is altogether different. I could see you'd enjoy it too much, and I didn't want to give you the pleasure."

"Aah. I see."

She brushed some imaginary dust from her knee and shifted uneasily in her seat. "Actually, I've got a little news, and now is as good a time as—"

"It must be serious."

"Not serious, exactly, just . . . I'm leaving. Leaving UNOAR, that is."

"Where are you going?"

"Vienna. There's a new psychotherapy unit for dysfunctional nation-states being piloted there. We'll be attempting to apply talking cures, looking at various events in the childhoods of the referred countries, that sort of thing."

"Sounds very . . . interesting."

"Oh, I hope so. Anyway, the Foreign Office wants me there, and well, I thought it was a good time to move on. Satesh will take over from me. He's very capable and I know you two get on. And you know what you're doing and the office is there and running on wheels. And anyway—"

"Jennie, you're not going because of . . . ?"

She scoffed. "A woman makes a career decision and it has to be because of a man?"

"Well, I—"

"No, Marc. It is not because of you. It's just . . . the right time. I was always bound to move on, sooner or later. A position like this was never forever."

She stood up and straightened her jacket and looked down at me. "We did some good work, Marc."

"Yes. And we had some fun. Don't forget that."

"Yeah. Some fun. You're right. We had some fun." And now, as if seeking an escape route: "They're looking after you well here?"

"Oh, sure. They think they've cracked it, actually. But they're keeping me in suspense."

"Well, if there's anything you need . . ."

"Franky and Alex are in and out five times a day."

She considered me uneasily, as if unsure of her next move. Then she leaned down and kissed me gently on the forehead. "Take care of yourself," she said.

An hour later my doctor came to see me. I was a rare case, he said. Very rare. Many people claimed to have my allergy, but there were few confirmed cases. One for the journals, actually. I was, he said proudly, allergic to the refined fruits of the *Theobroma cacao*.

I stared at him, openmouthed. "I'm allergic to chocolate?"

"Very good. Yes indeed."

"I can't be allergic to chocolate. I've eaten it all my life."

"But you have not eaten chocolate perhaps for the past few months?"

"Well no, but—"

"Your taste of good chocolate during the dinner made a reaction. Very interesting."

"Interesting? Interesting? It's a personal bloody tragedy."

But there it was: the jury was back in and I couldn't argue with the verdict. My own body had tried to do me in. It had studied my passions and identified one of the few things that defined who I was (or at least who I used to be) and said, Sorry, pal, but no more. It was very hard to deal with. If I'd been addicted to crack, if my septum had been corroded by cocaine or my arms gangrenous from heroin abuse, I would have understood. I would have been a victim of my own dysfunction. But chocolate? My dear friend chocolate, the one that had got me through so many dark nights and light early mornings when others had deserted me? How could chocolate be the professor in the library with the candlestick, the dowager duchess in the study with the pearl-handled revolver?

It didn't matter that I'd been off the bean these past few months. I was suddenly desperate for it: I wanted chocolate-covered Calabrian figs and white chocolate truffles; I wanted black chunks of Valrhona and wine jellies from L'Artisan; I wanted Madagascar Vanillas from the Chocolate Loft and perfect balls of creamy Lindt and even great fat bars of Cadbury's Dairy Milk. I wanted it all and I wanted it now, but I knew that if just the smallest square passed my lips, if I tasted the merest crumb, I could be dead. While I had been off circumnavigating the world in my Gulfstream V and grandstanding before the cameras, and eating caviar off my (now ex) girlfriend's hand, my body had taken a long hard look at who I was and what I was and what I did, and like my brother, it had said: We do not like who you have become. We do not like it one bit.

It was obvious what I had to do. I lifted the telephone and dialed Max's number.

Thirty-one

Abkhazia in the Democratic Republic of Georgia has impressive mountains, fine beaches, but no good restaurants. If you are going there it won't be for dinner. It was not always so. Abkhazia sits hard against the Russian border, and in the old days, the fattened pashas of the Communist Party used to come here from Moscow to vacation on the Black Sea coast, where they could eat charcoal-grilled bass, drink hefty Georgian wine, and make eyes at the famously pretty waitresses who were always willing to serve the Party. Then the Soviet Union collapsed like so many sandcastles before the tide, and the killing started. The Abkhazians demanded their independence from the Georgians, to whom they had been forcefully wed so many years before, and the tourism business suffered terribly. The charcoal grills were extinguished, the restaurants closed.

Today the only people who go to Abkhazia are peacekeepers or oil executives surrounded by their thick-necked bodyguards, for in the late 1990s, Abkhazia suffered further misfortune: oil was discovered on the coastal plain. Before the find Abkhazia was a scrappy place of beaches, mountains, and ethnic tension. Afterward it was a scrappy place of beaches, mountains, ethnic tension, and money. When the Georgian government awarded exploitation rights to Caucasia Oil and Gas, a Moscow-based corporation part owned by Russian billionaires with high-level connections to the Kremlin, Abkhazian separatist militias responded by taking small groups of

aid workers hostage. It was, they said, the only way to bring international attention to a gross injustice. An entire people was being
robbed of its birthright, they said. Later they alleged that Caucasia's
poor management of the oil find was poisoning the lakes and the
land, and that brutal private security companies were being used to
stifle dissent. They wrote mournful folk songs about their plight and
in London small theater companies performed evenings of poetry
and song, all proceeds going to the Free Abkhazia Campaign. These
theatrical events were, by all accounts, long and dull.

Eventually, of course, Caucasia Oil and Gas recognized that
something had to give. The cost of securing their oil pipeline to the
coast was proving prohibitive. The company kept being mentioned
on the evening news, and not in a good way. The evenings of poetry
and song were spreading to New York and Los Angeles and Paris.
Soon they would be in Berlin. Later Caucasia's chief executive officer declared that they were forced to act by the adverse publicity. I
can see now that this was my undoing. Without the media interest
none of it would have happened.

We called ourselves Olson, Rashenko, and Basset. I warned them
that the acronym, ORB, made us sound like a bunch of club DJs, but
it didn't matter, because the press dubbed us The Sorry Business
and it stuck. We had three offices. Max worked from Washington,
Rashenko went to Moscow, and I returned to a serviced suite in
London's Belgravia.

It was an awkward homecoming. When I was about ten years old
my mother had let me travel freely about the city. For a tiny sum, even
to me, even then, I could buy a day ticket that allowed unlimited use
of the red buses and I would ride whole routes just to see what was at
the end of them. I wanted to say I had been to London Bridge or the
Woolwich Arsenal, even though it was more interesting getting there
than arriving. After Dad died she withdrew the privilege as if afraid
that out of sight, I would also vanish and never come back. Life had
become unreliable and she didn't trust it to take care of me.

Now, so many years later, the thought of disappearing from view suddenly seemed very attractive. I wanted to slip back into London unseen and unannounced. I wanted to communicate with my mother by phone from undeclared locations, a free spirit who existed only as a voice on the line. It was never to be, of course. It is mothers who haunt their sons, not the other way round, and I knew that if I were to exorcise her from my guilty thoughts, I would have to visit her. Sons always go home to their mothers in the end, if only for tea.

I went every few days, for the train journey to the suburbs and the familiar smell in her house of lavender, which had quickly replaced the hot tang of stock after Dad went. I brought her news of what I was doing and she always managed to appear intrigued, although she knew most of it because she had read about it in the newspapers. This, she said, was one of the curiosities of my new life. In the past she knew what I was doing by reading my restaurant reviews. Now she could measure out my progress in headlines. I asked her if I had disappointed her, in the needy way of sons who hunger for reassurance, and she laughed and said she only wanted what all mothers want, which was for me to be happy, "though I'm not sure you are terribly happy at the moment, dear." I told her I was working on it.

I phoned Luke and asked him to have dinner with me. He agreed to come as long as I was paying. He also made me promise to order an offensively expensive bottle of wine. This seemed a reasonable deal, so I crashed the plastic on something big and French and tannic and then another bottle, until I was drunk enough to confess my sins.

"I'm afraid I was a bit of an arse in New York."

"You weren't a bit of an arse. You were both buttocks."

"Eh?"

"A complete arse, boy. A complete arse." I was too drunk to compete but I appreciated the sentiment. It felt good to be here in a London restaurant, being abused by my younger brother.

He told me that Lynne had met someone else so I didn't call her, though I was hungry to hear her voice. I wanted to talk to Jennie too and sometimes, when it was late and I knew the office was closed, I would dial her number in Vienna just to hear the outgoing message on her voice mail, which was calm and businesslike. For years I had always known there was a woman I could talk to. My relationship with Lynne had been one long conversation. It had been the same with Jennie, and I always felt that I was a better person than I might otherwise have been when I was talking to them. Now those dialogues had come to an end and I liked myself less as a result.

I rented an expensive apartment down by the river at Battersea, a place of glass walls and high ceilings, and I spent my evenings watching TV for the small pleasures of the English accent. If I was bored I would walk along the river or read the case files that Max sent my way. It was not gripping stuff and promised little substantial work. In time we held some seminars with pharmaceutical companies who had ill-informed their patients about drug side-effects, and we worked up apology strategies for a couple of personal investment companies which had mis-sold pension products. We even landed the contract to apologize on behalf of Dick's Dogs, which had recently expanded into Europe, but they had cleaned up their act and, much to my macabre disappointment, there were no burn victims requiring expressions of regret.

Until the Caucasia job came along the only apology we executed was delivered in-house. It was inevitable, really. I had heard the cough getting worse and worse. I had noticed, when we met, a sallowness to the cheeks and a thinness to his already thin hands. Nevertheless when Max told me, during one of our regular trans-Atlantic telephone conversations, that he had been diagnosed with a terminal cancer, I was shocked.

"Reward for a lifetime's committed smoking," he said, and he began one of those deep-lung laughs that soon slapped the breath out of him.

A few days later he flew to London. On diagnosis he had joined a class action against the American tobacco companies for failing to reveal what they knew about the links between smoking and cancers. The moment his name appeared in the suit, lawyers for Big Tobacco crumbled and agreed to apologize. They gave us the business and, to keep affairs tidy, agreed that Max could accept the apology. "I want you to do it," he said. "It's only right."

It was a moving ceremony. First came the formal signing of the share certificates. In his new book Schenke had argued that plausible apologibility in the private sector would come from the symbolic ownership of one, but only one, share in each corporation involved. The apologist was entitled, he said, to benefit from the apology process, but not from stock movements in the company itself. Mass share ownership was, he said, "antiempathetic." This made sense to me.

I lit and extinguished sixty-seven cigarettes, one for each year of Max's life, and told him the story of my ancestors' involvement in the tobacco business, in Jamaica and the Southern United States. "The irony is that you helped change my life," I said at the end. "And in return my family stole yours away from you. I am so terribly sorry." When I was done and we had chased any lurking smoke from the room, he said, "An apology like that is almost worth dying for," which was kind, if not true.

That was the day he told me about Caucasia. Some of it I already knew. I had watched news reports about the hostages. I recalled footage of the relatives being interviewed on the steps of the Foreign Office because that was when I first clocked Jennie, striding up behind them. I was shocked that they were still being held, and more shocked that I hadn't noticed, but I didn't immediately regard myself as the best candidate for the job. Caucasia, a Russian-owned company, wanted to offer an apology to the Abkhazian rebels for the damage done to their land and for acts of brutality committed by their security men. Afterward, compensation, in the form of a cut of the profits, would be negotiated. It seemed to me that, being Russian and having been a KGB heavy, Rashenko was better suited to the task than I.

Max placed one hand flat against his chest, as if soothing indigestion, and said, "He's been doing all the backchannel work, talking to both sides, settling terms."

"And you didn't think to mention this to me?"

"We were keeping your powder dry."

I should have become suspicious at that point. I should have smelled the deception. But that's the thing about the sorry business: it ruins your judgment. I had just come out of a ceremony marking the approaching death of my mentor. I was high on emotion, low on cunning, living in the moment. I was dead meat.

Two weeks later, on a bright, early spring morning, I flew to Istanbul, and from there in a private jet to the former Soviet airbase at Zugdidi, just south of the Abkhazian border. Max was waiting for me on the airfield, in the back of a heavy old Soviet jeep that smelled of oil and damp earth. At his side was a small oxygen tank from which he took gulps through a face mask. There was a young Irish nurse called Cathy with him, red hair cropped short, white nursing smock worn carelessly over jeans and sneakers. She was monitoring the dials on the gas canister as if waiting for a cake to cook, and occasionally she looked upward at the gray, cloud-quilted sky as though searching for something she recognized in this uncommon landscape. Max appeared even less substantial than the last time we had met, and his suit hung loosely from him in ugly folds which were too familiar to me to even deserve comment.

"You shouldn't have come, Max."

"Don't talk crazy. I wouldn't send you off on this one alone."

"He's a fool to himself, sir," Cathy said with an encouraging County Cork lilt. "A fool to himself."

"You should have listened to her."

"Cath takes good care of me," he said, patting her hand as if she were the girl who packed his bag at the supermarket. "She's on top of things."

I looked around. The broad airfield was restless with activity. On one side, personnel carriers were lined up in rows three deep, low slung and glowering, a dark smudge on the landscape. I could see a number of larger tanks on the other side with soldiers crawling all over them, and overhead double-rotored helicopters sucked up the air.

I leaned into Max's ear so he could hear me over the noise. "Is this all for me?"

Max gave me a conspiratorial wink. "Part of Vladimir's deal. Georgian military gets to conduct exercises down here while you go in there. The moment the apology is made and accepted"—he took a deep, uncomfortable breath—"they'll withdraw back to Tbilisi."

"And the other side are cool with that?"

"Sure," he said, and he took another gulp of air. "In this part of the world saber rattling is a spectator sport. They expect it."

"It still looks like they mean business."

"That's ninety-five percent of the military's job," Max said, "to *look* like they mean business."

He turned and gestured to Cathy, who pulled a sheaf of papers from her bag. The first was my single share in Caucasia, which I signed for. Next was a map showing the route into Abkhazia, a clear *X* marking each military checkpoint on this side of the border. The nurse then handed me a hefty mobile phone.

"A Thuraya satellite phone," Max said, nodding toward the kit in my hand. "Anytime, anywhere. Get the aerial up, point it south, and use the hands-free to speak. Turn it over." I did so. Taped to the back was a slip of paper bearing a phone number. "*My* sat phone. Dial it whenever you need to." He coughed. "Either me or Cath will pick it up. And I mean anytime, Marc. We're here for you. You understand?" I said that I did. "It's also equipped with a Global Positioning System so we can locate you if need be."

"That's reassuring."

"Don't worry."

"I'm not worrying. It should be . . . fun."

"Good. That's the spirit. You've worked on the apology?"

"It's a done deal."

"See you back here in a few hours?"

"Take care, Max." It seemed the right thing to say. I might be going off on a risky adventure, but he was the one in mortal danger.

Thirty-two

I was given my own oily jeep and offered the services of a driver, but I declined the company. I thought it might look too "corporate" if I were chauffeured to the meeting, when what was needed was humility. Instead I drove out alone through this landscape of pine forest and untended orchard to the battered town of Rukhi, where the streets were empty and each gray wall was scarred by bullet holes. A little way outside town, through a series of checkpoints manned by bored Georgian soldiers who waved me on, I crossed the Enguri River on a rusting iron bridge paved with steel sheeting. As instructed, I turned north to follow the line of the river, which soon dropped away into a gorge to my right. The road rose upward into tree-lined hills, and ten minutes further on, waiting in a siding, I came across two trucks. From a distance I could see large men lounging back against them, rifles slung loose over their shoulders, and as I neared, they clambered into their cabs and pulled onto the road, the first in front of me, the second behind. This too was part of the arrangement.

We drove along hard, unmetaled roads, occasionally fording streams, sometimes turning off onto little more than a dirt track and then emerging back onto something that had once been paved. We drove for so long that I missed lunch. This was when I realized that I was a long way from home, and searching for reassurance, I patted the phone in my pocket to make sure it was there, like a man checking his front door keys before a night on the town. Many years ago, when I was asked by friends why I wrote about restaurants, I said, "Because it's safer than writing about wars," and I meant it. The toughest assignment a restaurant critic could ever entertain was eating in one of those kebab joints in the outer London suburbs where the meat festered rather than cooked. Even allowing for Harry Brennan's moment of digestive distress, it was a safe business and this suited me fine. The only heroic act I was ever likely to perform in those days was finishing the last course of a Michelin-starred tasting menu. And yet here I was on an Abkhazian hillside being escorted by two truckloads of large men with guns. I found myself very impressive and wished Jennie were here to be impressed by me too.

In the early afternoon we pulled into a clearing. In the middle stood a large barn made of black wooden slats. I clambered out of the jeep and looked to my escorts for instructions. They remained in their vehicles but waved me forward to the doors of the barn, which were open. Inside, sitting on square bales of straw arranged as steps, picked out by beams of light from holes in the pigeon-roosted ceiling high above, were the hostages. There were, as I had expected, fourteen of them in all, for the most part young, for the most part thin, the men with beards, the women with their hair pulled back. They looked more weary than anxious. Further in was a trestle table, and waiting for me on the other side was a round-shouldered man with a large square head weighed down by a thicket of wild black hair. Even from a distance I could see that his mouth was a rock garden of crooked teeth. He looked like the kind of man who could get the tops off beer bottles with his thumbs. Sitting at the end of the table, her multipocketed jacket looking just the thing in this place of straw bales and bad teeth, was Ellen Petersen. She raised her eyebrows as if to say, "Well, here we are again," and turned back to the notebook in her hand.

I said, "Ellen, I didn't know you'd . . ." But she looked up and shook her head.

"Talk to Georgi," she said simply, nodding toward my host. I looked at him and he invited me forward. I sat down on a chair opposite.

I suppose I could tell you now exactly what I said, sitting there amid the half light and the smells of ripe animal and straw, with the pigeons fluttering and cooing in the rafters above me. I could tell you all about my speech on the evils of economic colonialism and unfettered mineral exploitation. I could even recount what I said about my family's part in this unequal game, but the truth is that everything I said that day was irrelevant. I might as well have read a shopping list.

In his first book Professor Thomas Schenke argues that the acceptance of an apology is dependent upon the passion of the apologist; that from the moment the exchange begins, nobody knows how the game will end. The Penitential Engagement groupies in the diplomatic service loved this because, in their business, everything else was agreed before the key actors ever reached the negotiating table. All an international summit had to do was keep to the script. An apology was special because, supposedly, it was an improvised drama that existed in and of the moment.

It wasn't like that this time. The decision to accept or refuse had been made long before the ceremony began. In fact it had probably been made before my plane had even taken off from Istanbul. Sadly, I didn't know anything about it until the man sitting opposite me placed a large manila envelope on the table and pushed it across to me with the muzzle of the oily black revolver that he held in his right hand.

I opened the envelope, pulled out the papers, and began flicking through them with the kind of rising dread I recalled from the days of adolescence and failed exams.

"You have to believe me, I didn't know."

Georgi was tapping the table with the tip of the gun. "Three million share . . . ?" he said in a ripe voice so deep it sounded like it started somewhere around his thighs. "You have three million share in Caucasia Oil and Gas and you don't know?"

I looked at the copies of the share certificates in my hand, willing them to change. "A guy came and he said sign these papers and I signed the papers and—"

"You have three million share? Three million?"

"I know, I know, it's a lot of shares and these are my signatures and that is my name there and there and—"

He lifted the revolver and pointed it at me. "You are one of them. You profit from our injustice and you come here to make more money and—"

"Georgi!" Ellen was up and leaning across the table, one hand gripping his thick forearm as if steadying herself. He looked at her, nodded slowly, and said, "I am only scaring."

"I think Mr. Basset is good and scared, Georgi. Good and scared."

I began going through the papers again, searching for something, anything, that might prove they were fakes, though I accepted that they weren't. From the quality of the print I could see they were faxes. I looked to the headers for identifiers, an originating fax number or a date, but there was just a line of zeros. The sending machine was either new or had been reset. I put the papers down on the table and rubbed my sweaty palms on my trousers. It struck me that the best approach when faced by a large man with bad teeth and a revolver would be to throw myself at his mercy.

"Georgi, I am guilty of stupidity. I didn't look at what I signed, and I should have and I am so, so sorry, but at the time I didn't know I was going to be apologizing to you and nobody—"

"Your apology is worthless."

"I can see it might look like that. But maybe"—I was thinking fast—"maybe we're both being set up here. Maybe someone is trying to sabotage our meeting? Isn't that possible?" I was searching around for a way out now, trying to talk the evidence of these papers into submission.

"Who? Who is this person?"

"I don't know. Maybe if you tell me who gave you the documents . . ."

He stared straight at me so directly that I was immediately moved to look to his left.

"Ellen, did you give him—"

"You know I can't reveal my sources."

"This is a setup, Ellen. I didn't know anything about this. I didn't know I owned more than the one share I signed for this morning."

"You didn't know you owned three million shares in Caucasia Oil and Gas?"

"Jesus, Ellen, don't you start. Just tell me who gave you the papers and—"

Georgi silenced me by standing up, his wooden chair creaking with relief. "Enough," he said. He shoved the revolver into the waistband of his canvas trousers. "We will see how much your rich friends want you back." From behind me I could hear mutterings of furious indignation from the hostages, and I couldn't blame them. I could see how it looked. This hadn't been my finest hour. I was finding myself less and less impressive by the minute. Georgi walked toward the door and Ellen got up to follow. She stopped at my shoulder. "Sorry, Marc, just doing my job."

"Ellen, please believe me. I knew nothing about this."

"Whatever."

She went after Georgi and I turned around in my chair to watch them go. At the doors he stopped and said, "Sorry. You too."

She shrieked. "You *what?"*

"You stay here too. It must be the way."

"Georgi, we had a deal. We had a fucking deal. We had a deal, a deal . . ."

He shrugged as if to say: This is the way. Night follows day. The river runs down to the sea. I have a gun in my waistband. You stay here.

Now the men who had been waiting in the trucks outside came into the barn, carrying blankets and metal cases marked with a red cross and half a dozen storm lanterns. They placed them in the middle of the floor and retreated back to their vehicles, leaving Georgi at the doors. He said, "A little longer, my friends." He went out too, locking the barn behind him. We listened to the thick metal clunk of the truck doors closing, the throat-clearing of the diesel engines, and stayed silent in there as the sounds pulled away into the muffled distance of the track through the woods. I picked the papers up off the table once more, willing the contents to change, but they remained the same. When I looked up, every person in the barn was staring at me.

I said, "Sorry?" They shook their heads and turned away.

Thirty-three

The situation might have been easier if the hostages hadn't been broadly sympathetic to the cause of their captors. They too thought Caucasia Oil and Gas represented the ugliest face of ugly big business, and had passed most of their captivity as teachers or health workers serving the isolated Abkhazian villages of the northern highlands. They wanted to go home but were prepared to wait until a favorable deal was done. My contribution that day did not represent a favorable deal. They avoided talking to me and busied themselves instead with hanging the lamps and sorting out sleeping areas for however long we were to be here, in this dank barn in the middle of this dank nowhere, five hundred miles from the nearest good restaurant.

Ellen talked to me, but it wasn't a conversation I wanted to have.

"You klutz, Basset."

"I wasn't the one who gave him the documents."

"And I wasn't the one who bought three million shares in the company."

"This is a setup, Ellen. Don't you see? A setup. I didn't know I owned those shares. If I had known—"

"Yeah? So someone wants you to be taken hostage?"

"Yes. No. I mean, I don't know. I—"

"You're a klutz, Basset."

I tried the sat phone, of course. I tried it for hours, but all I got was a long announcement in six different languages telling me no one was available and inviting me to leave a message. I left a message and then another and a third, each more frantic than the last. I tried Luke. I tried my mother. I even tried Lynne. But all I got was answering machines or failed calls as I screwed up the international dialing codes. When I called Jennie in Vienna I got the voice mail message again which only days before I had found comforting. Now her calm, measured tones infuriated me, for they were the sound of a woman oblivious to my predicament. Eventually, fearful that I might drain the battery and that nobody would then be able to call me back, I gave up.

As night fell and the lamps were lit, creating pools of light and leather black shadows in the corners of the ancient building, the Red Cross crates were opened. We were each handed a small sealed foil package the size of a paperback book. It was marked with another red cross and the words *Emergency Energy Ration.* I ripped it open hungrily, but quickly dropped the package onto the straw-strewn floor and dropped onto my haunches, my hands over my eyes to hide the horror.

"Not up to your usual gastronomic standards, Basset?" Ellen said, eating hers.

"It's chocolate."

"What were you hoping for? Roast swan?"

"I can't eat chocolate."

"Jesus, Basset, this is not the time to be a picky eater."

"I'm not being picky. I'm allergic to chocolate. There must be something else in the crate. I'm starving. There has to be something else . . ."

But there wasn't anything else. I took a blanket away into a corner by myself and curled up on it, my hands around the taunting emptiness in my belly. Somehow I fell asleep.

I was woken in the early hours by the deepest of thuds that made the earth beneath me shudder. It was followed, as I came to, by a second and a third. Ellen was already awake and sitting bolt upright, not far from me, staring into the darkness, chin up, mouth open, tip of tongue against bottom lip, like a cat tasting a scent on the air. I crawled over to her and whispered, "Thunder?" I looked upward at the great holes in the roof where the rain could come in.

She shook her head and whispered back, "No. Not thunder." There was another gut-shifting boom, louder and closer this time, and as I looked upward again, involuntarily, I saw a sudden flash in the darkness.

She said, "Munitions."

"Bombs?"

She nodded. "Aerial, I suspect." There was a roar as a jet passed low overhead. She turned to me with the kind of expression I was used to seeing only on the faces of wine connoisseurs after they have correctly identified a vineyard and vintage. "See?" she said, as if it were a good thing.

Everybody else was awake by now, and without much discussion, we moved to the corner of the barn that backed onto the woods, somehow believing it left us less exposed huddled there together. Throughout that night the air around us cracked with small arms fire and the fizz of bomb and blast, which made the old building shake on its meager foundations so that the lamps swung on their nails and the shadows danced on the walls. So this is how it ends, I thought. Here, in this barn, surrounded by people who hate me, in the backlit darkness with the air splitting open and the ground shaking and my stomach empty. This is where it finishes.

But the dawn came again, and with it, respite. The bomb blasts mellowed and then died away, like thunderstorms that had moved far out to sea. We were left with only the rattle of gunshot, followed later by another sound which was so unexpected and so shrill that it took me half a minute to realize it was my phone ringing. I snatched it up.

"Max?"

"They're coming to get you, kid."

"I've been taken hostage, Max."

"I know. They're coming to get you. It will be okay."

"They had papers."

"We know. They told us."

"I don't know how they got the papers, Max."

"Calm down."

"Calm down? I almost died tonight. I still might."

"They're coming to get you."

"Did you know I had shares in Caucasia, Max?"

"You've got a lot of investments."

"Did you know?"

"Kid, did they say where the papers came from?"

"Ellen Petersen gave them the papers."

"Petersen's there?"

"Yeah, yeah. She's here."

"How did she get them?"

"She won't say. She won't say anything."

"Was there anything on the fax header? Anything at all? A number? A code?"

"No, nothing. There was nothing. It's blank."

"Totally blank?"

"A line of zeros. The fax machine had been reset. Or it was new."

"Was there a date on the header?"

"I'm telling you, Max, there's nothing. Nothing at all. There was . . ."

I stopped and sat down on the floor of the barn, as if the air had been punched out of me. I closed my eyes to help me focus and said, "I didn't tell you they were faxes."

He coughed, and croaked, "Hang on." I heard him clearing his throat and inhaling deeply on the oxygen.

"Max, I didn't tell you." There was silence from the other end, save for the rush and suck of his congested breathing.

He said soothingly, "You're going to be fine, Marc. Try to keep your nerve."

"Did you give Petersen the papers?" I listened to the howl of static, the sound of empty noise bouncing between satellites.

He said, "We're in the private sector now, Marc. There are so many things to consider."

"What things?"

"Costs."

"What costs? Talk to me, Max."

"It's always a balance. What's cheaper, compensation or action?"

I began pacing the floor, watched by my fellow hostages, each of them regarding me with disgust. "You made sure the militia would have to refuse my apology?"

"Marc, it was a complex set of decisions."

"Did you know I would be taken hostage?"

"We thought it possible. But we made arrangements."

"So that the Georgians could launch a military assault?"

"And the Russians, Marc, and the Russians. They landed on the coast this morning at Sokhumi. It's all with United Nations approval."

This, I think, was meant to be the clincher; if the United Nations were involved it all had to be aboveboard, but it wasn't, of course. None of this could ever be aboveboard. At the time, though, hidden away in this locked barn, all I knew was that I was a victim, and that convincing others of my victimhood might prove difficult. Certainly Ellen Petersen was having none of it. I could see now that she really didn't know the identity of the person who had faxed her the papers, and without knowing the source she was in no position to accept my innocence, whatever I said. However, in her book, *A Very Sorry Affair,* published nine months after the Abkhazian incident, she did at least manage to trace the sequence of events.

For ten days prior to my arrival at Zugdidi, the Russians, acting for themselves and as proxies for the Georgians, had been secretly circulating a draft resolution around the United Nations Security Council. The resolution would sanction military action against the Abkhazian secessionist militias should my mission end in failure and the hostages not be released, although there was a general understanding that it would only be passed if I was under direct threat. Only if I too became a hostage would the Russians get the votes they wanted. It didn't matter that I was no longer the UN's Chief Apologist. As Petersen put it, I was "still family" and a figure of such renown that world opinion would swiftly swing behind any use of force. My fame, the fame Max had encouraged me to accept, had become the perfect excuse for starting a small war.

In this deal everybody won, except for me and the Abkhazians. With the help of the larger, more organized Russian forces, Georgia would take back control of Abkhazia once and for all. Russia in turn would get a local supply of cheap oil. And Caucasia Oil and Gas and its Kremlin-friendly owners had quietly agreed to underwrite part of the cost of the invasion, the first private corporation to do so. Their contribution to the military bottom line, although huge, was still far less than any compensation they might have ended up paying had my apology been accepted. And if the operation cost less, thanks to ORB arranging for me to be taken hostage in an entirely deniable manner, then my company's pay packet would only be greater.

For now, though, Max told me none of this detail. He simply said, "Our fee will be much bigger, Marc."

"I don't want the money, Max. And you don't need it. You're dying."

"Remember, Marc. Only losers die poor." He laughed until he was coughing and choking down the phone at me. "Hang on again."

"Max? MAX?"

"I'm here, Marc."

"The only thing I have is my reputation, Max. That's all I have. You have destroyed my reputation. Ellen's going to destroy me when she writes this up."

"Don't worry, my boy. I'll take responsibility. I'll say it was my fault. That I should have remembered your shares. Mistake of a sick old man. I'll resign from the company, make a statement, the moment we get you back." He coughed some more, so that it sounded like his chest was trying to escape from his body. "And don't worry about Petersen, either. I've set up a distraction for her. She won't be interested in the Caucasia story. Trust me."

"What have you done?"

"Trust me, Marc. It will all be fine."

I was shouting into the phone now, calling his name, telling him not to do any more, that he had already done enough, but the line was dead. There was another sound filling the barn. Everybody was on their feet now, watching the doors, as the noise of diesel trucks expanded into the space. Somebody was coming.

Thirty-four

We heard a shout of "Get down!" and did as we were told, throwing ourselves belly forward onto the cool bare earth. There was a flash and a bang and a rush of white smoke as the doors fell in, so that a little pale daylight reached into the barn, only to be snuffed out again by a rush of men in black jumpsuits and bulbous night-vision goggles, pointing rifles at the shadows and shouting at us. I put my hands over my head and pushed my nose into the dirt.

Lying next to me on the floor, Ellen shouted, "There are no gunmen in here, only hostages!," like she'd done this before. And again: "Only hostages, only hostages!" But the chaos still had a distance to run. The men surrounded us, filling out the space with their barrels and their barked commands. Just as I was easing into the noise and motion around me, there was a shout of "Above you!" A thick volley of ear-punching rifle shots bashed the air, chased into the echo by a series of thuds onto the barn floor, each one marked by squeals from a few of my companions. Slowly, as the noise died away, I opened my eyes. Lying on the floor in front of me was a fat wood pigeon, the place where its head should be a bloody, awkward stump. The floor was dressed with dead birds.

There was an embarrassed silence. Ellen stood up. "Well, guys, now that you've shot out the local wildlife, would you like to rescue us or shall we just stay here and pluck them?"

I pulled myself unsteadily to my knees and then upward onto my feet. The man in front of me stared down at the floor through his goggles and nudged the pigeon with the heavy toe of his heavy black boot, as if checking it no longer posed a threat.

"Believe me, it's dead," I said, inheriting a certain portion of Ellen's clumsy sarcasm. The man looked up at me quizzically, his goggles still in place. Now he pulled them off and, in one smooth action, the black cotton balaclava that lay beneath them. I stared at him, as if unexpectedly spotting my reflection across a room and finding the familiar face hard to place.

"Stefan?"

He frowned and looked around the barn shiftily, like a man meeting an unmourned ex-girlfriend at a party. He looked at everything except me. "Hello, Marc."

"I can't believe it. You're here. Rescuing—"

"It's what I do. It's what I'm paid for."

"Did you know I was—"

"No, I wasn't told. Just another contract. Count them, gentlemen. There should be sixteen hostages." He slipped his rifle high onto his shoulder.

"I mean, it's amazing to see you."

"Check for injuries. Then load up."

"Everybody's fine, Stefan. Nobody's hurt. We're just . . . it's great to see you. Really."

Ellen was at my shoulder now, breathless and excited. "This is him? This is the guy?"

"Yeah, my old mate Stefan. Er, Stefan Langley, meet—"

"—Ellen Petersen, *Time,* great to meet you. I've heard so much about you. Well, we all have. Haven't we?" She extended a hand for him to shake, but he looked at it and then at me.

He said, "You're the man who eats humble pie for a living?"

I smiled encouragingly. "Humble pie, crow. Take your pick."

He looked down at the ground and kicked the dead bird a few inches further toward me. "Sink your teeth into that, then," he said, and turned and walked back toward the shattered doors.

I stared at the bird. "It's a pigeon!" I shouted after him.

He muttered, "Fucking foodies," and walked out into the daylight like he owned it.

Ellen scribbled something in her notebook. "I sense a certain hostility," she said.

"It's been a while," I said. "He's probably just surprised to see me. I know I'm surprised to see him."

Waiting outside in the clearing, their engines marking time, were three gray armored personnel carriers. The hostages were being loaded into the back of them, but I knew I couldn't just sit there with the herd, playing passenger. I grabbed a front seat next to Stefan in the lead vehicle. As I was pulling the door closed, Ellen yanked it open.

"Room for one more?" she said, slipping in next to me without waiting for an answer.

Stefan opened his mouth to say something but thought better of it, and clenched his skinny jaw tight in the way he used to do when we were kids. He revved the engine, shoved the truck into gear, and shouted, "Seat belts. It may be a rough ride."

We moved off at high speed down the track through the woods, the carriers bucking and jumping over ruts and rocks as if nothing could unsteady them.

I said, "Is it dangerous?"

"The greatest risk is friendly fire," he said coldly. "Which reminds me . . ." He picked up a heavy radio from a compartment in the door. "We're rolling," he barked into the mouthpiece, and there was a crackle of message in reply.

"So we're okay?" I asked.

"They're all okay," he said, nodding backward to the people sitting behind us, necks craned forward to look over our shoulders like kids trying to catch a first glimpse of the sea. "Of course, there's always the chance that someone might want to shoot *you.*" He gave me a sarcastic smile which ended as quickly as it had begun.

"You saw my apology about you and Gaby and stuff, then," I said.

He didn't reply. Beside me Ellen was scribbling in her notebook, her whole body stiffening with the effort of getting our conversation down as the truck bounced along the road.

"I did mean it, you know. What I said, about what I did to you. I meant every word."

Still nothing. He shifted his hands a little further apart on the steering wheel to increase his grip as we turned downhill on a narrow rutted lane through pine trees. Something roared low overhead and I crouched down in the cab to hide from the noise. Some way off we heard the boom and stutter of bombs exploding. I flinched. Ellen sat bolt upright. Stefan screwed up his eyes slightly as if trying to keep the sun out of them.

"Are we safe?"

"We will be."

We drove in uncompanionable silence for a minute or two. I had another go. "I mean, I would have said sorry to you in person if I'd known where to find you, but—"

"Did you think about what would happen?"

"I . . ."

"Did you consider what would happen to me when that was broadcast?"

"Well, I . . ."

"It's a good question, Marc. Did you think about what would happen to Stefan when that apology was broadcast?"

"Shut up, Ellen."

"Did you for a moment think about how my mates would react when you broadcast every sodding detail of my sodding humiliation on global television and my picture appeared on-screen?"

"Well . . ."

"Did you?"

"God, Stefan. I didn't mean to embarrass you. I just thought—"

"What did you think? You didn't think, did you?"

"Did you think, Marc?"

"Ellen, please!"

The vehicle shook violently as if punched in the nose. My ears popped and the windscreen filled with a savage blast of light.

"What the . . . ?"

"Mortar," Stefan said. We had drawn to a halt. The road ahead was fractured by a deep crater latticed with shattered tree trunks. He picked up the radio and checked that everybody behind us was all right and then sat tapping his fingers against the steering wheel. We heard something whistle overhead and explode in the woods a few yards to our right. Again he didn't move.

"They're trying to locate us," Stefan said.

"Shouldn't we get off the road, then?"

He lifted his hands off the steering wheel. "You want to drive?"

"No, mate. No. It's just . . ." Another explosion, further back on the road behind us.

"Everybody who knows me saw that apology of yours."

"Maybe we could talk about this later when—"

"No. Let's talk about it now." I heard a rush of air and a fourth mortar exploded, this time on the road in front of us.

"Stefan!"

"Let's talk about you humiliating me in front of everybody I know."

"Stefan, I'm sorry I'm sorry I'm sorry."

"Oh sure, you're sorry. Now you're sorry. Now you think you're going to die you're bloody sorry. But at the time the only person you thought about was you . . ." I stared nervously at the trees around us, expecting bullets to spray from them at any moment. So *this* is how it actually ends: here on this blasted track with this man shouting at me and my stomach still empty. Thank you, Max. Thanks so much for setting Ellen up with this distraction; for reintroducing me to my boyhood friend the mercenary, a man who wants to assassinate my character before the mortars are given the chance to finish the job.

"We really should get off the road, shouldn't we?"

"Actually, Stefan, I think Marc's right."

He stared unblinking at Ellen as we listened in silence to the siren whir of another incoming mortar. "Fine," he said. "Off-road." He picked up the radio and barked an order. There was another blast to our side and we turned into the woods so that we were battering downhill through the trees, crashing through saplings, barreling over logs, and cutting through clearings toward whatever lay at the bottom. Involuntarily both Ellen and I shrieked. We let out a "Whoooooaaaaah!" that came from deeper and deeper inside our stomachs until it resonated with the growl of the overworked engine cranking out the power beneath our seats. At the bottom of the wooded hill we went headfirst into a deep gully and then up again and over a ridge. Then we broke through the tree line and emerged back onto a road running into open pastureland. Stefan spun the steering wheel and we steadied on the road, the other vehicles swiftly falling into line behind us.

We would be safe now, he said quietly, like a man who has known unsafe and can tell the difference. He told us that combat zones were a "patchwork of risk," particularly scrappy little combat zones like this one; a few mortars up in the hills, a sniper or two in the gorge, but nothing on the plain. The plain was the best place to be in a scrappy little war. I said "Oh!" and "Yes?" and "Really?" at what seemed like the right moments.

And suddenly I felt fourteen years old again. I was back in a sub-urban garden watching him dance slowly, his hands on some poor girl's ass and his trousers tented with lustful ambition. He was the man again, and I was the boy-child who needed rescuing. Out of my depth. Begging for help.

I said, "You're enjoying this, aren't you?"

"What?"

"Rescuing me. You like having to lord it over me."

"I'm doing my job."

"Sure you are. Playing the big man. You always had to play the big man."

Stefan jabbed one finger at me. "Do you know the problem with you, Basset? Do you want to know the problem?"

"Go on. Tell me. What's my problem?"

"You're obsessed with the past. That's your problem. You think it's more bloody important than the present." He leaned forward to talk across me to Ellen. "Has he bored the tits off you yet about his dad?"

"Well, he *has* mentioned—"

"I bet he has. Every time we went out for a drink, he'd have two pints and that would be it. Dad this, Dad that."

"That's not fair."

"Isn't it? Isn't it? You know what I thought when I heard you'd got the UN job? I thought: Perfect. Now he can wallow in the past. Now he can be paid to talk about his bloody dad."

"I don't wallow in the past."

"Yes you do. You luxuriate in it, mate. Shall I tell you the difference between you and me, pal? Shall I? Here it is: I live with my past; you live off it."

"Interesting point, Marc. Do you think you live off your past?"

"Leave it out."

We drove in silence now, all the way to the border and across the river and down to Zugdidi, where the air base was sodden with activity, its approach roads choking with tanks and armored personnel carriers all heading back the way we had come. Helicopters flew low overhead toward the Abkhazian hills, and in the distance, we could hear again the sound of mortar fire and gunshots. My war was progressing well, apparently.

Caucasia Oil and Gas had employed a team of doctors and nurses to look after the hostages, and when we parked they descended upon us, throwing unneeded blankets over our shoulders and offering us cups of hot sweet tea we didn't want. It was a few seconds before I realized Stefan was walking away without saying good-bye. I called after him.

"Stefan!"

He stopped but did not turn to look at me.

"I meant what I said, you know." He did not move. "I really am sorry."

He stayed there, his back to me, as if trying to remember where he was going, and then he began walking. He did not look back.

I found Cathy sitting by herself on the front seat of an old Soviet-era ambulance, all curves and dulled, dented chrome, parked up against one of the buildings. She was watching the parade of military vehicles passing before her as though it were for her benefit. I tapped my fingers against the window to get her attention and she wound it down.

"Where's Max?"

She bit her bottom lip and shook her head.

"Well, where was he when you last saw him, then?"

"Where he is now. I mean . . . I'm really sorry to tell you this, Mr. Basset. But he died an hour ago."

"He did what?"

"He was a very ill man, Mr. Basset."

"I know. But . . ." I looked around, half hoping to see him appear from around the side of the ambulance, his face fixed in a mischievous grin, cigarette up above his knuckle. "Did he give you anything for me? A letter? Something? A statement?"

"No, he didn't."

"Nothing at all?"

"It was very sudden, Mr. Basset. A coughing fit that turned into tightness of breath and . . ."

"Where's the body?"

"Behind me."

We went around to the back of the ambulance and she opened the doors. His corpse was strapped down beneath a red blanket that stretched up over his head.

"Would you like me to leave you alone with him for a moment?"

I ignored her. I was too busy bending over him, pulling back the blankets and rifling through his jacket pockets as his arm flopped down toward the floor, patting him down for a piece of paper or even just an envelope with a few scrawled notes, anything which might prove that I had been unaware of the Caucasia shares.

"Mr. Basset . . ."

"It has to be here somewhere."

"Mr. Basset, please! A little respect."

"He has to have left it somewhere. He said he'd clear me. He promised."

"Mr. Basset, if you don't control yourself I will have to ask you to leave."

I stood up. He lay there, eyes closed, his sharp, gray-stubbled chin pointing up at the ceiling, tie still tied, mouth just open in the suggestion of a smile as if to say, Well, son, at least I didn't die poor. Perhaps at that point I should have felt grief or regret at the loss of another father figure. But I didn't. I felt betrayed.

I bent down until the tip of my nose was almost touching his and shouted, "You bastard, Max!," like I might be able to wake him, but the only thing that moved was his hair, ruffled by my harsh, unfreshened breath. I was on my own.

Thirty-five

There were no elections in Germany, or anywhere else for that matter. The latest round of the world trade talks in Zurich rumbled on without conclusion and the planet was free of cataclysmic Acts of God. Would it have made much difference if volcanoes had erupted or rivers had flooded or hurricanes come ashore? I doubt it. I was always bound to make the cover of that week's *Time*.

Luke showed it to me when he arrived for breakfast at the Cock Tavern, one of those pubs in Smithfield which opens early to feed the porters from the wholesale meat market across the road. He wanted to meet elsewhere, but I told him that my experience of hunger in Abkhazia had been almost as traumatizing as the sound of bullet and shell; that I needed the encouragement of animal proteins to help me recover. Throughout that night in the barn I had dreamed endlessly about platefuls of the best Gloucester Old Spot bacon and coarse-ground sausages made from belly and loin, of grilled lambs' kidneys and crisply seared rounds of black pudding and slices of calves' liver that were still rosy pink in the middle. Just ordering it all made me feel alive.

"You might want a few pints of something very alcoholic to go with that," Luke said as he threw the magazine down onto the table. There was a big picture of me, grinning foolishly, and the headline: HOW SORRY CAN ONE MAN BE? Below that was the inevitable sub-head: *The rise and fall of Marc Basset*.

I took a sip of hot strong tea and said, "Nothing I didn't expect."

Luke turned the magazine around so he could examine it again. "Things must be pretty bad if this is what you expected."

"I'm not an idiot, Luke. I can see how it looks."

"*They* clearly think you're an idiot."

"Thank you. Now order your breakfast."

When his food had arrived, he said, "So, what are you going to do?"

"The only thing I'm qualified to do."

He laid down his knife and fork. "Oh god. You're going to cook a giant almond soufflé and offer it to the world."

"Kind of. Except without the soufflé."

He began eating again. "You don't think there's been enough apologizing?"

"What else can I do?"

"Shut up?"

"Once I've done this, I will. I promise." We ate in silence for a minute or two. "Will you help me?" I said. "I could do with a bit of moral support."

"Why should I?"

I thought for a moment. "Because I'm your brother?"

"Is that the best you can do?"

I nodded.

"Fair enough."

The next day we hired the Lancaster Room of the Savoy, partly for its size and partly because Dad had always admired the hotel. Once, when we were kids, he took us there for tea, to eat dainty sandwiches in the room overlooking the Thames and to worship at the place where the great Auguste Escoffier had cooked a century before. "Without Escoffier," he said with a gallant wave to the murals on the walls and the chandeliers and the mirrors, "the food in this country would be even worse than it still is." And then he bowed his head as if genuinely distressed by the thought. The Savoy felt to me then like the kind of place where nothing bad could ever happen, and it was natural that I should choose it now as the venue for my last heroic act.

When the hotel manager asked how many chairs we would need, I said 150, but Luke corrected me. We would need 600, he said, and he was right, or nearly right. The seats filled up quickly that afternoon with print and television reporters so that the photographers had to hunker down on the floor at the front, and both side aisles were filled with television crews like some detachment from the artillery corps taking aim at me with their cameras.

Luke and I sat behind a white-linened table, empty save for a jug of water and glasses and a single microphone attached to a public-address system. The hotel had offered to put a vase of flowers on the table but I had declined. This was not a moment for ornament.

Luke introduced me, said I would be making a statement, promised there would be time for questions, and then passed the table microphone across. I leaned down over it, and to the sound of whirring cameras, I gave them my version of events. I said I had known nothing of the shares and explained that, with regret, I had to blame Max Olson for my predicament.

"Unfortunately Mr. Olson died before he was able to exonerate me," I said, and I heard a huff of disbelief from the crowd, "so I have nothing to offer by way of proof. But I do know this: that I am not without guilt. It was stupid of me not to pay attention to my investments, stupid of me to take on face value everything I was told. I have been an idiot and for that I really am very sorry. A war that I never wanted, that horrifies me, has been started in my name, and I feel terrible about it. I hope the world will accept my apology because"—I folded up the piece of paper—"it is all I have to offer."

Luke tried to corral questions, but before he could identify the first speaker a voice called out from the front of the crowd.

"Mr. Basset, do you expect us to believe you when you say you didn't know you owned three million shares in Caucasia Oil and Gas?"

I shook my head. "I don't think I'm in a position to expect anything. I can only tell you how it is. I did a really stupid thing and I'm sorry."

Quickly Luke pulled up the next questioner, an American woman halfway down the room.

"Will you be apologizing to the people of Abkhazia also?"

"I'm hoping this apology will be heard and accepted by the Abkhazians too. But to be honest, I think the best thing I can do after today is just keep quiet."

"So are you retiring from the apology business?"

"Absolutely."

Another shouted question: "Mr. Basset, is it true that while Chief Apologist for the UN, you authorized your security detail to harass and intimidate members of the US Women's Olympic Paraplegic Team after your appearance with U2 at Veterans Stadium in Philadelphia?"

Luke turned to look at me as if I had just belched offensively. I blinked, swallowed, and leaned down into the microphone. "There was an incident at Veterans Stadium, yes, for which I am very, very sorry. It was a misunderstanding on the part of my security men, who felt I might be under threat. Obviously I'd like to apologize to the women involved for any distress that was caused. It was never my intention that anything like this should happen. I'm really sorry. Really."

Another question, from the other side of the room: "Mr. Basset, is it true you claimed to be the heir to the legacy of Willy Brandt, the late chancellor of the former West Germany?"

"Pardon?"

"We have a statement from a member of the civilian staff at Dayton Air Force Base in Ohio. He says that on the opening night of the inaugural UNOAR conference held there last year you had a private meeting with Mr. Olson at which you said, quote"—the journalist looked down into his notebook and back up again—" 'I am the new Willy Brandt.'"

I laughed nervously. I could feel the whole room recoiling from me.

"Well, no—I mean, yes, I did say that. But I think it was more of a question."

"What? You were asking if you could be the next Willy Brandt?"

"No. Yes. Look, it was a weird time and I was under pressure and I was having this conversation with Max—I mean, Mr. Olson— and . . ." I stopped and attempted to steady myself. "If I have offended anybody, anybody at all, by saying that, then I am, naturally, terribly sorry. I didn't mean it to be taken wrongly. I was just feeling my way and I thought it was a private meeting and—"

Luke grabbed the microphone from me. "Next question." He picked out a woman standing at the side of the room and shoved the mike toward me.

"Mr. Basset, is it the case that you cheated on your then girlfriend with two cocktail waitresses from Des Moines, Iowa?"

Luke pulled the microphone back toward him. "Oh yeah, that's true. He definitely did that."

I pulled the microphone over to my side once more. "Thank you, Luke." I turned to the audience. "Yes, I'm afraid something like that did happen . . ."

Under his breath I heard Luke mutter, "Something exactly like that."

". . . something exactly like that did happen. I suppose the thing is, you know, we all make mistakes in our private lives and those things stay private, but because of how I've been employed my life is a little less private than other people's, so . . ."

"Are you blaming the young women concerned for revealing what you did?"

"No, no, of course not. All I'm saying is, I didn't think through the consequences. It was a terrible thing to do, and you know, I welcome the opportunity to apologize here to all involved and I hope they're able to hear my words of regret and, well, I'm sorry."

I sat back and folded my hands in my lap. I was exhausted and the press conference had only been going ten minutes. I felt ambushed, overrun, drained, defeated. And there was still more to come. This time, it was a male French voice.

"Monsieur Bass*ay*—"

"Basset," I corrected.

"Monsieur Basset, the French government has announced that its ambassador to the United Nations will be proposing a motion to the General Assembly next week calling for the disbandment of the United Nations Office of Apology and Reconciliation. They say your activities have brought it into disrepute and they are proposing its replacement by the Nation-State Psychotherapy Unit being piloted in Vienna. How do you comment?"

"I, er, I know some of the people—well, *one* of the people involved in the psychotherapy project—and it's very promising and it's doing lots of good work. But I'd hate to think that UNOAR would come to an end just because of a few mistakes I made—" There was a short laugh of disbelief from the room. "Okay, okay, because of the many mistakes I have made. I think we did some great work at UNOAR and I think it has the potential to do much more."

A British journalist this time. "We're hearing from New York that Professor Thomas Schenke has issued a statement in which he calls you, and this is a direct quote, 'a lazy, feeble-minded shyster who has destroyed the good name of Penitential Engagement purely in the interests of greed.' What do you have to say?"

Now I was cross. "Oh, come on! Schenke's a madman. He's deranged, psychotic. You can't listen to a word he has to say."

"So your only response is to call the founding father of one of the most influential political movements of modern times a madman?"

I barked into the microphone, "Have you met Schenke?"

Luke pulled it away from me again. "Last question, please." He pointed to a man waving his arms furiously up by the public-address system control desk. "Mr. Basset, sir . . ." Another American journalist, his speech gilded with his country's common courtesies. "Mr. Basset, sir, Lewis Jeffries III of the African-American Slavery Reparations Committee, he's just made a statement to the media in Louisiana."

"What did he say?"

"Well, if it's okay by you, sir, we already have a recording here." He looked down to a technician sitting on the floor at his side, leaning over a laptop. "It's downloaded?" The man nodded. "Sir, we have the feed here and we could put it through the PA system for you to listen to and—"

I sat back and raised my arms as if to say, "Whatever." The crowd hushed and they each turned an ear toward the nearest speakers, which crackled and fussed with digital static. Jeffries' voice boomed out down the hall.

"Ladies and Gentlemen, I had hoped never to have need to make this statement," he said, "but I have concluded that in the present circumstances to withhold the truth would be to further amplify the offense of which I am talking today." I closed my eyes and waited out one of Jeffries' dense theatrical pauses, for what I knew was to come. He sighed deeply, as if the weight of history were on his shoulders. And then: "It is with great regret that I must tell you today that the apology for the Atlantic slave trade made on behalf of the Federal Government of the United States and other colonial powers by the Chief Apologist of the United Nations here at Welton-Oaks was not Mr. Basset's own work." There was a gasp from the room, followed by a quick burst of shushing so that not a word should be missed. "Mr. Basset did present an apology, but it was neither robust enough nor elegant enough for the purposes of the process with which we were engaged, and for the sake of that process, I wrote the apology myself." Another gasp. "Mr. Basset just wasn't up to the job. It is, I fear, in the nature of the relationship between African-Americans and the rest of the US that we should be required to draft our own apology for the hurt we have suffered at their hands, but I hope, indeed trust, that now that a settlement has been reached, we may as a people be able to move on from the sorry charade over which Mr. Marc Basset has presided."

There was a little more static hiss as the recording came to an end. I opened my eyes. The room was silent. The photographers had lowered their cameras and were staring at me. The reporters were staring at me. Luke was staring at me.

Slowly I bowed my head over the microphone. "What can I tell you? I'm just so bloody sorry."

There was a second's silence before a voice from somewhere in the hall boomed out, "Who wrote that apology for you, Basset?" and the Lancaster room exploded into mocking, exclusive laughter. I pushed myself back from the table and watched as, shaking their heads at the idiocy of it all, at the constant, charming ability of the world to confound their expectations, the press corps rose as one and left the room. So this is how it *really* ends, I thought, here in this grand room with its mirrored doors and its fussy lighting and its row upon row of emptying chairs. Next to me Luke stood up. He looked down at me, opened his mouth to say something, but then closed it as if he had thought better of it. He shook his head and walked away.

It was, I suppose, inevitable. I had made my name, and my fortune, by saying sorry, and I had said it with such intensity and to so many people and so often that eventually nobody wanted to believe me anymore. No one could be that sorry. No one ever was. Not even Marc Basset.

Soon the journalists had departed to file their reports, leaving behind the camera operators to coil up their cables and the sound boys to unplug their microphones. There was just one person left sitting at the back of the phantom audience, her head down. I stood up and walked through the vacant aisles to sit down next to her. I stared up at the podium.

"Well," I said quietly, "that went okay."

Lynne nodded. "It could have been worse."

"You think so?"

"Oh, sure. They could have stormed the front and ripped you limb from limb."

"That's true. There was no limb rippage."

She smiled. "Indeed. No limb rippage." She looked around the room, now being emptied of its chairs by Savoy staff.

I said, "Luke tells me you're seeing someone else."

She shook her head. "He had little hips. I could never waste too much time on a man with little hips."

"Right." And then: "Thank you for coming."

"You know me. Always one for a good show."

"Yes."

"You hungry?"

"I'm starving."

"Come on."

She hailed a cab from the front of the hotel and told the driver to take us to our old flat in Maida Vale, and I didn't question her. Inside she led me to the kitchen, where she opened the fridge and retrieved two bottles of a fine New Zealand sauvignon blanc.

"Two bottles?"

"You'll need one to cook with," she said, and she reached further into the fridge to retrieve a hunk of pancetta and a net bag of clams. "There's Parmesan and flat-leaf parsley in the bottom of the fridge and you know where the dried chili and garlic are."

She left the room and I went to work. I heated the olive oil and threw in the flakes of chili and, while they were cooking, chopped up the pancetta into small bite-sized pieces. I added them to the oil too, where they writhed and bucked pleasurably in the smoking oil. When the bacon fat was almost rendered and crisp and golden brown, I threw in a crushed garlic clove and followed that with the white wine, which fizzed and offered up an impressive sheet of blue flame which soon dissipated.

Finally, I tore open the little net and I threw in the clams, which rocked in the simmering liquor and slowly began to open until they were smiling up at me and at last I was content and in control. I knew what I was doing and how the cooking process would end. What's more, I had done nothing for which I needed to apologize in at least the last half hour. I was guilt free. I was making dinner. I was home.

Epilogue

There is one last thing you should know: I have lied to you. I would like to claim it was a small lie, but if I'm honest—and I am trying to be—the size of the falsehood doesn't matter. The fact is, Lynne didn't take me back to the flat at the end of the press conference and I didn't cook her dinner. We went to some small, bog-standard trattoria in Covent Garden and ate mediocre pasta. I told her how bad I felt about everything and she observed me as if I were some naughty schoolboy who had finally admitted his sins. At the end of the evening we went our separate ways.

I suppose I wanted to give you an ending less dripping in pathos, a sense that not all was lost, and in my attempt to do so, I tumbled into fantasy. Of course you would be entitled now to wonder what else I have lied about, to question whether I am an unreliable narrator, but I think we all know that I've told the rest of it as it happened. The story hardly does me any favors, and even the lie I told didn't ring true. How would my dad have described Lynne? A sensible girl. She's not the type to just take me back, is she?

It seems I am not terribly gifted when it comes to manipulating people's opinions of me. The day after the press conference, for example, I issued a statement saying I would be donating every penny I had earned from the Caucasia contract to the Free Abkhazia Campaign. I thought this would do my image no end of good. Unfortunately, I didn't earn anything. Rashenko declared that by speaking out, I had breached the confidentiality clause in my ORB contract. He then siphoned off all the funds, dissolved the company, and went to live with his therapist in a dacha outside Moscow. Apparently he's very happy these days.

Meanwhile I'm doing okay. I've started writing the occasional restaurant review for Hunter, who is, I think, endlessly amused by the way things turned out. And I still see Lynne. We meet up for dinner every now and then (she says she wants to get some meat back on my bones) and she told me a few nights ago that I wasn't a total idiot, so there may be hope for us yet.

As to the lie I told you, well, I know what I should do now. It is the thing I am most qualified to do, isn't it? The one thing at which I am practiced. But will you understand if I say I no longer have the stomach for it? That the luster has gone? I think I've said the *S* word enough for all of us over the past year or so. I've certainly said it enough for me. So I'm hoping I don't have to say it again. I'm hoping you'll be understanding if it's not the last word on this page. I'm hoping you'll give me a break. Tell me I don't have to say it again. I don't have to say it again. Do I?

Acknowledgments

A lthough this is a work of fiction not everything in it is invented. Most of the dishes on the chocolate menu in chapter 29 are real and the chefs responsible must get the credit. The white chocolate and caviar buttons and the chocolate delice with popping candy with which the meal begins and ends are to be found at Heston Blumenthal's remarkable restaurant The Fat Duck, at Bray in Berkshire. I was advised on the game, chocolate, and chili soup by Henry Harris of Racine, 239 Brompton Road, London SW3, although he serves nothing like it, preferring instead his own brand of classy French country cooking. The lobster with cocoa powder is available at Vineet Bhatia's groundbreaking Indian restaurant Zaika, 1 Kensington High Street, London W8. The roast venison in a chocolate sauce is similar to, if not exactly the same as, a dish served at London's only establishment with three Michelin stars, Restaurant Gordon Ramsay, 68 Royal Hospital Road, London SW3.

Marc's favorite chocolatier, L'Artisan du Chocolat, is to be found at 89 Lower Sloane Street, London SW1, and the salt caramels are as good as he says they are. The Chocolate Loft, home of Garrison Chocolates, is located at 119 West 23rd Street, New York, NY 10011. Sandor's, which supplies the stocks for Lewis Jeffries' meal in chapter 20, is at 2984 South County Highway 395, Santa Rosa Beach, FL 32459. The Destin Seafood Market, which supplies the scallops, is not far away from Sandor's at 9 Calhoun Avenue, Destin, FL 32541. The Houston branch of Central Market mentioned in chapter 20 is to be found at 3815 Westheimer, though there are others across the state. The Cock Tavern, where Marc and Luke have breakfast in the last chapter, is on East Poultry Avenue by London's Smithfield Market and is one of the few pubs in the city licensed to sell beer from 6:30 AM. All other restaurants mentioned or reviewed are fictional.

I would also like to thank: members of egullet.com's South-eastern US bulletin board for advice on food suppliers in the region; Steven A. Shaw for gastronomic directions around New York; Julian Barnes for his thoughts on wines; Simon and Robin Majumdar for the napkin test (it's not much but it is theirs); Sam Daws and Carne Ross for their knowledge of the United Nations; Fergal Keane and Jonathan Freedland for their understanding of Bill Clinton's trip to Rwanda; Marina Warner for her work on the culture of the international apology; Claire Rayner for her medical knowledge. Eric Schlosser's book *Fast Food Nation* was the source on the early days of McDonald's, mentioned briefly in chapter 13.

Gary Younge and Maureen Mills read the manuscript and made incisive comments. They are not, however, responsible for any of its contents. My agents, Pat Kavanagh at PFD and Sam Edenborough and Nicki Kennedy at ILA, both in London, and Joy Harris in New York, were always enthusiastic and supportive. I was cheered on by all my editors but particularly fortunate to have in Toby Mundy of Atlantic Books an editor of rare precision and tact. He showed me how to make this a much better book than it might otherwise be. He also didn't blame me when he experienced food poisoning after we went for dinner one night to a place of my choosing.

Finally, my wife, Pat Gordon Smith, not only put up with my moods but read every chapter as it was written, told me how to improve it, and poured the wine when it became necessary, which was often. I couldn't have done it without her.

About the Author

Jay Rayner is an award-winning journalist and broadcaster who is now the *London Observer*'s restaurant critic. He is married and lives in London.